Samuel P. Newman

A Practical System of Rhetoric

or the principles and rules of style inferred from examples of writing - to which is

added a historical dissertation on English style. Sixtieth Edition

Samuel P. Newman

A Practical System of Rhetoric
or the principles and rules of style inferred from examples of writing - to which is added a historical dissertation on English style. Sixtieth Edition

ISBN/EAN: 9783337312954

Printed in Europe, USA, Canada, Australia, Japan

Cover: Foto ©Andreas Hilbeck / pixelio.de

More available books at **www.hansebooks.com**

A

PRACTICAL

SYSTEM OF RHETORIC

OR THE

PRINCIPLES AND RULES OF STYLE,

INFERRED FROM

EXAMPLES OF WRITING

TO WHICH IS ADDED A

HISTORICAL DISSERTATION ON ENGLISH STYLE

BY

SAMUEL P. NEWMAN,

PROFESSOR OF RHETORIC IN BOWDOIN COLLEGE.

SIXTIETH EDITION

IVISON, BLAKEMAN, TAYLOR & CO.,

NEW YORK AND CHICAGO.

1873.

INTRODUCTION

The advantages proposed to be attained by the study of
*Rhetoric.**

1. Some acquaintance with the philosophy of rhetoric.
2. The cultivation of the taste, and in connexion, the exercise of the imagination.
3. Skill in the use of language.
4. Skill in literary criticism.
5. The formation of a good style.

By the philosophy of rhetoric, I here refer to those principles in the science of the philosophy of mind, and in the philosophy of language, on which are founded those conclusions and directions which are applicable to literary criticism, and to the formation of style. Obviously, then, it will be said, an acquaintance with the science of intellectual philosophy, and with the philosophy of language, should precede the study of rhetoric. Hence, no doubt, Milton and others assign to this branch of study the last place in a course of education.

But it is known to all, that the prevalent opinion and practice are different from those recommended by Milton; so that our inquiry should be, what is the best practical method of acquainting the young with the philosophy of rhetoric — those whose minds are not accustomed to philosophical investigations, and who are ignorant of those sciences on which the art is founded?

I answer, that, while the attention should be directed to but few principles, and those most essential in a practical view, instruction should be imparted principally by familiar,

---

* Extracted from a lecture delivered in Boston before the American Institute August, 1830

talking lectures. A text-book, if one is used, should contain but a mere outline, — some general principles plainly stated and well illustrated.

Here I would more fully state, what I mean by familiar, talking lectures. Suppose I wish to make the student understand what I mean by taste, and in so doing, I have occasion to speak of the judgment, sensibility, imagination, emotions of beauty and sublimity. Now, should I attempt to effect my purpose by a definition, or an extended technical explanation of these terms, there would be little reason to hope for success. I would rather refer him directly to the operations of his own mind, point out to him instances where he forms a judgment, where his sensibility is excited, his imagination called into exercise, and emotions of beauty and sublimity kindled up in his own soul. It is true he may not, after this, be able to give me an exact definition of these faculties and intellectual operations, but he has learned what is meant by the proposed terms; and when I have occasion to use them afterwards, I have no fears of not being understood.

That instruction in this part of rhetoric is attended with difficulty, no one will deny. The subjects themselves are intricate; hard to be understood, and still harder to explain, especially to those whose minds are immature and unaccustomed to philosophical reasonings. Here, then, is room for much ingenuity in the instructor; and without a skilful effort on his part, the efforts of the pupil will be of little avail. Above all things, let not the mockery of set questions and set answers be practised, in teaching what pertains to the philosophy of rhetoric.

After all, it must be allowed, that with the most skilful instruction, and the best text-book, young students will obtain but imperfect ideas in what pertains to the philosophy of rhetoric. Still, what is thus imperfectly acquired, will be of importance to them as opening some interesting fields of thought, which, with strengthened powers, they may afterwards explore; and further, as aiding them in better understanding the nature of the rules and directions founded on these important and somewhat intricate principles.

I have stated as a second object to be attained by the study of rhetoric, the cultivation of a literary taste, and, in connexion, the exercise of the imagination.

The cultivation of a literary taste must evidently depend principally on a familiarity with those productions, which are esteemed models of excellence in literature. In this respect, there is a close analogy to the cultivation of taste in painting, or in any of the fine arts. We may also learn something on this subject, from the course pursued by painters in the improvement of their taste. They visit the most celebrated galleries, and seek for models of excellence in their art; and these they make the object of close, long-continued and patient study. They inquire what there is to excite admiration in these paintings, and dwell on their different prominent beauties, and in this way cultivate and improve their tastes. Now it is in the same way that a literary taste is to be cultivated. And that the student may skilfully use his models of excellence in literature, and unite with his observation of them the application of those principles on which they depend, he needs the assistance of an instructor.

In stating the details of the course here recommended, I remark, that, by the aid of a text-book prepared with reference to the proposed method of instruction, the student may have brought to his view examples of those instances, where there is most frequent occasion for the exercise of literary taste. I here refer to what are termed the ornaments of style. In connexion with these examples, the nature of whatever in literary productions comes under the cognizance of literary taste, may be explained. The different ornaments of style may be pointed out to his notice, and he may be led fully to see why attempts of this kind are in some instances successful, and in other instances fail.

When the examples thus cited, and the comments upon them, have become familiar to the student, let his attention next be directed to finding examples in English writers, which may exhibit similar ornaments of style, and in the examination of which, there is opportunity for the application of the same principles. Here it is that important aid may be rendered by the instructor, since, in conducting these inquiries and forming his decisions, the student needs both guidance and confirmation.

To make myself fully understood, I will here illustrate my remarks. Suppose that a student finds in his text-book the following comparison from the writings of Locke:—

'The minds of the aged are like the tombs to which they

1*

are approaching; where, though the brass and the marble remain, yet the inscriptions are effaced by time, and the imagery has mouldered away.'

This comparison, he is told, is *naturally suggested;* and in connexion with the example, the meaning of this phrase is fully explained to him. And not only is he made to see what is meant by a comparison's being naturally suggested, but to feel, that in the absence of this trait, the pleasure to be derived from it, as exciting an emotion of taste, would be impaired. Let the student now be directed to bring forward from any author, instances of comparison, which are in the same manner naturally suggested; and in this way let him become familiar with the principle stated, and with its application. In the same manner, by directing the attention in succession to the different traits in the various ornaments of style, and illustrating, in connexion with examples, the various principles on which these attempts to excite emotions of taste are founded, the pupil is led to a full acquaintance with this part of rhetoric. He is enabled at once, when reading the productions of any author, to perceive the beauties of style, and to classify and arrange them—in other words, he acquires a good literary taste.

But there is another point connected with this part of my subject, to which I will for a moment direct your attention. I refer to the exercise thus given to the imagination. In our courses of study, we have discipline for the memory, for the reasoning powers in their various forms, and for the invention. But no regard is paid to the exercise and improvement of the imagination. And this, not because this faculty of the mind is useless, or because it admits not of being strengthened and improved by exercise. The impression is, that there is no method which can be adopted for the attainment of this end. Now I would ask, if, by the course here recommended, the imagination will not be called into exercise, and strengthened? These attempts to excite emotions of taste are addressed to the imagination; they are understood by the imagination, and it is a just inference, that the plan of study I have now recommended, will furnish a salutary discipline to the imagination.

Of the favorable tendency of the method of instruction, I can from my own experience as an instructor, speak with some confidence. I have ever found, that my pupils engage in this part of their rhetorical course with interest. They get new views of the nature of style, are led to notice their susceptibilities of emotions, of which before they have been unmindful. They also become conscious of their own powers of imagination, and learn something of the nature and offices of this faculty; and with these views and this consciousness, they find that a new source of pleasure is opened to them. Thus they both derive important aid in becoming writers themselves, and are prepared to read with increased interest the writings of others.

Before concluding my remarks on this head, let me say, that what is here recommended, is perfectly practicable. It is an employment, which any student with common powers of mind may pursue; and it requires, on the part of the instructor, only that degree of literary taste, which every one profe-sing to teach rhetoric should possess.

The third object proposed to be obtained by the study of rheto c, is skill in the use of language. Here I refer both to the choice of words, so far as purity and propriety are conce ned, and to the construction of sentences.

Instruction in this part of rhetoric should be conducted with reference to two points, — to acquaint the student with the nature and principles of verbal criticism, and further to lead him to beware of those faults in construction, to which he is most liable.

The former of these appertains to the philosophy of rhet oric, and is included under my first head : but I here offei an additional remark. It was stated, when speaking of giving instruction on the philosophy of rhetoric, that difficulties attend this part of the course. These difficulties exist but in a slight degree, when exhibiting what is connected with the philosophy of language. Here is such abundant opportunity for illustration, and examples are so easily adduced, that every principle may without difficulty be made perfectly intelligible. Neither is this part of the study uninteresting to students. Curiosity is fully awake to whatever pertains to the nature of language, and to the rules that govern its use. And here I may be permitted to mention a work which, in what pertains to this part of rhetoric, I regard as of the highest authority. I refer to Campbell's Philosophy of Rhetoric, — the ingenious, elaborate production of the Quinctilian of English literature

To lead the student to beware of those faults in construction which are of most common occurrence, — the other object in view in this part of the course, must evidently be effected by adducing examples of these faults. From the nature of the case, the endless forms of correct construction cannot be stated. On the obvious principle, then, that where one has erred, another will be liable to leave the right way, we direct the attention to these wanderings, and connect with such instances the cautions they naturally suggest. The object here in view may be accomplished for the most part by the text-book. All that is incumbent on the instructor, is, to lead the pupil fully to see what in every example adduced the failure is, and how it is to be remedied. This part of a text-book does not require to be dwelt upon in the recitation-room. It is rather a part to be referred to by the student, when, hesitating as to the construction of sentences, he needs guidance and assistance.

I mention in the fourth place, as an object to be obtained by the study of rhetoric, skill in literary criticism.

Under this head, I include whatever pertains more particularly to style, its nature and diversities, as seen in the writings of different individuals, and in different classes of literary productions. Our inquiry is, What can be done by the instructor most efficiently, to aid the pupil in acquiring skill in literary criticism, as thus explained?

Style has been happily defined by Buffon as 'the man himself.' If I wish to become acquainted with any individual, I seek an introduction to him; I endeavor to learn from personal observation the peculiar traits in his character. I may, indeed, from the description of a third person receive some general and perhaps just impression respecting this individual; but all this, though it might prepare the way for my better understanding his peculiarities when in his presence, would alone make me but imperfectly acquainted with him.

The same holds true, if I wish to become acquainted with the peculiarities of those of different nations. You might describe to me the national traits of the French and of the Spanish; but a visit to those countries, and familiarity with their inhabitants, would be of far more avail in learning their national traits of character.

This illustration suggests the best practical method of

giving instruction in what relates to literary criticism. A text-book or an instructor may describe, with accuracy and fulness, the peculiarities of style, as they are seen in the writings of different individuals, or found in different classes of literary productions. But this is not enough. That the student may clearly discern these characteristic traits, and understand their nature, and the causes on which they depend, his attention must be directed to these writings. He must in some good degree become familiar with them, and thus learn wherein they differ, and what there is in each to approve or condemn.

It may be thought, that to bring to the view of the student in this manner the peculiarities of different styles, may require too much time and labor. But with the aid of the text-book, much of the work may be performed by the student himself. What is most necessary on the part of the instructor is, to direct the attention to specimens of different styles, and in some few instances to point out characteristic traits. The student, with this aid, will soon acquire sufficient knowledge and skill to apply the remarks found in the text-book himself.

This leads me to remark generally on the importance of reading good authors in connexion with rhetorical studies This part of education is, I fear, in most of our schools and colleges, too much neglected. From his inability to judge of the merits of writers, the student needs guidance in selecting those which may be most useful to him, and this guidance the instructor should feel it is incumbent on him to supply. To read over occasionally with the pupil some choice specimens of style, may also be of essential advantage. To learn how to read, is no easy acquisition. Of course, I refer, not to the pronunciation of the words, or the inflections of the voice, but to the quick and true apprehension of the meaning, and a susceptibility to the beauties of style.

In this connexion, too, the student may be taught the true nature of literary criticism. It looks not for faults. It cherishes not a censorious, captious spirit. Its eye is directed after what is excellent and praiseworthy — after what may inform the mind, give grateful exercise to the imagination and refinement to the taste. And when it discerns excellences of a high order, as if dazzled with what is bright

and imposing, it sees not minute and unimportant defects.
It is indeed nearly allied to that charity which is kind, and
which, where she discovers what is truly worthy of her regard,
throws her mantle of forgiveness over a multitude of sins.

I proceed now to notice the last mentioned advantage proposed to be obtained by the study of rhetoric. I refer to the
formation of style.

This part of a rhetorical course of instruction is not particularly connected with the use of a text-book, further than
that it furnishes opportunities for the application of principles and rules, which are there found. The aid furnished
by an instructor, is principally in the correction of attempts
in composition, with such general guidance and advice, as
the intellectual habits and peculiarities of the individual may
require. I offer, therefore, on this head, merely a few practical suggestions.

1. It is highly important, that the attention of the student,
in his first attempts, should be directed to the management
of his subject. I would require of him to exhibit a plan, or
skeleton, stating the precise object he has in view, the divisions he proposes to make with reference to this point, and
he manner in which he designs to enlarge on each head.
In this way, he will not only be aided in forming habits of
methodically arranging his thoughts, but will be led to adopt
the easiest and most direct method of proceeding, in writing
on any subject.

2. I have ever found, that, so far as the construction of
sentences is concerned, and here I refer both to the division
of a paragraph into sentences and to the phrases and forms
of expression, — I remark, that, in relation to this part of
the work of composition, I have ever found, that students
derive important aid from translating select passages from
the writings of good authors in other languages. Every one
knows, that in this way a command of languages is acquired
And I would extend the meaning of the phrase, so as to
include, not only that *copia verborum*, and that power of nice
discrimination in the use of words, which are generally un
derstood to be implied by it, but also the right arrangement
of words, and the correct construction of sentences. Other
things being equal, he who, during the first six months
in which the attention is directed to composition, should
devote half of his efforts to the writing of translations

would, I doubt not, be in advance of him, all whose exertions had been employed in the work of composition.

3. I would further recommend a familiar mode of correcting the first attempts of the student. If practicable, the instructor may with advantage read over with the pupil his productions, and alone with him freely comment upon its defects and excellences. While in this way needed encouragement is given, the attention of the student is directed to that point where there is most need of improvement. Besides, it not unfrequently happens, that the efforts of the student have taken some wrong direction. He has some erroneous impressions as to the nature of style, or as to the manner in which a good style may be formed. It may be that he is laboring too much on the choice and arrangement of his words, or the construction of his sentences; or, assigning undue importance to the ornaments of style, he may be seeking principally after what is figurative, and the elegances of expression; or, again, with false notions of what is original and forcible, he may be striving after what is sententious and striking. Sometimes, too, there exists a fastidiousness of taste, which is detrimental. The student is kept from doing any thing, because he is unable to do better than he can do. In other instances, there is an injurious propensity to imitation. The student has fixed upon some writer as his model, and, servilely copying his master, his own native powers are neglected. Now, in all these instances, the advice of the instructor may be of essential benefit.

One general remark is all that I have to offer further on this head. It should ever be impressed on the student, that, in forming a style, he is to acquire a manner of writing to some extent, peculiarly his own, and which is to be the index of his modes of thinking — the development of his intellectual traits and feelings. It is the office of the instructor to facilitate the accomplishment of this important end, both by wisely directing the efforts of his pupil, and by removing every obstacle in his way.

The following work having been republished in England, and introduced into the schools of that country, and having come into extensive use in the United States, the publishers, grateful for the favor with which it has been received, are induced to present it to the public in an improved and more permanent form. It has been stereotyped, with the hope that its circulation may thus be extended and its usefulness increased.

Andover, September, 1838.

CHAPTER FIRST

ON THOUGHT AS THE FOUNDATION OF GOOD WRITING

Plan of the work.

WHEN we read the production of one who is justly accounted a good writer, we are conscious that our attention is engaged, — that we are pleased, and if the subject is one which can interest the feelings, that we are moved. If from being conscious of these effects we are led to search for their causes, we find, that our attention is engaged by the valuable thoughts and just reasonings that are exhibited ; we are pleased by what gives exercise to our imagination, — by happy turns of expression, — by well introduced and well supported illustrations. We are moved, because the writer, whose productions we are reading, is moved, and our feelings of sympathy cause us to be borne along on the same current, by which he is carried forward. But we now ask, what may be hence inferred in relation to the writer ? Do we not discover, that his mind has been stored with knowledge ? that his reasoning powers have been strengthened and subjected to salutary discipline? — that his imagination is active and well regulated, and his heart alive to emotion ? and is it not from his possessing these resources — these intellectual and moral habits, that he is able to

2

engage our attention, to please and to move us, and consequently has acquired the reputation of a good writer ?

If this view be just, we may infer, that the foundations of good writing are laid in the acquisition of knowledge, —in the cultivation of the reasoning powers, — in the exercise and proper regulation of the imagination. and in the sensibilities of the heart.

But let us now suppose, that two writers, who possess those qualities, which I have called the foundations of good writing, in equal degrees, should write on the same subject There might still be important differences between them One might use words with correctness and skill, selecting always the best term ; the writings of the other might show improprieties and want of skill. The sentences of the one might be smooth in their flow, perspicuous in their meaning, gratefully diversified in their length, and well suited to the thought that is conveyed ; those of the other might be rough, obscure, ambiguous, and tiresome from their uniformity ; and while we are engaged and pleased in reading the production of the former writer, we soon become wearied and disgusted with that of the latter. Here then we have a new cause in operation, and this obviously is the different degrees of skill in the use of language, possessed by these two writers.

From this statement, we may learn the objects of attention to the critic, in examining a literary production. He would judge of the value of the thoughts, of the correctness of the reasoning, especially of the method observed in the discussion of the subject. He would next apply the principles of good taste, and notice what is addressed to the imagination, and judge of its fitness to excite emotions of beauty, or of grandeur, or other emotions of the same class. He might then direct his attention more immediately to the style, and examine its correctness, perspicuity, smoothness adaptation to the subject, and the various qualities of a good style.

The course here marked out, as that of the critic in the examination of a literary production, suggests the objects of attention and the method pursued in the following work. In the first part, a writer is regarded as addressing himself to the understanding of his readers, and the importance of being able to think well, as including the number and value of the thoughts and the proper arrangement of them, is considered. The writer is then regarded as addressing himself more immediately to the imagination, with the design of interesting or pleasing his readers. Here the nature of taste, which directs in what is addressed to the imagination, is explained, — the proper objects of its attention in a literary work pointed out, and some instructions given which may aid in its cultivation. Skill in the use of language is next made the object of attention, so far as this is necessary for the accurate and perspicuous conveyance of the thoughts. In the remaining part of the work, the qualities of a good style are enumerated, and the different circumstances on which they depend, are mentioned. Through the whole work, the inductive method is observed as far as practicable. Examples are given, and rules and principles are inferred from these examples. At the close of the work also exercises are found, the analysis of which may call forth the skill of the learner, and make him familiar with the rules which are stated.

It will at once occur, that in each of the particulars mentioned, Rhetoric is connected, in a greater or less degree, with other departments of instruction. The Grammarian gives us rules for the attainment of correctness in the use of language; and Logic informs us of the different modes of conducting an argument. The intellectual philosopher also explains to us the phenomena of mind, particularly of those emotions with which taste is connected. This connexion has been borne in mind, and hence it is, that on some parts, comparatively little is said, and that of a general nature Other parts, which are thought to belong more appropriately to Rhetoric, are more fully treated.

Extensive Knowledge essential to the good writer.

It is a received maxim, that to write well we must think well. To think well, implies extensive knowledge and well disciplined intellectual powers. To think well on any particular subject, implies that we have a full knowledge of that particular subject, and are able to understand its relations to other subjects, and to reason upon it.

In saying that extensive knowledge is essential to the good writer, the word knowledge is meant to include both an acquaintance with the events and the opinions of the day, and with what is taught in the schools. That this knowledge is necessary to the good writer, may be inferred from the intimate connexion between the different objects of our thoughts. It is impossible for a writer to state and explain his opinions on one subject, without showing a knowledge of many others. And if, in the communication of his opinions, he endeavors to illustrate and recommend them by the ornaments of style, the extent of his knowledge will be shown by his illustrations and allusions. Were it necessary to establish this position, it might be done by analysing a passage of some able writer, and by showing, even from the words that he uses, the knowledge which its composition implies.

He, then, who would become a good writer, must possess a rich fund of thoughts. The store-house of the mind must be well filled; and he must have that command over his treasures, which will enable him to bring forward, whenever he occasion may require, what has here been accumulated 'or future use. To make these acquisitions, is not the work of a month, nor of a year. He who would gain much knowledge, must possess habits of diligence and attention. He must be always and every where a learner. Especially must he seek after a knowledge of facts, and distinct views of received opinions on important subjects. He will be mindful, that the extent of his knowledge will depend more on his manner of reading, than on the amount read, and on h's attention to the facts which fall under his observation, than on the number of these facts.

Discipline of mind essential to the good writer.

In saying that the discipline of the mind is essentia' .o the good writer, particular reference is had to the reason-ing powers. In other words, the good write .must have sound sense. He must be able to examir subjects, and pursue a connected train of thought with power and cor rectness. That this is essential, may be inferred from the rank, which is held by the understanding among the differ-ent faculties of the mind. A man may have invention, memory and imagination, but if he cannot reason accurately and with power, he will not interest and inform his readers, and thus acquire the reputation of a good writer. It is also well known, that many of the faults of style arise from in-distinctness in the thoughts, and an inability to discern their relations to each other. Both these causes of defects in writing are removed by the discipline of the mind.

The improvement of the reasoning powers, is the appro-priate object of the study of the sciences. The ability to reason justly and ably must be acquired by practice. There may be physical strength of mind as of body, but the strength of the giant will not avail him in rearing a stately edifice, unless his strength be combined with skill; and neither can he giant mind rear its structure without the guidance of

2 *

skill, acquired both by instruction and practice. And how can this skill be better acquired, than by the study of those sciences, which require patient and careful research for hidden principles, or furnish instances of close and long-continued trains of argumentation? Hence the fondness for metaphysical and moral investigations, and for the exact sciences, which is ever felt by those who excel as sound reasoners. And the student, who in the course of his education is called to search for truth in the labyrinth of metaphysical and moral reasonings, and to toil in the wearisome study of the long and intricate solutions of mathematical principles, is acquiring that discipline of the mind, which fits him to distinguish himself as an able writer.

But in addition to the exercise and improvement of the reasoning powers, there are certain intellectual habits, which form a part of the mental discipline of the able writer, and are worthy of particular consideration. To these I now propose to direct the attention.

Habit of patient reflection necessary.

He who writes for the instruction of others, seeking in this way to enlighten and influence his readers, offers to them the results of his own investigations and reflections Unless then he is able to state new facts or to present new views of facts and opinions already known, he has no claim on the attention of other minds. Hence arises the necessity of habits of investigation and reflection. The good writer is a man of thought; he is accustomed to observe accurately the phenomena, both in the natural world and in the scenes of life, which come under his notice, and to seek an explanation of them; and whatever statements or opinions he finds in the writings of others, or hears advanced by them, he is wont to examine them, to test the validity of the arguments brought forward in their support, and the objections which are made, or which rise up in his own mind.

The habits of thought here recommended, are not easily formed or generally possessed. The attention of most minds is so much engrossed with the objects and occurrences around them, that there is little inclination or ability to look in upon their own thoughts and trace out their connexions and relations. Even educated men are too ready to be satisfied with superficial views of subjects, and to shrink back from that intellectual effort, which a more thorough investigation requires. But there can be no doubt, that habits of research and reflection have done more towards enlightening and improving men, than all the brilliant sallies and sudden efforts of genius. It is indeed this ability to think, joined with a favorable constitution of mind, which gives its possessor a claim to the name of genius. It is said, that when the great Newton was asked, how he was enabled to make the greatest discoveries that any mortal had ever communicated to his fellow men, he answered, *by thinking.*

A habit of patient reflection should especially be enjoined upon the young writer. Let him remember, that his danger is from a slight and superficial acquaintance with his subject, and not enter too hastily on its treatment. He sits down to reflect, and finds that he has some floating thoughts on what he intends to discuss. This is not enough. He must direct his thoughts to some definite object, and find out all that may be made useful in exhibiting and enforcing his opinions. Neither let him be discouraged, if difficulties offer themselves and first-efforts are vain. Often, in the course of such investigations and patient examination of a subject, new views and valuable thoughts will present themselves. We make new discoveries. Our minds become filled with the subject, and our thoughts flow forth in order and abundance.

It is by thus carefully and patiently reflecting on his subject, that the writer prepares himself to read with advantage what has been written by others. Having his own views and opinions, which are the result of patient thought and thorough examination, he is enabled to make comparisons between the opinions he has formed and those of other men. Wherein the opinions of others coincide with his own, he feels strengthened and supported. Wherein they differ, he is led to a more careful examination; and thus the danger of falling into error himself, and of leading others astray, is diminished. Often also, in reading the productions of others, some new views will be brought before the mind, or some aid derived for illustrating and enforcing what is designed to be communicated. In this way, too, the writer is less liable to be biased by the authority of a name, and to become the retailer of the opinions of other men. These remarks are designed to answer the inquiry, how far we ought to read what others have written on a subject, before attempting to write ourselves. We should read, not so much with the design of furnishing our minds with ideas, as to test the value of our own thoughts, and receive hints, which may be dwelt upon and thus suggest new views and thoughts.

There can be no doubt, that the practice of most young writers is contrary to what is here recommended. Immediately upon selecting a subject on which to write, they read what others have written, and thus instead of trusting to the resources of their own minds, they look to books for thoughts and opinions. The injurious effect of this habit is seen in that want of originality and vigor of thought, which in later periods of life characterizes the efforts of these servile minds

Method.

Another intellectual attainment essential to the success of the writer, is the power of methodically arranging his thoughts. It is well known, that the thoughts in their passage through the mind, are connected together by certain principles or laws of association; and these laws are different in different minds. In the mind of one man these associations are accidental. One thought introduces another, because it has happened to be joined with it, having before been brought to view in the same place, or at the same time. Another man thinks in a more philosophical manner, and looks at the causes and consequences of whatever passes under his observation. When his attention is turned to any subject, there is some leading inquiry in view, and the different trains of thought which pass through his mind, are seen in their bearing on this leading object. As a necessary result, he has clear and connected views of whatever subject he examines, and is prepared to place before the minds of others, the conclusions to which he has arrived, with the reasonings by which they are supported.

To attain this power of methodically arranging the thoughts, or as it is sometimes termed, of looking a subject into shape, it is recommended to study with care the works of those, who are accustomed to think with order and precision. It may be of advantage, often to make a written analysis of such productions, stating in our own language the proposition, which is the design of the writer to establish, and the different arguments which he has brought forward in its support. This exercise will be found advantageous, not only as it aids in forming a valuable intellectual habit, preparatory to the work of composition, but as it enables us to possess ourselves, in the best manner, of the opinions and reasonings of well disciplined minds.

It is also recommended for the attainment of method, to exercise the mind in the work of forming plans. The impression is too common, that all which is necessary for becoming a good writer, is to direct the attention to the manner of conveying the thoughts by language. But this is an erroneous impression. While it is the design of Logic to aid in the investigation of truth, it is one purpose of Rhetoric, to give directions for exhibiting to others what is thus discovered. Hence the plan, or the right division of a composition and the arrangement of its several parts, becomes a prominent object of attention and study. The young writer, especially, should a.ways be required to form and state his plan, before writing; and, as here recommended, it will be found advantageous to make this a distinct exercise. In this way, habits of consecutive thinking will be formed, and a principle of order established in the mind, which is imparted to every subject of its contemplation.

Amplification.

Another qualification of the good writer, which has its foundation in the thoughts and is connected with the intellectual habits, is the power of enlarging upon the positions and opinions advanced. When any assertion has been made, whether it be a leading proposition, or a subordinate head or division, the writer is desirous, that what is thus advanced should be understood and received by his readers. He endeavors therefore to exhibit his proposition more full; to support it by argument, and to enforce it upon the consideration and observance of others. His attempts to effect these objects, constitute what is called amplification.

To state the various ways, in which writers enlarge upon the propositions which they advance, is impracticable. Ingenuity is continually in exercise, seeking to arrest the at tention and awaken the interest of readers. There are however a few general principles, which may be stated, at the same time that some suggestions are made, as to the best ways of attaining and improving this power of amplification.

One leading object of amplification, is the more full exhibition of the meaning of what is asserted. This is effected in the following ways;

1. By formal definitions of the words, or phrases, used in stating the proposition, or head of discourse. This is necessary, when the words or phrases are new, or uncommon, or used in a sense differing in any respect from common usage.

2. By stating the proposition in different ways, at the same time shewing what limitations are designed to apply to it, and wherein there is danger of mistake, which it is necessary to guard against. This we often do in conversation, when we fear that an assertion we have made, is not fully and rightly understood.

3. By stating particular cases, or individual instances, and thus shewing what is meant by a general proposition.

4. By illustrations, especially by formal comparisons and historical allusions. What is familiar to our minds, is thus made to aid us in understanding what is less obvious and less easily discerned.

A second object of amplification is to support by argument the proposition or assertion advanced. Here, of course, the amplification will vary with the nature of the argument used. The more common forms are,

1. When the proposition to be established is of the nature of a general truth, and the writer supports it by an enumeration of the particular instances, on which it is founded, or from which it has been inferred. This is called Induction.

Paley treating on the goodness of Deity, lays down the

following proposition, that in a vast plurality of instances in which contrivance is perceived, the design of the contrivance is beneficial. To prove this proposition, he looks at the different parts of animals as they are subservient to the uses of the animal, and also at the various orders of animal existence; and thus from particular instances infers a general conclusion. This is an example of inductive reasoning.

2. When a proposition is established by a statement of facts, or an appeal to acknowledged authorities. Thus Addison, when endeavoring to shew that a middle condition in life is to be chosen as favorable to the cultivation of the moral virtues, introduces the prayer of Agur. This is an argument from Testimony.

3. When similar cases are stated, and the inference is made, that what is proved or acknowledged to hold true in the one case, is true also in the corresponding case. This is an argument from Analogy.

Illustration. In observing different orders of animal life, we notice important changes as to their modes of existence. Such is the transition of the caterpillar to the butterfly, and of the bird from its confinement in the shell to its full fledged state. Bishop Butler hence derives an argument from analogy in favor of the existence of man in a future state.

Other forms of argument are occasionally resorted to, in proof of propositions and assertions. Those which have been mentioned, are in most frequent use : and we learn from them the nature of amplification, so far as it is of an argumentative kind.

A third object of amplification is to persuade. A writer would recommend, or enforce, what he advances. He would induce his readers to think that what he proposes to them, is desirable; and further, that the course which he recommends for its attainment is practicable and will be successful.   Here then the amplification becomes in part hortatory, and in part argumentative.

So far as the amplification is hortatory, it consists of appeals to some leading principles in the constitution of man — to his conscience, or his sense of what is morally right and wrong — to his selfish propensities, or the desire for his own welfare and happiness, and to his feelings of benevolence. Other passions are also appealed to in particular cases. In making these appeals to the sense of justice, and the selfish and social principles of our nature, there is frequent occasion to view one proposition in its connexion with others, to make inferences from what is felt and acknowledged to be true in cases of frequent occurrence, to that which is more rarely witnessed. (See Exercise II with remarks.)

Appeals are also often made in this kind of amplification to common sense. By this it is meant, that the writer endeavors to recommend and enforce his proposition by accounting for it, that is, by assigning the causes or reasons on which it rests. It is asserted, for example, that men profoundly versed in science are usually negligent in attending to the common transactions of life; and in supporting this proposition, the writer dwells on the nature of habits of abstraction, and assigns the existence of these habits as a cause of the negligence referred to. Thus he accounts for what is asserted in his proposition, and every man of common sense perceives the reasonableness of the cause assigned. Appeals of this kind to the common sense of readers, which are sometimes called arguments from cause to effect, are more frequently used to instruct and influence those of candid minds, than to convince opposers. They gratify also the strong propensity of man to know the causes of things, and thus dispose the mind to the reception of any proposition which they are brought to support.

The inquiry may here arise, what kinds of composition and what circumstances, require a brief, and what demana an extended amplification? It may be said generally. in reply, that writings designed to excite emotion, and to influence the will, require a more extended amplification than those which are argumentative, or those addressed directly to the understanding. In the former case, it is desirable, that the mind should be led to dwell on what is presented before it, and to notice whatever is fitted and designed to excite the desired emotion. Hence copiousness of detail,. and a full and minute statement of attending circumstances. are required. — On the other hand, an argument should be stated concisely and simply; in this way it offers itself in a form most striking and convincing to the mind. Sometimes, however, it is necessary to modify these general directions. An argument may be abstruse and complex, and hence may require to be stated at greater length; or those, for whom the production is designed, may be men of uncultivated minds, and unaccustomed to connected reasonings In these instances, it may be well to depart from the general rule, and to expand and repeat the argument stated.

The nature and object of amplification may be learnt from what has been stated. The inquiry remains, How is this power of enlarging upon a topic attained? or rather, upon what intellectual habits and qualifications, does the successful exercise of it depend? And here I mention,

1. Extent and command of knowledge.

It was stated at the commencement of this chapter, that extent of knowledge is essential to the good writer. But it is not sufficient, that the mind is well stored with facts. — Our thoughts must be at command. They must come at our bidding, and be made to effect the purposes for which they are needed. This power of producing and applying our knowledge as occasion demands, evidently depends on the intellectual habits, especially on the etentiveness ar. readiness of the memory.

2. Closely connected with the command of the thoughts, is the power of illustration. Successfully to perform this part of amplification, the writer needs to be familiar with objects and scenes in the natural. world, with passing events, and with the whole circle of science and literature. He needs also an active imagination. Liveliness of fancy is no less conducive to the clear and striking exhibition of the thoughts, than to ornaments of style. Hence the cultivation of this class of the powers is equally important to the practical and to the elegant writer; to him who aims to enlighten the mind and improve the heart, and to him who would gratify the taste and please the fancy of his readers.

3. Another requisite for success in amplification, is defi niteness of thought in our reasonings. There are men of strong minds, who reason ably, and, if we look at the con clusions to which they arrive, correctly, but who are unable to follow out in their own minds, or to state to others, the train of argument they have pursued. To do this, requires a mental discipline, to which their intellectual powers have not been subjected. On the contrary, those who are accustomed to look in upon the operations of their own minds, and to think with precision and accuracy, are able to state their reasonings definitely and fully to others; and this, as it has been said, is the kind of amplification, which in argu mentative writings is required.

4. Another requisite for success in amplification, is copi ousness of expression. This phrase includes both a command of words and of construction, and he who excels in this particular, has one important qualification for enlarging upon the topics on which he writes, especially when joined with the other qualifications that have been mentioned. Copiousness of expression is acquired by a familiarity with

good authors; and the differences, which in this respect
are found among writers, are principally to be traced to
some diversities in their literary advantages and habits.
Those, who in their early years are familiar with books,
and accustomed to listen to the conversation of literary
men, usually acquire, with little effort, copiousness of expression. Much advantage in this respect is also derived
from translations, whether written or oral, from foreign languages into our own.

Different kinds of composition.

Writings are distinguished from each other, as didactic,
persuasive, argumentative, descriptive and narrative. These
distinctions have reference to the object which the writer
has primarily and principally in view. Didactic writing, as
the name implies, is used in conveying instruction; the
common text-books used in a course of education are examples. When, in connexion with instruction, precepts are
enjoined, and rules laid down for the observance of those
who read, we have an example of didactic preceptive writing (Ex. i.) When it is designed to influence the will,
the composition becomes of the persuasive kind; the proposed object is made to appear desirable, and the reader is
urged to pursue it. Of this class, are sermons and most
discourses addressed to deliberative assemblies. (Ex. ii.)
Another kind of composition, and one which is found united
with most others, is the argumentative. Under this head,
are included the various forms of argument, the statement of proofs, the assigning of causes, and, generally,
those writings, which are addressed to the reasoning faculties of the mind. (Ex. iii.) Narrative and descriptive
writings relate past occurrences, and place before the mind.

'or its contemplation, various objects and science.   (Lx. iv
and v.)

These different kinds of composition are often found
united together in the same discourse. In ancient systems
of Rhetoric, they became distinct objects of attention, and
appropriate directions were given for the composition of
each part. It is not, however, designed to treat, in this chapter, on the management of the subject in an extended regular
discourse. Nothing more is attempted, than to state and
illustrate some general remarks, pertaining to this topic.
The kind of composition more immediately in view, is an
essay, or treatise, in part argumentative, and in part persuasive, — such as is adapted to defend and enforce the
opinions of a writer on any subject he would present to the
consideration of his readers

Selection of a subject.

It is a direction of Horace,

> Sumite materiam vestris, qui scribitis, æquam
> Viribus.*

The meaning of this maxim evidently is, that we should not
attempt to write on subjects which are beyond the reach of
our mental powers, and to the treatment of which, from our
habits of thought, we are not fitted. Rightly to understand
and discuss some subjects, requires a previous knowledge
and powers of reasoning, which are not commonly possessed;
and when these essential prerequisites do not exist, our labor
must be in vain.

The injunction of Horace, as thus explained, admits of
being applied to the selection of subjects for young writers

---

* Examine well, ye writers, weigh with care,
  What suits your genius; what your strength can bear.

FRANCIS

3 *

And on this point, two important directions may be given
they should be topics which they are capable of fully under
standing, and which are interesting to them. Let a pupi.
be required to write on a subject which is above his comprehension, and his composition becomes either a succession
of vague and disconnected assertions, or a collection of
thoughts and sentences from different authors. In either
case, the exercise, though laborious perhaps, is injurious to
the intellectual habits of him by whom it is performed.
The subject selected should also be interesting, one within
the usual range of the writer's studies and conversation,
and which may have to him an air of reality. Descriptions
of scenes and occurrences which have come under immediate observation, are for these reasons recommended, or if
the composition be of a didactic kind, the attention may be
directed to subjects of an ethical nature.

The neglect of what is here recommended may lead to
much vain and fruitless labor, and perhaps to fatal discour-
agement. Young writers not unfrequently get the impression, that they have not a genius for writing, or that in their
case there are peculiar difficulties and hinderances, when the
true difficulty is the wrong selection of subjects for their first
attempts in composition.

Introduction.

Whether a composition should have a formal introduction
or not, must be determined by the good sense of the writer.
In short essays, it is generally best to commence with a
statement of the subject, and to enter at once on its discussion. There should at least be a proportion observed between the introduction and the rest of the performance. A
huge portico before a small building, always appears out of
place When an introduction is used, it should be striking

and appropriate. Often the opportunity is improved, to correct some mistake, or remove some prejudice connected with the subject to be discussed, — or a statement is made of facts, the knowledge of which is important to the right understanding of what follows, — or general remarks may be made, designed to impress the reader with a sense of the importance and interest of what is advanced. But whatever be the nature of the introduction, it should be written with great care. Before the minds of readers become engaged in the discussion of the subject, the attention is at liberty to fix itself on the skill shown in the choice of words and the modelling of the expression. It is also well known, that first impressions are important. A happy turn of expression, or a well timed allusion in the commencement of a performance, may effect much in arresting the attention of readers and conciliating their good will.

The following introduction to Webster's Address, delivered on Bunker's Hill, is striking and appropriate

"The uncounted multitude before me, and around me, proves the feeling which the occasion has excited. These thousands of happy faces, glowing with sympathy and joy, and, from the impulses of a common gratitude, turned reverently to Heaven, in this spacious temple of the firmament, proclaim that the day, the place, and the purpose of our assembling have made a deep impression on our hearts."

The speaker seems aware of the thoughts and feelings which have taken possession of every heart, and giving utterance to these thoughts and feelings, he arrests with consummate skill the attention, and conciliates the good will of those whom he addresses. The expression, too, " in this spacious temple of the firmament," though not striking from its novelty, is yet, from the circumstances under which t was uttered, happy and truly appropriate.

On the statement of the subject.

The first and leading object of attention in every compo
sition of an argumentative kind, is to determine the precise
point of inquiry — the proposition which is to be laid down
and supported Unless the writer has steadily before him
some point which he would reach, he will ever be liable to
go astray — to lose himself and his readers. It is not til
he has determined on the definite object of inquiry, that he
can know what views to present, and how long to dwell on
the different topics he may discuss.

It is recommended to him, who is considering what proposition shall be laid down, and in what form it shall be
stated, to ask himself the three following questions; 1. What
is the fact? 2. Why is it so? 3. What consequences
result? Suppose as an illustration, that my thoughts have
been turned towards the manifestations of wisdom, goodness and power in the works of creation around me, and
I wish to lead those whom I address, to be mindful of
these things. I ask myself, 1. What is the fact? In reply, it may be said, — that in the material world there are
numerous indications of infinite wisdom and benevolence,
and of almighty power. I ask, 2. How is the existence of
these works to be accounted for? What is the cause? I
answer, God hath created them. I ask again, 3. What
should be the consequence? Again I reply, men should
live mindful of God. I embody the results of my inquiries
in the following proposition; Men who live in the midst of
objects which shew forth the perfections of the great Creator, should live mindful of Him.

It is not always necessary, that the proposition to be sup
ported, should be thus formally stated, though this is usually
done in writings of an argumentative nature. Sometimes it
is elegantly implied, or left to be inferred from the introduc

tory remarks. When however any doubt can exist as to the object proposed, or there is any danger that the reader may mistake the design of the writer, the precise object of discussion cannot be too distinctly and formally stated. In the management of the subject, as in the expression of the thoughts, elegance should always be sacrificed to perspicuity. Half the controversies and differences of opinion among men, arise from their not distinctly understanding the questions on which they write and converse.

It is a common impression with young writers, that the wider the field of inquiry on which they enter, the more abundant and obvious will be the thoughts, which will offer themselves for their use. Hence, by selecting some general subject, they hope to secure copiousness of matter, and thus to find an easier task. Experience, however, shews that the reverse is true — that as the field of inquiry is narrowed, questions arise more exciting to the mind, and thoughts are suggested of greater value and interest to the readers. Suppose, as an illustration, that a writer proposes to himself to write an essay on literature. Amidst the numerous topics which might be treated upon under this term, what unity of subject could be expected? How commonplace and uninteresting would be the thoughts advanced! But let some distinct inquiry be proposed, or some assertion be made and supported, of which the extract among the Exercises, entitled a " Defence of literary studies in men of business," is an instance, and there is a copiousness of interesting thoughts, presented in a distinct and connected manner

On the plan or divisions.

Having before his mind the precise object of inquiry, and having stated also, either in a formal manner, or by impli cation, the proposition to be supported, the writer now turns his attention to the formation of his plan; in other words, he determines in what order and connection his thoughts shall be presented. Thus are formed the divisions cf a composition, which will correspond in their nature to the leading design and character of the performance. In argumentative discussions, the heads are distinct propositions or arguments, designed to support and establish the leading proposition. In persuasive writings, they are the different considerations, which the writer would place before his readers, to influence their minds, and induce them to adopt the opinions and pursue the course, which he recommends. In didactic writings, they are the different points of instruction. In narrative and descriptive writings, they are the different events and scenes, which in succession are brought before the mind.

It is obvious, that no particular rules of general application, can be given to aid the writer in forming his plan. It must vary with the subject and occasion. Here then is room for the exercise of ingenuity; and the habits of consecutive thinking mentioned in a former section of this chapter, are the best preparation for this part of his work. But though no specific rules can be given, there are a few general directions, which will now be stated. It will be seen, that they apply principally to those writings, which are of an argumentative nature, and which alone admit of an extended plan.

1. Every division should have a direct and obvious bear ing on the leading purpose of the writer.

2. The different divisions should be distinct, one not in cluding another.

3. The divisions should to a good degree exhaust the subject, and taken together should present a whole.

Let us suppose, in illustration of these rules, that it is

proposed to write an essay on Filial duties As the object of the essay, the writer designs to shew, that children should render to their parents obedience and love. His division is as follows. Children should render obedience and love o their parents,

1. Because they are under obligation to their parents for benefits received from them.

2 Because in this way they secure their own happiness

3. Because God has commanded them to honor their parents.

In this division there is a manifest reference to the object of the writer. The different heads are also distinct from each other, and taken together give a sufficiently full view of the subject. It is in accordance then with the preceding directions.

Let us now suppose that the following division had been made ;

Children should render obedience and love to their parents,

1. Because they are under obligations to them for benefits received from them.

2. Because their parents furnish them with food and clothing

3. Because in this way they secure their own happiness

4. Because there is a satisfaction and peace of conscience in the discharge of filial duties.

This division is faulty, since the different parts are not distinct from each other. The second head is included under the first, and the fourth under the third.

A third division might be made as follows ; Children should render obedience and love to their parents,

1. Because they should do what is right.

2. Because in this way they secure their own happiness.

3. Because God has commanded them to honor their parents.

It may be said of the first part of this division, that it has no particular reference to the object of the writer. It is a truth of general application, and may with equal propriety be assigned in enforcing any other duty as that of filial obedience. It is also implied in the other heads, since children do what is right, when, in obedience to God's command, they seek to secure their own happiness.

The question may arise, Is it of importance distinctly to state the plan which is pursued? Should there be formal divisions of a discourse? To this I answer, that in the treatment of intricate subjects, where there are many divisions, and where it is of importance that the order and connexion of each part should be carefully observed, to state the divisions is the better course. But it is far from being always essential. Though we never should write without forming a distinct plan for our own use, yet it may often be best to let others gather this plan from reading our productions. A plan is a species of scaffolding to aid us in erecting the building. When the edifice is finished, we may let the scaffolding fall.

Arrangement.

In the discussion of a subject, which is of an argumentative nature, the direction is generally given, that the arguments should rise in importance. In this way the attention, excited by novelty at first, may continue to be held, and a full and strong conviction be left on the mind at the conclusion of the reasoning. This, as a general rule, may be observed, but the more obvious occurrence of an argument or some other cause, will often require the skilful writer to depart from it.

Another rule of more importance is, that arguments from cause to effect, or those which account for what is asserted in the leading proposition, supposing it to be true, should precede those of a stronger or more convincing kind, such as arguments from testimony or induction. Even this rule, however, is not without its exceptions.

An inquiry of some importance pertaining to arrangement, is, whether the proposition to be supported, should in all cases precede the proof, or whether the proof should precede the formal announcement of the proposition. Men usually assert their opinions, and then assign the reasons on which they are founded, and this, without doubt, is the best arrangement, unless special reasons exist for adopting some other. If what is asserted is likely, either from its being novel, or uncommon, or from its being opposed to the prejudices of the reader, to disaffect him, and to prevent his due consideration of the arguments brought forward, it is better to depart from the general rule, and to defer the formal statement of the proposition maintained to the close.

Another inquiry relates to the proper place for introducing the refutation of objections. On this point, the general rule is given, that objections should be considered near the commencement of a composition. In this way, the prejudices of opposers may be eradicated, and their minds left free to give full attention and due weight to the arguments advanced. Often, however, it is necessary to bring forward some views of the subject, preparatory to the examination of objections; in these instances, their refutation is found in the midst, or deferred to the close of the composition.

Transitions.

Transitions from one part of a composition to another, are also important objects of attention. The general direction is often given, that transitions be natural and easy. By this it is meant, that they be in agreement with the common modes of associating the thoughts. In argumentative writings, where the different parts are connected by a common reference to some particular point, which they are designed to establish, this common relationship will be sufficient to prevent the transition from one argument to another from appearing unnatural and abrupt. Still, as has been intimated, there may be skill shown in the arrangement of the arguments, and one may appear to arise happily from another. But in writings which are not argumentative, much skill is often displayed in the transitions. With the design of exhibiting some happy instances of transitions and thus showing what is meant by their being natural and easy, I shall notice those in Goldsmith's Traveller, to which these epithets are often applied. His description of Italy closes with the mention of its inhabitants, feeble and degraded, pleased with low delights and the sports of children The transition to the Swiss is thus made;

> My soul, turn from them; — turn we to survey
> Where rougher climes a nobler race display.

The principle on which the transition is here made, is that of contrast. And since the mind is often wont to look at objects as opposed to each other, it naturally, in this way, passes from the Italians to the Swiss.

The transition from Switzerland to France is thus made;

> Some sterner virtues o'er the mountain's breast
> May sit like falcons, cowering on the nest:
> But all the gentler morals such as play
> Through life's more cultured walks, and charm the way
> These far dispersed, on timorous pinions fly,
> To sport and flutter in a kinder sky.
>
> To kinder skies, where gentler manners reign,
> I turn — and France displays her bright domain.

In this instance, the transition, like that before mentioned, depends in part on the principle of contrast, but seems more immediately to rest on the accidental mention of the words *kinder sky*.   Such accidental associations are frequent, especially in familiar intercourse, and in the easy flow of the thoughts; and though they would not be approved in the grave discussion of a subject, in a descriptive epistle, which is the nature of the production we are examining, they strike us favorably.

Resemblance, cause and effect, contiguity as to time or place, may be mentioned as other principles of association on which transitions are often easily made.

Conclusion.

If it be of importance, that the attention be arrested at first by a well written introduction, and sustained by well connected and increasingly important arguments, it will be readily allowed, that a happy conclusion is no less desirable. It is then that a decision is about to be made, and the mind of the readers should be left impressed with a favorable opinion of. the writer, and with the justness and truth of what has been told him.   Here then the writer should exert all his skill, and put forth all his powers.

As an example of a well executed conclusion, the following passage, which is found at the close of an eulogy on Adams and Jefferson, may be cited ;

" Their statues are men · living, feeling, intelligent, adoring man, nearing the image of his Maker; having the impress of divinity. Their monuments are the everlasting hills which they have clothed with verdure — their praises are sounds of health and joy, in vallies which they have made fruitful — to them incense daily rises, in the perfumes of fragrant fields, which they have spread with cultivation — fair cities proclaim their glory — gorgeous mansions speak their munificence — their names are inscribed on the goodly habitations of men ; and on those hallowed temples of God, whose spires ever point to the heaven, which, we trust, has received them."

Narrative and Descriptive Writing.

The directions given in this chapter on the management of a subject, refer principally to argumentative composition. We are not to expect in narrative writings the regular divisions of a discourse, as in didactic and argumentative productions. Still there will be some prominent or leading event, and the different parts of the narrative will tend to exhibit it fully and clearly. These parts will be the circumstances of the event, such as led to it, such as accompanied it, or such as follow from it ; and the writer will dwell upon them in proportion to their importance and connexion with his main design. Occasional reflections may also be made, and inferences drawn, and whatever can illustrate, or throw an interest around the principal event, will be introduced. As to transitions, they will often depend on the order of occurrences in the succession of time, or as one occurrence is accounted to be the cause of another. (Ex. iv.)

In descriptive writing, it is the purpose of the writer, as has been stated, to place before the view of his readers some object or scene. In its design, it nearly resembles both historical and landscape painting, and there is a resemblance, too, in the particulars on which the successful exertion of each depends. A happy selection of circumstances is of importance. A few prominent traits, well chosen, and strongly exhibited, will produce a much better effect, than the enumeration of many particulars. In this kind of writing, much is found, which is designed to assist the distinctness of the mind's conception, and when the writer dwells on different parts, it is with this purpose. The transitions, as in argumentative writings, are often abrupt, and it is thought sufficient connexion, that the different parts tend to the same end. The narrative and descriptive are often found united. (Ex. v.)

CHAPTER SECOND

ON TASTE.

Were men simply intellectual beings, and weie it the
n ly design of the writer to convey instruction to his readers,
what has been said in the preceding chapter, would be all
that is required, preparatory to the consideration of the qualities of a good style. But men have imagination, and are
susceptible of emotions; and it is often the purpose of the
writer, to cause the imagination to be exercised, and emotions of various kinds to be excited. To give pleasure in
this way, may be the immediate object of the writer, or
he may seek to please his readers, merely to arrest their
attention, increase the distinctness of their views, and favorably incline them to the reception of the opinions he communicates.

From this statement, the definite object of this and the
following chapter may be learnt. It is to aid in judging of
whatever is thus addressed to the imagination in connexion
with certain emotions of which men are susceptible. To
direct in all that thus pertains to the imagination and these
emotions, is regarded as the office of Taste. Hence the
nature of taste in general will first be considered. This will
be followed by some account of what is implied by a literary
taste, including an enumeration of those different properties
in literary productions which are objects of its attention,

4 *

with such ren arks and directions as may aid in its acquisition and improvement.

Definition of Taste.

T.ie decisions of taste are judgments passed on whatever
is designed to excite emotions of beauty, of grandeur or of
sublimity. The power of thus judging is founded on the
experience of emotions of the same class, and is called taste;
and hence he who exercises this power successfully, is called
a man of taste. By judgment, as the word is here used, 1
mean the determining of the fitness of particular causes fcr
producing certain effects. The chemist would produce a
mixture having certain properties, — a certain degree of hard-
ness, a required color or taste. With this view he unites
several simples; and in selecting the simples that are to be
united for producing the required mixture, and in determining the quantity of each to be used, there is judgment. In
the same manner. where taste is exercised, there is a certain
effect to be produced, and in determining the fitness of
means for producing this effect there is judgment.

For a full account of the emotions here mentioned. the student must be referred to works on the philosophy of the mind.
But it is necessary, that a short statement of what is meant
by them should here be given.

If we reflect on the different emotions, of which we are
conscious in the notice of actions and objects around us, we
find that some of them are of a moral nature, and we speak
of the actions which excite them as virtuous or vicious. —
Other emotions are included under what are called the passions, and we speak of the objects which excite them as objects of desire or aversion — of fear or remorse, or of some
other passion. We think also of such objects as affecting
our happiness. But distinct, both from emotions of a moral
nature, and from those included under the passions, there is

a third class of emotions, which is particularly referred to in the preceding definition of taste, and these will now be exhibited.

When the sun goes down in the west, the surrounding clouds reflect to our view a rich variety of colors. We gaze on the splendid scene, and there is a pleasant emotion excited in our minds.

In reading the story of the two friends, Damon and Pythias, who were objects of the cruelty of Dionysius, we are struck with the closeness of their friendship; and while we think on the fidelity of the returning friend, and on their mutual contest for death, a pleasing emotion arises in the mind.

When examining Dr. Paley's reasoning in proof of the existence of the Deity, and observing how every part is brought to bear on the particular object in view, while one example after another gives additional strength to the argument, we admire the skill of the reasoner and the perfection of his work, and in view of this skill and this finished work a grateful emotion arises in the mind.

It will be observed in these examples, that the emotion excited is not strong, — that it is of a grateful kind, and that it may continue for some time. This is called *an emotion of beauty.*

The traveller, when he stands on the banks of the Mississippi, and looks upon that noble river, flowing on with the power of collected waters, and bearing on its bosom the wealth of the surrounding region, is conscious of emotions, which, as they rise and swell within his breast, correspond to the scene on which he looks.

Burke has given the following biographical notice of Howard the celebrated philanthropist.

"He has visited all Europe,— not to survey the sumptuousness of palaces, or the stateliness of temples; not to make accurate measurements of the remains of ancient grandeur; not to form a scale of the curiosities of modern art, not to collect medals, or collate manuscripts; — but to dive into the depths of dungeons; to plunge into the infection of hospitals, to survey the mansions of sorrow and pain; to take the gauge and dimensions of misery, depression and contempt; to remember the forgotten, to attend to the neglected, to visit the forsaken, and to compare and collate the distresses of all men in all countries. His plan is original; and it is as full of genius, as it is of humanity. It was a voyage of discovery, a circumnavigation of charity."

No one can read this passage, and not feel a high degree of admiration in view of the devotedness and elevation of purpose it describes.

When the orator stands up before collected thousands, and for an hour sways them at his will by the powers of his eloquence, who, in that vast throng, can regard the speaker before him and feel no admiration of his genius?

The emotions excited in these and similar instances, have been called *emotions of grandeur*. They differ from those of beauty in that they are more elevating and ennobling.

Byron, in his description of a thunder storm in the Alps has the following passage ·

> " Far along,
> From peak to peak, the rattling crags among,
> Leaps the live thunder! — not from one lone cloud,
> But every mountain now hath found a tongue;
> And Jura answers through her misty shroud,
> Back to the joyous Alps who call to her aloud."

Who in the midst of Alpine scenery could thus listen to the voice of the leaping thunder, and not start with strong emotion?

We are told, that when Washington appeared before Congress, to resign his military power at the close of the war, " he was received as the founder and guardian of the republic. They silently retraced the scenes of danger and distress, through which they had passed together. They recalled to mind the blessings of freedom and peace pur chased by his arm. Every heart was big with emotion. Tears of admiration and gratitude burst from every eye."

In the presence of this august assembly, the Commander in chief of the armies of the United States, after piously recounting the blessings, which divine providence had conferred on his country, and commending that country to the continued care of its Almighty Protector, advanced, and resigned the great powers, which had been committed to his trust. How much must this closing act have added to the deep interest of the scene!

We are told, that when Newton drew near to the close of those calculations, which confirmed his discovery of the laws, by which the planets are bound in their courses, he was so overwhelmed with emotion, that he could not proceed, and was obliged to ask the assistance of a friend. No one can think of the mighty intellectual work that was then accomplished, and not feel as he did, an overpowering emotion.

To the emotions excited in these last mentioned examples is applied the epithet *sublime*. They are less permanent than those of grandeur, but more thrilling and exalting.

In these examples, the emotions which are excited, arise neither from a moral approbation of the objects or actions as virtuous, nor from a personal interest in them as affecting our happiness. How, then, are they excited?

The answers to this inquiry have been numerous. Some have said, that there is a distinct sense, which enables the mind to discern in objects something which is fitted to excite emotions of taste, and which is suited to this purpose in the same manner as the sense of hearing is suited to sounds. Others have attempted to resolve the whole into the principle of the association of ideas, and have said, that in every instance where an emotion of the kind mentioned is excited, some associated thoughts connected with our happiness, are brought before the mind. Thus, in the second of the examples given, they would say, that the grateful emotion arises from the thought of our own past friendships, or of how much we should enjoy in the possession of a faithful friend. Others account for these emotions by referring them to what are called primary laws of our nature. So far as these emotions are excited in view of natural objects and scenes, they say, that our Creator has so formed us and adapted us to the world in which we live, that the view of certain objects and scenes is fitted to excite in the mind certain corresponding emotions. — At the same time they allow, that much influence is to be ascribed to the principle of association. In reference to works of art, another original principle is also recognized, which is called the love of fitness or adaptation. The last theory is that of Brown, and is the one now generally received. For a full explanation of it, the student is referred to his work on Intellectual Philosophy. It is enough for my present purpose to have pointed out the class of emotions which comes under the cognizance of taste, and to have referred to some of the attempts to explain them.

It will be observed, that the examples which are given, are drawn from three different classes of objects, natural moral, and intellectual. But since, in the classification of emotions, as those of beauty, grandeur and sublimity, we obviously refer to the emotions as they exist in the mind, and not to the objects by which they are excited, this diversity in the exciting objects is not regarded. Neither is it of importance, that these different classes of emotions should here be separately considered. It is difficul in many cases to mark the transition from one to another, and to decide whether the emotion excited be an emotion of beauty, of grandeur, or of sublimity. These three classes of emotions are alike objects of the attention of taste ; and the principles and rules established in reference to one class. admit of application to the others. Hence the attention is principally directed to emotions of beauty, and emotions of each class are sometimes called *emotions of taste.*

I return now to the definition of taste. Every instance of judgment implies knowledge of those subjects, on which it is exercised. The chemist cannot form his mixture, that shall possess certain required properties, without a knowledge of the properties of the several simples which are ingredients. In those instances of judgment also which are included under taste, there is in the same manner knowledge implied; but as this is the knowledge of emotions, and can be acquired only by experience, taste is said to be founded on the experience of past emotions.

Though taste, in the definition which has now been explained, is called judgment, it is not meant, that in the exercise of taste, the mind is ordinarily conscious of deliberation or of the balancing of reasons, as in some other instances of judgment. It is true, that this deliberation may be rapidly passed through in all instances, and in some, as in the case of the artist employed in designing and executing his work, there may be a consciousness of the process But most frequently, judgment on objects of taste seems to be passed instantaneously. As the result of past experience of emotions, certain principles seem fixed in the mind, and when taste is called into exercise, it is the immediate application of these principles to particular instances. The analogy is close between the exercise of taste in the works of the fine arts, and of taste, as the word is literally applied to the sense of taste. Take for example the case of wines The wine merchant is able at once to decide as to the qual ity of the wine presented to him, and to detect any foreign ingredient. He has acquired his ability to do this by past experience, and he brings the results of this past experience, which seem to exist in his mind as certain fixed principles, to the particular instance in which his judgment is required.

Sensibility as connected with taste.

From the definition that has been given of taste, we may learn in what way sensibility is connected with its attainment. By sensibility, is meant a high degree of susceptibility of the emotions of beauty. And since taste is founded on the experience of these emotions, sensibility, as thus defined, must aid in the formation of a good taste. It must be supposed, that so far as the emotions of beauty result from original tendencies of the mind to be pleased in view of certain objects, they are in some degree common to all men in their earliest years. But it is a well known fact respecting all our emotions, that if neglected, they lose their strength, and if entirely disregarded, they will soon cease to be felt. On the contrary they are strengthened by being regarded and cherished. Hence it is, that while some men are susceptible of emotions of beauty in view of objects and scenes around them, others, the circumstances of whose life have been different, look upon the same objects and scenes without any emotion of this nature. So far, too, as these emotions result from associated thoughts and feelings, there is an equal cause of diversity among different individuals. One, from the scenes and events that have fallen under his observation, may have many associations connected with a particular object, which another may have never formed.

These remarks admit of illustration. Addison, when he

went forth in the evening, and gazed upon the starry heavens and the moon walking in her majesty, felt emotions of sublimity. In accounting for the rise of these emotions, we might say, that he was a man of sensibility — from the original constitution of his mind he was susceptible of emotions of taste to a high degree. His intellectual habits also, and the circumstances of his life, were such as to cherish and strengthen these original tendencies of his mind. Astronomy had taught him something of the size and number and uses of these heavenly bodies; and in this way, or in other ways, many associations were connected with them. On the same evening, perhaps, and in the same neighborhood, the laborer returning from his daily toil, looked upon the same starry and moon-lit firmament, but felt no emotion of beauty or sublimity. Still this individual might have been originally constituted with as much sensibility as Addison; but such has been his lot in life, that this sensibility has been lost, and he thinks of the moon and stars only as lighting him homewards from his toil.

Standard of taste.

The inquiry here arises, whether a sensibility to emotions of beauty may not exist, and still the individual possessing it be destitute of good taste? And if this inquiry be answered in the affirmative, as it must be in accordance with facts, it may be still further asked, how this want of taste is consistent with the statement, that taste is founded on the experience of emotions of beauty and sublimity? The resolution of this apparent difficulty brings to view what is termed the STANDARD OF TASTE. It is the case, as we have seen, that from the peculiar circumstances of individuals, their original tendencies to emotions of beauty may be perverted and blunted, or strengthened and increased. The associations also connected with the same objects and scenes may be very different in different minds. From both of these causes, and from others not mentioned, the emotions excited in the minds of different individuals in the view of the same objects, will differ, and consequently, their experience as to past emotions will vary. In this way we account for diversities of taste among individuals, and here is the ground of the maxim so often quoted, *de gustibus non disputandum.* But amidst all these diversities, there are some objects and scenes, which do uniformly excite emotions of beauty in the great majority of those, who have any degree of sensibility. And where there are cases of exception, some sufficient reason may generally be assigned. In the assertion then that taste is founded on the experience of past emotions, reference is made to this common experience, and not to the experience of individuals, or of any particular country or age. Hence then we infer, *that the standard of taste is the agreeing voice of such as are susceptible of emotions of beauty, both of those who lived in past ages, and of those now existing.*

To illustrate these remarks, I may refer the student to the statue of Washington, which has been recently placed in the metropolis of New England, and which represents him in the drapery of a Roman hero. Should it be asked, why he is thus represented, rather than in the dress, which as a military commander, or a civil leader, he was accustomed to wear? or in such attire as was used by military and civil leaders in Europe two hundred, or five hundred, years ago? it might be answered, that though such drapery might have been approved at the period when it was worn and thus have been in agreement with the taste of the age at the present time it would appear unbecoming to the hu man form. But such is not the case with the Roman toga This is a drapery, which at all times, and to all men, ap pears graceful and excites emotions of beauty. This fact, then, both proves, that there is a standard of taste, and illustrates what is meant by it.

Hence we learn one object and use of models of excellence in the fine arts. It is principally by means of these, that we obtain a knowledge of the standard of taste, or rather they are the standard, since in them the decisions of men in different periods and portions of the world are found embodied. To illustrate this by an example, I will refer to West's painting of Christ in the exercise of the charities. We know that this painting was universally admired in England. It has been regarded with like admiration in this country. All those who are susceptible of emotions of taste, have felt these emotions when looking upon this production of art. Here, then, is found the united voice of men of the present age; and the artist knows, that so far as his production exhibits what excites emotions of beauty in this painting, it is in agreement with the general opinion of men now living, or the standard of the taste of the age. Had this picture existed through successive ages, and been uniformly admired, this would give it higher authority, and the artist, in conforming his work to it, would know, that what he produces, is in agreement with the opinions of men of different ages of the world. He might then hope, that his work, being conformed to this general standard of taste, would please all men every where, and of every age, who are susceptible of emotions of beauty, and whose minds are not under the influence of some particular bias. In models of excellence, then, in the fine arts, is expressed the experience of mankind respecting emotions of beauty; and in studying these models, the man of sensibility learns to correct any peculiar influence which circumstances may have had on his own emotions, and thus acquires a taste which is n conformity with the general standard of taste

Taste as affected by the intellectual habits.

Taste, as it exists in different individuals, is affected by the intellectual character and habits. We might expect this to be the case from the fact, that it implies discrimination, and that the same intellectual habits will be brought into exercise in judging of what is fitted to excite emotions of taste, as in those instances where judgments are formed on other subjects. It is in this way, that we may in part account for the diversities of taste in different individuals. He whose mind is enriched with various knowledge, and whose intellectual powers have been strengthened and improved, and who is wont to take large and comprehensive views of subjects, will manifest the greatness of his mind and the liberality of his views, in his judgment of what is fitted to excite an emotion of taste. He whose attention has been restricted to philosophical speculations, and who has been accustomed to reason with the precision of mathematical accuracy, will in like manner bring his habits of reasoning to subjects of taste, and will be less bold and more severe in his judgment of what is fitted to excite emotions of this kind.

Locke and Burke are striking examples of the justness of these remarks. Locke was an accurate thinker, and a close reasoner. His judgment, where he forms an opinion, is based on careful and minute examination. Hence his taste was severe. He used but little ornament, and that simple and illustrative. Fearful also that it might betray him, he condemned the use of it in the writings of others. Burke, on the contrary, was a man of much refinement. He possessed extensive classical attainments — had large and liberal views of subjects, and, susceptible to a high degree of emotions of taste, he was ever prone to indulge in the excitement of these emotions. But then he approved only of what is truly beautiful and sublime, and his judgment of what is fitted to excite these emotions, evidently felt the influence of his enlarged and liberal views on other subjects, or, in other words, of his intellectual habits.

Objects on which taste is exercised.

Taste, as thus explained, employs itself in judging both of the objects and scenes in Nature, and of works in the Fine Arts, and in both cases it determines as to the fitness of what is presented before it to produce emotions of beauty. Suppose several individuals, who are susceptible of emotions of beauty, to be travelling through some region of our country, which presents a rich variety of natural scenery. One of them, in advance of the others, upon rising an eminence, is struck with the view opening before him, and is led to exclaim as to the beauty of the prospect. The others, upon coming up, are impressed in the same manner They declare the scene before them beautiful, and they unite in pronouncing him who first pointed it out, a man of taste. All that is meant by this expression is, that the individual to whom it is applied, is able, from his experience of past emotions, to form a judgment respecting the fitness of objects in natural scenery to produce emotions of beauty, which is in agreement with the general judgment of mankind.

Suppose further, that the same individuals, in the course of their journey, stop to examine a gallery of paintings. One of them, in looking round on the different pictures, selects a painting which he pronounces beautiful. The attention of the others being called to it, they express the same opinion, and again they unite in calling the individual who has pointed out the painting, a man of taste. Here, as in the former case, all that is implied is, that the individual

called a man of taste, is able to judge of the fitness of cer
tain works of art to produce emotions of beauty.

But let us now suppose, that instead of speaking of the
individual who pointed out the painting to their notice, they
are led to speak of the work itself, and to call it a work of
taste. This might be said of a work of art, though not of
a scene in nature; for in this expression reference is evidently had to the artist by whom the work was executed,
and we never think of the Creator as guided by taste in the
work of creation. In this then, as in the preceding case,
all that is implied is, that the artist has shewn by the design
and execution of his work, that he is able to judge correctly
as to the fitness of objects and scenes to produce emotions
of beauty. But to shew more fully the nature of taste, and
to point out its connexion with the imagination, I shall
here describe the manner, in which it guides the artist in
designing and executing his work; and in doing this, I
shall confine the attention to works in the art of Painting,
since the mind conceives most eas'ly and distinctly objects
of sense

Connexion of taste with the imagination.

Let us first suppose, that the scene or object represented
by the painter, is an exact imitation of some scene or object
in nature. In this case, we might be pleased with the work,
and say that it discovers good taste. We might be pleased,
because the original scene is one fitted to excite emotions
of beauty, and we might ascribe good taste to the painter,
from his having selected a scene of this kind to be represented. Besides, we might be gratified with the skill that
is shewn in the execution of the work. Emotions of beauty
might be excited in view of the closeness of the imitation,
the justness of the coloring, and the truth of the perspective

and we might say, that taste has guided the artist in his ex-. hibition of what are usually called secondary beauties of painting.

But the most admired works in the arts of painting are not exact imitations. They are the creations of the painter, and have no archetype in nature. And it is in designing these original works, that the presence of taste is most needed, and her influence felt.

To show in what way taste guides the artist in designing his work, I shall here introduce an account given by Cicero of the course pursued by Zeuxis, when employed by the Crotonians to paint the picture of a beautiful female. The city of Crotona was celebrated for the beauty of its females Zeuxis requested, that those esteemed most beautiful might be assembled at the same place. From these he selected five, who in his estimation excelled all others in beauty, and by combining in his picture the most striking traits of beauty in each of these five, he executed the task assigned to him.

Now in the whole of this process, taste was evidently the guide of the artist. The selection of the five most beautiful virgins, the choice of the most beautiful traits in each, are both instances of judgment, founded on the experience of past emotions. But this is only the preparation for his work. What has been thus selected must now be combined together, and so combined, as to produce one harmonious effect. Instead of an assemblage of beautiful limbs and features, an air and proportion must be given to the form, and a cast to the countenance. Here is exercise for the designing powers of the artist, and over this part of the work also taste must preside. Different modes of combination present themselves before his "mind's eye," and of these different combinations, one is to be selected as most beautiful. The making of this selection is evidently an in-

stance of judgment, founded on the experience of past emo
tions of beauty. Zeuxis was familiar with forms of beauty,
and had fixed in his mind those principles of judging
which enabled him to decide with readiness and correct
ness. Hence, no doubt, his celebrity as a painter of the
female form.

From this example, we learn, why the most admired productions of the painter are not exact representations of objects and scenes in nature. In natural objects and scenes,
that which is suited to excite emotions of beauty, is mingled
with objects of indifference and disgust. The artist, under
the guidance of taste, collects together these scattered fragments of beauty, and combining them in one view with harmonious effect, presents to us objects and scenes more
beautiful than those which can be found in nature.

But it is by no means the case, that the artist is confined
to objects and scenes of nature for the materials of these
new combinations. It is here that the office of imagination
and its connexion with taste, may be seen. By this faculty
of the mind, the objects of past sensations are modified and
combined anew, and images of objects and scenes, that exist
only in this airy creation, rise up before our view. But
while gazing on these visionary things, the same grateful
emotions of beauty are excited, as when the objects before
us have more of reality. Hence, when the artist would
represent to us a scene, which shall strongly excite our
emotions of beauty, he calls in imagination to his aid. She
brings to his view a bright assemblage of forms of beauty.
She presents them in different lights ; combines and modifies
them variously. And while these shifting scenes are flitting
before him, he selects, under the guidance of taste, the most
beautiful forms and happiest combinations, and fixes them on
the canvass for our view.

From these united efforts of imagination and taste he

artist presents to us models of excellence, superior to what can be found in the works of nature, or in the productions of artists that have preceded him. By the efforts of genius, he is enabled to make such combinations as others have never made; and taste, by exercising itself in the study of these visions of the mind, reaches a degree of perfection, to which it could never have attained in the study of existing models, or of the scenes of nature. But if imagination thus assists in the cultivation and improvement of taste, taste in return repays the assistance of imagination, by acting as director in the new creations which she forms. Imagination might be furnished with a thousand different forms of beauty, as the materials of her work, and unite them in ten thousand different combinations; but without taste to preside and direct, she could never reach that harmoniousness of effect, that unity of expression, to which nature often attains.

Value of models of excellence in the arts.

From this analysis of the manner in which works in the fine arts are produced, the assistance, which the artist must derive from the study of models of excellence in the arts, may be learnt. Here he sees presented before him, the representations of those beautiful forms of nature, the knowledge of which, without this assistance, he could have obtained only by frequent and tedious processes of observation and analysis. The *beau ideal* is delineated to his view, and he forms his taste from the contemplation of perfect forms of beauty, instead of those imperfect forms where beauty is mingled with deformity. He sees also the most happy combinations of these forms. He has before him the results which others have made, and is thus placed in advance of

those who are not favored with similar means of improvement.

The man, who is thus permitted to form his taste from
models of excellence around him, may be said to exist in
a new creation. He lives where the sun sheds a brighter
day, where the clouds are skirted by more brilliant colors,
and where nature's carpet shows a richer green. Angelic
forms are about him. He ever stands on some chosen spot,
and each new scene that presents itself, gives but a varied
hue to the emotion of beauty that he feels.

Explanation of the word Picturesque.

We may learn also in this connexion, and by the aid of
the principles which have been stated, what is meant, when
it is said of some countries, that they present scenes more
picturesque than those found in others. This epithet, when
applied to natural scenery, relates primarily and principally
to the harmoniousness of effect produced on the mind, and
implies such a prominence and combination of objects as
give an expression or character to the scene. Nature seems
in such instances to perform that work of combination,
which, when represented to us on canvass by the skilful
painter, we say he has designed by the aid of imagination
and taste. The view may or may not present surpassing
forms of beauty. We look not at objects individually, but
regard them as grouped together and exerting a combined
influence. Neither is it implied that the prospect is extensive, and that it embraces numerous and varied objects.
On the contrary, picturesque scenes are most frequently
those of limited extent, and which contain but few prominent parts.

Revolutions in Taste.

On the principles which have been stated in this chapter, the revolutions of taste may be easily explained. As peculiar circumstances have their influence on the tastes of different individuals, so the manners and customs and peculiar circumstances of different ages, exert their influence on the taste of these ages. The power of these adventitious circumstances is so great, that what in one age is esteemed and pronounced beautiful, in a succeeding age of more refinement, is regarded with disgust. Still it is true, that in this case, as in the diversities of the taste of individuals, there are some works of art, which rise superior to the influence of these accidental causes, and wherever they are known, excite emotions of beauty.

Different qualities of taste explained

I shall close this account of taste in general with a short explanation of the qualities, which are most frequently ascribed to it. These are three; Refinement, Delicacy, and Correctness.

We speak of Refinement of taste in reference to different ages and different periods in the life of an individual. It implies a progress, so that what is pleasing in one age, or one period of life, is not so in another. The sculptured monument, which in the early ages of a country is regarded with admiration and called beautiful, at a later period is unheeded, or considered rude and unsightly. — The pictures, which in our childish years we gazed upon with pleasure, at a more mature time of life, are passed by with neglect. This difference in the feelings with which the same object is regarded at different periods, is found connected with differ ent advances that have been made in knowledge, and in the cultivation and refinement of the intellectual powers. The emotion of pleasure, felt by the ignorant and half-civilized man when gazing on some rude monument or unsightly picture, is of the same nature as that felt by the man of knowledge and refinement, while viewing a finished work of sculpture or of painting. But the latter has become habituated to the exhibition of skill in the works of art. He has become familiar with monuments and paintings, that are better in their design and execution, than those that have been seen by the former; and hence it is, that the production of the artist, which at an earlier period of life would have excited emotions of beauty, is now disregarded. Refinement in taste, then, denotes a progress in the knowledge of what is excellent in works of art, and results from the study of models of excellence.

Delicacy of taste implies a quick and nice perception of whatever is fitted to excite emotions of beauty. He who possesses it, will detect beauties both of design and execution, which pass unnoticed by common men; and when others pronounce a scene beautiful from the general effect on their minds, he will discover and point out all that tends to the production of this effect. This quality of taste results from a habit of careful and minute observation, joined with a quick susceptibility of emotions of beauty. It is also most frequently found in connection with moral purity of feeling, and in its common acceptation, is sometimes used as opposed to what is indelicate.

Correctness of taste evidently refers to an agreement with some standard. What this standard is, has been already shewn. It is the agreeing voice of those, who, from their experience of past emotions, are able to form a judgment on what is fitted to excite emotions of beauty. He, then, who has correctness of taste, feels and judges, in reference to

objects which come under the cognizance of taste, in ag.ee
ment witl. he only true standard of taste.

Different uses of the word Taste.

It will at once be seen, that in the preceding account of
taste, the word is used in a sense, different from that oiter
applied to it in its common acceptation. We speak of a
taste for some particular occupation, for some amusement or
study, when all that is meant to be expressed, is, that there
is a fondness, or inclination of the mind, for the pursuit, and
the word fondness or inclination would better convey our
meaning. It must be obvious to all, that the rhetorical use
of the word is quite different.

The definition here given of taste is also different from
that found in Blair's Lectures on Rhetoric, which, as a text
book, is in most frequent use. He defines taste to be the
power of receiving pleasure or pain from the beauties or deformities of nature and art. The definition which has been
given of it in this chapter, makes it of a more discriminating
principle. It implies, that the man of taste is able to discern
what in nature and art is fitted to excite this feeling of pleasure and pain, while the power of receiving this pleasure is
called sensibility. That there is ground for this distinction,
is evident from the fact already stated, that some men are
highly susceptible of emotions of beauty, who, at the same
time, are utterly destitute of good taste.

Technical Taste.

Neither is it the case, that in all instances where the
word taste is used, reference is had to the standard, which
has been stated in this chapter to be the true standard of
taste. A man is sometimes called a man of taste, when his

judgment extends no further than to a decision, whether in any particular production, or performance, the rules of his art have been observed. This may be illustrated in the case of an epic poem. Aristotle has fully and with precision laid down the rules, according to which this species of writing should be composed, deriving them from Homer, the great master of the art. It is evident, that one, who has made himself familiar with these rules, may sit in judgment on the Æneid of Virgil, and the Paradise Lost of Milton. With his line and his compass, he may take the dimensions of an Epic Poem, as readily and easily as of a building. In fact, he does nothing more than apply to the work he examines, the measures which have been taken from some other work that has been admired, and in this way decide as to the merits of the poem. This is the lowest kind of criticism, and he who exercises it, may be called a man of technical taste

Taste of Comparison.

It is also sometimes the case, that the productions of some admired author, or artist, are the standard, to which all attempts of the same nature must be brought. The admirer of Byron, whose mind is filled with his delightful horrors, and who is wont to admire his master-strokes of passion, in examining the productions of other poets, will pronounce on their excellence, from their comparative effect on his own mind, and will approve or condemn, as they agree with those of this great master of the art. This may be distinguished as the taste of comparison. It is often found among those, who devote their time to visiting galleries of paintings, and other collections of works in the fine arts. This kind of taste is a source of enjoyment to its possessor, and is often found united with merit as an author or artist. Some men succeed better, when they take the taste of another for their guide, than when they rely on their own. — *"Velles eum suo ingenio dixisse, alieno judicio."* *

Philosophical taste.

But the man of taste, in the true use of the word, does not, like the mere critic of technical skill, only apply the rules of his art. Neither, in forming his decisions, does he bring every object of which he judges, to some favorite standard of excellence. Truth and nature are the models which he has studied, and he has found them alike in the objects of creation around him, in the scenes of real life, and in the creations of genius. Like Numa of old, he has his Egeria in the woods, and after holding high converse with this mysterious revealer of the secrets of nature, he comes forth to the world, and discloses, as if by inspiration, the principles of the empire of taste, and the laws of her dominion. To him belongs the prophetic eye of taste. He can not only decide with correctness on the scene spread before him, but surveying the visions of his own mind — the scenes that exist only in the world of imagination, he can anticipate with unerring certainty their beauty and effect. There is also an unchanging uniformity in the decisions of philosophical taste. Even the eternal principles of morality are not more fixed and determinate. What met the approbation of the man of philosophical taste two thousand years ago, meets the approbation of the man of philosophical taste now, and will continue to be thus admired till the end of time. On this principle Quinctilian has said, " *Ille se profecisse sciat, cui Cicero valde placebit.*"† On this principle Homer, and Virgil,

---

* You commend the genius of the writer, but prefer, that it should be guided by another's taste, rather than by his own

† Whoever can discern the excellences of Cicero, may hence learn that he has himself made proficiency as an orator.

and Demosthenes, and Cicero, have been adm'red, wherevei
they have been known.   Here also is the only foundation of
hope to the aspirant after literary immortality.

The Fine Arts are so closely connected with the subject
of taste, that I subjoin to this chapter a short account of
what is meant by them.

The Fine, Elegant, or Polite Arts, for these epithets are
synonymous, are so called in distinction from the Useful
Arts.   The former are designed to please; the latter aim
at the supply of human wants.   It is true, that works in the
useful arts may be so constructed as to please, at the same
time that they subserve our necessities.   And on the other
hand, works that please and are designed to please, may be
useful.

Hence it may be difficult in regard to some productions
in the arts, to say to which they belong, the Useful, or the
Elegant; still there is ground for the distinction that has
been made, and according to the design — to please, or to be
useful, we say that some arts are elegant and others useful.

Of the Fine Arts, some are imitative, and others symbolical.   Some exhibit an exact representation of the object
or scene they would present before the mind; such are
Painting and Sculpture.   These are called imitative fine
arts.   Others make use of signs which have been agreed upon
among men for the representation of objects; such as Music
and Poetry.   These, in distinction from the former, may be
called symbolical fine arts.

It has been stated, that the design of works in the fine
arts, is to please.   This may be effected in two different
ways.   The object or scene brought before the mind, may
be such as is suited to excite grateful emotions, or the mind
may be pleased with the skill that is shown in the execution
of the work.   In the former case, when the object or scene

represented has no original in nature, but is a creation of
the artist's mind, while we regard the object of the work,
and notice how the different parts of it tend to the promo-
tion of this object, we are said to observe the primary beauties, or the beauties of design. But whether the scene or
object represented be an exact copy of some original in nature, or a creation of the artist's, if the attention is directed
only to the skill shewn in the execution of the work, we are
said to observe secondary beauties, or the beauties of execution. The art of writing or composition, whether elegant
or useful, is one of the symbolical arts. There is no exact
imitation of what is designed to be brought before the mind,
but objects and scenes are represented by words as symbols.
This must evidently increase the difficulty of the artist, or
writer; for though he may have in his own mind distinct
views of what is fitted to excite emotions of taste, and may
connect these views with the signs which he uses, yet, if the
reader do not attach the same views to the signs used, they
will fail to excite in his mind the emotions designed to be
produced. Much then will depend upon the skill with which
these signs are used, and hence it is, that in literary productions, so much attention is paid, with the design of pleasing,
to the execution of the work.

We may here also see a reason, why the beauties of design in literary productions, are said to be addressed to the
imagination of the readers. As we have seen in the last
chapter, it is by the aid of the imagination that the artist is
able to design those objects and scenes, which are the creations of his own mind. When these creations have been
formed, they are represented by the signs that are used.
Now it is obviously the imagination of the reader, which must
interpret these signs. They are intended to set his imagination in exercise, and to cause it to present before the mind
an object or scene, similar to that which the writer had in

view when using these signs; and if the reader have no powers of imagination, the attempt of the writer to place before him a scene fitted to excite grateful emotions will be vain.

It is an easy inference from what has been said in this chapter, that the cultivation and improvement of taste in the several fine arts, will be promoted by a familiarity with models of excellence in those arts. He who would cultivate a taste for painting, or music, or fine writing, will seek after the works of those who excel in these different departments But it may here be remarked generally in respect to taste, that it is improved by whatever gives enlargement and improvement to the mind. Taste, as judgment, calls into exercise various intellectual faculties; comparisons are to be instituted, inferences to be made, and conclusions to be drawn; and the more perfectly this work is performed, the higher is the order of taste possessed. Education, then, furnishing mental discipline, and accustoming the mind to processes of analysis and investigation, s conducive to the improvement of the taste. And since, as has been stated, much that comes under the cognizance of taste is addressed to the imagination, especially in the symbolical fine arts, the cultivation of this faculty of the mind will conduce to the same result

CHAPTER THIRD

ON LITERARY TASTE.

Literary taste is the judgment of whatever of a literary nature is designed to excite emotions of beauty, grandeur and sublimity, founded upon the past experience of emotions of the same kind. It is the object of this chapter to explain the nature of literary taste as thus defined, and to offer, in connexion with examples, such directions and cautions as may aid in its improvement. The word literature is most frequently used in distinction from science. In this sense, it refers to certain classes of writing. Such are Poetry and Fictitious Prose, Historical, Epistolary and Essay writing. On the other hand, a treatise on Optics or Electricity, or a work on Intellectual Philosophy, is classed under the head of science. In examining this division, we find that those works are classed under the head of literature, in which it is a leading object of the writer to interest and please the mind by the mode of exhibiting objects and scenes to its view; while those, which are designed only to elucidate and establish principles in any branch of knowledge, or to give exercise to the reasoning powers, are denominated science.

There is however a more extended scene, in which the word literature is used. It is often intended to refer more-ly to the use of words as a mode of exhibiting the thoughts and views of the mind, and thus embraces all that is committed to letters. In this sense of the word, we might speak of Euclid's Elements of Geometry as a literary work and say of the literature of any particular age, that it is of a scientific kind.

As it is not the object of this part of the work to direct the attention of the student to particular classes of literary productions, I shall here consider the word literature as used in its most extensive sense, and consequently, in treating of attempts of a literary kind to excite emotions of taste, I shall refer to what is more particularly connected with the style.

If now we examine the various classes of literary productions, we find attempts to excite emotions of taste which are common in some degree to all. Such are well chosen words, well turned expressions and happy illustrations. These are called the ornaments of style, and though not essential to the communication of the writer's thoughts, they are often highly useful. They allure and fix the attention, and aid in the full and clear exhibition of what is communicated.

Of these ornaments of style, some have been classified, and have received appropriate names. Such are Similes, Metaphors, Allusions and Personifications; others are of a more incidental nature. The former will be examined in the present chapter; of the latter, some mention will be made, when treating of the different qualities of style.

Before entering upon the examination of the classified ornaments of style, I wish to bring distinctly to view the different principles, on which these attempts to excite emotions of taste are founded. In this way, the student will be enabled more fully to understand the reasons of the different directions and cautions which may be given, and to discern more clearly the nature and objects of literary taste.

It was stated in the last chapter, that from the original constitution of the human mind, we are fitted to feel emotions of beauty and sublimity in view of objects and scenes in nature. A passage of descriptive writing will enable me to illustrate what is here meant.

The following description of the rising sun is taken from one of Gray's Letters.

"I set out one morning before five o'clock, the moon shining through a dark and misty autumnal air, and got to the sea-coast, time to be at the sun's levee. I saw the clouds and dark vapors open gradually to the right and left, rolling over one another in great smoky wreaths, and the tide (as it flowed in on the sands) first whitening, and then slightly tinged with gold and blue, and all at once a little line of insufferable brightness, that before I can write these five words is grown to half an orb, and now a whole one, too gloric us to be distinctly seen."

This is a representation of a scene in nature, and the writer, in looking on this scene, felt an emotion of grandeur. Should it be asked, why this emotion is thus excited, the only cause to be assigned is, that it is natural to us to feel this emotion in view of this and similar scenes. Our Creator has so constituted us. Should we now further inquire, why the *description* of the scene excites an emotion of the same kind in the minds of its readers, we have to assign in answer the same cause. The writer addresses himself to the imagination of his readers, and by the use of words as symbols brings the scene distinctly before their minds, and an emotion of grandeur is excited in view of it as thus described, on the same principle, as when this emotion was excited in view of the original. Now this is often done, when the ornaments of style are introduced. A word, or an illustration, brings before the mind an object or scene, which from the original constitution of our mind, excites an emotion of beauty or sublimity. This principle then in the original constitution of the human mind is to be considered as one of those principles, to which the writer addresses him self, with the design of exciting emotions of taste.

It was still further stated, that emotions of beauty and sublimity are often excited on the principle of association. Objects and scenes, which are not fitted from any original tendencies of the mind to excite these emotions, may still excite them from their being associated in our minds with what is thus regard. 1; or where they are fitted to excite these emotions in some degree, they may excite them in a higher degree, because of such associations. The traveller, in passing the river Rubicon, might regard it as a common stream; but should it be told him, that he is standing where Cæsar stood, when he decided the destinies of Rome, the scene before him from association excites an emotion of sublimity. Here then is another principle, to which the writer addresses himself in the introduction of the ornaments of style, with the design of exciting emotions of taste. He brings before us that which from association is fitted to excite in our minds an emotion of beauty or sublimity.

On the principles which have been stated, the ornaments of style may excite emotions of taste distinct from their con-nexion, as found in a literary production, and as tending to the accomplishment of the design of the writer. Regarding them in this latter view, another cause of the emotions of taste which they are fitted to excite, is brought to notice. I refer to what is called fitness or adaptation.

When we look at any work of art, a piece of cabinet work for example, we may think of it in relation to some purpose which it is designed to answer, and from perceiving that it is admirably well adapted to answer this purpose, we may on this account regard it with admiration. We may still further examine it as to the proportion of its parts, their fitness to the whole work, and the skill with which they are formed and arranged; and in this view of the work we may feel a similar emotion. Thus we are led to pronounce the work beautiful. Now in these instances, we feel an emotion of beauty in view of fitness or adaptation. Should it be asked, why the emotion is felt, it must, as before, be referred to a primary law of our nature. We can only say, that our Creator has so constituted us. As it is highly important that the student should clearly understand this principle, and as it is the foundation of the rules by which we judge of descriptive writing, I shall attempt its more full development in connection with illustrations of this kind. I would remark, however, that it is not my design to state the rules and principles which apply to descriptive writing, any further than is necessary for the illustration of the principle of adaptation, which is now to be explained.

The following passage forms part of the description of a fatal contest between two Highlanders, who encountered each other on a narrow and dangerous pass.

"They threw their bonnets over the precipice, and advanced with a slow and cautious step closer to each other; they were both unarmed, and stretching their limbs like men preparing for a desperate struggle, they planted their feet firmly on the ground, compressed their lips, knit their dark brows, and fixing fierce and watchful eyes on each other, stood there prepared for the onset. They both grappled at the same moment; but being of equal strength, were unable for some time to shift each other's position, — standing fixed on a rock with suppressed breath, and muscles strained to the 'top of their heart, like statues carved out of the solid stone."

The object of the writer in this passage, is to place before us a distinct view of the combatants as they entered on the contest; and in answer to the inquiry, why the passage strikes us favorably, and, as a description, excites an emotion of beauty, I would assign as a cause, the adaptation of the description to this design. We admit it because both the selection and arrangement of circumstances, and the use of

words, are such as to bring the scene directly and clearly
before the view. Here then is one instance, where an emo
tion of beauty is excited in view of fitness or adaptation to a
particular design, and that design is the distinct and striking
representation of a scene.

The accurate and vivid delineation of objects and scenes
here exemplified, is sometimes called *truth to nature.* The
representation of common and familiar scenes in this way
excites emotions of beauty ; but the power of truth to nature
is most deeply felt, when the writer lays open to our view
the hidden workings of the mind, and the strong affections
of the heart. That the student may more fully understand
what is meant by the phrase, " truth to nature," which is of
frequent occurrence, I here introduce two passages, which
happily illustrate its meaning, — one a description of a familiar scene ; the other, of the affections.

The following description of a country inn is from Gold
smith's Deserted Village.

> Imagination fondly stoops to trace
> The parlor splendors of that festive place ,
> The white-washed wall, the nicely-sanded floor,
> The varnished clock that ticked behind the door ;
> The chest contrived a double debt to pay,
> A bed by night, a chest of drawers by day ;
> The pictures placed for ornament and use,
> The twelve good rules, the royal game of goose ;
> The hearth, except when winter chilled the day,
> With aspen boughs, and flowers, and fennel gay ;
> While broken tea-cups, wisely kept for show,
> Ranged o'er the chimney, glistened in a row.

Mrs Hemans thus describes a mother's love ;

> There is none
> In all this cold and hollow world, no fount
> Of deep, strong, deathless love, save that within
> A mother's heart. - —— You ne'er made

Your breast the pillow of his infancy,
While to the fulness of your heart's glad heavings
His fair cheek rose and fell; and his bright hair
Waved softly to your breath! — You ne'er kept watch
Beside him, till the last pale star had set,
And morn, all dazzling, as in triumph broke
On your dim, weary eye ; not yours the face
Which, early faded through fond care for him,
Hung o'er his sleep, and duly, as heaven's light,
Was there to greet his wakening! You ne'er smoothed
His couch, ne'er sung him to his rosy rest,
Caught his least whisper when his voice from yours
Had learned soft utterance; pressed your lip to his,
When fever parched it; hushed his wayward cries,
With patient, vigilant, never-wearied love!
No! these are woman's tasks!

The following example is taken from Everett's description
of the Pilgrim Fathers on their voyage to America.

"I see them driven in fury before the raging tempest, on the high
and giddy waves. The awful voice of the storm howls through the
rigging. The laboring masts seem straining from their base;—the
dismal sound of the pumps is heard; the ship leaps as it were madly
from billow to billow;—the ocean breaks and settles with engulfing
floods over the floating deck, and beats with deadening, shivering
weight, against the staggered vessel."

The design of the writer in this passage, is to excite emo
tion in the minds of his readers. He would have them
shudder in view of the dangers, by which the frail bark he
describes is encompassed, and regard with deep commiseration the noble adventurers it bears. If now we notice the
circumstances which make up the description, as they tend
to this design of the writer, we may learn at once, why the
passage, as a description, excites our admiration. The
" howling voice of the storm," " the straining of the masts,"
" the dismal sound of the pumps," " the leaping of the ship,"
" the overflowing of the deck," and " the deadening shock

of the ocean," all tend to impress the mind most deeply with horror at the scene, and with commiseration for those who were exposed to its dangers.

I give one example more, in which it is the design of the writer to excite emotions of a ludicrous nature. It is Irving's description of Ichabod Crane.

"He was tall, but exceedingly lank, with narrow shoulders, long arms and legs, hands that dangled a mile out of his sleeves, feet that might have served for shovels, and his whole frame most loosely hung together. His head was small, and flat at top, with large ears, large green glassy eyes, and a long snipe nose, so that it looked like a weather-cock perched upon his spindle neck, to tell which way the wind blew. To see him striding along the profile of a hill on a windy day, with his clothes bagging and fluttering about him, one might have mistaken him for the genius of famine descending upon the earth, or some scarecrow eloped from a cornfield."

Now there is no one, who, in reading this passage, does not admire it as a description. And any one, in assigning the reason of his admiration, would at once pronounce it a fine description, because all the circumstances mentioned tend so admirably to the design of the writer.

The examples which have been stated and examined, are amply sufficient to illustrate and establish the position, that in descriptive writing emotions of beauty may be excited in view of adaptation to a particular design.

I now wish to exhibit this same principle differently applied. I would show, that an emotion of beauty may be excited in view of the fitness or adaptation of the different parts of a description to the whole. For this purpose I introduce the following passage :

"The sun gradually wheeled his broad disk down into the west. The wide bosom of the Tappaan Zee lay motionless and glassy excepting that here and there a gentle undulation waved and pro longed the blue shadow of the distant mountain. A few amber clouds floated in the sky, without a breath of air to move them. The horizon was of a fine golden tint, changing gradually into a pure apple green, and from that into the deep blue of the mid-heaven. A slanting ray lingered on the woody crests of the precipices that overhung some parts of the river, giving greater depth to the dark blue and purple of their rocky sides. A sloop was loitering in the distance, dropping slowly down with the tide, her sail hanging uselessly against the mast; and as the reflection of the sky gleamed along the still water, it seemed as if the vessel was suspended in the air."

Now in answer to the inquiry, why this description is regarded with emotions of beauty, it may at once be said, that the scene itself is one fitted to excite emotions of this kind, and also, that it is most clearly exhibited to our view. But in looking at the different circumstances which make up the description, it may be still further noticed, that they all correspond with each other,—they are of like importance, and produce a similar effect on the mind. The " glassy bosom of the lake,"—the " amber clouds,"—the " varying tints of the horizon,"—the " light and shades on surrounding objects," and the becalmed vessel, apparently " suspended in the air," are prominent objects in the scene, each worthy of notice, and each producing a similar effect on the mind. That the emotion of beauty felt in reading this description, is to be ascribed in part to the correspondence and fitness of the several parts, may be made evident, if we attempt to introduce an object of a different nature. Suppose that after mentioning the clouds floating in the sky, the writer had said, —the Dutch farmers were driving home their cows from pasture, who would not say at once, that the beauty of the description is gone? An emotion of beauty may then be excited in view of the fitness of the parts of a description to the whole, on the same principle, as in view of the fitness of the whole to some particular design.

The application of the principle of fitness or adaptation

in accounting for emotions of taste, may be carried still
further. From the different circumstances of a description,
we may proceed to notice the words, and we shall find
that part of the effect of passages of descriptive writing, as
fitted to excite emotions of taste, is to be ascribed to what
is usually called the happy choice of words, or the choice
of those words which are best suited to the design of the
writer. In the examples already given, we have full illustration of the correctness of this statement. I would direct
the attention particularly to that where the writer says,
the ocean beats with "deadening, shivering weight, against
the staggered vessel." How much of the beauty of this
part of the description is to be ascribed to the choice of the
epithets here used! To be persuaded of this, we have only
to make some alteration in this respect, to substitute one
word for another, and the charm is broken. Had the writer
just quoted said, The ocean beats with a stupefying, shocking
weight, against the shattered vessel, who, in reading the description, would have felt an emotion of beauty?

If, in what has now been stated in connexion with passages of descriptive writing, the student has been led fully
to understand what is meant by fitness or adaptation, and
to see, that it may be regarded as one of those principles on
which are founded attempts to excite emotions of taste, the
design of their introduction has been answered. It will be
shewn in the examination of the ornaments of style, that,
whether we regard them only as parts of the literary production in which they are found, or look on them as tending to
produce some designed effect, we may in part account for the
emotion of taste which they excite, on this same principle
of adaptation.

I have thus brought to view three distinct principles, on
which are founded attempts on the part of the writer to excite emotions of taste in the minds of his readers. They

are as follows; 1. Primary laws or original tendencies of our natures. 2. Association. 3. Fitness or adaptation. Full opportunity for illustration is found in the remaining part of the chapter.

In examining the classified ornaments of style, I begin with the SIMILE OR FORMAL COMPARISON.

EXAMPLE 1. — "Wit and humor are like those volatile essences, which, being too delicate to bear the open air, evaporate almost as soon as they are exposed to it."

In this example, as in all instances of the Formal Comparison, different objects are brought together, and the resemblance which they bear to each other is formally stated. My design, in its introduction, is to shew the student the kind of resemblance on which the Comparison is founded. It will at once occur to him, that wit and humor are in their nature different from volatile essences. The latter are perceived by one of the senses; the former exist only in the mind. Still there is a resemblance between them as they are here viewed, and it is a resemblance which is discerned with pleasure. Had the wit and humor of one man been compared with the wit and humor of another, we might have derived information from the comparison; but the effect upon us as a pleasing comparison would have been unfelt. It is the unexpectedness of the resemblance which pleases us. Hence then we infer the caution, *that the resemblance on which the Simile or Formal Comparison is founded, should not be too obvious.*

EXAMPLE 2. — "The minds of the age. are like the tombs to which they are approaching; where, though the brass and the marble remain, yet the inscriptions are effaced by time, and the imagery has mouldered away."

This beautiful passage is introduced to shew, that it is a trait of a good comparison, that the object, to which a resemblance is traced, be naturally suggested. We say that the object is in this case suggested naturally because the transition is easy from the minds of the aged to the tombs, which they are approaching. The image brought to our view is in consonance with the feelings, which the thought to be illustrated had excited. Suppose now, that the object of resemblance, instead of mouldering tombs, had been the canvass on which images had been drawn in fading colors. This would have been illustrative, but what man of taste would not say, that the beauty of the comparison is impaired? While then, as before stated, we guard against drawing our comparisons from objects to which the resemblance is too close, it should be remembered, *that it heightens the beauty of the comparison, to discover that the object to which a resemblance is traced, is naturally suggested.*

In applying this direction, we are to take into view, not only the nature of the subject, but the circumstances with which the writer is surrounded. Some of the most admired compositions in our literature are those, in which the resemblance is obviously suggested by an object immediately before the writer. Thus Burke, describing the effect produced upon him by the loss of his son, says; " The storm has gone over me; and I lie like one of those old oaks which the late hurricane has scattered about me. I am stripped of all my honor; I am torn up by the roots and lie prostrate on the earth ! "

When a comparison is thus naturally suggested, there is found in it a fitness or adaptation to the subject and occasion on which it is introduced; and in such instances, the emotion of taste which is called forth, may be traced in part to this principle of adaptation as its exciting cause. More fully to shew that this fitness must exist, that a comparison may be approved, I introduce another example

Suppose that in a discourse from the pulpit the following sentence should be found ;

" Curses, like chickens, always come home to roost."

This comparison is founded on an unexpected resemblance, and is illustrative ; but if we regard it in relation to the occasion, there is a want of fitness. It is not in consonance with the sober, elevated train of thought and feeling, which should characterize a religious discourse ; and the man of literary taste at once condemns it, because of its want of fitness to the occasion.

The principle here stated is fully illustrated in the nature of the comparisons, which are most frequently introduced in different departments of writing. In pastorals, resemblances are traced to objects and scenes in rural life ; in epic and tragic poetry, to such as are of a more exalted and ennobling kind ; in comic, to those of a familiar nature. Now in all these instances, the resemblances are said to be naturally suggested, — there is in them a fitness to the occasion and to the thoughts and feelings of the personages introduced.

Example 3. — " The style of Canning is like the convex mirror, which scatters every ray of light which falls upon it, and shines and sparkles in whatever position it is viewed ; that of Brougham is like the concave speculum, scattering no indiscriminate radiance, but having its light concentrated into one intense and tremendous focus.

This comparison strikes us favorably, and should the inquiry be made, why it excites an emotion of taste, we at once refer the pleasure it gives us to its fitness to the design of the writer. He would have us perceive the different characteristic traits of the styles of Canning and Brougham, and every one must see with admiration, how much is effected by the illustration which is introduced.

To illustrate, is most frequently the design of the Comparison: and when in this way the writer seeks to increase the distinctness of the reader's views, the object of resemblance should always be more familiarly known, or such as to be more distinctly conceived by us, than the object to be illustrated. In the example given, an object of thought is compared to an object of sense, and since objects of sense are generally more distinct to the mind than objects of thought, the effect of the comparison is favorable. Hence, in good illustrative comparisons it will generally be the case, *that when objects of thought and sense are brought to view, the former is illustrated by the latter.* In those exceptions to this principle which strike us favorably, some reason may generally be assigned, as in the following example. Scot describing Loch Katrine, says,

> " The mountain shadows on her breast
> Were neither broken nor at rest ;
> In bright uncertainty they lie,
> Like future joys to fancy's eye."

In this instance, it may be said, that our consciousness of the uncertainty of those future joys which fancy presents, is so strong, that our conceptions of the wavering of mountain shadows on the lake, is aided by the comparison.

In determining whether an object is familiarly known, regard must be had to those who are addressed. In a production on a literary subject addressed to literary men, it would be proper to bring to view objects of resemblance, which should not be referred to in writings addressed to children or to the unlearned. Neither, in what is addressed to a learned audience, would it be proper to introduce as an object of comparison, a principle in science, or a process in some art, which is comparatively of little importance, and known only to those who are learned in a particular branch of knowledge, or adepts in a particular art.

The object of resemblance in the example we are now considering, is sufficiently familiar to all who are capable of understanding the production in which it is found, and this is all that is required.

EXAMPLE 4.—"Thus it is with illustrious merit; its very effulgence draws forth the rancorous passions of low and grovelling minds, which too often have a temporary influence in obscuring it to the world; as the sun, emerging with full splendor into the heavens, calls up, by the very power of his rays, the rank and noxious vapors which for a time becloud his glory."

This is called an analogical comparison, and if analysed, it will be found to contain an argument from analogy. We all know that it is the fervor of the sun, which calls up rank and noxious vapors from the earth; and reasoning analogically, we are led to the conclusion, that it is the effulgence of illustrious merit, which draws forth the rancorous passions of low and grovelling minds.

Comparisons of this kind strike us favorably. They aid the writer in imparting to others the opinions he may entertain, and the reasonings on which these opinions are founded. Some men are accustomed to reason in this way, and such are usually eminently successful as instructors, since they are thus enabled to make themselves easily and readily understood. This indeed is the appropriate object of analogical comparisons; and it is a fitness to this design, which causes us to regard those which are well conducted with emotions of taste.

EXAMPLE 5.—"He lived a wanderer and a fugitive in his native land, and went down, like a lonely bark foundering amid darkness and tempest,—without a pitying eye to weep his fall, or a friendly hand to record his struggle."

Th s comparison is found at the conclusion of the account, given by Irving, of King Philip. He has made mention of his heroic qualities and noble achievements, and he would excite in the minds of his readers a feeling of compassionate regret at his miserable and untimely fall. The comparison pleases us. The resemblance on which it is founded, is not too obvious; and it is naturally suggested. But the principal cause of the emotion of beauty which it excites, is its adaptedness to the design of the writer. When we think of the lonely bark, 'foundering amid darkness and tempest,' it is with strong emotions of compassion and regret; and by causing the mind to bring this object before its view in connexion with King Philip in his adversity, the writer derives much aid in leading us to regard the latter object with the same emotion.

In this manner any object or occurrence, which, either from the original constitution of our minds, or from association, is wont to excite an emotion of a particular kind, may be introduced by the writer, and thus a higher interest is thrown over the thoughts he communicates, and increased influence exerted over the minds of his readers. And while the man of literary taste is led to notice the skill and power which is thus displayed, he feels, in view of such comparisons, emotions of beauty.

Example 6. — "He was a little, meagre, black-looking man, with a grizzled wig that was too wide, and stood off from each ear; so that his head seemed to have shrunk away within it, like a dried filbert in its shell."

In this comparison, it is the writer's design to increase the emotion of a ludicrous kind, with which the object he is describing is in itself regarded. The comparison is therefore approved by the man of literary taste, on the principle of fitness, as in the last example. All similar attempts a

wit and humor must evidently come under the cognizance
of literary taste. But there is a peculiarity in many comparisons, introduced with the design of exciting emotions
of the ludicrous, which requires particular notice. Often
there is nothing in the object compared, or in that to which
a resemblance is traced, which is fitted to excite emotions
of the ludicrous; but when they are viewed together, an
emotion of this kind is produced. In such instances, the
effect of the comparison is to be ascribed to the strangeness
of the resemblance which is traced out. An example will
more clearly show what is here stated. Of Hudibras it is
said :

> " We grant, although he had much wit,
> He was very shy of using it ;
> As being loath to wear it out,
> And therefore bore it not about ;
> Unless on Holidays, or so,
> As men their best apparel do."

Now there is nothing ludicrous in the assertion, tnat a
man possesses wit, but does not often show it. Neither is
there any thing ludicrous in saying, that a man wears his
best apparel only on holidays. But when the objects are
brought together and compared, the comparison excites an
emotion of a ludicrous nature. Still, in such instances, as
in those of which an example was before given, it is the fitness of the comparison to the design of the writer, which
causes it to be approved by the man of literary taste.

Example 7. — " Bramins and sooders and castes and shasters will
have passed away, like the mist which rolls up the mountain's side,
before the rising glories of a summer's morning, while the land on
which it rested, shining forth in all its loveliness, shall, from its
numberless habitations, send forth the high praises of God and the
Lamb. '

In the part of the discourse from which this comparison

is taken, the writer is dwelling on the influence which must attend the spread of the Gospel in Asia. He would have us regard the thoughts he expresses on this subject with grateful emotions, and by introducing the comparison which has been stated, he evidently does much towards effecting this design. Hence the man of literary taste approves the comparison, from its fitness to the design of the writer. But it is to be noticed, that the scene is one, which in itself, distinct from its adaptation to the subject, is fitted to excite an emotion of beauty. "A land shining forth in its loveliness, beneath the rising glories of a summer's morning, while the mists are rolling up the mountain's side," is a scene, which, from the original constitution of our minds, is regarded in this manner. In this example, then, we find an illustration of what was stated in the former part of the chapter, that in the introduction of the ornaments of style, with the design of exciting emotions of taste, the writer sometimes addresses himself to the original tendencies of the mind to feel such emotions in view of objects and scenes in the natural world. Comparisons of this kind are called embellishing comparisons, and when naturally suggested, and in agreement with the subject and occasion, they excite strong emotions of beauty.

Example 8. — "The poetry of Milton, exhibiting the most sublime conceptions and elevated language, intermingled with passages of uncommon delicacy of thought and beauty of expression, reminds us of the miracles of Alpine scenery. Nooks and dells, beautiful as fairy land, are embosomed in its most rugged and gigantic elevations. The roses and myrtles bloom unchilled on the verge of the avalanche."

This example, like the preceding, unites the various excellences of a fine comparison. The resemblance on which it is founded is not too obvious, and is naturally suggested the comparison is also illustrative; — it aids in effecting the

design of the writer as connected with his subject, and i
brings before the mind a scene, which, partly from the original constitution of the mind, and partly from association,
is fitted to excite an emotion of taste.

From the remarks now made, and the principles stated,
the student is prepared to judge of comparisons as ornaments of style. In examining a particular instance, he will
first consider the nature of the resemblance on which it is
founded, — whether it be not too obvious — whether it be
naturally suggested, and whether the object to which a resemblance is traced be sufficiently familiar. He will next
inquire as to the kind of comparison, — whether the instance under examination is illustrative, or analogical, or
embellishing, or designed to excite some particular emotion;
and thus he will judge of the propriety of its introduction
in the place where it is found, and of its bearing on the
leading design of the writer. He may then ask more generally, on what principle is the instance founded, as an attempt to excite an emotion of taste — whether on fitness, or
association, or on some primary law of our nature.

From the consideration of the Formal Comparison, I proceed to the Implied Comparison, or Metaphor.

Let us suppose, that a writer wishes to show his readers,
how soon the effect of sorrow on the minds of the young is
done away. While this thought has possession of the mind
some principle of association brings up to his view a young
and vigorous tree, in the bark of which an incision has
been made, but the wound, from the rapidity of the growth
of the tree, is fast closing over. The resemblance between
he thought in his mind and the object thus presented, his
taste approves as illustrative and striking, and he wishes to
place it before the view of others. The most obvious
method of doing this is as follows; " As the wound made
in the bark of the young and healthy tree soon closes over,

so sorrows in the minds of the young, are of short duration."
By this formal comparison, the object of the writer would
be effected.   His readers would perceive the resemblance,
and their good taste would approve this attempt to aid the
distinctness of their view.   But let us suppose, that instead
of this formal comparison, he expresses himself as follows:
'What are the sorrows of the young!   Their growing
minds soon close above the wound."   This expression
brings before the mind the same objects as are brought by
the comparison; the same resemblance is traced, and the
same aid is given to the distinctness of our view.   But the
resemblance, instead of being distinctly stated, is implied.
Upon reading the passage, it at once occurs to us, that some
of the words used are applied to objects, to which they are
not usually applied.   We are not wont to speak of the
mind as growing, and of the wounds of the mind as
closing over.   From this unusual application of words, the
imagination is set in action, and brings up to view the resemblance, just as the writer designed it should be seen.
This, then, is what is called an IMPLIED COMPARISON or a
METAPHOR.

So far as the comparison and metaphor are the same, it
is unnecessary to repeat the principles and rules stated with
reference to the former, since they apply alike to both.
But in thus implying a resemblance by the unusual application of language, there is an exertion of skill, which is
not found in its more formal statement.   And hence, when
the metaphor is extended through different clauses, an emotion of taste may be excited in view of the fitness of the different parts in their connexion with each other, and with
the whole.   There is also need of cautions which are not
required in the use of the comparison.   Some happy instances of the metaphor will therefore be pointed out, and

such cautions given as may guard us from faults in the un usual application of language.

EXAMPLE 1.—" She had been the pupil of the village pastor, the favorite lamb of his little flock."

The latter part of this sentence is a metaphor. We are at once aware, that the fair maiden here referred to, is not meant to be called a lamb of a little flock in the literal application of the word. The implied comparison is readily suggested. The imagination brings before us the lamb of a little flock, and we think of the tenderness and care with which it is nurtured, and the strong interest, which from its youth and simplicity it excites; and we trace out the resemblance to this pupil of the village pastor. We are pleased with the comparison as one easily and naturally suggested, as illustrative, and as bringing before the mind an object which it regards with an emotion of beauty.

·Though this example of the Metaphor is faultless, it does not excite in the minds of most readers a strong emotion of beauty. This is easily explained, and is an illustration of a principle which should be borne in mind in all ·our judgments of attempts of this nature. So frequently do we compare what is tender and delicate and innocent to the lamb, that we have become familiar with the comparison, and it has lost its effect upon us. We may learn then from this example, that the introduction of common comparisons and metaphors will add little to the beauty of style. They will not be defects, but having lost by repetition their power of pleasing, they will be passed by unnoticed. *Novelty is not then to be regarded as a source of emotions of taste; but the want of novelty will prevent such emotions from being felt.*

Example 2. Burke, in his description of Atheists, says,

" They abhor the author of their being. He never presents him self to their thoughts, but to menace and alarm them. They can not strike the sun out of the heavens, but they are able to raise a smouldering smoke that obscures him from their eyes.'

From the connexion, we learn, that this last sentence is not meant to convey what is expressed by the words as they are usually applied. This leads us to inquire, in what way they are designed to be understood, and imagination at once traces out a resemblance between the sun in the heavens, and that glorious Being, who shines forth in the brightness of his perfections; and we continue to trace the resemblance between the attempt of mortals, to obscure the brightness of the sun to their own view by raising a smouldering smoke, and the attempt of Atheists, to obscure to their own minds the existence of the Deity, by their darkening speculations. As this is a representation of objects of thought by objects of sense, the effect in giving increased distinctness of view is favorable.

Example 3. Byron has the following striking Metaphor

" Man!
Thou pendulum betwixt a smile and tear."

Here is evidently an implied comparison, and one that pleases us from the unexpectedness and appropriateness of the resemblance on which it is founded The example also brings to notice a characteristic trait of the Metaphor. I refer to its boldness. The writer, under a deep impression of the varieties in the life of man, in a sudden, striking manner, calls him a pendulum, and leaves it to the excited imagination of the reader to trace out the resemblance. Hence it is, that the use of the Metaphor is not well adapted to a calm, deliberate, reasoning state of mind. In this respect it differs from the Comparison, which is sometimes called the figure of description, while the Metapho- is term ed the figure of passion.

Example 4. Irving, while wandering amidst the silent and gloomy scenes of Westminster Abbey, hears .he souna of busy existence without. He thus describes the effect on his feelings.

" The contrast is striking; and it has a strange effect, thus to hear the surges of active life hurrying along and beating against the very walls of the sepulchre."

" The surges hurrying along and beating," at once suggests to the imagination the comparison here implied, and there is a sublime emotion which takes possession of the mind, as the resemblance is traced.

These examples are sufficient fully to show the nature of the Metaphor, or Implied Comparison. With the design of exhibiting the skill which is requisite when language is thus used figuratively, a few more examples will now be given.

Example 5. Of Mr. Roscoe it is said in the Sketch Book,

" He found the tide of wealth flowing merely in the channels of traffic; he has diverted from it invigorating rills to refresh the gardens of literature."

This is an example of a well supported metaphor. If we notice the different words, by the unusual application of which the metaphor is here implied, we shall find, that they are in agreement with each other, and all tend to aid the imagination in bringing up the object of comparison and tracing out the resemblance. We have before our view the " tide flowing in channels," and then the " rills are diverted to refresh the gardens." In saying that these words are in agreement with each other, reference is had to the use of them in their common application, and this is necessary that the metaphor be well supported Let us suppose that the writer had said, "He found the tide of wealth flowing merely in the channels of traffic, and took out large sums to support and encourage literature." We might in this case have made out his meaning, but what confusion is there in the attempt of the imagination to trace out the comparison which is implied! The reason of this confusion is obvious. In the former part of the sentence, the words are used figuratively, and in the latter, literally. Hence then we derive the following rule. *That in Metaphors, we guard against joining together language applied figuratively and literally.*

Example 6. A writer in the Edinburgh Review, with the design of showing in what way the early state of society is favorable to poetical excellence, says,

" Poetry produces an illusion on the eye of the mind, as a magic lantern produces an illusion on the eye of the body. And as a magic lantern acts best in a dark room, poetry effects its purpose best in a dark age. As the light of knowledge breaks in upon its exhibitions, as the outlines of certainty become more 'and more definite, and the shades of probability more and more distinct, the lines and lineaments of the phantoms which it calls up, grow fainter and fainter."

This example commences with a formal comparison, and afterwards changes into a metaphor. It is introduced to show the admirable skill, which is displayed in the application of words. " The breaking in of light," the " outlines becoming more definite," the " shades more and more distinct," and the " lines and lineaments of the phantoms growing fainter and fainter," are expressions, which may be literally applied to the objects presented by the magic lantern, and at the same time, as applied by the imagination to the creations of poetry, they present a distinct and complete view. There can be no doubt, that part of the pleasure derived from reading this passage, results from the skill displayed in this happy application of language, continued as it is through several clauses. Suppose that the latter part of this example had read, As the light of knowledge breaks in upon its exhibitions, as the outlines of certainty become more and more definite, as the weight of probability increases, the lines and lineaments of the phantoms which it calls up, grow fainter and fainter." Here would be what is called mixed metaphor. The imagination, in its attempt to trace out the resemblance and bring a distinct image before th mind, when it comes to the clause — "the increasing weigh of probability," is led astray, and the whole image become confused. This then suggests the caution, *that in contin ued metaphors, we should guard against applying words ir such a manner, as to bring up two or more different resem blances, and thus produce confusion in the view presented to the imagination.*

And here I introduce an example of mixed metaphor, in detecting which, the student may more fully see the nature of this fault.

"We are constantly called upon to observe how the noxious pas-sions, which spring up in the heart like weeds in a neglected garden are dissipated by the light of truth."

Example 7. The same writer, in describing the sophistry and unfair statements of those, who tell us to judge of Civil Liberty from the outrages and violent acts which attend rev-olutions, says,

"It is just at this crisis of revolution that its enemies love to ex-hibit it. They pull down the scaffolding from the half-finished edi-fice; they point to the flying dust, the falling bricks, the comfortless rooms, the frightful irregularity of the whole appearance; and then ask in scorn, where the promised splendor and comfort is to be found."

This example is different from the preceding. It is only in the first part of it, that the words are designed to be figu-ratively applied to the system of government, by which civil liberty is secured.　We may speak of civil government as an edifice, and of the helps used in rearing it, as scaffolding. But if we try to trace out that which may correspond to the flying dust, the falling bricks, the comfortless rooms, and other circumstances mentioned, it is without success.　Still the metaphor strikes us favorably; for though the imagination cannot trace out the particulars, it is aided in bringing to the mind a general view of the effect.　Let us now suppose that the example had read, "They pull down the scaffolding from the half-finished edifice, they point to the dust of dispute, the falling bricks of contention, the comfortless rooms of an exhausted treasury, the frightful irregularity of the whole appearance of government; and then ask in scorn, where the promised splendor and comfort is to be found."　This would have been pursuing the metaphor too far; it would be called strained, and good taste would condemn it.　Hence then we derive the caution, *not to pursue the figurative application of language too far.*

ExAMPLE 8.　"Half round the globe, the tears pumped up by death
Are spent in watering vanities of life."

The metaphor in this passage, though it may catch the attention because of its novelty and ingenuity, will not be pleasing to the man of correct literary taste.　It is not founded on a resemblance which is obvious and easily traced out, or, as the phrase has been explained, naturally suggested. *Hence metaphors of this kind are said to be forced, or far fetched, and the use of them should be avoided.*

Example 9.　The celebrated passage, in which Burke describes the fall from power of Lord Chatham and the rise of Charles Townsend, unites in it all the excellences of the metaphor.

'Even then, before this splendid orb was entire'y set, and while the western horizon was in a blaze with his descending glory, on the opposite quarter of the heavens arose another luminary, and for his hour became lord of the ascendant."

In this fine passage, the resemblance implied is such as to be highly illustrative; there is a grandeur in the object presented which elevates the mind, and the language, in its figurative application, is skilfully and happily managed.

In the examples of the Metaphor which have now been given, it has been shewn, that it is in its nature the same as the Comparison, — that it differs from it, in that the resemblance is not formally stated, but simply implied, — that the mode of implying it is by the application of language in an unusual manner, which is called applying it figuratively, — that several cautions are to be observed in this figurative application of words, and that strained and forced metaphors are to be avoided.

It has been common to mark a distinction between the metaphor and the allegory, the latter being defined a continued metaphor. But as both are founded on the same principles, and require the same cautions and directions in their use, the distinction is regarded as one of little practical importance.

There is a mode of illustration and embellishment, often found in the productions of good writers, which, though of the nature of the comparison, is worthy of separate attention. I refer to what are called ALLUSIONS. It will at once be seen, that though they differ in form from the comparison, they are of the same nature, and their introduction depends on similar principles. Like comparisons they are illustrative, and give us pleasure from the discovery of unexpected resemblances, or coincidences of thought, or expression. If, too, the comparison, when drawn from some fair scene in nature, or some finished work of art, gives us pleasure by directing the mind to that which causes a grateful emotion, the same is true of the allusion. Our attention is directed to some classical writer, or to some well known popular writer of the day, or to some recent event, — the imagination is set in exercise, — grateful associations are excited, and the effect is happy. Some examples of the Allusion will now be given.

Example 1. Burke, in his character of Lord Chatham, has the following passage:

"His is a great and celebrated name; a name which keeps the name of this country respectable over any other on the globe. It may be truly called,

Clarum et venerabile nomen
Gentibus, et multum nostræ quod proderit urbi."

This is called a classical allusion, and to those who have classical associations, such allusions are always pleasing. They are connected with the days of our youth, and with scenes, the memory of which is grateful to us. They refer us also to those pages, where our tastes have been formed, and our minds disciplined and furnished with knowledge

It will at once occur, that allusions in the form of the example given, should never be made, except in productions which are primarily addressed to those who are familiar with the language of the quotation. Should a preacher of the present day imitate in this respect the sermons of Jeremy Taylor, he would justly incur the charge of pedantry. But in addresses to deliberative assemblies, or to literary associations, or on public national celebrations, or even where classical scholars are found, allusions of this kind may occasionally be introduced with a happy effect.

Example 2. In some instances of classical allusions there a reference to facts found in classical writers, without quotation in a foreign language. Of this an example is given by Burke in his speech on the Carnatic war

"Every day you are fatigued and disgusted with this cant — The Carnatic is a country that will soon recover, and become instantly as prosperous as ever. They think they are talking to innocents, who believe that by the sowing of dragon's teeth, men may come up ready grown and ready made."

In classical allusions of this form, the writer is not confined within so narrow limits, as in those of the preceding. Still, care should be had, that what is thus alluded to should be generally known. Miss H. More is a writer, who has not sufficiently observed this caution. We not unfrequently find classical allusions in her writings, of which even to the classical student, it is no shame to be ignorant.

Example 3. A writer, describing the influence of the American revolution, says,

"From our revolutionary struggle, proceeded the revolution in France, and all which has followed in Naples, Portugal, Spain and Greece; and though the bolt of every chain has been again driven, they can no more hold the heaving mass, than the chains of Xerxes could hold the Hellespont vexed with storms."

This is a historical allusion. In most instances of this kind the design is to illustrate. The caution then is peculiarly necessary, that in historical allusions the facts alluded to be such as are generally known. Otherwise such allusions will only throw a deeper shade on those objects, which they were designed to illuminate.

Example 4. There are some instances in which historical allusions are designed not only to illustrate, but to awaken grateful emotions. Such is the following from Everett's Address;

"Lincoln, and Greene, and Knox, and Hamilton, are gone, the heroes of Saratoga and Yorktown have fallen before the only foe they could not meet."

Historical allusions of this kind, which bring to view im-

portant events or characters in the history of a nation, are
ever grateful to the people of that nation. Hence they are
so often found in public addresses on occasions of national
celebrations, and serve to gratify the pride of national feeling. One caution may well be given respecting allusions
of this kind — that they be not worn out, or such as are too
commonly made.

Example 5. The following is an English classical allusion. Milton, who was a contemporary with Cromwell,
was a zealous republican. He wrote much and ably against
the monarchical and aristocratical institutions of his time
and, in so doing, condemned many of those elegant amusements which were congenial to his own feelings.

"He sacrifices his private tastes and feelings, that he might do what
he considered his duty to mankind. It is the very struggle of the
noble Othello. His heart relents, but his hand is firm. He does
nought in hate, but all in honor. He kisses the beautiful deceiver
before he destroys her.

This allusion is to the Othello of Shakspeare; and such
is the rank and antiquity of his writings, that allusions to
passages found in them, are regarded much in the same
manner as classical allusions. We have in fact our English
classical writers, who have outlived their century, and who,
from their preëminence, may be supposed to be familiarly
known by every English scholar. To such writers it is law-
ful to make allusions as those whose works should be known;
and such allusions, when happily introduced, will please us
in the same manner and degree, as those made to the an
cient classics.

Example 6. The following example is from Irving, and
is taken from his account of James of Scotland, the " Royal
Poet."

" James is evidently worthy of being enrolled in that little coa stellation of remote, but never failing luminaries, who shine in the highest firmament of literature, and who, like morning stars, sang together at the bright dawning of British Poetry."

This beautiful passage affords an example of a Scriptural allusion, and is highly pleasing. Allusions of this kind will always be well understood, and often, from their elevated nature, add much to the beauty of writings. But there is need of caution in their use.

With the example that has been given, no fault can be found. It is rather to be commended as an embellishment. But too frequently is it the case, that the same innocency cannot be affirmed of allusions to our sacred writings. This remark is not meant to imply, that such allusions should never be made, except when the subject of discourse is of a serious or religious nature. It is enough that the subject be one of importance, that it have some dignity attached to it, and that there be nothing ludicrous or trifling Let ludicrous or trifling associations be connected with a passage of Scripture, and whenever this passage meets our attention, even in our most sober hours, there will be danger that these associations will come with it, and exert an unfavorable influence on the state of our feelings. Besides, there is something which savors much of profanity in such allusions to Scripture; it shows, that that reverence is not felt for it, which, as God's word, it should command.

These remarks are intended to be applied with most strictness to the introduction of the language of Scripture. There may be instances in which we may innocently make use, in the way of allusion, of historical facts found in Scripture when the introduction of a phrase or sentence from the same source, would manifestly be improper. The reason of this distinction is obvious. Our associations with particular forms of expression are close and strong; with facts, much less so. There is more need of caution also, because the temptations in one case are much more frequent than in the other. From the antiquity of our translation of the Bible, there is often a quaintness in its expressions, and their introduction may give a point to some satirical remark, or furnish a striking form for some sally of wit. But we should beware. Scripture is a pure stream, flowing forth from the throne of God, and it should never be made to reflect the fantastic images of human folly.

In the productions of writers of taste, there are many allusions made to the literature of the times. When any literary production gains celebrity, it is supposed to be known to literary men; and allusions may be made to such writings without incurring the charge of obscurity, and often with a favorable effect. Such allusions form a kind of bond between literary men. They are the language of the fraternity, and one cause of the pleasure which they afford, is found in the complacency and pride which are felt in being able to understand them. It is unnecessary to give many examples of this class of allusions. Two only will be brought forward, which furnish opportunity for some additional remark.

Example 7. The following passage is from Greenwood on the eternity of God:

" A stone perhaps may tell some wanderer where we lie, when we came here, and when we went away; but even that will soon refuse to bear us record : ' time's effacing finges ' will be busy on its surface, and at length will wear it smooth."

The quotation in this passage is from one of the popuar poets of the day. The allusion to the admirable description where it is originally found, will be perceived and relished by every man of taste who is familiar with the writings of Byron; and the pleasure, with which the passage that has oe en cited, will be read, is much greater, than if the same thought had been expressed without the allusion.

We have in this instance an example of a method often resorted to by writers in prose to embellish their productions. Poetry is the language of the imagination. Its aim is to please; and hence the happy introduction of poetical language is justly considered an ornament of prose. Poetry also allows of inversions of clauses, and of the use of words forbidden to prose; and hence it enables a writer to convey a thought in a sententious and striking manner. But here the caution may be given, not to introduce poetical expressions with great frequency. To say in verse what might as well be said in prose, and thus to be continually introducing scraps of poetry, may shew a familiarity with poetical writers, but is no evidence of a good literary taste.

Example 8. As another example, I quote the following passage :

" No sooner does he (W. Irving) catch a glimpse of the venerable Kaatskill, lifting its shaggy head over its white ruff of ambient clouds, and frowning on the glorious Hudson as it rolls below ; no sooner do the antique gable-roofed domes of the Manhattoes and Albany, and the classic shades of Communipaw rise upon his fancy, than his foot is on his native heath, and his name is M'Gregor."

Here the allusion is to one of the popular romances of the day, and hence it is understood and is pleasing.

Example 9. The following example is from a review of the works of Milton. The author is stating the fact, that while, in the time of the English rebellion, others were desirous only of reforming some prevalent abuses, it was Milton's aim to attain the freedom of the human mind — to deliver men from moral and intellectual slavery.

" Milton was desirous that the people should think for themselves, as well as tax themselves, and be delivered from the dominion of prejudice, as well as from that of Charles. He knew, that those who with the best intentions overlooked these schemes of reform, and contented themselves with pulling down the king and imprisoning the malignants, acted like the heedless brothers in his own poems. who, in their eagerness to disperse the train of the sorcerer neglected the means of liberating the captive. They thought only of conquering, when they should have thought of disenchanting.

> O, ye mistook. Ye should have snatched the wand.
>   Without the rod reversed,
> And backward mutters of dissevering power,
> We cannot free the lady that sits there,
> Bound in strong fetters, fixed and motionless.'

To reverse this rod, to spell the charm backwards, to break the ties that bound a stupefied people to the seat of enchantment, was the noble aim of Milton."

In this example, a striking passage selected from the works which the reviewer is examining, is used as an illustration, and the effect is good. The pleasure which it affords us, is similar to that derived from a sprightly turn in conversation. We all know, that it adds much to the point of a witty remark, when its author has founded it on an expression just dropped by another. There is a suddenness about it, which is an evidence that it is not premeditated, and which is pleasing to us. Something of the same kind of pleasure, is without doubt felt, in meeting with allusions of the class to which the preceding example belongs.

Example 10. I shall give but one example more of the Allusion, and that is worthy of notice from the manner of its introduction. It is sometimes the case, that a writer meets with a suitable object of allusion in the productions of some author, whose writings are either in a language unknown to most of his readers, or not of sufficient reputation o be regarded as classical. In such instances, the only way is to state the fact or story, and then on this statement found the allusion. One caution in such cases should always be remembered. Be sure that the allusion is of sufficient importance to justify so formal an introduction. And if ever this is the case, it surely is so in the following example:

"Ariosto tells a pretty story of a fairy, who, by some mysterious law of her nature, was condemned to appear at certain seasons in the form of a foul and poisonous snake. Those who injured her during this period of her disguise, were forever excluded from participation in the blessings she bestowed. But to those, who, in spite of her loathsome aspect, pitied and protected her, she afterwards revealed herself in the beautiful and celestial form which was natural to her; accompanied their footsteps, granted all their wishes, filled their houses with wealth, made them happy in love, and victorious in war. Such a spirit is Liberty. At times she takes the form of a hateful reptile. She grovels, she hisses, she stings. But woe to those who in disgust shall venture to crush her. And happy are those, who, having dared to receive her in her degraded and frightful shape, shall at length be rewarded by her in the time of her beauty and glory."

In the arrangement of the preceding examples of allusion, reference is had to the division of our associations into universal and arbitrary, which has been made by intellectual philosophers. Classical allusions, whether to standard authors in our own or foreign languages, Historical allusions, and Scriptural allusions, come under the head of those of universal association. Other instances are those of arbitrary associations. From noticing this distinction it may be seen, why, in the writings of our best authors, — those who write with the hope of being read when other writers of the age are forgotten, — allusions of the former class are much more frequent, than of the latter. The passing events of the day, and the ephemeral productions of the age, will soon be forgotten; and though an allusion to them may at first cast some light on the passages where they are found, at a later time, and in a different place, such allusions will only tend to darken what before they illuminated. Not so with allusions founded on associations that are universal. While the works from which they are derived go down to posterity, gathering new admiration in their progress, these allusions are understood, and constitute a bond of connexion between the literary men of different ages, being drawn from the same common storehouse of imagery and facts.

The Comparison, Metaphor, and Allusion, are founded on the fondness of the mind for tracing unexpected resemblances. There are other relations which give rise to other attempts to please. One thing is the cause of another; here is the relation of cause and effect. One thing is the symbol of another; here is the relation of the sign to the thing signified. We look on the goblet, and we think of the generous wine with which it is wont to be filled; here is the relation of the container to the thing contained. Again, one thing is part of another; here is the relation of a part to the whole. One thing is a species in relation to another which is its genus; here is the relation of the species to the genus.

The relations which have now been stated, are not often formally referred to with the design of illustration or ornament; but instances frequently occur, in which they are implied and suggested to the mind by the peculiar use of a word. The manner in which this is done, has been already shewn in the case of the Metaphor.

To give examples of the different tropes, or figures, founded on these several relations, would be of little practical advantage. Besides, in these instances, the writer does not found his attempts to please solely on the fondness of the mind for discovering unexpected relations. Most frequently it is his wish to increase the distinctness of the reader's view, or in some other way to excite an emotion of taste. Instead then of making these different figures, as the Metonymy, Synecdoche, Metalepsis and others, disti objects of attention, I shall more fully explain the nature the figurative use of language, and in another chapter, when treating of vivacity, as a quality of style, give examples of the most important of these figures.

A word is said to be used literally, when it is used in a manner, which is authorized by the general consent of hose who speak and write with correctness the language, in which it is found A word is used figuratively, when, though it retains its usual signification, it is applied in a manner different from its common application. When I speak of the pillar which supports the edifice, I use the word *pillar* literally, or as it is usually applied by those who speak the English language. If I say of a man, that he is the pillar of the State, I still use the word *pillar* in its common signification, as denoting that which, firmly fixed, gives a solid support, but I apply the word to an object different from those to which it is usually applied. Instead of a solid mass of wood, or stone, the object to which it is applied, is an intelligent being; and instead of supporting a material edifice, it is the support of the State. This, then, is an example of the figurative use of language.

It might be expected, that from their being often used ir a manner different from their common literal use, the significations of this class of words would in time be subject to change. And this, in examining the history of a language, is often found to be the case. In our own language, there are many words, which were at first literally applied to material objects only, and figuratively used to denote those which are intellectual. Many of these have now altogether lost their original meaning, and retain only that derived from their figurative use. Who would now speak of the *apprehension of a chair*, or of the *ardor of his fire?* But such, in their original signification, was the common use of these words. In other instances, where the signification of the word in its literal use has not become obsolete, the meaning derived from its figurative use is more readily suggested.

It may be said, if this change is progressive, and the

meaning of a word, as used figuratively, supersedes the original literal signification, how are we to determine, in respect to a word thus changing, whether it be used figuratively or literally? The answer is, that whenever a word of this class ceases to have any influence on the imagination, in leading it to trace out an unexpected relation, it is no longer used figuratively, but its figurative meaning has become its literal.

The changes in a language introduced by the figurative use of words, are attended with inconvenience, so far as they cause uncertainty in the signification of terms. But this inconvenience is amply compensated by the advantages resulting from the same source. Some of these I shall here mention;

1. The figurative use of words increases the copiousness of a language. It has already been stated, that when a word is used figuratively, its original meaning is retained, but this meaning is modified by the new application which is made. These new applications, then, are to be regarded as modifications of the original meaning of the word, and the effect is similar to the multiplying of derivatives from the radical terms of a language. The following uses of the word " tide " illustrate this remark.

> " What a tide of woes come rushing on this woful land '
> " The tide of blood in me hath proudly flowed in vanity. '
> " There is a tide in the affairs of men."

Now these different applications of the word *tide* do in fact so modify its meaning, that the effect is the same, as if so many new words had been introduced into the language Thus it is that a language is made more copious.

2. As a necessary consequence from the preceding, the richness of language is increased. We have a greater variety of terms and expressions for conveying the same

thought, or describing the same object, and are enabled to
mark with distinctness minute shades of difference in our
thoughts and in the appearance of objects. To illustrate
this remark, I introduce several different ways in which the
shining of the Sun is represented ;

> " Behold, the Sun hath burst the Eastern gates,
> And all his *splendor floods* the towered walls."
> " And when the Sun begins *to fling*
> His flaring beams."
> " Right against the eastern gate,
> Where the great Sun *begins his state*
> Rob'd in flames and amber light."
> " Thou'rt *purpling* now, O Sun, the vines of Canaan,
> And *crowning with rich light* the cedar tops of Lebanon '
> " Thou Sun,
> *The quiver* of thy noontide rays
> *Exhaust* in all their fiery blaze."
> —— " a dazzling *deluge* reigns."
> " The western *waves* of ebbing day
> *Rolled* o'er the glen their level way,
> Each purple peak, each flinty spire,
> Was *bathed in floods* of living fire."
> *Phœbus bade farewell* to every leaf and flower.

The aid derived from the figurative use of words in pointing out minute differences in the appearance of objects,
may be learnt from the following expressions which describe
the passage of light.

" A peculiar melancholy reigns over the aisle where Mary lies
buried. The light *struggles dimly* through windows darkened by
dust."

" The last beams of day were now *faintly streaming* through the
painted windows in the high vaults above me."

" The time shall come, when the garish sunbeam *shall break* into
these gloomy mansions of death."

The advantages derived from the figurative use of words

in giving copiousness and richness to a language, are not confined to descriptive writing. Without aid of this kind, it would be difficult for the intellectual philosopher to con duct his reasoning and explain the phenomena of the mind.

3. The increased power of language may be mentioned as a third particular, in stating the advantages arising from the use of figurative terms. By the increased power of language, I here refer to its influence on the distinctness of our views, and in exciting the feelings and emotions of which we are susceptible. The passages quoted when treating of vivacity as a quality of style, illustrate this remark. I shall therefore state but few instances here, and these without comment.

—————— " Men looked up
With mad disquietude on the dull sky,
  The *pall* of a past world."
    " Thoughts rush in *stormy darkness* through the soul.
  " It broke the *Sabbath* stillness round."
  " The heavens present an immense concave *reposing* on the circular boundary of the world."

A fondness for life and animated beings in preference to inanimate objects, may be stated as one of the principles in man, on which attempts to excite emotions of taste are founded. Whenever, therefore, a writer causes the imagination of his readers to regard inanimate objects, or such as have an existence in the mind only, as living and acting, or having the properties of a living being, such attempts, if authorized by the subject and occasion, are approved by lit erary taste This is called PERSONIFICATION.

There are different ways in which the imagination is led to give life to inanimate objects. Sometimes it is by a direct address to them as listening, sometimes by a description of them as acting, and sometimes by merely ascribing to them the properties of intelligent or animated beings

Examples of these different methods will be given, accompanied with such remarks as may fully shew the nature of such attempts and the cautions to be observed in their use.

Example 1. The following much admired instance of personification is from Milton. It is the language of Eve on leaving Paradise.

> " Must I leave thee, Paradise? thus leave
> Thee, native soil, these happy walks and shades,
> Fit haunts of Gods! where I had hoped to spend,
> Quiet though sad, the respite of that day
> That must be mortal to us both? O flowers,
> That never will in other climates grow,
> My early visitation, and my last
> At even, which I bred up with tender hand
> From the first opening bud, and gave you names,
> Who now shall rear you to the sun, or rank
> Your tribes, and water from the ambrosial fount?

In this example, the garden with the different objects it contains, are addressed as having life and intelligence. Eve parts from them, as from friends with whom she has long been familiar, and whom she fondly loves. What is most prominent in all instances of this kind of personification is, that they result from strong emotion; and this suggests one important rule respecting them. *Personifications of the bolder kind should never be introduced, except when there is strong excitement.*

Personification, both of inanimate objects, and of such as have an existence only in the mind, are frequently found in the commencement of poetical effusions. The poet, struck with them as objects of beauty, or grandeur, or sublimity, becomes highly excited, and breaks forth in an address to them, as if they could hear his strains, and receive his praises.

Example 2. The following example of this kind is from Akenside.

> " Indulgent Fancy ! from the fruitful banks
> Of Avon, whence thy rosy fingers cull
> Fresh flowers and dews, to sprinkle on the turf
> Where Shakspeare lies, be present."

In this example, there is a personification of a faculty of the mind — that which exists only as an object of thought or consciousness. Instances of this kind are common, and from their frequency do not appear so bold, as those of inanimate material objects; but they are often justly regarded as happy attempts to excite emotions of taste. Like comparisons in which intellectual are illustrated by material things, they assist the mind in the distinctness of its views. They also often bring before the mind an object or scene, in the view of which, from some original tendency of the mind, or from some association, an emotion of beauty is excited. In the instance just stated, imagination causes a fair form to rise before us, whose occupation it is to " cull fresh flowers from the banks of the rivers," and " sprinkle dews on poets' graves," and we regard the image presented with an emotion of beauty.

The most important caution to be observed in the introduction of personifications of the kind we are considering is, *that the object addressed be one of sufficient dignity and importance.* Should a writer address his inkstand, or his paper, as beings of life and intelligence, the effect would be unfavorable.

It will be noticed, that in the examples of personification which have been cited, inanimate objects and objects of thought are addressed as living agents. The writer calls upon them as beings that can hear and act. Examples will now be given, in which inanimate objects and objects of thought are described as acting and possessing the qualities of living beings. These instances form a second class of personifications, being less bold than those before stated

Example 3.   The following example is from Milton;

> " So saying, her rash hand in evil hour
> Forth reaching to the fruit, she plucked she ate.
> Earth felt the wound, and Nature from her seat,
> Sighing through all her works, gave signs of woe
> That all was lost."

In this example, Earth, an inanimate material object, is described as feeling, and Nature, an object of thought, as acting.   Though so high an excitement of the mind is not required to justify the introduction of a descriptive personification, such as is here given, as is necessary to authorize a personification of the preceding class, still that excitement must exist to a considerable degree.   Had not the occasion been one of great importance, and the event one regarded with deep interest, the personifications of the earth and of nature here found, would not be approved.   But so important was the occasion, and so momentous the event, that the method of description here adopted, is in agreement with our excited feelings.   Hence, then, the caution given in reference to the former class of personifications, is applicable in some degree to this.

Instances, in which objects of thought are represented as acting and exhibiting the qualities of active and intelligent beings, are frequent.   One principal design of such personifications, as before remarked, is to aid the mind in the distinctness of its conceptions.

Example 4.   The following example of this kind is from Hooker;

" Of law, there can be no less acknowledged, than that her seat is the bosom of God, her voice the harmony of the world.   All things in heaven and earth do her homage; the very least as feeling her care, and the greatest as not exempted from her power.   Both angels and men and creatures of what condition soever, though each

in different sort and manner, yet all with uniform consent, admiring
her as the mother of their peace and joy.

No one can read this passage without a consciousness,
that the personification gives a unity and distinctness to his
conception of the nature and offices of law ; and this advantage is in addition to the pleasure, which is felt in the view
of the venerated form of an intelligent being.

In connexion with this example, one caution may be
given, as applicable to descriptive personifications. There
should be consistency between the different parts ; the language used throughout the whole description should be such
as can be applied to an active, intelligent being ; and the
traits of character ascribed to it, should harmonize with
each other. This is admirably exemplified in the instance
before us. An intelligent being may have her seat, she may
utter her voice, she may receive homage, and be called a
mother. The traits of character are also consistent. Well
may she, whose resting-place is the bosom of God, and whose
voice is the harmony of the world, receive the homage of all
things in heaven and earth, and be admired as the mother
of peace and joy.

It may be here remarked, that personifications are often
found united with metaphors. Of this the following passage
from Thomson is an example ;

> " The mountain thunders ; and its sturdy sons
> Stoop to the bottom of the rocks they shade."

Here the trees are called the sons of the mountain. This
will at once be recognized as the metaphor, and it happily
introduces the personification, by which the trees are represented as stooping. That the author speaks of the trees
as acting, and not of the sons, is evident from the latter
part of the sentence, in which mention is made of the shade

Instances of this kind are frequent, and upon examination
of them, it will generally be found, that they occur where
inanimate objects are wont to have some motion imparted
to them from an external cause, or where some other circumstance connected with them, gives ground for the personification.   This is seen in the following examples:

> " Low the woods
> Bow their hoar heads."
> " The sky saddens with the gathered storm."
> " The cherished fields
> Put on their winter robe of purest white."

All these instances of personification are evidently founded on a resemblance between what is literally true of the
object presented to our notice and an imagined animated
being.   Hence such instances are said to partake both of the
nature of the metaphor and personification.   Personifications
of this kind are naturally suggested, and do not imply so
high a state of excitement as those before mentioned.   Hence
they are frequently found.

Instances in which some of the properties of intelligent
and animated beings are ascribed to inanimate objects, are
very frequent, especially in poetical productions.   Our language, from its philosophical distinction of gender, is well
suited to personifications of this kind.   We have only to apply
to an object one of our pronouns, thus giving to it a gender,
and it " becomes a thing of life."   The same is also effected,
by connecting, as a predicate, with an inanimate object,
a verb, which in its received use implies life and action, or
by joining to an inanimate object some epithet expressive of
life.   Thus when we say of a ship, that she sails ; of a book,
that it speaks to us ; or when we call the wind, the whisper-
ing wind, we afford examples of this class of personifications.
Instances of this kind of personification are common, and
conduce much to the animation and beauty of writing.

.On the principle, that the mind is pleased with animated beings in preference to those which are inanimate, a writer sometimes calls on the dead, or absent, as if living or present. This is termed APOSTROPHE.

The following example is from Webster's Address on Bunker's Hill:

"Him! cut off by Providence in the hour of overwhelming anxiety and thick gloom; falling, ere he saw the star of his country rise; pouring out his generous blood, like water, before he knew whether it would fertilize a land of freedom or of bondage! how shall I struggle with the emotions that stifle the utterance of thy name! Our poor work may perish; but thine shall endure! This monument may moulder away; the solid ground it rests upon may sink down to a level with the sea; but thy memory shall not fail!"

It will be observed in reading this passage, that the Orator, after speaking of the "first great Martyr in the cause of Independence," as of one absent or dead, suddenly changes the train of his thought, and addresses himself directly to the same personage as one present and listening. It is this sudden turn from one manner of speaking of a subject to another, that is referred to by the word Apostrophe, which etymologically signifies a breaking off, or turning from one object to another.

Attempts of this kind to excite emotions of taste, are but seldom made. They are evidence of strong excitement, and are found in prose only in high flights of oratory. In poetical writings, they are more frequent. The same cautions and directions may be applied to them, as to personifications of the bolder kind.

It may be remarked, that the word Apostrophe is often used in a more general signification, than that here ascribed to it. Thus we have in Byron an Apostrophe to the Ocean, and also to Mount Parnassus. All that is meant in this use of the word is, that the author turns himself to these objects with a direct address to them. So far as these instances come under the examination of literary taste, it is as examples of personification of the bolder kind.

Writers under the influence of strong excitement, sometimes break forth in incoherent and extravagant expressions, which will not bear the examination of common sense, and which, unless viewed as the language of passion, would be condemned by good taste as unnatural and inconsistent. Such expressions however are excused as the language of passion, and to instances of this kind the name of HYPER-BOLE is applied. But as such instances are of rare occurrence, and are not subject to rule, one example only will be given. It is extracted from the Siege of Valencia.

> " Flow forth, thou noble blood!
> •   Bathe the land,
> But there thou shalt not sink! our very air
> Shall take thy coloring, and our loaded skies
> O'er the infidel hang dark and ominous,
> With battle hues of thee! And thy deep voice,
> Rising above them to the judgment-seat,
> Shall call a burst of gathered vengeance down,
> To sweep the oppressor from us! For thy wave
> Hath made his guilt run o'er "

To call upon the blood of youth to ' bathe the land,' or to speak of it as ' tinging the skies,' and ' uttering a voice,' is an extravagance, to be excused only on the ground of the wildness of passion; but when the character of the individual by whom these expressions were uttered, and the circumstances in which he was placed, are known, the language used is not only allowed but approved.

But there is another form of the Hyperbole, which comes more strictly under the cognizance of literary taste. It is when a writer, with the design of producing a strong impression on the mind, and thus gratifying a fondness for dis-

tinct and vivid views of objects, exaggerates what he relates.
Instances of this kind are frequent in common conversation ;
but such instances, from their frequency, lose their influence
on the imagination, and are regarded as common forms of
speech. Of instances less common, a few examples will
now be given The following is from the Siege of Valencia;

> " A rescued land
> Sent up a shout of victory from the field,
> That rocked her ancient mountains."

This is evidently exaggeration, and it is the language of
an excited mind; but since the occasion authorizes this excitement, and the effect of the strong expression used, is to
produce a clear and vivid conception of the event described,
it is approved by good taste. It will be noticed in examining examples of this kind, that there is some apparent foundation for the exaggeration used. What is asserted does
not at once strike the mind as improbable, though upon reflection it is seen to be impossible. Hence, when an exaggeration appears at first view both improbable and impossible, the effect is unfavorable. Such is the example given
by Dr. Blair ;

> " I found her on the floor
> In all the storm of grief, yet beautiful,
> Pouring out tears at such a lavish rate,
> That were the world on fire, they might have drowned
> The wrath of heaven, and quenched the mighty ruin."

The following is from Milman's Belshazzar ;

> " Oh maid ! thou art so beauteous
> That yon bright moon is rising, all in haste
> To gaze on thee."

This example evidently differs from the preceding, since

it is rather the language of adulation than of passion. In the use of Hyperboles of this kind, much skill is necessary. They should appear to be naturally suggested, and not be too bold, nor pursued too far. This last caution is one of general application to all instances of exaggeration; for even to the extravagance of passion there is a limit, and if this limit be passed, the effect must be to disgust. What this limit is in any particular case, the good sense of every one must determine.

It has been my object in this chapter to direct the attention of the student to those attempts to please by exciting emotions of taste, which are of most frequent occurrence. At the same time, such cautions and directions have been given, as are of most practical importance. There are besides certain nameless graces, which are the objects of the attention of literary taste. But these, except such as may be mentioned in describing the qualities of a good style, must be left to be pointed out by the instructor.

In concluding this chapter, I would recommend to the student the study of models of excellence in literature. The value of these models to the learner, and the manner in which the study of them tends to the improvement of a literary taste, may be inferred from what was said n a preceding chapter. It is not enough that the productions of good writers are read. They must be studied as models of style. Let the student in literature imitate in this respect the course pursued by the artist in the acquisition of skill in his profession. The painter does not rest satisfied with a single look at a fine picture. He emphatically studies it, both as to its design and execution. Knowing that it is fitted to give pleasure, he would discover wherein its excellency consists; and thus derives from the study of it, rules which may guide him in his own efforts, and assist in his judgment of the works of others. At the same time, from his famil

iarity with works of excellence, his taste becomes in a manner assimilated to the tastes of those who are the masters of
the art.   The same is true in literature, and hence it is,
that familiarity with the best literary productions, both of
our own language and of other languages, is so highly conducive to excellence as a writer.   The remark is often made,
that the best writers are almost uniformly the best classical
scholars.   The connexion here stated, may easily be explained.   The models of fine writing, which have come down
to us from former periods of the world, furnish ample opportunity for the exercise of the imagination and the improvement of the taste.   To him then who aspires to become a
good writer, I would recommend the study of those ancient
models, with all the earnestness of Horace, *Nocturna versure
manu versate diurna.*

CHAPTER FOURTH.

ON SKILL IN THE USE OF LANGUAGE.

VALUABLE thoughts, extensive knowledge, the ability to reason justly, and good literary taste, are essential to form the good writer, in whatever language he may compose. They are therefore rightly called the foundations of a good style. But it was stated in the Introduction, that in addition to these requisites for good writing, there must be skill in the use of language. This then is the next object of attention.

To use the English language skilfully, implies that the writer selects his words and composes his sentences, in a manner, which accurately and clearly conveys to those able to read this language, the thoughts existing in his own mind. With the design then of aiding the young writer in the acquisition of this skill, I shall treat of the nature and principles of Verbal Criticism, and afterwards state the rules and cautions to be observed in the composition of sentences

SECTION 1.—ON VERBAL CRITICISM.

Nature and necessity of Verbal Criticism.

When Cortez landed on the Coasts of South America, information was immediately given to the king of Mexico of his arrival and of the appearance of his troops. The despatches which were sent, consisted of pictures representing the appearance of the ships, the disembarking of men, their arms and equipments and military array. Had Montezuma, with a company of his subjects, arrived at the same period of the world on the coasts of England, an account of his arrival and appearance would have been sent to the king of that country; but in this case, instead of pictures words would have been used in conveying the information; and the king of England, upon looking on the words, would have had as correct and distinct information of the arrival and appearance of Montezuma and his troops, as was obtained in the former instance from looking on the pictures. Hence we infer, *that words answer the same purpose as pictures: they bring up to the mind subjects and thoughts which they are designed to represent.*

Suppose next, that Montezuma, with his troops, after leaving the coast of England, had visited those of Spain. Information of his arrival and appearance would have been sent to the monarch of that country; and in sending this information, as in the case of the king of England, words would have been used. But though the words used for conveying this intelligence, would in this case have been different from those before used, still they would represent the same objects, and be as readily understood. Different words then in different languages represent the same objects. Hence we infer, *that there is no natural connexion between words and the objects which they represent.*

Suppose next, that the event of Montezuma's arrival on the English coast had occurred during the thirteenth century, instead of the sixteenth. In this case, an account might have been sent to the king of England in writing, as before, but the words used, would not be intelligible to those who speak and write the English language at the present aay.   This we infer from the fact, that some fragments of writings of that period in the English language, which now remain, are not intelligible.   Hence we learr., not only that different words are used to express the same thoughts in different languages, but *that at different periods different words are used in the same language, as the symbols of the same object.*

Now from these facts, that words are but signs — that there is no natural connexion between them and the objects which they represent — and that the words of a language are changing, some becoming obsolete, and others gaining admission, arises the necessity of verbal criticism ; the object of which is to establish those principles, and lay down those rules, which may direct writers in the selection of right words for expressing their thoughts.   If words, like pictures, were the exact representatives of objects, or the same word always, in every period in the history of a language, and whenever used, had the same thought attached to it by all who speak or write the language, there would evidently be no necessity for verbal criticism.   In learning a language, we should acquire the knowledge of the correct and uniform use of each word, and we should then be in no danger of using it incorrectly.

Good use the standard of appeals in all decisions of Verbal Criticism.

Suppose that in a recent publication, I should meet with the following expression; "When the trial came on, he occupied this man as a witness."   I at once say, that the word *occupy* is here incorrectly used.   Should any one ask me, on what authority I make this assertion, I should answer, that the signification given to it, is different from that which it has in the writings of those, who are esteem ed good authors in the English language. I should turn to several passages in the writings of Addison, Swift, Jeremy Taylor, and perhaps others of the same repute, and show him, that the common meaning of the word, is *to possess — to hold or to keep for use*, and I would then challenge him to shew me the word, as used in the passage in dispute, in the writings of these authors, or of any author who is reputed a good writer.

Suppose, now, that my opponent should say, that he had found the word *occupy*, used in the sense *to make use of*, in the writings of Sir Thomas More, who wrote at the close of the fifteenth, or near the commencement of the sixteenth century; and at the same time acknowledge, that he could not find it thus used in any writer, since that period; I should tell him in reply, that this is no authority for its being used in this sense at the present time. If for three centuries the word has ceased to be thus used by English writers, it is not now a part of the English language. It has become obsolete, and to English readers, it is no longer the sign or symbol, with which the idea *to make use of* is connected.

Suppose, next, that my opponent should assert, that he has found the word thus used in some newspaper, and that he considers the editor of that newspaper a good writer. I should answer him, that it is not enough, that one individual esteems the editor of the newspaper in which the word n question is found, a good writer. He must generally be reputed as such. And even if he were so reputed, it is not enough that one good writer has thus used the word in dispute. This will not make the word, as thus used, a part of the English language, and cause it to be generally understood in this sense.

Suppose, once more, that my opponent should assert, that the word *occupy* is thus used in his own neighborhood, acknowledging at the same time, that he had not heard it so used in other parts of the country. I should answer him again, that this local use of it does not make it a part of the English language. It may be a part of the language of the town where he resides, but it would not be right to use it in this signification, in a work intended to be read by all those who read the English language. It would not convey a right meaning, or be intelligible to any, excepting those of a single town or village in the country.

The case would be similar, supposing my opponent should assert, that lawyers, or those of any particular profession, are wont to use the word in the sense for which he contends I might allow that the word *occupy* is thus correctly used, and at the same time contend, that this professional usage does not authorize its introduction with the same signification into works addressed to all who read the English language. Lawyers, and those of other professions, have many terms in use, which are peculiar to the profession, and which are not expected to be understood by those unacquainted with its mysteries.

From these statements, we learn in what manner each word in a language becomes the symbol of a particular object. It is by conventional agreement. All who speak the language, are supposed to have entered into an agreemen' to use and understand the word in this sense. When therefore we would know in respect to any particular word, whether it belongs to a language, we are to inquire, if it is found in the writings and heard in the conversation of those who write and speak the language. If it is not thus found, the use of it is called *a Barbarism*, and is to be avoided.

We learn further from the views now given, in what manner we may ascertain the proper use of those words which belong to the language. It is by an appeal to Good Usage. We are first to inquire, how the word in question

is used by those who are generally reputed good writers
This is called *reputable usage*, and is opposed to vu.gar usage
on the one hand, and to partial or limited usage on the
other.   We are in the next place to ask, whether the writings to which we look as authorities, are reputed to be
good by those who at the present time speak and write the
language.   This is *present usage*, and is opposed to ancient
or obsolete usage.   The inquiry further arises, whether the
word in question is used in the sense ascribed to it, wherever the language to which it belongs, is spoken; and this is
national usage, as opposed to foreign, to provincial or to
professional usage.   Thus Good Usage includes *reputable,
national, and present usage ;* and when a word is found in
a sense which is not supported by good usage, as thus ex
plained, it is called *an impropriety*, and is to be shunned

Nature and design of a Dictionary.

From this view of the standard in verbal criticism, may
be learnt the nature and design of a Dictionary.   When
wishing to show my opponent, that the word *occupy* is used
by authors of reputation, in a different sense from that
which he defends, instead of seeking for passages, in which
 he word is used by different authors, I should have turned
to the word in my Dictionary, and there have found the result, to which the compiler of the Dictionary had been led
from an examination, such as I proposed.   Hence it may
be seen, why Johnson's Dictionary is sometimes called the
standard of the English language.   He has carefully investigated the meaning of words, as used by authors of reputation, and has given us the results, to which, from these investigations, he has been led; and confiding in his fidelity
and good judgment, we appeal to him as a standard

Manner in which changes in a language are effected.

From this view also, may be learnt the manner, in which old and long established words become obsolete, and new ones are introduced. When a word, from the harshness of its sound, from any indefiniteness in its meaning, from its being no longer needed, or from any other cause, ceases to be in use by writers of reputation, for a considerable time, it is said to become obsolete, and is no longer considered a part of the language.

On the other hand, every new word that is introduced into a language, must be first proposed by some author of reputation. If it is thought necessary — if it expresses the meaning attached to it better than any other word, or is more harmonious than another word before used in the same sense, it is adopted by other writers of reputation, and thus becomes a part of the language. If it is thought un necessary, it is not adopted, and the attempt to introduce it fails. While then inconvenience is experienced from the changes of language, in that the authors of one period are thus rendered unintelligible at another, this evil is balanced by the introduction of more significant and harmonious words. No new word however should ever be admitted, which is not decidedly an improvement. On the other hand, a word which is unharmonious in its sound, or which, from any newly associated idea, becomes unfit for the use formerly made of it, though its use be supported by the authority of good writers, should be objected to by critics, and be suffered by writers to become obsolete. These remarks hold true, whether the word in question be entirely of new formation, whether it be made up of two or more words compounded together, or be introduced with or without modification from some other language.

It may here be asked, — for how long a period must a word have been disused by the reputable writers in a language, to make it obsolete? To this inquiry, no definite answer has been given. Campbell has proposed, that a generation, or age of human existence, should be considered a limit, and this rule is generally adopted.

Greater liberty however is given to poetical writers in the use of ancient words, and to scientific writers in the invention of new terms, than to those who are authors in other kinds of writing. The same word, which in a prose writer would be objected to as an obsolete term, might in poetry be received as supported by good authority. This indulgence is granted to poetry in consideration of the embarrassments of rhyme and of measure, which require a copiousness of language. On the other hand, science is progressive. New terms must be found to express new discoveries and inventions. The use of old words in new significations, would obviously create obscurity and mistake, and it is thought better, that new words should be introduced when new objects are to be represented. It is also common for writers on scientific subjects, to define the most important words in their works, especially those which are new or peculiar to the science. This liberty is given them, and it is expected in return, that they will be uniform in the use of the word in the sense defined.

In connexion with these remarks, the influence of criticism on language, may be mentioned. Its object is the improvement of the language — the avoiding of all harsh, unharmonious words, and of those also which, from their etymology, or any other cause, are peculiarly liable to be misunderstood. This object is effected, not by the exercise of any authority, but by pointing out the offensive word to the notice of the public, and dissuading from its use

*Good use not always uniform in her decisions; rules which
should guide us where these decisions are at variance with
each other.*

Suppose that I should meet with the following sentence.
' Beside he was a cotemporary writer of great delicateness
of expression, and highly approved of." I might object to
', and say that *besides* would be better than *beside* — con-
temporary than *cotemporary* — *delicacy* than *delicateness*,
and *approved* than *approved of.* Should I, in support of
my criticisms, appeal to good usage, and mention several
authors of reputation, in whose writings the forms of these
words which I prefer, are uniformly used, it might be said
..a reply, that those forms which I condemn, are also found
in the writings of authors of equally good reputation ; and
this could not be denied. In these instances good use is
not uniform in her decisions; and it is necessary that some
other principles should be referred to, in determining which
of these forms of words is preferable. I might say then, that
the word *beside* is used often as a preposition, and that
where there are two forms of a word, each of which is supported by the authority of good authors, but one of these
forms is sometimes differently used, it should be restricted
to this particular use, and the other form alone used in that
sense, which has hitherto been common to both. Both
perspicuity and variety evidently require this.

In preferring *contemporary* to *cotemporary*, I might plead
the analogy of the language. Whenever the inseparable
preposition *con* precedes a consonant in composition, the *n*
is retained; we say *conglomerate, conglutinate, concomitant*
To this, *copartner* is the only exception. But if this par
ticle in composition precedes a vowel, we use the form *co*

11 *

as *cocqual, cocternal.** Hence in the present case, the anal
ogy of the language requires that we say *contemporary.*

For preferring *delicacy* to *delicateness,* supposing the au·
thorities on either side equal, I can give no other reason, than
that it is more agreeable to the ear. Here then harmony of
sound is the principle on which a decision is made.

In the other instance of criticism, where I prefer *approved*
o *approved of,* simplicity of expression is the ground of
choice. It is well known, that the use of numerous particles is a defect of our language. It weakens the strength
of expression. The more simple and brief the form which
is used, the better.

In instances then where good use is not uniform in her
decisions, perspicuity and variety as leading to appropriate
words to one uniform signification, — the analogy of the language, harmony of sound, and simplicity of expression, are
the principles to which we should refer.

These principles are stated in the following rules, which
may be applied to the examination of the examples referred
to at the close of the chapter.

Rule 1. When two forms of a word have been used with
the same signification, but one of them is sometimes found
used in a different sense, the latter form should be restrict
ed in its use to this latter meaning, and the other form used
in that sense which has hitherto been common to both.

---

* Appeals are so often made to the *analogy of the language,* in
determining questions which pertain to the use of words, that it is
important the student should rightly understand the meaning of this
phrase. In reasoning from the analogy of the language, we first
assign a word to a class of words, to which, from some similarity in
its form, its derivation, its composition, or some other circumstances
it bears a close resemblance. We then apply the rules and principles
of this class of words to the individual word. Thus we assign the
word *contemporary* to a class of words compounded of the inseparable
particle *con* as a prefix. We then, as in the text, apply a rule of the
class to the individual word. Departures from the analogy of the
language are called *Anomalies*

Rule 2. Of two forms of a word which are each supported by a good use we should prefer that which is agreeable
to the analogy of the language.

Rule 3. If two forms of a word are supported by equal
authority, and in other respects equally appropriate, the
sound may determine us in our choice.

Rule 4. In doubtful cases, when no one of the preceding rules will apply, simplicity should be the ground of preference.

*Cautions against the most frequent violations of the princi-
ples of Verbal Criticism.*

From the statements that have now been made, we learn
that to use words with propriety, is to use them in that manner which is authorized by writers of reputation. The most
important of those rules, by which we are to be governed
in cases where authorities are divided, have also been stated.
Some of the most frequent violations of the principles of
verbal Criticism will now be enumerated, and those cautions
given which are most needed on this subject.

" The lamb is tame in its disposition." — Here the word
tame is incorrectly used for *gentle ;* — *tameness* is superin-
duced by discipline — *gentleness* belongs to the natural disposition.

" Herschel discovered the telescope." — In this sentence
the word *discover* is incorrectly used for *invent.* We discover what was before hidden ; we invent what is new.

" Caius Mucius displayed courage, when he stood un-
moved with his hand in the fire."

Here *courage* is incorrectly used for *fortitude.* It is
courage that enables us to meet danger ; but fortitude gives
us strength to endure pain.

In these instances, the words which are substituted, resemble in meaning those which are displaced. Such words are said to be synonymous. They agree in expressing the same principal idea, but some accessory circumstance produces a shade of difference in their meaning. As the English language is characterized by copiousness, there is great danger of confounding terms which are synonymous. *Hence in the use of words, care should be had, lest we confound those which are synonymous.*

" The observation of days of Thanksgiving is common in New England." — Here the word *observation* is evidently used instead of *observance*, which it resembles in sound.

" The endurance of his speech was for an hour." — Here the word *endurance*, which signifies suffering, is used for *duration*, which implies length of time. It is true, that if a speech is dull, and continues for an hour, we may speak of the endurance of those who listen to it. But in the example which is given, the word is wrongly used for duration.

In these instances, a similarity of sound has led to mistake. *Hence, in the use of words, we should avoid confounding those which are similar in sound.*

" Meanwhile the Britons, left to shift for themselves were forced to call in the Saxons to their aid."

" He passed his time at the court of St. James, currying favor with the minister."

The expressions *left to shift for themselves* and *currying favor*, found in these sentences, are most frequently heard in the conversation of men destitute of refinement and information. They are beneath the dignity of the historical style. Like clowns when admitted to the society of polite, well informed men, they appear out of place. Other expressions equally significant, and better suited to the subject, might be substituted. *Hence then we learn, that low words and phrases, or such as are usually termed vulgarisms, are to be avoided.*

We are liable to err in violation of this rule, from the circumstance, that many words are used in common conversation, which are not suited to the dignity of a written discourse. I might hence infer the importance of keeping good company, and being choice in the selection of our words. Evil communications not only corrupt good manners, but good language.

"I have considered the subject in its integrity."

The writer here means, that he has considered the whole of the subject; but in expressing this idea, he uses a word in its Latin signification. *Integrity*, in the sense of *wholeness*, is not in common use by those who correctly write and speak the English language. Other instances might be cited, in which words have ascribed to them a meaning derived from the Greek, French, or some other language. Hence such instances are called Latinisms, Grecisms, etc. Besides the obscurity, which must thus be caused to those who are ignorant of the meaning of the word in its native language, there is an air of pedantry about expressions of this kind, which renders them disgusting. Hence then the caution may be given, *Avoid using words in foreign significations.*

We not unfrequently find in reputable English writers words and phrases which belong to a foreign language Among those most frequently introduced are the following; coup d'œil — corps de reserve — stans pede in uno — miscere utile dulci. Sometimes this practice is carried to an extent, which savors of pedantry, and to one unacquainted with the language of the quotations, obscures the meaning. Foreign words and phrases, when thus introduced, are designed either to convey some striking thought in a more bold, sententious manner, than could otherwise be done, or to give a happy turn of expression. Hence we infer the proper limit to be observed in their introduction. When ever we have in our own language a word or phrase equally expressive and striking, a writer cannot be justified in supplanting it by the use of one that is foreign.

The most frequent instances of the violation of the principles of Verbal Criticism, are in the introduction of new words. So much however has been said on this point, that it is unnecessary to give either examples or rules.

The inquiry may here arise whether Johnson's Dictionary, or any other, is to be regarded as a standard, to which we may in all cases refer for the decisions of Verbal Criticism? To this inquiry I answer, that since the words of a language are ever changing, some becoming obsolete and others coming into use, it is impossible, from the nature of the case, that any Dictionary can continue, for a long time, to be a standard of good usage. In regard to Johnson, there are many words now in good use, which are not found in his Dictionary, and many there found, have become obsolete in the sense he has ascribed to them. Where then is the standard? The principles stated in this chapter give the answer. There is none, except that which the finished scholar forms for himself from his familiarity with good models of writing. And if he possesses this familiarity, he may conclude, that if a word strikes him as new or strange, it should be considered a word used without good authority, and which, unless some necessity for its use exists, should be avoided.

Section II.—On the Composition of Sentences.

The design of this section is to treat of the composition of sentences, so far as the clear conveyance of the author' meaning depends on skill in the use of language.

Sentences are either simple or complex. A simple sen

tence consists of a single member. A complex sentence consists of several members, and these members are sometimes subdivided into clauses. "The sun shines." This is a simple sentence. "The sun, that rises in the morning and sets at night, gives light to all those who dwell on the face of the earth" This is a complex sentence, and consists of two members, each of which is made up of two clauses.

The principle by which the writer is guided in dividing a discourse into sentences, is, that where he makes this division, he considers the exhibition of his thought as complete. Sometimes in making this exhibition several members are necessary; and where these members are so closely connected, that the reader cannot stop before the conclusion of the sentence with any distinct thought in his mind, the sentence is called a period. If there is one or more places, where he may stop, a distinct thought having been stated, the sentence is called a loose sentence. This distinction will be clearly seen in the following examples. "If in America, as some of England's writers are endeavoring to convince her, she is hereafter to find an invidious rival, and a gigantic foe, she may thank those very writers, for having provoked that rivalship and irritated that hostility." This is a period; and it will be noticed, that though there are several members and clauses, there is no place before the close, where the reader may stop with a distinct view in his mind. This account of the period is in agreement with the etymology of the word. It signifies a circuit, and the thought winds round, as it were, among the different members and clauses, till it is brought out full at the close. The following is a loose sentence. "These minor comforts are all important in the estimation of narrow minds; and they either do not perceive, or will not acknowledge, that they are more than counterbalanced among us by grea and generally diffused blessings." Here it is evident, that we might stop at the word *minds*, and the thought would be complete; but had a full stop been placed there, what follows would not, in its present form, constitute a distinct sentence.

The principles of construction in our language are equally favorable to the period and the loose sentence. Hence in the productions of those esteemed the best writers in the language, sentences of both forms are found intermingled. Some writers incline more to the periodic structure; others to the loose sentence. The prevalence of the former gives to style strength and power of expression, accompanied with a degree of stateliness and formality. On the contrary, where the loose sentence prevails, the style is generally characterized by ease and familiarity. Either, when long continued without interruption, becomes tiresome and dull Hence the inference will be readily made, that neither form should prevail to the exclusion of the other; and further, that there should be an accommodation in this respect to the subject and occasion.

Since sentences are made up of many words, and of clauses and members, it will readily occur, that the forms which they assume, will be many and various, and some of these forms will be best suited to one subject and occasion, and others to a different. Vain then would be the attempt to prescribe rules which should govern the writer in the composition of his sentences. Instead of this, those instances have been noticed, in which perspicuity is most frequently violated from want of skill in the use of language, and from the examples given, such cautions have been inferred, as may guard against similar violations of perspicuity.

The examples first given are of simple sentences and of the members and clauses which make up complex senten ces.   These are classed under the following heads; 1 Equivocal words and phrases. 2. Ambiguous constructions. 3. Wrong arrangement of adverbs and adverbial phrases.

The composition of complex sentences is next examined with reference to the same object.   Connectives are afterwards separately considered.

1. Equivocal words and phrases.

A word or phrase is called equivocal, when on the authority of good usage different significations are at different times applied to it.   The true meaning of such words is to be determined from their connexion with other parts of the sentence.   Hence the danger of obscurity in their use.

Examples of the preposition.

"I am persuaded that neither death nor life — shall be able to sep arate us from the love of God."

In this sentence, *the love of God*, may signify *God's love to us* or *our love to him*.   This equivocation may be avoided by changing the last clause into the following form — *from our love to God; of* being more correctly used before the subject, and *to* before the object of a passion.   The design of prepositions is to express the relations between different words, and since many of the prepositions express different relations, there is much need of caution lest they be used equivocally.

Example of the conjunction.

"They were much more ancient among the Persians than Zoroaster or Zerdusht."

In this example, the *or* is equivocal.   It may either be understood as coupling together Zoroaster and Zerdusht, as two synonymous words, or, as a disjunctive conjunction, it may imply that Zoroaster and Zerdusht are two different things.   Were the latter the meaning of the writer, the word *either* should be inserted before Zoroaster. But if he designs to use the word as a copulative, when the words thus connected are not generally known to be synonymous, some clause may be thrown in to denote that they are thus used In the example given, it might have read — *than Zoroaster, or, as he is also called, Zerdusht. When, in such instances, the first noun follows an article or preposition, or both, the equivocation may be avoided, by repeating the article, or preposition, or both, before the second noun, if the conjunction be used disjunctively, and omitting to repeat it, if it be used copulatively.*

Example of the noun.

" Your majesty has lost all hopes of future excises oy their consumption."

The word *consumption* may be either passive or active. It may mean, either by their being consumed, or by their consuming. The equivocation in this sentence results from the double use of the word *consumption*. Words of this kind are not to be avoided, when the connexion plainly determines which of the meanings is intended ; but when this is not the case, some other word, or some other form of expression, should be selected. In the example given, it should be read, *on what they may consume.*

Example of the adjective.

" As for such animals as are mortal, or noxious, we have a right to destroy them."

It is the design of the writer to use the word *mortal* as signifying destructive, or causing death, whereas the meaning most obviously suggested, is *liable to death.* This may be more correctly called an impropriety than an equivocation ; since it results from the application of a qualifying word in a sense different from that, which is authorized by good usage We speak of a mortal poison, or of a mortal disease, meaning a destructive poison or disease; but when we speak of a mortal animal, it is always in the sense of an animal liable to death. This example suggests the need of caution in the use of adjectives, when usage has given them different significations as applied to different nouns.

Example of the verb.

"The next refuge was to say, it was overlooked by one man, and many passages wholly written by another."

The word *overlooked* may here signify *revised*, or it may signify *neglected*. The equivocation in this example, like that in the example of the noun, results from the use of a word to which usage has given a double meaning. It may here then be said, as in that instance, that if the connexion does not readily suggest which of these meanings is intended, some other word or form of expression should be chosen. In this example, the meaning of the author would be expressed without equivocation by the word *revised.*

Of equivocal phrases, the following may be mentioned, *not the least — not the smallest.* These phrases may signify in direct opposition, *not any,* or *very great.* But it is unnecessary to give examples of the use of these and similar phrases, as they are made the subjects of grammatical criticism. It may be said generally, that such equivocal phrases should be avoided.

2. Ambiguous constructions.

By construction, as the word is applied to sentences, is meant the forming of the sentence in such a manner, that the relations and connexions between the different parts of it may be made known. The standard of correctness in the construction of sentences, as of propriety in the use of words, is good usage. Every language has certain forms of construction, either peculiar to itself, or in common with other languages.   What these forms are, may be learnt from the conversation and writings of men of refinement and knowledge, who speak and write the language.   But as the Lexicographer has given us, in his Dictionary, the result of his inquiries after the proper signification of words; in the same manner, the Grammarian gives us, in his Grammar, the results of his investigations as to what are the correct forms of construction.   Correctness, then, in the construction of sentences, is to be learnt from the rules and principles of syntax.

But a sentence may be correct in its construction, and still may carry to the reader a meaning different from that designed to be conveyed by the writer.   In such instances, since the sentence is so constructed that two different meanings may be received from it, the construction is said to be ambiguous.   Ambiguous constructions most frequently arise from the use of those words which are called connectives, and these, it will be remembered, are to be separately considered.   Some instances in the use of other parts of speech will now be given.

Examples of the adjective.

"God heapeth favors on his servants ever liberal and faithful."

Is it God, or his servants, that are ever liberal and faithful?   It is obvious, that the construction would bear either meaning, and of course it is ambiguous.   The ambiguity may be removed by altering the arrangement of the words. God, ever liberal and faithful, heapeth favors on his servants; or God heapeth favors on his ever liberal and faithful servants.   This altering of the arrangement of he word is in our language a change in the construction of the sentence.   In languages where adjectives and substantives have correspondent changes of termination, the reader may in this way most generally determine to which noun the ad jective belongs; but in languages, as in the English, where adjectives have no change in their terminations, it is their arrangement, which must determine the nouns, with which they are to be connected. Hence then the caution may be given, *To avoid ambiguity in the use of the adjective, let it be placed as near as practicable to the noun it is intended to qualify.*

There is another case, in which there is danger of ambiguity in the use of adjectives. Sometimes, when two adjectives are used in connexion with the same noun, it is difficult to determine, whether they are designed to express different qualities belonging to the same thing, or qualities belonging to different things, but which are included under the noun as a generic term. This is illustrated in the following example: "The ecclesiastic and secular powers concurred in those measures." Is it meant, that the powers which concurred, had both the qualities expressed by the adjectives, *ecclesiastic* and *secular?* or that one class of these powers was ecclesiastic, and the other secular? The latter meaning is no doubt that of the writer; and it should have been expressed, "The ecclesiastic powers, and the secular, concurred in those measures."

In cases of this kind, the following rule should be observed: *When the adjectives are designed to qualify the noun as expressing one thing, the noun should either precede or follow both adjectives; but when the adjectives are to be understood as qualifying different things included under the noun, the noun should follow the first adjective, and may be repeated or not after the second, as the harmony of the sentence may require; and in this latter case, when an article or preposition precedes the first adjective, it should be repeated before the second.*

By this rule, the following version of a passage in the Bible, is to be censured. "Every scribe, instructed into the kingdom of heaven, is like an householder, who bringeth out of his treasury things new and old." It should read *new things and old.*

Instead of saying, "Death is the common lot of all, of good men and bad," the passage should read, " of good men and of bad."

Instead of saying, "How immense the difference between the pious and profane," it should read, " between the pious and the profane."

Example of the preposition.

" You will seldom find a dull fellow of good education, but (if he happen to have any leisure on his hands) will turn his head to one of those two amusements for all fools of eminence, politics, or poetry."

On first reading this sentence, we are led to connect *politics* and *poetry* with *eminence,* and make them all the objects of the preposition *of.* But the true meaning of the writer is expressed, by inserting *to* before the words *politics* and *poetry.* The ambiguity in this case arises from the omission of the preposition, which leads the mind to supply the copulative conjunction, and thus causes mistake. Hence the general remark may be made, that *clearness in the construction of a sentence, is often secured by the repetition of a preposition ; and the writer may be cautioned against its omission in such instances.*

Example of the noun.

" The rising tomb a lofty column bore."

Did the tomb bear the column, or the column bear the tomb ? Ambiguities of this kind result from the principles of our language, which makes no distinction in termination between the nominative and objective case, but leaves the construction to be determined by the arrangement of the words. In prose, therefore, such ambiguities will rarely occur, because the nominative will be placed before the verb, and the objective will follow it. But in poetry, where inversions are allowed, they will occur; and the danger of mistake can be guarded against only by the connexion, except in instances, where, the possessive pronoun being used, it may determine the nominative by referring to it as its antecedent; as in the following example:

"And thus the son his fervent sire addressed.'

Here the pronoun *his* most naturally refers to son as its antecedent, and thus determines which is designed as the nominative, and which as the object of the verb.

3. I proceed now to mention the wrong position of adverbs and of adverbial phrases, as affecting the clearness of the sentence. Faults of this kind, it may be thought, are included under the solecism or grammatical blunders, since the rules of Syntax require, that adverbs should be placed near the words they are designed to qualify. But such instances are of so frequent occurrence, that a few will be mentioned.

"The Romans understood liberty, at least as well as we."

In hearing this sentence read aloud, with the emphasis upon liberty, we should be led to connect the adverb with this word. But should the emphasis be placed on the adverb itself, we should connect it with the concluding part of the sentence. It is better to change the position of the adverb, so that there can be no danger of mistaking the true meaning of the writer. The sentence is then more correctly constructed as follows: "The Romans understood liberty, as well at least as we."

"Theism can only be opposed to polytheism or atheism.

" Theism can be opposed only to polytheism or atheism."

" There is not perhaps any real beauty or deformity, more in one piece of matter, than in another.'

" There is not perhaps any real beauty or deformity in one piece of matter, more than in another."

" Not only Jesuits can equivocate."

" Jesuits can not only equivocate.'

My design in stating this last example, is to shew, that the same word, according to its position in a sentence, may be either an adverb or an adjective, and consequently an essential difference in the sense be made. The meaning of the sentence, as first given, is, that Jesuits are not the only persons who can equivocate. In the second form of the sentence, the meaning is, Jesuits can not only equivocate, but they can do other things in addition. Hence then may be inferred the need of additional caution in the use of those words, which may be regarded either as adverbs or adjectives, according to their position in the sentence.

Adverbial phrases are to be considered as adverbs, and should be placed near the word whose meaning they are designed to affect. Much skill is often requisite in so placing them, that the sentence may be easy and harmonious in its sound, and still retain its perspicuity. They are well compared to unsightly stones, which try the skill of the builder. As several examples will be given while treating of complex sentences, the further notice of them is here omitted.

I proceed now to consider complex sentences, in reference to perspicuity, so far as this quality depends on skill in the use of language; and without arranging the faults which are mentioned under distinct heads, I shall give instances of sentences that are deficient in perspicuity, and infer from the examination of such instances several cautions.

The following example is introduced, to shew the injurious effect on both the smoothness and perspicuity of a sentence, of separating prepositions from the words with which
they are grammatically connected.

EXAMPLE 1.—"Though virtue borrows no assistance from yet it
may often be accompanied by, the advantages of fortune."

It occurs to every one in reading a sentence constructed
in this manner, that the easy flow of expression is checked,
at the same time that we feel a sort of pain from the violent
separation of two things, which ought to be united. In
State papers, and legal instruments, where there is need of
uncommon precision, sentences of this form may be allow
ed, but on other occasions they should be avoided.

EXAMPLE 2.—"After we came to anchor, they put me on shore,
where I was welcomed by all my friends, who received me with the
greatest kindness."
"Having come to anchor, I was put on shore, where I was wel
comed by my friends, and received with the greatest kindness."

Should the question arise, who, or what, is the predomi-
nant subject of discourse in the first form of this sentence
it may be difficult at first view to answer. *We*, *they*, *I*, and
who, referring to friends, are in different parts of this short,
complex sentence, made the governing or leading words.
In the corrected form there is one leading word, and all the
parts are constructed with reference to this. In this way,
the sentence is made more simple, and the meaning is more
obvious. Hence then we infer, *that there should be one
leading word or clause in every sentence, and that the different members and clauses should be so constructed and
connected, as to be made subservient to this leading word or
clause*

Example 3. — " He had been guilty of a fault, for which his mas
ter would have put him to death, had he not found an opportunity
to escape out of his hands, and fled into the deserts of Numidia.
———— and to flee into the deserts of Numidia."

In the first form of this sentence, are found two clauses,
" to escape out of his hands" and " fled into the deserts of
Numidia," which have the same relation to the other part
of the sentence, and are constructed differently. In one,
the form is that of the infinitive: in the other, of the past
participle. In the sentence as corrected, this diversity is
not found, and the meaning is more obvious. From this
and similar examples may be inferred the following direction; *When two or more clauses have the same relation to
other parts of the sentence, they should, if possible, be made
similar in their construction.*

The two directions, that have now been given, should be
particularly regarded in the composition of long sentences.
It is generally supposed, that in long sentences there is always danger of obscurity, and that they should be avoided.
But let the two directions that have been given, be observed — let there be a leading word or phrase in the sentence,
and all the parts be similarly constructed, and have a common reference to this leading part, and the sentence may be
long without becoming obscure. This is seen in the following example :

" He can render essential service to his country, by assisting in
the disinterested administration of the laws ; by watching over the
principles and opinions of the lower classes around him ; by diffu-
sing among them those lights which may be important to their we.
fare ; by mingling frankly among them, gaining their confidence
and becoming the immediate auditor of their complaints ; by inform.
ing himself of their wants, and making himself a channel through
which their grievances may be quietly communicated to the proper
sources of mitigation ; or by becoming, if need be, the intrepid and

·ncorruptible guardian of their liberties, the enlightened champion of their wants."

EXAMPLE 4.—"If he delights in these studies, (Mathematics,) ne can have enough of them. He may bury himself in them as deeply as he pleases. He may revel in them incessantly, and eat drink, and clothe himse'f with them."

———"He may revel in them incessant y, and eat them, drink them, and clothe himself with them."

In the first form of this sentence, there is a solecism, arising from the ellipsis. According to the statement there made, a student may eat and drink himself with Mathematics. The second form of the sentence is grammatically correct, and expresses the meaning of the writer. This example then suggests the necessity of caution in the use of elliptical expressions.*

EXAMPLE 5.—"Whatever renders a period sweet and pleasant, makes it also graceful; a good ear is the gift of nature; it may be much improved, but not acquired by art; whoever is possessed of it, will rarely need dry critical precepts to enable him to judge of a true rightness and melody of composition; just numbers, accurate proportions, a musical symphony, magnificent figures, and that decorum which is the result of all these, are unison to the human mind; we are so framed by nature that their charm is irresistible."

To make this sentence perspicuous, it would be necessary to entirely remodel it. It is an example of the violation of those principles, on which a discourse is divided into sentences. It neither has one subject, nor is there a connexion between its different parts We may infer from it the general direction; *Not to unite in the same sentence those thoughts and statements which are distinct, and but remotely connected with each other.*

EXAMPLE 6.—"It is not without a degree of patient attention and

---

* See Rule 22, Syntax of Murray's Grammar

persevering diligence, greater than the generality are willing to be
stow, though not greater than the object deserves, that the habit can
be acquired of examining and judging of our own conduct with the
same accuracy and impartiality as that of another."

"The habit of examining our own conduct as accurately as that
of another, and of judging of it with the same impartiality, cannot be
acquired, without a degree of patient attention and persevering dil
igence, not greater indeed than the object deserves, but greater than
the generality are willing to bestow."

This sentence is long, and the objection may be made to
the first form of it, that no distinct meaning is conveyed to
the mind, till we arrive nearly at its close. This prevents
its being readily and fully comprehended. In the corrected form, the different parts are so arranged, that we take in
the meaning of the different clauses as we proceed, and
without difficulty or delay comprehend the full meaning of
the entire sentence. The example then suggests the important caution; *That the different parts of long sentences
be so constituted and arranged, that each part may be un
derstood as the sentence proceeds, not leaving the meaning
of the different parts as well as of the whole sentence to be
gathered at its close.*

Most of the faults in the composition of complex sentences, are connected with those clauses, which express some
circumstances of the actions or objects mentioned. Some
of these clauses are less intimately connected with the main
thought expressed in the sentence than others, and the writer should always avoid crowding into one sentence more
clauses expressing circumstances, than are absolutely necessary. But writers, sometimes, instead of observing this
rule, bring into the same sentence circumstances, which
are but very remotely connected with the leading thought
of the sentence. One of our daily papers, in an account of
a man frozen to death, says: "His head was supported by
a bundle of clothing, but all efforts to revive the vital spark

were fruitless." Now it may be asked, what connexion the circumstance, that the man's " head was supported by a bundle of clothing," has with the want of success in attempts to restore him to life.

But since there is difficulty in the right position of clauses, some directions will now be given, which may aid in their arrangement.

EXAMPLE 7.—" The moon was casting a pale light on the nume rous graves that were scattered before me, as it peered above the ho rizon, when I opene' the small gate of the church yard."

" When I opened the small gate of the church yard, the moor, as it peered above the horizon, was casting a pale light on the nume rous graves that lay scattered before me."

Any one will allow, that the image brought before the mind in the second form of this sentence, is more distinct and vivid, than that presented in the first. Upon comparing the two forms of the sentence, it will be seen, that all that has been done, is to alter the position of clauses expressing the circumstances of the action. Instead of being introduced near the close of the sentence, they are placed at its commencement. From this and similar instances it is inferred that *clauses expressing circumstances, must be placed as near as practicable to the beginning of a sentence.* It is obvious that this direction will apply principally to those clauses expressing time or place, and not to those which are designed to affect the meaning of particular parts of the sentence.

EXAMPLE 8. — " There will therefore be two trials in this town at that time, which are punishable with death if a full court should attend."

" At that time, therefore, if a full court should attend, there will be two trials which are punishable by death."

The first form of this sentence conveys a meaning differ-cut from that intended to be conveyed by the writer. According to this statement, the criminals might earnestly wish that a full court should not attend. This wrong meaning is given, by connecting the clause "if a full court should attend" with the wrong part of the sentence. In the corrected form, the place of this clause is changed, and the meaning of the writer is clearly conveyed. Hence then the rule may be inferred, that *clauses expressing circumstances of the action, should be placed near that part of the sentence the meaning of which they are designed to affect.*

EXAMPLE 9.—"Are these designs, which any man who is born a Briton, in any circumstances or in any situation, ought to be ashamed or afraid to avow?"

"Are these designs, which any man, who is born a Briton, ought, in any circumstances or in any situation, to be ashamed to avow?"

This sentence consists of two members, the former ending at *Briton*, and the latter commencing with *ought*. The phrase " in any circumstances or in any situation," is in the first form thrown in between the two members, and may be connected with either. By changing its position, and connecting it with the latter member of the sentence, all ambiguity is removed. Hence we may infer the following rule: *A clause or phrase expressing a circumstance, ought never to be placed between two principal members of a sentence.*

Under the head of CONNECTIVES, are included those words, which are used to connect different sentences, or to connect different clauses and members of the same sentence. Much of the clearness and finish of style will depend upon the skilful use of this class of words. It is true, they are the articulations, or joints of a discourse: but in a well written production, they are like the joints in the human frame which show forth the skill of the Maker, and are essential to the perfection of the work.

A connective may be defined, *as that word in a sentence or clause, which being neither expressed nor implied, it could not be discovered, that what is said in the sentence, or clause, has any connexion with what precedes.* To show more ful the nature of a connective, the following examples are given

" It is difficult for the most wise and upright government to con ı ect the abuses of remote delegated power, productive of unmeasured wealth, and protected by the boldness and strength of the same ill-got riches. These abuses, full of their own wild native vigor, will grow and flourish under mere neglect."

The connexion between the latter sentence and the preceding, in this example, is denoted by the demonstrative pronoun " these," followed by the word " abuses," which expresses the subject of the former sentence. That the connexion is expressed in the pronoun, is evident from the fact, that if the pronoun be omitted, what remains of the sentence expresses a distinct proposition without any connexion with what precedes. In some instances, the noun is not repeated after the demonstrative pronoun, and in others, some synonymous word, or some word which brings to view the object of the preceding sentence, is joined to the pronoun Sometimes also the definite article, or possessive pronoun. is used for the demonstrative pronoun. But in all instances of this nature, the connexion is in the pronoun itself.

" A true aristocracy is not a separate interest m the state, or sep arable from it. It is an essential integrant pai of any large body rightly constituted."

Here the personal pronoun *it* is the connective. Examples of this kind are frequent, and need no comment.

" The air, the earth and the water, teem with delighted existence In a Spring noon or a Summer's evening, on whichever side we turn our eyes, myriads of happy beings crowd upon our view."

This latter sentence, in this example, is intended to be il
lustrative of the former, and though no connective is ex
pressed, there is one easily supplied.   Instances of this kind
are also frequent.

"Let not the passions blight the intellect in the Spring of its ad
vancement, nor indolence nor vice canker the promise of the heart
in the blossom.   Then shall the Summer of life be adorned with moral
beauty."

In this instance, the connecting word is *then*, which is a
particle usually called an adverb, though by some gramma-
rians considered as a conjunction when used, as in this instance, to connect sentences.   But by whatever name it
may be called, it is evidently one of those words, which, in the
improvement of language, are inserted to save circumlocu-
ion, and is here equivalent to the phrase, *Let this be done.*
Instances in which adverbs are used as connectives, may be
resolved in this way into a phrase containing a demonstrative pronoun.

"I certainly have very good wishes for the place of my birth
But the sphere of my duties is my true country."

The connective in this example is the particle *but*, which
is a conjunction.   Should this be resolved, as in the last example, into what it is designed to express, it would be found
equivalent to some phrase like the following; *To this su-
peradd.*   Of this mode of resolving conjunctions, I shall
presently speak, and endeavor to shew, that where the conjunction is used as a connective, a pronoun is implied.

The examples which have been given, are instances shewing the manner of connecting different sentences.   The
same means, together with relative pronouns, are used for
connecting the different members and clauses of the same
sentence.   Of this common use of the relative pronoun no

example is needed. From this short view of the nature of connectives, I now proceed to give some cautions to guard against their wrong use.

1. Of demonstrative and other pronouns except the relative.

It has been already remarked, that when pronouns of this class are used as connectives, it is generally the case, that either the noun which expresses the subject of the preceding sentence, is repeated, or some synonymous word is used. When this is done, there can be little danger of mistake. The only caution needed, is the general one, that whenever adjective pronouns are used as connectives, and the noun to which they belong is left to be supplied by the reader, care should be had, that this noun be obvious. To effect this, the word to be supplied should be, 1. A word which the mind is accustomed to supply in similar cases. 2. The leading word of the discourse. 3. A word that has just been mentioned, and is thus fully in the view of the reader. An example of each kind is subjoined.

"The citizens of a free government must be enlightened and virtuous. To effect this, schools and the institutions for religious instruction must be supported."

Here the mind readily supplies the word *object*, referring to what is mentioned in the preceding sentence.

"This was not the triumph of France."

The subject of the discourse, from which this sentence is taken, is the removal of Louis XVI. from Versailles to Paris. The mind, in reading the passage, readily supplies a word or phrase expressing this subject.

"He received the papers from the Secretary. These he is now unwilling to return."

13 *

In this example the word *papers*, having been recently mentioned, is easily supplied after the pronoun.

Excepting in cases similar to those now mentioned, there is danger of obscurity in omitting the noun, which is designed to be connected with the pronoun.

2. Of the relative pronoun. Under this head are included relative pronouns, properly so called, and other pronouns used as relatives. The danger of obscurity in the use of this class of pronouns as connectives, arises from uncertainty as to the antecedent. To prevent this in the construction of sentences, some cautions will now be given.

"It is folly to pretend to arm ourselves against the accidents of life by heaping up treasures, which nothing can protect us against, but the good providence of God."

"It is folly to pretend, by heaping up treasures, to arm ourselves against the accidents of life which nothing can protect us against, but the good providence of God."

In the first form of this example, the mind is led to refer the relative *which* to the word *treasures*, immediately preceding it. Upon examining the sentence, we perceive that the relative is designed to refer to *accidents*, and that we have been led astray by the intervention of a clause between the antecedent and relative. The position of this clause is different in the corrected form of the sentence, and the true sense is then evident. Hence we infer the following rule *In arranging the members and clauses of a sentence, the relative should be placed as near as possible to its antecedent.*

"But I shall leave this subject to your management, and question not, but you will throw it into such light, as shall at once entertain and improve your readers."

In this sentence, the personal pronoun *it*, which is here a relative, is removed to some distance from the noun to

which it refers. It would be difficult to make any alteration in the sentence, which would place it nearer. Neither
is this necessary for the attainment of perspicuity, since
we are in no danger of mistaking the right antecedent.
Here then we are governed by a different principle from
that which has just been mentioned; and this principle is,
the rank which different words hold in a sentence. The
nominative and accusative, as the agent and object, are of
more importance in a sentence, than other nouns which are
dependent upon them. In the example given, the word *subject* is the accusative, and of higher rank in the sentence,
than the word *management*, which is connected with the
accusative by a preposition, and thus made dependent upon
it. Hence then we infer the following rule; *When the
sentence cannot be so modelled, that the relative may be
placed in close connexion with the antecedent, it should be
made to refer to the leading noun of the sentence.*

"The orator deserves no credit for those benefits, however important, which result from the subject and occasion, which are often
the true cause of that effect, which is generally supposed to be produced by the man himself."

"The orator deserves no credit for those benefits, however important, which result from the subject and occasion. These are often
the true cause of that effect, which is generally supposed to be produced by the man himself."

In the first form of this example, the relative is used three
different times, and in each instance with a different antecedent. This causes a want of perspicuity in the sentence.
The pronoun is a substitute for the noun, and the effect of
using the same relative with different antecedents in the
same sentence, is a violation of perspicuity, similar to that
which arises from the use of the same word in different
senses. The difficulty is removed in the second form of
the example by a division of the sentence. Hence then we

٭crive the direction, *Avoid using the same relative twice ท oftener in the same sentence with different antecedents.*

The preceding rules are designed to assist in so con structing the sentence, that no doubt may exist as to the right antecedent of the relative. But cases will occur, when it is impossible to prevent all ambiguity in the use of the relative pronoun. In such cases the noun itself may be repeated, or a division be made of the sentence, or in some other way the use of the pronoun may be avoided. Scme-times ambiguity in the use of the relative, may arise from a different source, as is seen in the following example.

" I know that all words which are signs of complex ideas, furnish matter of mistake and cavil."

" I know that all those words which are signs of complex ideas, furnish matter of mistake and cavil."

In the first form of this example, though the relative is rightly placed in reference to the antecedent, still the true meaning of the author is not conveyed. He did not mean to say " that all words are signs of complex ideas," which is expressed by the words used ; but his design is, to affirm something of those words which are signs of complex ideas. Here then is ambiguity arising from a cause which has not been mentioned. To state this cause, it is necessary to mention a distinction between clauses introduced by the relative as explicative of the meaning of the antecedent, and those introduced as determinative of its meaning. " Man who is born of a woman, is of few days and full of trouble." " The man that endureth to the end, snall be saved." In the former of these sentences, the clause introduced by the relative is explicative. It merely points out some property of the antecedent, but does not affec٭ ٭ts meaning as used in the given instance. It might be said of man that he is of few days and ful of trouble, though he were not born of a woman. In the other example, the relative introduces a determinative clause, which affects the meaning of the antecedent. It is not said that all men shall be saved, but only "he that endureth to the end;" and the clause introduced by the relative cannot be removed without changing entirely the meaning of the sentence. Now the clause introduced by the relative in the example at the head of this paragraph, is designed to be determinative in its effect on the antecedent. It has this force in the corrected form of the example, which is given to it by the insertion of the demonstrative pronoun *those* before *words*. The same effect would have been produced by the insertion of the definite article. Hence then we infer the rule, *That whenever a clause which is designed to be determinative in its effect on the antecedent, is introduced by the relative, the antecedent should be preceded by the demonstrative pronoun, or the definite article.*

3. Of conjunctions, and other particles.

Every one acquainted with grammar, knows that adverbs are not essential parts of language, but that they might be dismissed, and the same meaning expressed by circumlocutions. It has been shewn by a late eminent philologist, that conjunctions are of the same nature. They are obsolete forms of verbs, and in the use of them an ellipsis is implied, in supplying which, where they serve the purpose of connectives, a pronoun is used. This is shewn in the following example; "Faith cannot be perfect unless there be good works." Here, *unless* is to be considered as the imperative of the obsolete verb *onlessan*, the signification of which is *to dismiss*. In supplying the implied ellipsis, the sentence will read; "Faith cannot be perfect *to this dismiss* there be good works." In this then, as in the preceding examples, the real connective is a pronoun

In agreement with this account of conjunctions, it is found, that besides implying connexion, they express the manner of connexion, or the relation of one clause or member to another, or of one sentence to another. In doing this, they retain their original meaning, and hence the different classes into which they are divided; as the copulative, disjunctive, causal, illative, etc.; all of which names are intended to shew the nature of the relation expressed by the conjunctions included under them.

Skill, in the use of conjunctions, both as connectives and as shewing the relation between parts connected, is to be acquired from practice in writing, and from familiarity with good writers. It is also most frequently found united with clearness of thought, and accurate habits of reasoning. Hence no directions are here given to guide the writer in their use, but simply a few remarks offered, the reason and propriety of which, sound sense and good taste must perceive.

1. Long conjunctions are to be avoided. Such are the words, *nevertheless*, *notwithstanding*, *furthermore*, *forasmuch*.

The improvement of our language has caused most of these conjunctions to give place to others, which are shorter; and as such words are but secondary parts of sentences, it is desirable that they should not occupy more room, and become more conspicuous, than is absolutely necessary.

2. The frequent recurrence of the same conjunction is to be avoided; especially if that conjunction consists of more than one syllable. The reason of this direction, as of the preceding, is to prevent conjunctions from appearing too prominent.

3. The accumulating of several conjunctions in the same

clause is to be avoided, unless their coalition be absolutely necessary. To aid in forming a judgment of what propriety and the idiom of the language allow in such cases, the following remarks are made:

Two conjunctions may follow each other, when one of them serves to connect the sentence with what precedes, and the other to connect one clause in the sentence with another clause. "I go to prepare a place for you. And if I go and prepare a place for you, I will come again and receive you to myself." *And* is the connective of the sentences, and *if* of the clauses.

Conjunctions of the same class may be united, but such coalitions are often unnecessary, and should be avoided. Examples of this kind are *but however, and further, yet nevertheless,* etc. In each of these instances, one of the conjunctions used is unnecessary.

Conjunctions of different classes are often found united, and sometimes necessarily, but at others, when more care in the construction of the sentence would have rendered their union unnecessary. Of the propriety of such coalitions, a knowledge of the usage of the best writers, and of the original meaning of the conjunction, will enable us to judge.

Conjunctions may often be left to be supplied by the reader.

To use a conjunction wherever the sense would allow of one, would render a style heavy, and conduce but little to its perspicuity. Here, as in the former instance, the usage of good writers must decide. On the one hand, we are to guard against the omission of connectives to that degree which might render the style defective and obscure. On the other, we are to avoid the too frequent use of them, which would render our manner of writing awkward and defective.

To these remarks on connectives, it may be added, that the abbreviations i. e., e. g., and viz., are in dignified composition to be avoided.

CHAPTER FIFTH

ON STYLE

STYLE is defined by Dr. Blair, to be "the peculiar manner in which a writer expresses his thoughts by words. It
is a picture of the ideas in the mind, and of the order in
which they exist there." Buffon has more boldly and nap-
pily said, "Style is the man himself." Let two individuals
write on the same subject. We see in their productions
their peculiar modes of thinking — the extent of their knowledge — their tastes and their feeling. The portrait executed
by the most skilful painter, does not more fully represent
the countenance, than the productions of the pen exhibit the
characteristics of the mind.

Consistently with this account of what is meant by style,
the attention has been directed to thought as the foundation
of good writing — to the nature and objects of literary taste,
and to skill in the use of language. From what has been
said on these different heads, it may easily be inferred, that
there are some qualities of style, which are common to all
good writers. But since style depends on the intellectual
habits and acquirements — on literary taste, and on skill in
the use of language, each of which is possessed by different
individuals in different degrees, it must be obvious, that the

14

modes of writing peculiar to different authors, will differ according to their characteristic traits. Other diversities in style, arising from the subject and occasion, and characteristic of different classes of writing, will also be found. I purpose, therefore, in this chapter, to consider in three different sections, 1. The qualities of style common in some degree to all good writers; 2. The different modes of writing which characterize different individuals; 3. The kinds of style suited to some of the more common classes of writing. To this will be added some general directions for improvement in style.   .

.Section 1.   *On the qualities of a good style.*

Correctness, as a quality of style, implies the use of words that are purely English in their true and proper sense, and the construction of phrases and sentences according to the rules of Grammar. Thus it is opposed to the Barbarism, or the use of foreign words; the Impropriety, or the use of words in a wrong sense; and the Solecism, or grammatical blunder. Enough has been said in the section on Verbal Criticism, to guard the writer against the two former faults; to prevent the latter, is the appropriate object of Syntax, and does not come within the limits of Rhetoric.

Attention to this quality of style should be urged upon all those who would become good writers. It is equally necessary in all kinds of writing, and though it is not regarded as a high excellence, the absence of it is ever thought disgraceful. Incorrectness in the use of words and in the construction of sentences, like inaccuracies of pronunciation, is considered as evidence of careless intellectual habits and an unfinished education. There is also something of the nature of incivility, when a writer asks us for our attention, and addresses us in language we cannot understand. Hence it is, that the faults which are opposed to correctness are pardoned with least willingness, and furnish occasions to critics for raillery at the expense of guilty writers.

The different feelings with which we regard an instance of incorrectness in conversation and in writing, are worth our attention. If, in the ardor of conversation, a word is improperly used, or a sentence wrongly constructed, we are ready to ascribe the incorrectness to the impetuosity and hurry of the thoughts, or to the rapidity of the expression, and we overlook it. Not so in writing. Here is time for reflection, for the due arrangement of the thoughts, and the right modelling of the expression; and though one or two instances of incorrectness may be forgiven, yet if they are of frequent occurrence, their effect on our opinion of the writer is unfavorable.

It is unnecessary to repeat here what was said at the close of the section on Verbal Criticism, on the importance of familiarity with authors of reputation, that we may attain propriety in the use of words. But it is not amiss to urge the necessity of a critical knowledge of the rules and principles of syntax.

These rules, it is true, like those which relate to the choice of words, derive their authority from good usage, and the principles which they enjoin may be learnt from the study of good models in writing; still they are valuable, since they direct the attention to those cases where there is most danger of error, and give us the results to which those have been led who have carefully studied the subject. Let then an intimate knowledge of the principles and rules of syntax be considered essential toward forming a good style.

Perspicuity is the next quality of a good style to be considered. It implies that the expressions used are such as to convey, and clearly to convey, the true meaning of the writer

Thus defined, it is opposed to ambiguity and obscurities of every kind, from whatever source they may arise.

In every system of Rhetoric, Perspicuity is dwelt upon as an essential quality of a good style. The argument, by which its observance is enforced, is simple and unanswerable. We write to communicate to others our thoughts; and, if we do not make ourselves understood, we fail of our object in writing. Neither is it enough that, by study, a meaning may be made out of the expressions that we use. The meaning of a passage should be so obvious, as not only to prevent mistake, but to become evident at the first glance — so evident, that we cannot help discerning it. On this point Quinctilian has happily said, "Oratio in animum audientis, sicut sol in oculos, etiamsi in eum non intendatur, occurrat." * Perspicuity is a word of similar import to transparency, which is applied to air, to glass, and to water, or to any substance, through which, as a medium, we are wont to look at objects. Now it is well known that, if there be any defect in the medium through which we look, so that we do but imperfectly discern the object of our survey, we are liable to be deceived in our estimate of it; our attention is also taken off from the object itself, and we are led to notice the want of perfect transparency — to account for it, and to judge of its effect on our view of the object before us. But, on the other hand, if the medium be perfectly transparent, our undivided attention is directed to the object itself; and, while we see it distinctly, and judge of it correctly, we think not of the medium through which it is viewed. This illustration admits of close application to style.

But the question may be asked; Do not instances sometimes occur, in which a degree of obscurity is desirable

---

* The meaning of a discourse should strike the mind, as the light of the sun does the eyes, though they are not intently fixed upon it.

Are there not some delicate turns or bold forms of expres
sion, which lose nothing of their pertinency from the degree
of obscurity which characterizes them? and may not a regard for delicacy, or even decency, sometimes prevent the
distinct enunciation of a thought? To these inquiries, it
must be answered in the affirmative. Still such instances
are but of rare occurrence, and upon examination of them,
it will generally be seen, that the thought intended to be
conveyed, is rather left to be inferred from what is said,
than obscurely expressed in the words themselves. The
expression itself perspicuously conveys what it was designed
to convey.

The following instance of a delicate turn of expression
happily illustrates this remark. Fontenelle in his address
to Dubois, who was guardian to Louis XV, in his mi-
nority, says to him, "You will freely communicate to our
young monarch that knowledge, which will fit him one day
to govern for himself. You will strive with all your efforts
to make yourself useless." This last phrase may be consid
ered obscure. Fontenelle designed to say, "You will labor to impart so much knowledge to your ward, that your
services will no longer be needed by him." But this is
rather an inference from what is said, than what is conveyed
in the words themselves. There is no obscurity as to the
meaning of the expression itself. It is a singular fact, that
a critic, in remarking on this passage, asserted, that no doubt
Fontenelle said, or designed to say, *useful* instead of *useless*,
and that the present reading is probably a typographical error. From such critics may we be delivered!

But another inquiry on this subject has arisen, May not a
writer be too perspicuous, and not leave enough to exercise
the ingenuity and reflection of his readers? This question
has arisen from ascribing the weariness and disgust, which
are felt in reading some productions, to a wrong cause

Some writers are minute to a fault. They mention every little circumstance in a narrative — state with formality common and trivial thoughts — supply every step of an ar gument, and dwell upon what the ingenuity of their readers could better have supplied; and such writers are always te dious. But our ennui and disgust in reading their works, do not arise from the perspicuity of their expressions, but from their saying what had better been omitted. The fault is not so much in the manner of saying, as in what they say. Often also is it the case, that these prolix and minute writers add to their other faults that of obscurity, and leave us to labor and search after that, which when attained does not reward our exertions. When then a writer is complained of as too perspicuous, we may safely ascribe the fault to futility of thought, and not to excessive clearness of expression. We never complain that glass is too transparent, and no more can style be too perspicuous.

So far as perspicuity, thus explained, depends on the selection of words and the construction of sentences, the rules and principles found in the preceding chapter, are designed to aid in its attainment. An additional direction of some practical importance may here be given; that in the selection of words and forms of expression, the writer adapt himself to those, for whom his production is primarily de signed. A story, or tract, intended for children, or for il literate persons, should be expressed in the most common and familiar language. On the other hand, in those works which are strictly of a literary and scientific class, and which are addressed to scholars, words and expressions of less frequent occurrence and less obvious import, may oe introduced. Often, however, a production is designed for a promiscuous assembly, and here much skill may be exhib ited in its adaptation. The point to be aimed at, both in the reasonings and language, is, that while there is nothing tedious or disgusting to any, the production may be level to the comprehension of all. It may be well, in writings of this class particularly, to select words of Saxon origin, ir. preference to those of foreign derivation, even though the latter should be in more common use among educated men. A different practice in this respect accounts for the fact, that some public teachers are much better unders ood by men of common education than others. Indeed a difference of this nature is observed in the writings of the same individual, comparing his early productions with those written at a later period in life, when, by intercourse with the world, he has become more familiar with the language and modes of thinking of those around him. Some quaint, but judicious remarks on the selection of words, are found in the extract from the Rhetoric of Thomas Wilson in the history of English style at the close of this work, to which the student is referred.

It is obvious to all, that distinctness and order in the thoughts, are essential to perspicuity. Let a writer's view of the subject be indistinct — let him but imperfectly understand what he would communicate to others, or let his thoughts be without method, and there will necessarily be indistinctness and confusion in his productions. This confusion of thought will betray itself in long, involved sentences, made up of loose and redundant expressions, the meaning of which it is difficult to divine. It sometimes seems as if the writer, aware of the indistinctness of his thoughts, would conceal it by the use of many words, thus hoping to throw the blame of obscurity, either on his subject, or on the discerning powers of his readers. Against violations of perspicuity arising from this source, the observance of what was enjoined in the first chapter of this work, will be a sufficient security. Let habits of patient, persevering and connected thinking be acquired, and it will seldom be the case that a want of perspicuity will arise from confusion of thought.

It was stated, when treating of the illustrations and ornaments of style, that when heterogeneous objects are brought together, a confused and disproportionate image will rise to the view of the mind. Here is another source of obscurity Such attempts at illustration and ornament are called an affectation of excellence, and tend to darken and deform those objects, around which they are designed to throw light and beauty. It is unnecessary here to give examples of faults of this kind, or to repeat what was before said. The remedy for such violations of perspicuity is improvement of the taste.

Before leaving the subject of perspicuity, the student should be reminded, that writers become obscure, not only from indistinctness and confusion in their conceptions, but from the reverse — from familiarity with their subject. They forget that what, from having long been the object of their contemplation, is known to them in all its relations and in all parts, is often to their readers new and strange, and hence they omit those parts of a statement, which are essential to its being fully understood. From this cause also, writers are often led to construct long and involved sentences, the full meaning of any part of which cannot be known till the reader has reached its close. (See page 143.) To prevent obscurity from this source, a revision, when the ardor of composition has passed away, will be advantageous

A good style, in addition to Correctness and Perspicuity, will be characterized by VIVACITY. This quality of style implies, that the thoughts are exhibited with distinctness before the mind of the reader, and in a manner which arrests and fixes his attention. It gives evidence that the writer is interested in the subject on which he treats, and springs from a desire to awaken the same interest in the minds of his readers. Viewed in this light, it is an effort on the part of the writer to supply, in a written discourse, what is effected, in conversation, by the tones of the voice and the expression of the countenance. As it is a quality of high excellence, and conduces much to the success of the writer, the different circumstances which are favorable to its attainment, will be distinctly considered.

Vivacity is promoted by the happy choice of words. Under this head I mention,

1. The use of specific and appropriate terms, in preference to those which are more general and extensive in their meaning, and of well-chosen epithets.

The following passage, found in one of the Waverley Novels, affords opportunity for illustrating and establishing what is here stated.

" The moon, which was now high, and twinkled with all the vivacity of a frosty atmosphere, silvered the windings of the river, and the peaks and precipices which the mist left visible — while her beams seemed, as it were, absorbed by the fleecy whiteness of the mist, where it lay thick and condensed, and gave to the more light and vapory specks, which were elsewhere visible, a sort of filmy transparency resembling the lightest veil of silvery gauze."

An inferior writer, describing the same scene, might have said, —

" The moon, which was now high, and shone with all the brightness of a frosty atmosphere, lighted the windings of the river, and the tops and steep sides of the mountains which the mist left visible — while her beams seemed, as it were, absorbed by the whiteness of the mist, where it lay thick and condensed, and gave to the more light and vapory little collections of mist, which were elsewhere visible, a sort of transparency resembling a veil of gauze."

In directing the attention to the diversities in the two forms of the preceding sentence, the use of the word *twinkled* for *shone* first occurs. Every one will allow, that the word *twinkled*, as here used, is more expressive than the word *shone:* since it not only conveys what is conveyed by the word *shone*, but something more. It informs us of the manner in which the moon gave forth her rays. The next instance is the use of the word *vivacity* for *brightness*. The reason of our preference of the former, is the same as in the preceding case, though not so obvious; the word *vivacity* conveys to us more than the word *brightness*. There is a cheerfulness and animation in a wintry scene, lighted up by the rays of moonlight, which is well expressed by the word *vivacity*, but not brought to view in speaking of its *brightness*. In the same way, *silvered* instead of *lighted*, informs us of the manner in which the rays were reflected from the river. *Peaks and precipices* mean the same as the *tops and steep sides of the mountains*, but they are preferred as terms appropriated to these objects. *Specks* also has the same meaning, since the connexion determines that specks of clouds are referred to, as the phrase *little collections of vapors*, but it is preferred, not only as shorter, but as exhibiting more distinctly the appearance of the clouds. It will be still further noticed, that in the second form of the passage, the epithets *fleecy*, applied to the whiteness of the mist, — *filmy*, applied to transparency, — and *silvery*, applied to gauze, are omitted. The effect of this omission, in each case, is to take away something, which, when expressed, adds much to the distinctness of the view.

From the preceding examination of the different forms of the passage used for illustration, the following inferences may be made.

1. That specific terms and phrases are to be preferred to those more general in their signification. By a specific word or phrase, is meant a word or phrase used in comparatively a definite and limited sense. This distinction be-

tween specific and generic terms, as fully explained in books
on Logic. It is also there stated, that a specific term conveys a more full and distinct meaning to the mind than that
conveyed by a generic term; and hence the use of such
terms conduces to vivacity of expression. Of the instances
mentioned, *shone* is the generic term, and *twinkled* the specific. *Vivacity*, as expressing the appearance of a scene, is
a specific term in relation to *brightness*. *Silvered* is specific
in relation to *lighted*.

2. That when words have been appropriated to particular
objects, as their signs, it is better to use such words, than
to convey the same meaning in more general terms. It gives
a more definite view to the mind to speak of *peaks and precipices*, than of the *tops and steep sides of mountains*, and of
specks than of *little collections of mist*.

3. That the use of well-chosen epithets contributes much
to vivacity of style. So much depends on the successful
use of this class of words, that I shall bring forward several
examples, illustrating the different ways, in which they produce the effect here ascribed to them.

Epithets increase the distinctness of the view:

1. By directing the attention to some striking and char
acteristic quality of the object, with which they are con
nected.

> EXAMPLE: "The wheeling plover ceased
> Her plaint."

In this example, the epithet *wheeling* directs our atten
tion to that kind of motion, which is characteristic of the
species of bird mentioned. By thus bringing before our
minds the characteristic property of an object the distinctness of our conception of that object is aided

2. By directing the attention to those qualities of objects which are most obvious in the view taken of them.

EXAMPLE: "Happiness is found in the arm-chair of dozing age, as well as either in the sprightliness of the dance, or the animation of the chase."

In this example the epithet *dozing* brings before the mind that characteristic of age, which the writer designed should be prominent, when speaking of the happiness found at this period of life. In this way, it increases the distinctness of the reader's view, and leads him more fully to feel the force of what is asserted.

3. By leading the mind to trace out illustrative com· parisons.

EXAMPLE: "I have felt the bitter satire of his pen."

The epithet *bitter* is literally applied to that which is an object of the sense of taste. By its application to an object of a different kind, the mind is led to trace out an illustrative comparison. Consequently, in this way the distinctness of the reader's conception of the object, to which the epithet is applied, is increased.

4. By affording a more full description of an object.

EXAMPLE: "The rays of the setting sun were just gilding the gray spire of the church."

The epithet *gray*, in this example, might have been omitted, or a different word, as *dark-blue*, might have been substituted for it, and the proposition would have been true. Still the effect of its use is favorable, since the mind has more definiteness in its view of the object, on which it fixes its attention. Every spire must have some color, and mention of this color, whatever it may be, aids the mind in the

distinct conception of the object to which it belongs. It is
in this way then, that an epithet, by a more full description,
aids the distinctness of the view.

To these illustrations of the nature and power of epithets,
I would subjoin the remark, that compound epithets are
sometimes introduced with favorable effects. The following are instances of this kind; " — silver-tongued hope,'
— " much-abused man." The caution, that they be not too
frequently introduced, may not be amiss.

Under the head of a happy choice of words as conducive
to vivacity, I mention,

1. The use of language in a figurative manner. While
giving examples in illustration of this position, I shall direct the attention to' what are called tropes or figures of
language.

" An ambition to have a place in the registers of fame, is the Eurys
theus, which imposes heroic labors on mankind."

In this example, Eurystheus, the name of an individual,
is put for a class of men. The same idea would have been
expressed, had the word *taskmaster* been used. But by in
troducing the word *Eurystheus*, besides the pleasure derived
from the classical allusion, a more distinct idea of what is
imposed by ambition on its slaves, is given to the mind. This
is an instance, where an individual is put for the species, and
is a form of the synecdoche.

" When we go out into the fields in the evening of the year, a different voice approaches us."

The word *evening*, which is properly applied only to the
close of the day, is here used in a more extended signification Instead of being a specific, it becomes a general
term In the same manner, we speak of the evening of life

In this example, besides the increased distinctness of view
there are pleasing images and associations connected with
the close of the day, which are brought before the mind.
This example may be classed under either the metaphor or
synecdoche.

In the two examples now given, we have instances, where
greater distinctness is given to the view, by using a word in
a more general sense than that usually applied to it.

> "O! 'Tis a thought sublime, that man can force
> A path upon the waste."

In this passage, the word *waste* is used for *ocean*, a quality
for a subject to which it belongs. This is called synecdoche.
From the connexion are seen at once the design and effect
of the change. What is it that makes it difficult for man to
force a path upon the ocean? Is it not because it is a vast
desert — a wide spread waste, where all is trackless? How
much then does it add to the vividness of our conception of
what the author here says, that he fixes our attention on that
quality, which he designs should be immediately in view, and
on which his assertion is founded!

> "We wish that labor may look up here, and be p oud in the midst
> of its toil."

In this example, the abstract is used for the concrete —
labor for the laborer. This is called synecdoche, and its
tendency is to increase the distinctness of our view. In
reading the word *laborer*, there are many circumstances
which rise to the view of the mind. We think of the man,
his station in life, and the relations he sustains; but in the
use of the abstract term, our attention is directed to the
humble and wearisome occupation.

> " All hands engaged, the royal work grows warm

The word *hands* in this example is used to signify men.
.t may be considered either as a synecdoche, when a part
is put for the whole, or metonymy, when the instrument is
put for the agent. In either case, it directs the attention
to what the writer designed should be a prominent circumstance.

Many other examples might be given, in which the attention is in different ways directed to the most prominent circumstance. One caution is necessary in all attempts of
this kind — that the whole form of the expression be suited
to the design of the writer. If it had been said, that the
waste dashes and foams, that we wish labor may regain its
health, and that all hands walked out, the expression would
at once strike us as faulty.

"The last fond look of the glazing eye, turning to us even from
he threshold of existence."

In this example, the word *threshold*, which is usually applied to the extreme part of the passage to a building, is applied to the close of life. As the ground of this different application of the term is resemblance, the figure will at once
be recognized as the metaphor. It is an instance, where
that which is an object of thought is represented to the
mind by that which is an object of sense. This, as was remarked when treating of the metaphor, aids the distinctness
of the view, and what was there said needs not be repeated.

"It is curious to get at the history of a monarch's heart, and to
find the simple affections of human nature throbbing under the ermine."

The word *ermine* is here used for majesty, or royal estate.
The ermine is the dress of royalty — it is the symbol which
indicates its presence. Here then the sign is put for the

thing signified.   This is an instance of the metonymy.   We
notice also, that it is of the same nature as the preceding
example — that which is an object of thought is represented by that which is an object of sense.   The same favorable
effect on the distinctness of our conception, is also exerted.

2. Vivacity is often attained by a departure from the
common arrangement of the words in a sentence.

Every language has some manner of arranging the words
of a sentence, which, from the frequency of its occurrence,
may be called its common mode of arrangement.   Especially
is this true of the English language, in which the grammatical construction is often made to depend on the juxtaposi-
tion of words.   That vivacity of expression is caused by departing from this common arrangement, is learnt from the
following examples.

Peter, observing the grammatical order, would have said
to the lame man who asked alms, "I have no silver nor
gold to give thee."   But how much more vivacity is there in
the expression, "Silver and gold have I none."   In the
same manner, our Saviour, following the common order,
would have said, "The pure in heart are blessed."   But
oy departing from this order, he has conveyed the same
thought with increased force and vivacity — "Blessed are
the pure in heart."

In these and other expressions of the same kind, it is not
difficult to account for the effect of the change in the order
of the words on the vivacity of the expression.   What is
most prominent in the mind, is thus made to occupy the
first place in what calls forth the attention.   The imploring
look of the beggar had asked for silver and gold, and Peter
in his answer discovers, that he fully knew the meaning of
that look, and lets the attention first rest on that, which is
first in the mind's view.   In the same manner, it is to the
blessedness of the pure in heart, that the Saviour would di

ect the attention, and this is effected by the arrangement of the words in his declaration.

The alteration of the arrangement of the words for the attainment of vivacity of expression, is not confined to words of primary importance in a sentence. It is extended to adverbs and conjunctions, and the whole class of secondary words. On the same principle also, in the arrangement of the clauses and members of complex sentences, that clause or member, which is most prominent in the view of the mind, is made to hold a conspicuous place.

3. Vivacity is promoted by the omission of unnecessary words and phrases.

This is what is called precision, and is opposed both to Tautology, or the repetition of the same sense in different words, and to Pleonasm, or the use of superfluous words. The nature of precision may be learnt from the following examples:

"It is clear and obvious, that religious worship and adoration should be regarded with pleasure and satisfaction by all men."

"It is obvious that religious worship should be regarded with pleasure by all men."

"He sat on the verdant green, in the umbrageous shade of the woody forest."

"He sat on the green in the shade of the forest."

"He succeeded in gaining the universal love of all men."

"He succeeded in gaining the love of all men."

"They returned back again to the same city from whence they came forth."

"They returned to the city whence they came.

In the corrected form of these examples, those words are omitted, which are redundant, or add nothing to the meaning of the sentence. That the effect of those alterations on the vivacity of the style is favorable, will be readily allowed. As a general rule it may be said, that the fewer the words used, provided perspicuity be not violated, the greater will be the vivacity of the sentence.

It may occur, that there are instances, where the repetition of words nearly synonymous in their meaning, adds force and strength to the expression. Of this many examples are to be found in tragedies, and wherever exhibitions of strong feelings are made. Such is the following passage:

> " Oh Austria!
> Thou slave, thou wretch — thou coward,
> . Thou little valiant, great in villany,
> Thou ever strong upon the strongest side."

This and similar expressions are the language of passion. The mind is full — the feelings too strong to find utterance, and we may truly say, that out of the abundance of the heart the mouth speaketh. These passionate expressions are of course free from the law, by which, in more sober compositions, we should be governed.

It is important here to remark, that in reviewing our writings for the purpose of striking out redundant words and phrases, we should remember that every expletive is not to be struck out. There are some, which, instead of impairing, increase the vivacity of an expression; and others, the meaning of which we can hardly define, that cannot be omitted without giving an air of stiffness and awkwardness to the sentence. Of the former, *do*, in the following declaration of Othello, is an example.

> " Perdition seize thee, but I *do* love thee "

Of the same nature are the redundant forms of speech which are found in ancient writers; — "I have seen with mine eyes." "I have heard with mine ears."

As examples, where the removal of an expletive endangers the smoothness of the style, the many sentences in which the expletive *there* is found, may be mentioned.

4. Vivacity is sometimes attained by the omission of conjunctions and the consequent division of the discourse into short sentences.

A single example will show what is intended by this re mark.

" As the storm increased with the night, the sea was lashed into tremendous confusion, and there was a fearful, sullen sound of rushing waves and broken surges, while deep called unto deep."

" The storm increased with the night. The sea was lashed into tremendous confusion. There was a fearful, sullen sound of rushing waves and broken surges. Deep called unto deep."

In the second form of this example, the conjunctions are omitted; and instead of one long sentence, as in the first form, we have several short sentences. The effect on the vivacity of the passage will be perceived by every one. The reason of the increased vivacity is also obvious. What is thus expressed in short sentences, stands out more prominent and distinct to the view. There is also more of conciseness, since all unnecessary words are omitted, especially those which are injurious to vivacity. But it is not here meant, that short sentences are to be preferred to long ones. The most important direction that can be given on this subject is, that there should be variety. Long sentences and short ones should be intermingled, since the continued repetition of either becomes tedious and wearisome. Besides, it is sometimes the case, that conjunctions cannot be omitted without danger to perspicuity, which, as a quality of a good style, ranks higher than vivacity. But when conjunctions may be better omitted than expressed, as in the example given, and when the division into short sentences is not con

tinued too far, such a division of a discourse is to be rec
ommended as conducive to vivacity.

5. Vivacity is sometimes attained by the use of certain
forms of sentences, which might in distinction be called figures of sentences. Of these I mention the Climax, Antithesis, Exclamation, Repetition and Interrogation. Some examples with accompanying remarks will be given.

The following instance of the Climax is from a writer
against infidelity.

"Impose upon me whatever hardships you please; give me nothing
but the bread of sorrow to eat; take from me the friend in whom I
had placed my confidence; lay me in the cold hut of poverty and on
the thorny bed of disease; set before me death in all its terrors; do
all this, only let me trust in my Saviour, and I will fear no evil — I
will rise superior to affliction — I will rejoice in my tribulation."

In this example, and other sentences of a similar construction, one clause is accumulated upon another, each surpassing in importance and power the preceding, till it seems
as if nothing could resist their united force. As an illustration, I would refer to a deep and full flowing river, opposed
to whose current some obstacle has been placed. The re-
sisted waters are heaped on each other, and each successive
wave bring an addition to their power, till the collected
mass can no longer be withstood — the obstacle is swept
away, and the river resumes its course with the rapidity and
momentum of a torrent.

There can be no doubt, that this form of sentence is
highly conducive to vivacity. It should, however, be but
rarely introduced, and never, except when it seems required
by the occasion and subject. It is evidence of an excited
mind, and should seem to result from this excitement. If
the subject does not require it — if the form of sentence does
not have its foundation in the thought itself, it will have the

air of something artificial, and instead of exerting an influence favorable to vivacity, it will have a different effect.

Of the Antithesis, I give the following example. The subject is the steam engine.

"It can engrave a seal, and crush masses of obdurate metal before it; draw out, without breaking, a thread as fine as gossamer, and lift up a ship of war like a bauble in the air. It can embroider muslin and forge anchors—cut steel into ribands, and impel loaded vessels against the fury of the winds and waves."

A second example, more finished in its composition, is from Beattie on poetry.

"In the crowded city and howling wilderness; in the cultivated province and solitary isle; in the flowery lawn and cragged mountain; in the murmur of the rivulet and in the uproar of the ocean; in the radiance of summer and gloom of winter; in the thunder of heaven and in the whisper of the breeze; he still finds something to rouse or soothe his imagination; to draw forth his affection and employ his understanding."

This form of sentence is founded on the principle of opposition or contrast. A figure in black is never more distinctly seen, than when placed upon a white ground-work. Campbell has very happily illustrated the effect of Antithesis, by an allusion to a picture, where the different objects of the group are not all on one side, with their faces turned the same way, but so placed that they are made to confront each other, by their opposite position. He says, that in such instances, there is not only the original light which is suited to each object, but that also which is reciprocally reflected from the opposed members. In the examples of the Antithesis that have been given, it will be noticed, that there is a balancing of the clauses. Not only is there opposition in the thought, but in the form and length of the clauses in which this opposition is expressed.

In connexion with this remark the caution against the appearance of an artificial construction, which was given in reference to the climax, may be repeated. Let the form of the sentence always arise from the thought itself, and not be the result of an attempt after vivacity. Of the two examples given, though the latter is more perfect and finished, the former is to be preferred as most natural and easy.

The Interrogation and Repetition are the language of an excited mind. Where the former is used, the writer seems so impressed with the truth of what he asserts, that he is not content to state it in the cold form of a proposition, but utters it in a manner, that challenges any one to regard it with doubt.

The Repetition also gives evidence of a full conviction of the truth of what is asserted, and of a deep sense of its importance, and is well calculated to convey these impressions to the reader in a striking manner. Both these forms of sentences are more frequently found in discourses intended for delivery, than in those designed to be read only, and when well pronounced, are often powerful in their effects on the hearers.

The Exclamation is to be regarded as the mere burst of feeling, and will rarely be found in the productions of good writers. Writers of inferior order sometimes attempt to give an air of animation and feeling to their style by the use of it; but such artificial means must fail of success, and by the man of good taste will be regarded with disgust.

6. Vivacity is promoted by the use of those forms of construction, which represent past actions and events as transpiring at the present time, and absent individuals as present, speaking and listening. This has been called Rhetorical dialogue, and is found most frequently in narra tive writing.

The following example, the latter form of which is that of

Rhetorical dialogue, both illustrates this remark, and furnishes evidence of its justness.

"Two hereditary enemies, among the Highlands, met face to face on a narrow pass. They turned deadly pale at the fatal rencontre Bendearg first addressed his enemy, and reminded him, that he was first at the top of the arch, and called on him to lie down that he might pass over. He was answered by an assurance from Cairn, that when the Grant prostrates himself before a Macpherson, it must be with a sword through his body. Bendearg then proposed to him to turn back, if he liked it.'

———— They turned deadly pale at the fatal rencontre. "I was first at the top," said Bendearg, "and called out first ; lie down that I may pass over in peace." "When the Grant prostrates himself before Macpherson," answered the other, "it must be with a sword through his body." "Turn back, then," said Bendearg, "and repass as you came." "Go back yourself, if you like it," replied Grant.

Though several circumstances have been thus mentioned as conducive to vivacity of style, it should be remembered, that the foundation of this quality of style is in the mind of the writer. What has now been said is designed only to point out some of the different ways in which the excited feelings manifest themselves. The best direction, then, which can be given for the attainment of vivacity of style, is to become interested in the discussion of the subject itself.

EUPHONY, or smoothness of sound, is the next quality of a good style to be considered. This is attained by the use of such words as in themselves, and in their succession in the sentence, are grateful to the ear. .

There can be no doubt that this quality of style is acquired more by imitation than by the observance of rules. Hence, any directions for its attainment are of little practical importance. Still it may be useful for the writer to remember, that the intermingling of long and short syllables, the frequent occurrence of open vowel sounds, and the avoid-

ing of those successions of consonants which are difficul
of utterance, are favorable to smoothness of style. He
should know also, that certain successions of syllables are
well suited to that cadence, or falling of the voice, which
marks the close of the sentence. And, as a general remark
it may be said, that what it is easy to read, is smooth in its
sound to the ear. But the best and most practical direction,
which can be given, is, to attune the ear by the frequent
reading aloud of those writings in which this quality of style
is found.

It should make no difference with respect to the attention
paid to the smoothness of style, that our writings are designed to be silently read, and not pronounced aloud. So
closely is the sound of words associated with their appearance to the eye, that, though no voice is uttered in reading
them, they are mentally pronounced, and the ear passes its
judgment on the smoothness of their sound.

The attention of writers is rarely directed to this quality
of style any further, than to the avoiding of faults. But it is
sometimes found to that extent, that it becomes a positive
excellence and a high recommendation. The following
sentence of Sterne has been pronounced one of the most
musical in our language :

" The accusing spirit, which flew up to heaven's chancery with
the oath, blushed as he gave it in, and the recording angel, as he
wrote it down, dropped a tear upon the word, and blotted it out forever."

Young writers, in their attempts after harmony of style,
sometimes fall into a measured manner of writing, which
may here be noticed. It is characterized by the occurrence
of successive sentences, and sometimes paragraphs, which
may be scanned, the regular return of the accented syllable
being in accordance with the rules of versification. Espe

cially is this the case in those passages, where the writer be-comes excited, and thoughts are conveyed, which are fitted to affect the feelings and call into exercise the imagination. This measured manner, since it violates one of the distinc-tive differences of prose and poetry, is a fault in prose wri-tings, as much so as the absence of it is a defect in poetry. And when, as is sometimes the case, it is united with ex-travagances of thought and bombastic forms of expression, it is to a high degree disgusting. In such instances there is a radical deficiency of literary taste. But sometimes pas-sages thus measured will be found in the writings of those, whose style is not otherwise to be censured; and here it will generally be a sufficient remedy to direct the attention to the fault.

The epithet *natural* is frequently applied to style. Our works on Rhetoric want a noun to express the quality here implied. *Simplicity* is sometimes used; but as this word is more frequently found in a different sense, I shall introduce the term *naturalness*.

Naturalness, as a quality of style, implies that a writer, in the choice of his words — in the form of his sentences — in the ornaments he uses, and in his turns of thought and ex-pression, commends himself to every man of good sense and good taste, as having pursued the course best suited to his subject and occasion. In this way it is opposed to affecta-tion of every kind. But the following illustrations will aid in more fully stating in what sense the word is used.

When we look on some of the beautiful remains of an-cient statuary, we pronounce them natural in their appear-ance By this expression we mean nothing more than that their appearance is such, as, in our opinion, it should be — such as is in consonance with our experience and observa-tion. There is no violent contortion of the features nor forced attitude with the design of producing effect, but the

image stands and appears as a man should do, in the circumstances and situation in which it is placed. In the same
manner, we say of a graceful dancer, who from long practice has learned to move gracefully and apparently without
effort or rule, that he moves naturally, and we mean the
same as in the former instance. Now, should we say of the
image, that there is much naturalness in its appearance,
and of the dancer, that there is much naturalness in his
movements, we should use the word in the same sense in
which it is here applied to style. The writer who has naturalness of style, expresses himself in that easy, unlabored
manner, which commends itself to our favor. He selects
and uses his words, and forms and connects his sentences,
just as we should suppose any man might do, who should
write on the same subject — just as we think perhaps we
could and should do, unless we attempt to imitate him. We
seem to hear him thinking aloud, and his thoughts flow forth
to us in the same order, and with the same clearness, with
which they sprung up in his own mind. He appears never
to stop for a moment, to consider in what way he shall express himself, but thinks only of what he shall say. Let but
one far-fetched expression, one forced comparison, or one
extravagant thought be found, and the charm is gone.

The inquiry may here be made, whether by naturalness
of style may not be meant that mode of writing, which is
suited to the intellectual habits and attainments of an author
— a style in which a writer shews himself, whatever his intellectual character may be. To this it may be answered,
that, if this were the correct use of the term, naturalness,
instead of denoting the highest excellences of style, would
often express its greatest deformities and faults.

The word is here used as referring to a common standard,
which is found in the mind of every man whose taste is not
perverted and vitiated. This may be clearly shewn by re-

ferring to the illustration before introduced. Every one while looking on the performance of a graceful dancer would say that his movements are easy and natural. Bu should one unacquainted with the rules and practice of the art attempt to dance, his movements might be natural to him, but no one would think of applying to them the word *natural*, in the same sense as in the former instance. In the same way, a manner of writing may be natural to a writer, when we should not think of ascribing to him the merit of naturalness of style.

This illustration may be still further continued, with the view of shewing in what way this quality may be obtained.

Were it asked in what way the awkward dancer may attain the easy and graceful movements of the other, it would be answered, by pursuing a similar course of instruction and practice. Some, either from the form of their bodies or their previous habits, would acquire these easy and natural movements more readily than others, and a few perhaps might need but little practice and little aid from the rules of the art. But these would be regarded as exceptions to what is more generally the case. In the same manner, to acquire naturalness of style, there is need of instruction and practice. A few, either from the original constitution of their minds, or their previous habits of thought and conversation, fall into it easily. Others, in their first attempts, are far from it, and it is with them the fruit of long practice in writing and a careful observance of rules. It may appear paradoxical, that what is called natural should be the result of art and labor. But this difficulty is removed, if we remember, that the object of this art and labor is to bring us back to nature Naturalness of style is not confined to any species of wriing. It is found alike in the most artless narrations, and in the most elevated descriptions — in the story that is open to the understanding of a child, and in the sublime raptures

of Milton. The best examples of it are among ancient wri
ters. This is the spell which binds us to the page of Ho
mer, of Sophocles and Theocritus, of Xenophon and He·
rodotus. And a reason may easily be assigned, why naturai·
ness of style should be found in these ancient writers
They lived, as it were, near to nature. With them all is
originality. Their thoughts and expressions are their own.
With most modern writers it is otherwise. It is ofter. re
marked, that in modern times there are few original ideas.
We tell in different words what has often been told before,
and, that we may avoid a coincidence of expression, we
leave the natural, and seek after the more labored forms of
speech. Hence it is, that less of naturalness of style is
found in modern writings.

The following are instances in which naturalness of style
is most frequently violated ;

1. When there is an evident attempt after ornament
What are called the ornaments of style should ever appear
to be naturally suggested, and to be most intimately con·
nected with the subject and occasion. They should offer
themselves for our use, and not be sought after.

2. When the writer seeks after elegances of expression,
or, as they are sometimes called, felicities of diction. Some,
with the design of being thought elegant writers, studiously
avoid old, genuine English words and idioms, introducing,
so far as practicable, those which have been derived from
other languages. Others have what may be called a sen-
timental manner of expressing themselves.

3. Some violations of naturalness' of style arise from at·
tempts to be forcible. Under this head are included extrav·
agances of expression, sweeping assertions and forced illus·
trations.

4. Writers still further affect a fulness and flow of expression. Because some men of powerful minds and strong

feelings, have expressed themselves in long, flowing, full sentences, many, the current of whose thoughts is neither strong nor deep, would have them flow forth in an equally full and irresistible stream.

SECTION 2   *On the modes of writing, which characterize the productions of different individuals.*

It is the design of this section to treat of the different modes of writing, which characterize the productions of different authors. These, it has been stated, arise from diversities in their intellectual habits, in their tastes, and in their skill in the use of language. They are denoted by different epithets, which are applied to style; and while the meaning of these epithets is explained, the attention should be directed by the instructor to such examples as furnish illustrations.

It is sometimes said of a style, that it is IDIOMATIC AND EASY. These epithets are generally found in connexion, and where the former is justly applied, the latter denotes a natural consequence. A style which is idiomatic, will appear to have been easily written, and will be easily understood; and this is all that is meant by ease as a quality of style. By an idiomatic style is meant a manner of writing, in which, in addition to purity in the use of words, the phrases, forms of sentences, and arrangement of the words and clauses, are such as belong to the English language. Every language, as has been already stated, has peculiarities of this kind by which it is characterized, and the style in which they abound, is said to be idiomatic.

Dr. Paley's style may be mentioned as idiomatic. The following sentence is from his writings; " A Bee amidst the flowers of spring is one of the most cheerful objects that can be looked upon." This expression is just what we should have used in conversation for conveying the same thought. A writer whose style is less idiomatic, would have said, "Of the different objects, which, amongst the flowers of spring, arrest the attention, the bee is the most cheerful that can be looked upon." This mode of stating the thought is more formal and stately, but less easy and idiomatic. In another place, when speaking of the fry of fish that frequent the margins of our rivers and lakes, he says, "They are so happy, that they do not know what to do with themselves." Every English reader fully knows, and, I may say, feels, what is here expressed. It is a form of every day's occurrence, and its introduction shows the style of the author to be idiomatic.

It is not meant, that expressions like the last, would be proper on all occasions and subjects. We vary the forms of expression in conversation. In conversing on grave subjects, we should not use the lively and familiar forms of expression, which are suited to an hour of gayety; and we should be equally far from imitating the stately and involved modes of expression, which characterize a foreign language. There are idiomatic expressions in English which are suited to the grave style, as well as those which are suited to the lively. In the writings of Dr. Paley, those of either kind are to be found, when required by his subject.

There is danger, lest a writer, in seeking to be idiomatic, become careless in his style. We often use expressions in conversation, which are incorrect in construction, and obscure in their meaning. But they are understood from the accompanying look, or some attending circumstance, and the incorrectness is forgiven, because of the hurry of the moment. But when the same expressions are found in a written discourse, they are justly censured. An idiomatic style is most strictly correct in construction and perspicuous in its meaning

It has been said, that an idiomatic style is the style of conversation. Still it must be confessed, that there is hardly any one, that has not more formality in his writings, than in his familiar, oral intercourse. The distinction may be illustrated by referring to reading aloud. A good reader will, on the one hand, be far removed from artificial, or, as they are called, "reading tones;" on the other, though his tones are natural, they will differ in some respects from the familiar tones of conversation. In the same manner, a style may be idiomatic, and rise in some degree above the most common forms of conversational intercourse.

An idiomatic style is always grateful to the reader. It requires no labor to understand a writer of this class. His forms of expression are those with which we are familiar — those which we use in the most artless, free communication of our thoughts, and we collect his meaning from a glance at the sentence.

An abuse of the idiomatic style, to which no particular epithet has as yet been applied, is sometimes found at the present day. It is in fact rather the want of style, than a well-characterized manner of writing. Like the conversation of a man who is hasty in his conclusions, and all whose thoughts and views are ill defined, this style is loose and rambling, utterly disregarding all smoothness and polish and often violating the most common principles both of Rhetoric and Grammar. There is a mixing together of low cant words and phrases, with foreign, abstruse and strangely compounded terms, and sometimes with lofty and imposing forms of expression. The figurative language especially, and all that is introduced with the design of illustration and ornament, wants consistency and uniformity. Odd conceits, vulgar illustrations, and undignified figurative ex-

pressions, are found in the same sentence with figures an.
anguage, striking and pertinent, and sometimes chaste and
beautiful. The same inequalities mark different passages
and parts of the composition. One paragraph is trite and
common-place both in thought and expression. The next
is original, bold, startling and impassioned.

An analysis of this mode of writing shews us that it is an
unsuccessful attempt to be idiomatic and striking. It is in
fact a species of literary coxcombry, and those who affect it
would pass themselves off as men of superior powers and
attainments. Their leading motto is, " Never think twice,"
and the first thoughts and expressions which they give us,
are such as might be expected. It is not necessary to state
the remedies, which should be applied to the faulty style
that has been described.

Opposed to the easy and idiomatic manner of writing,
which has now been described, is the labored style. This,
as the epithet imports, appears to have been written with
much pains on the part of the writer, and requires close attention and effort that it may be understood. The arrangement of the words and clauses is often inverted, and the
whole composition of the sentence is artificial. A labored
style, when carried to excess, will be highly faulty. It will
want perspicuity, smoothness, and naturalness. But it is
often the case that a style, which is in some degree labored,
has redeeming qualities, which recommend it, and give
some degree of reputation to a writer. The style of Dugald
Stewart may be mentioned as an instance of this kind. His
manner of writing is evidently labored; but there are qualities to be found in it which save it from censure.

For the correction of a labored style, and the attainment
of a more idiomatic and easy manner of writing, it is recommended; 1. To compose with greater rapidity. Ordinarily
that form of expression, which presents itself to the mind

with the thought to be communicated, will best convey this thought to others; especially is this the case, when a writer's views of his subject are clear and well defined. But the labored writer is not willing to use this obvious and easy form of expression. He must stop to select less common words, less simple and obvious phrases, to invert his clauses and new model his sentences. But a habit of writing with greater rapidity, will tend to correct this propensity and the consequent faults of style.

2. There are some kinds of composition, the frequent practice of which will aid in the attainment of ease of style Epistolary writing may particularly be mentioned. He who often communicates his thoughts to his friends in the easy, artless style of letter writing, will insensibly be led to use the same forms of expression on other occasions. The writing of a journal, or the noting down of our casual thoughts and feelings, or the sketching of short descriptions of scenes and occurrences presenting themselves to our notice, when done simply for our own amusement and benefit, without any intention of submitting what we write to the inspection of others, will be of service in the same way.

3. Aid will be obtained in the correction of a labored style from a familiarity with those writers, who are distinguished for their easy and idiomatic manner of writing. Goldsmith, Addison, Steele, Swift, and many of their contemporaries, are of this class.

The epithets CONCISE and DIFFUSE are often applied to style. It may be said generally, that these qualifying terms refer to the number of words used by a writer for conveying his thoughts; but these different kinds of style merit a more particular description.

A writer whose style is concise, expresses his thoughts in few words. There is a vividness and distinctness in his views, and he endeavors by a single and sudden effort to exhibit these views to others. His words are well chosen, and his turns of expression short and bold. No unnecessary expletive, no redundant phrase is found. Grammatical ellipses are common, and his sentences are usually short. The thought is presented in but one light, and much is left to be inferred. As to ornament, there is no room for it. Sometimes a short, plain comparison, or a bold metaphor is found. These, however, are always highly illustrative, and seem designed to save the necessity of a fuller statement.

A diffuse style is the opposite of the concise. The thought is expressed in comparatively many words. It is not meant by this, that a diffuse writer employs more words than are of use in conveying his thoughts. A writer may be diffuse, and be free from the charge of Tautology and Pleonasm. But he does not, as in the former case, leave any thing to be supplied. The statement is not only clear, but full. He dwells on the thought presented, exhibits it in different lights, and enforces it by repetition in different language, with many and varied illustrations. His words are poured forth in a full and uninterrupted stream, and his sentences, though long, are usually harmonious and flowing.

These different kinds of style are respectively suited to different subjects and occasions. The concise style is often used in short biographical notices, or what is sometimes called character painting — in the detail of facts, and in proverbs and sententious remarks. The diffuse, on the contrary, is used in the statement and discussion of novel opinions, especially on subjects that are uncommon. It is also well suited to discourses, which are designed to be delivered, and not to be read. Still it is often difficult to determine the degree of conciseness or diffuseness which is desirable. On the one hand, an excess of conciseness endangers the perspicuity of the style; on the other, an excess of diffuseness renders it heavy and tiresome. Whately recommends to combine the two — to state the thought first in a diffuse manner, expanding the sense so that it may be distinctly understood, and then to convey the same idea in a more compressed and sententious form. This expedient produces the effect of brevity, and at the same time, what is said is fully comprehended, or, as he has well expressed it, " the reader will understand the longer expression and remember the shorter." Passages in the writings of Burke and Johnson illustrate this remark.

The epithets BARREN and LUXURIANT are applied to style to denote defective modes of writing nearly allied to conciseness and diffuseness. The former epithet implies a nakedness and want of connexion in the thoughts and expressions. The trains of thought which are started, are but partially followed out, and the production has in this respect a half finished appearance. The expressions, too, want fulness and flow. Repetitions of the same words and phrases are frequent, and all that pertains to the use of words and the forms of expression, is common place.

What is thus described as barrenness of style, may owe its origin, either to a want of fertility of invention or to a deficiency of ideas or of words. Where there is a deficiency of ideas, when the subject is within the compass of the writer's powers, further research and reflection are needed. When barrenness of style arises from want of copiousness of expression, or command of language, it is a defect, which much reading of good English authors and persevering efforts after improvement will overcome. This defect is most frequently found in those whose acquaintance with literature has commenced late in life, and such especially need make persevering efforts to supply the deficiencies of their early education. In other instances, barrenness of style arises from a want of fertility of invention. The writer is unable to trace the relations between his thoughts, to make inferences and draw conclusions, to explain and exhibit. Barrenness of style, when arising from this source, will be remedied by increased maturity of the mind and improved discipline of its powers. It may be of service also to direct the attention to the modes of amplification used by those, who in this respect excel.

A *luxuriant* style, which is the opposite of that just described, is characterized by a redundancy of words and phrases, especially by a profusion of imagery and exuberance of figurative language. The writer, instead of selecting that which is choice and best fitted to the subject and occasion, seems to give us all his thoughts, and the different conceits, both as to form of expression and ornament, which have offered themselves to his mind. Sometimes, also, there is an attempt to write in a commanding and imposing manner, which manifests itself in many and extravagant epithets and figures, and an affected fulness and flow of expression

Luxuriance of style, in young writers, is ascribed to the glow and excitement of mind natural to the early period of life. It is looked upon as the overflowings of youthful feelings, and often pronounced to be ominous of good; for it is anticipated, that when more maturity of mind *shall have been obtained, and the ardor of youthful feeling cooled, what is exuberant and extravagant will give place to richness and force of expression.

Another cause, to which this mode of writing is sometimes ascribed, is the temperament of the individual writer He belongs to a class of men who are wont to be easily and strongly excited. Hence, whatever may be the subject or occasion on which he writes, he becomes at once impassioned in his style.

In other instances, and those in which perhaps a remedy may most easily be applied, luxuriance of style may be traced to some erroneous impressions as to wherein a good style consists. An undue importance is ascribed to figures and ornaments, and the writer prides himself on his command of language and the rapid and ready flow of his expressions. Having been struck with the fervency and imposing character of some admired passages in his favorite authors, he endeavors on all occasions and subjects to manifest an equal warmth and power of expression. Thus the rules and principles of good taste are violated, and the writer becomes extravagant and verbose.

To correct the faults of a luxuriant style, a strict and careful revision is enjoined. Not only should all unnecessary words and phrases be struck out, but in some instances it may be required to recast the whole sentence. Particular attention should also be given to whatever is of a figurative nature in the composition. Nothing of this kind should be introduced, which is not strictly chaste and fitted to the subject and occasion. It may further be recommended to the luxuriant writer, occasionally to select some familiar and common topic as the subject of his composition. In this way the impropriety of any uncommon elevation and luxuriance of style, will become obvious to the writer himself.

Forcible and vehement. We apply the epithet *forcible* to a style of writing, which, in a plain, distinct and irresistible manner, urges upon us the opinions and views of the writer. It is an evidence of excitement. The writer is interested in his subject, and is desirous that others may have the same feelings with himself. But it more especially implies a full persuasion of the truth and importance of what is said, and such an exhibition of the reasons of this persuasion, as cannot fail to produce conviction on the part of the reader. Hence it is dependent in a great degree on the intellectual habits, and implies a wel disciplined mind — a mind accustomed to comprehensive, methodical and strong views of subjects. It requires also skill in the use of lan-

guage, but derives little aid from what are called the orna
ments of style.

When to sound and convincing arguments, clearly and
forcibly exhibited, is added a highly excited state of feeling
vehemence of style is the result. It is from this deeper
current of feeling, implied by the latter term, that the shade
of difference between a forcible and vehement style arises.
This excitement of feeling may spring from the greater
importance of the subject, or from the more intense interest
felt in it by the writer. An able political writer, in a production on an electioneering question, might be forcible in
nis style. But let this same writer be called to treat on some
subject deeply affecting the welfare of his country, and he
becomes vehement.

The forcible and vehement styles are well suited to the
discussion of political subjects; and in the past history of
our country, especially about the time of our revolution,
many examples are to be found. Among others, the writings of Patrick Henry, of James Otis, and of President
Adams, may be mentioned. Controversial writings on other
subjects are also often forcible, and our age has furnished
some good examples of the vehement style among divines
Chalmers may be mentioned as a writer of this class.

Opposed to the forcible and the vehement style, is that
manner of writing which is called *feeble*, and *languid*. A
distinction may be made between these epithets, similar to
that made between forcible and vehement. The former has
reference to strength of reasoning, and energy of thought:
the latter to the degree of excitement which is manifested.
Hence it is, that a feeble and languid manner of writing is
indicative of the whole character of the writer. The man
whose style is feeble and languid is usually slothful in his
habits, and inefficient in his plans and conduct. His view
of his subject is cold and indistinct. His words are general,

and destitute of that vivacity which results from the use of more specific terms. His sentences are often long, and the clauses and members loosely connected. The parenthesis is much used; and not unfrequently we find at the close of a sentence an appendage, which is evidently designed to save the trouble of forming a new sentence.

Attempts after force and vehemence of style, when unsupported by strength of thought and real feeling, become rant and declamation. In such instances, instead, of strong reasoning, we have confident assertions; and for clear, impressive views of the subject, we have frequent repetitions, and bold declarations of its clearness. Instead of being left ourselves to discern the depth of the writer's feelings, we are told how deeply he feels; and all the artificial helps of vivacity, as exclamation, interrogation, antithesis and climax, are called to his aid. But while force and vehemence of style, like a deep and powerful current, sweep every obstacle before them, rant and declamation are fitly represented by the broad and shallow stream, specious and noisy, but powerless.

ELEVATED and DIGNIFIED. The foundations of an elevated style are laid in the thoughts. And these have more of originality and sublimity about them, than those which flow through the minds of less gifted men. There is also a fervor by which the writer seems to be urged onwards — not an impetuous and violent feeling, but calm and powerful

Ordinarily, in reading a production in an elevated style our attention is too much engrossed by the thoughts, to permit us to regard the language in which they are conveyed; and if at any time we stop with this object in view, it is but to feel and express our admiration. The words used are those, which, from the associations connected with them, are well suited to the feelings and thoughts that have possession of our minds. But the selection of these words seems not the result of effort and care. They have sprung up in the mind simultaneously with the thoughts themselves, and we regard them as the language in which the author ordinarily thinks a id converses.

The sentences are full and flowing, but at the same time unlabored, and simple in their composition. There is also a uniformity about them, which is characteristic of an elevated style. In more common styles you will find here and there a striking thought, or a bold expression, while other parts are thrown in as subsidiary or as connecting the more prominent thoughts. But in the elevated style, every sentence has its meaning and its importance. The whole abounds in thought, and there is a majesty and grandeur in the quiet but resistless power, with which it holds its undisturbed and even way.

We can hardly with propriety speak of the ornaments of an elevated style. This word implies something put on with the design of pleasing ; but in the kind of style I am describing, figurative language, and all that is included under the head of ornament, seems rather to arise from a kind of inspiration, than from any design of pleasing ; and the effect produced in the mind of the reader is a grateful exaltation of feeling. The definition which Longinus has given of sublimity, is in such instances happily exemplified. We seem to put ourselves in the place of the author, and as if the thought were our own, we glory in the grandeur and nobleness of the conception.

In applying the epithet *dignified* to style, there is a reference to true dignity, in distinction from the air of importance which sometimes assumes this name. Considered in this light, it is allied to the elevated style, but differs from it, in that here is less of ease and naturalness in its character The attitudes and movements of dignified men, are often the results of design and study, and similar art and labor are

found in the style of the dignified writer. He seems conscious, that he is treating of weighty matters, and laying
down important conclusions, and there is something in his
very air, which tells us it is a great work he is carrying on.
Hence uncommon and learned words are chosen, and there
is a stateliness and formality in his sentences. The phrase,
which the idiomatic writer would select as most happily
expressive of his meaning, the dignified writer rejects as
beneath his style. Instead of distinctness and ease of expression, there are inversions and involutions of clauses.
Many circumstances are introduced, which give preciseness
to the meaning, but which break up the continuous flow of
the sentence. A tiresome uniformity in the length and form
of the sentence, is also found, giving to the whole production the appearance of the enunciation of successive, distinct
propositions.

The dignified style admits of ornament, and that of a high
kind. But there is something of parade attending its use.
Instead of the sprightly metaphor, or well timed allusion,
we have the protracted allegory, or the formal comparison.
But then the images which are brought to view, are not
only illustrative, but often ennobling and exalting. It is not
a common pageant that passes before the mind, but one of
those splendid scenes that can give pleasure to the great.

For examples of the elevated style, I may refer to the
writings of Robert Hall of England, and of Dr. Channing
of Boston. Of the dignified style, the philosophical writings
of Dugald Stewart may be mentioned.

Unsuccessful attempts after the elevated or dignified
manner of writing, result in what is called the *pedantic* or
pompous style. A pedant is one fond of showing book-
knowledge; and a pedantic style is characterized by the
use of such terms and phrases, as are obsolete, uncommon,
or derived from the dead languages. The pompous style is

usually associated with the pedantic, and is characterized
by the use of long and sonorous words, by circumlocutions,
by the frequent use of synonymes, and by the repetition of
the same thought in different words. Instead of any further
description of these styles, it may be sufficient to refer
to Weems's Life of Washington. There are plants which
in the language of husbandmen, grow rank in certain
soils. They spread wide their branches, and are covered
with thick foliage. But it is only after a long and wearied search, that any fruit can be found, and then it is not
of sufficient value to repay the toil. These plants are apt
emblems of the productions of pompous writers.

NEAT and ELEGANT. These epithets are applied to style
with particular reference to what is called the turn of expression. They denote also, especially the latter, the nature
of the ornament used. We well understand their force, as
they are applied to a production in the arts. By the application of the former to any article of ornament or use, we
declare that it is not only free from faults, but that it is
executed in a manner that pleases us, and shows skill on
the part of the artist. In applying the other epithet, we express admiration. The work is not only faithfully and skilfully executed, but in a manner which excels. They have
the same meaning when applied to style. In saying that a
style is neat, we mean that the turns of expression are such,
as happily convey the thoughts, and are well suited to the
subject and occasion. In saying that a style is elegant, we
declare that there is the same happy and well adapted mode
of conveying the thoughts, and to a degree that is uncommon.

The turn of expression must necessarily depend both on
the choice of words, and the composition of the sentence.
It is also closely connected with the thought that is conveyed. Thus in the forcible and vehement style, we have

bold turns of expression;—in the elevated and dignified, we have sublime and grand turns of expression. In the neat style, there is sprightliness and justness in the thoughts, and a vivacity and finish in the mode of conveying them. At the same time, the writer is careful to avoid every fault. The neat style, as thus explained, is ever pleasing, and to some classes of writing peculiarly well suited. But it differs essentially from the easy and idiomatic style before described, in that it gives evidence of labor in its construction. It seems the result, to which mediocrity of talent has attained, by patient and praiseworthy exertions.

Elegance, as has been stated, implies that which is choice and select. In this sense it may be applied to words, forms of sentences, and the various ornaments of style. Especially does it require that all coarse and homely words and phrases should be avoided, even though their use might give more vivacity to the expression. The sentences also are harmonious and flowing, and while they are polished, and easily understood, they are alike removed from the stiffness and awkwardness of the labored style, and the looseness and familiarity of the idiomatic. But it is in the imagery that the characteristic trait of the elegant style is found. Beautiful and expressive epithets and turns of expression, with embellishing comparisons, and other formal ornaments of style, often occur, and excite emotions of taste. It is manifest that all is fitted and designed to please. Writings of this class are referred to under the next head of ornamented styles, where the import of elegance, as applied to the ornaments of style, is more fully exhibited.

In considering an author's manner of writing as addressed to the imagination, or as designed to please, we say that his style is PLAIN, or that it is ORNAMENTED. As the words obviously imply, the former of these epithets refers to a des-

titution of ornament, and the latter to its presence. Bu
between an absolutely plain style and one highly ornamented,
there are various degrees; and different epithets have been
applied to different kinds of writing, according to the nature
and amount of ornament used.

In attempting to explain the most common of these epithets, I shall direct the attention to different authors in
whose writings the ornaments of style abound.

W. Irving, whose literary productions have acquired a
deserved celebrity, may be first mentioned. Most of his
works are addressed to the imagination, with the design of
pleasing rather than of instructing. This kind of writing
admits of much ornament, and the reader of the Sketch
Book and of Bracebridge Hall will find that his expectations of pleasure from this source are not disappointed. But
though in these writings there is a profusion of ornament,
it is of that modest, chaste, unobtrusive kind, that never
cloys. It does not dazzle the mind, nor fill it with admiration, but excites emotions more calm and permanent. It is
either the unstudied metaphor, or the embellishing and illustrative comparison, which are always welcome, as they cast
new light and beauty on the objects of our view. Sometimes also a metonymy, or a synecdoche, or a personification
of the humbler kind, gives increased vivacity to the expression. In reading the works of this author we seem not to
be passing through a region, where gorgeous palaces, artificial parks and lakes and shrubbery, are successively meeting
our attention, till we are wearied by their uniform splendor;
but it is rather a land of rural elegance, and we look upon
the neat villas — the highly cultivated fields with their haw-
thorn hedges, while over the whole country is spread, in rich
profusion, those simple but graceful ornaments, with which
nature knows how to deck her own fields. I would then
call the style of Irving, in reference to its ornament, simple

and elegant;— simple, as free from all that is affected — elegant, as being choice in its selection of ornament. This is one of the most grateful forms of the ornamented style, and denotes both delicacy and refinement of taste.

As an example of an ornamented style, in which elegance is found, but not in connexion with simplicity, that of Alison may be mentioned. In his writings, as in those of Irving, there is a profusion of ornament, and it must be said, that this is less acceptable in sermons and philosophical treatises than in fictitious writings. There is also manifestly something of art in the ornaments of Alison's style. They have been put on, and are not a part of what they adorn. They are flowers that have been planted, and not those that have sprung up spontaneously. Still no one will deny that Alison excels in the figurative use of language, and that the ornamental figures of style that he introduces, are often beautiful and striking; and he justly bears the name of an elegant writer.

The style of Phillips, the orator, affords an example of an ornamented style differing from those which have been mentioned. From the nature of his productions we should expect to find in them figures of the bolder kind; and many splendid passages are found. But too often it is the case, that it is all splendor — mere show without solidity. Many of his figures are figures of words, and nothing more. If we attempt to bring up before the mind the image he presents, and to see whether it be distinct and perfect, we too often find that we have something glittering before us, but it is without form or comeliness. His style may be called brilliant but specious. We are ready to apply to it the common proverb, " It is not all gold that shines."

Hervey, the author of Meditations, is often mentioned as a florid writer. This epithet denotes a superabundance of ornament, and not of the choicest kind. His work is a mass of metaphors and comparisons. There is evidence of an active imagination, but it wants the guidance of taste. There is also ingenuity, but it manifests itself in strange conceits and far-fetched illustrations.

From these instances we learn what is meant by the epithets *simple*, *elegant*, *specious*, and *florid*, as applied to style; and these epithets denote the most common qualities of those styles in which ornament abounds.

SECTION 3. *On modes of writing suited to different subjects and occasions.*

It is the design in the preceding chapters to treat of the principles and rules of good writing. An examination of the different classes of literary productions, and of the style suited to them, may form a second part of this work. All that will now be attempted, is to give in a short section some practical directions, which may aid the writer in those kinds of composition which are most common. Such are Epistolary writings, Essays, Historical and Fictitious writings, Argumentative Discussions, and Orations.

EPISTOLARY WRITINGS are communications between individuals, which serve as a medium both of friendly intercourse and of transacting the business of life. They hold a middle rank between the unrestrained flow and carelessness of conversation, and the preciseness and formality of dignified composition, approaching, however, nearer to the former than to the latter.

Authors sometimes assume the form of letters in their publications when nothing more than the form is designed to be used. Such letters, though addressed to individuals, are in fact written for the public, and dropping the addresses prefixed to them, differ in no respect from the essay or dissertation. These are not included in the class of writings I am now describing.

Letters of friendly intercourse should be written in an easy, artless style. Sprightliness of thought and vivacity of expression, are appropriate to this class of writings; but the more formal ornaments of style should be rarely introduced. At least, it may be said, that such ornaments must be managed with uncommon skill, not to injure the simplicity that is required. In the conversation of the man of taste and intelligence, we look for a correct use and happy choice of words, and for an easy, idiomatic and simple phraseology, avoiding alike the cant of the vulgar, the verbosity of the pedant, and the sickening refinement of the sentimentalist. The same propriety in words, the same artlessness in expression, are required in his letters, with the additional care which must always be caused by the thought *manent scripta.*

The letter of business should have strictness of method and perspicuity of style. Its object should be promptly stated, and nothing unnecessary be introduced.

It is not sufficient to insist upon a simple and artless style, and to caution the writer against a stiff and labored manner of composition. There is danger of negligence and carelessness. Some, presuming on the good nature of their friends, write their letters in a hasty, disconnected manner as to the thoughts, while their words are often incorrectly used, and their expressions are slovenly. Such may be called rattlers. They run on from one subject to another — their words and sentences but half written out, and their letter, from its beginning to its close, is a perplexing enigma. To such a letter, the lines of Cowper may be applied;

<blockquote>

' One had need
Be very much his friend indeed,
To pardon or to bear it."

</blockquote>

It may be added that the man who can write better, is thus doing injustice to himself. An improper expression in conversation may be forgotten, an awkward movement may be overlooked, but a carelessly written letter is an abiding witness against its author.

English literature furnishes many good models in this species of composition. Cowper may be mentioned as a writer who excels. His solid common sense, his judicious reflections, his lively wit, his playful poetical fancy his warm affections, his melancholy but deeply interesting feelings of piety, all conspire to give a charm to his letters. Add to this a style, chaste, simple, and sometimes elegant, and it is no wonder, that his productions of this kind are ever read with interest.

Essays are writing , which are usually addressed to the public periodically, and which are brief in their extent and humble in their pretensions. The Essayist does not promise a full view of his subject; nor does he seek to exert a strong influence over the minds of his readers. His arrangement is professedly desultory; his arguments are probabilities and inferences from facts that are stated. He makes no appeal to the passions, but tells his story and leaves his reader to his own feelings and reflections. The characteristics which recommend writings of this kind to public attention, are the following:

1. The thoughts should have novelty and importance. It can hardly be expected, that readers will direct their attention to so humble a class of writings as the Essay, unless they are to be compensated, either by the pleasure of novelty or by an increase of valuable knowledge. Hence the difficulty of ably conducting periodical publications. To do this successfully, requires a mind well furnished with rich and varied stores of knowledge. Addison has said, that it is more difficult to write a series of periodical essays, than to compose a book on some definite subject; and he spoke from experience He is said to have spent much time in

preparation, and to have collected three manuscript volumes of interesting facts and references, before he commenced the writing of the Spectator. The issuers of proposals for publishing periodical essays, who with limited resources are wont to make ample promises, should know this anecdote of Addison.

2. The flow of thought in the essay should be discursive and animated. To writings of this kind, the maxim *ars est celare artem*, may be well applied. Every well disciplined mind will form its plan, but as it has been already remarked, it is not necessary in all cases, that this plan be formally stated. Much skill is also required in the frequent transitions from one subject to another. By dwelling too long on one part, the production becomes tedious; by passing too rapidly from one to another, it appears sterile and abrupt. Wit and sprightliness are also expected in the Essay. We look for the efforts of the active, playful mind rather than for the deep-laid and well-matured reflections of the philosopher. Sprightliness and discursiveness are so essential to productions of this kind that those, who from their intellectual habits, or from the constitution of their minds, are destitute of these qualities, should abstain from all attempts in this species of writing.

3. The style of the Essay may be easy and idiomatic, or more labored and neat. I have already explained what is denoted by these qualifying terms.

The absence of those adventitious causes, which excite a strong interest and arouse the attention, is a reason, why writings of this class should in some degree be addressed to the imagination. There are few minds willing to seek after knowledge, unless some peculiar interest in the subject of inquiry, or some striking charms in its representation, allure them to the task. Hence, so far as is consistent with the calm and simple manner of the essay, the allusions should be frequent and happy, the illustrations pertinent, and the figurative expressions profuse and pleasing.

In the literature of no country, do we find more perfect and numerous specimens of Essay writing, than in that of England. From some favorable circumstances, this species of composition early became popular in that country. The minds of those who devoted their time and talents to it, were well suited to the employment, while the state of morals, manners and literature, afforded fit and copious subjects. Hence the Spectator was well received, had a wide circulation, and became a part of the literature of the country. Numerous, and some of them able periodical publications of this class, have since been issued and well received.

HISTORY is the record of past events. It may treat separately of the government and political relations of a country, —of its literature, or of its religion; and may hence receive the epithet of Civil, Literary, or Ecclesiastical History. As examples, we have Pitkin's Civil History of the United States, Dunlop's History of Roman Literature, and Mosheim's Ecclesiastical History. So intimate, however, is the connexion between civil government, literature and religion, and so great is their reciprocal influence on each other, that writers most frequently view them in connexion, and give us the General History of a country;—such is Hume's History of England.

A further division of historical writings, is founded on the different modes of stating events. One is a simple relation of facts; the other views facts in their connexion with each other, as cause and effect. The former is termed Narrative History; the latter Philosophical History.

In examining the merit of a historical production, we direct our attention, 1. To the skill shown in the selection and arrangement of facts. 2. To the fidelity of the writer. 3. To the style. Each of these topics will now be briefly noticed.

1. The skill shown in the selection and arrangement of facts.

No employment perhaps requires such various and extensive knowledge, as the writing of history. The historian is to view the actions of men in connexion with their causes: and to do this, he must well know the secret springs of human action He is to judge also of occurrences as affecting communities, and this requires an intimate knowledge of the different forms of government, and of the principles of civil polity. He needs further to be familiar with literature in its different departments, and with religion in its various forms. But all these are but remote and indirect preparatives for the work. With the particular country and portion of time, which are the subjects of his history, the writer must have a thorough and intimate acquaintance. He must seek access to the fountain sources of knowledge, — must examine authentic documents and original authorities, and become familiar with the institutions, and manners, and opinions, of the age and people of whom he writes.

When, as the result of patient, continued research, and careful investigation, the writer has collected the materials of his work, his attention is in the next place directed to the selection and arrangement of facts; and here he will be guided by the proposed object of his work. If it be his design to write a narrative history simply, he will place before us such facts, as may fully inform us of whatever of importance pertains to the people of whom he writes. He wi.. also have reference to what is fitted to excite interest in his readers, to gratify their curiosity and furnish them profitable instruction. But in philosophical history, the writer has some leading design in his work. He would show us the origin and progress of certain civil and religious institutions, or he would trace the effects of opposing opinions on a community, and show us in what manner public measures have been influenced, and the welfare of the nation affected by contending parties. Any definite object of this kind, must evidently become a ruling principle to the historian in the selection of his facts.

The success of a historian, will also depend much on the clearness of his method and the strictness of his arrangement. In narrative history, the order of time will be principally observed. In philosophical history, the arrangement, us well as the selection of facts, will depend on the leading design of the writer. His statements, like the different parts of an argument, must all be brought to bear on some common point.

Some writers divide their histories into successive eras, and give a full and distinct view of the condition of a nation at these epochs. Such is the arrangement of Henry's History of England. Divisions of this kind are favorable to perspicuity, but, by breaking up the natural connexion of events, they diminish the interest of readers.

Many of the ancient historians are deficient in their plan. Herodotus, the father of Grecian history, though possessing great merit as a narrator, observes but little order in his narrations. He passes hastily from one nation to another, and often introduces in a parenthetical form, the events of many years. Thucydides also has in this particular shown little skill, and often, that he may strictly observe chronological order, interrupts in a painful manner the course of his narrative. After recording the events, which have occurred during a period of time in one part of the world, he breaks off abruptly, and proceeds to the narration of what has taken place, during the same period, in another part. A more skilful writer would have found some connecting link. Livy and Tacitus have more merit in this respect, and, as narrative historians, are good models in the selection and arrangement of facts.

2. Fidelity as a trait of the historian.

Cicero has said that two things are incumbent on the historian — to avoid stating what is false, and fully and fairly to place before us the truth. These two things the historian professes to do, and fidelity implies that he is true to his professions. He promises us the results of careful, thorough, fair investigation; and if he is faithful, he seeks access to every possible source of knowledge, and free from carelessness and indolence, makes a fair use of the materials he may obtain. Fidelity further implies, that a writer does not designedly deceive us. It is indeed hardly to be supposed, that one wishing to obtain confidence as a writer of history, should designedly deceive. But it is not enough that a historian may not have laid to his charge designed misrepresentations. He must be free from the influence of prejudice, and his statements must be fairly made. In philosophical history, there is often strong temptation to misrepresent, and so various and apparently unimportant are the ways in which this may be done, that there is much need of watchfulness The selection of some facts in preference to others — the dwelling on favorite views of subjects — the manner of representing facts, even. the epithets used, may give a decided cast to a historical statement, and strongly manifest the bias of the writer's mind. We almost expect, that when a historian writes of his own country, or attempts to account for the origin and to exhibit the nature of those political or religious opinions, which he himself is accustomed to maintain or oppose, he will be partial. From this source. no doubt, arise the greatest defects in Hume's History of England. Sometimes, also, the influence of cherished opinions will be felt, when writing the history of a nation extinct, and with which the historian himself has no connexion. Thus Gibbon's infidelity has colored his representations of what pertains to the Christian religion. In the same manner, Mit-

18 *

ford's monarchical principles are seen in the account, given in his History of Greece, of the democracy of Athens. In fact, such are the subjects on which the philosophical historian is called to pronounce an opinion, so connected are they, either directly or indirectly, with his own private views and opinions, that we can hardly expect more than an approximation to uncorrupted truth. The historian should be a man of no party, either in politics or religion, of no partialities or aversions, with no avowed or secret aim but naked truth; and rarely indeed can such a man be found.

3. Style of historical writings.

In examining a historical production of modern times, we find that there is a diversity in its different parts, requiring variety in the style in which it is written. Some portions are simply narrative; others argumentative. There are found relations of striking and imposing occurrences, and descriptions of natural scenery and of works of art. Some histories also contain descriptions of men, or character-painting. Here evidently is occasion for variety of style. Narration and argument require chasteness and simplicity. Descriptive writing allows a freer range to the imagination. This is in fact a species of historical painting; and though it must be true to the original, it admits the adornings of fancy.

It may be said, in general, of the style of history, that it should have simplicity and gravity. Instruction is the appropriate employment of the historic muse; still she would allure us to the study of the lessons which she teaches. She may well be styled a matron among the muses; and the words which she utters, and the aspect which she wears, are those of maternal simplicity and endearment. It is well known, that ancient historians proposed the amusement of their readers as a prominent object of their efforts. When Herodotus wrote, he had in immediate view the assembled throng at the Olympic games. Indeed it may be said, that

histories are among the most polished and elegant produc·
tions of ancient literature.   And even now that History and
Philosophy are found in alliance, much of the polish and
elegance of former times is retained.

In tracing the progress of historical writings, we are led
to notice varieties in their form, which occur at successive
periods.   The earliest records of nations belong to their
poetry, and the connexion between epic poetry and narrative
history is close.   This is seen, not only in the style, but in
the incidents narrated.   Such are the marvellous exploits of
heroes, uncommon and striking occurrences, and events,
both in the natural and moral world, approaching the mi-
raculous.   Amusement, and not instruction, is evidently a
leading design of the writer.   The resemblance between
ancient histories and modern historical novels, is striking.
Both aim to carry us back to former periods, and to make
present to us the scenes which then transpired.   Of these
ancient histories, but few have come down to us.   Herodo
tus is usually placed in this class, though the accuracy of his
geographical statements, and the amount of true information which he gives, might entitle him to a higher rank.

In the next period, are placed those rightly styled narrative historians.   In these writings, we find true accounts
of occurrences distinctly and fully stated in regular succession.   The course of the narrative and the style are natural and easy.   There has apparently been little effort on the
part of the writer, and little is required on our part in following him.   It is a plain, easy route, and we advance in it
pleasantly, gathering instruction as we proceed.   Xenophon
among the Greek, and Livy among the Latin historians,
may be mentioned as excelling in this form of historical
writing.   The easy, artless, natural manner, which charac-
ierizes their works, — the simple story which they tell, are
fitted to excite grateful emotions, and recommend them highly to all their readers.

In the third class of historical writers, we see the beginnings of philosophical history. The writers allow themselves in some remarks on the events which they relate. They begin also to regard occurrences in their connexion with each other. Still there is not found any guiding, leading principle, which runs through their works; neither is there displayed that knowledge of politics and of man, which is found in philosophical history. Thucydides and Tacitus, especially the latter, are admirable instances of this class of historians.

The transition from such writers as Thucydides and Tacitus to philosophical history, is easy. Some of the Italian writers lay claim to be regarded as the earliest philosophical historians. Macchiavelli particularly is mentioned, as uniting the elegance and poetry of ancient history with the wisdom and gravity of philosophy. But it is to English literature that we are to look for models in historical writing. Hume, Robertson, and Gibbon, are masters in the art.

BIOGRAPHY is a branch of Historical writing, being designed to place before us the characters and important events in the lives of distinguished individuals. It is a kind of writing, which, from the subjects on which it is employed, excites much interest. The reader expects to see how one has conducted in scenes, the same, perhaps, or similar to those, with which he himself is conversant. At least, he is to have exhibited before him the workings of the human mind, the views and feelings of one of like passions with himself. He is to learn something of the private character and of the retired hours of one, who as an actor in the more public scenes of life, or as an author and a scholar, has been the object of his admiration. The following practical directions may be given, to aid those who attempt compositions in this class of writings.

1. In the selection of incidents to be narrated, the writer

of Biography should restrain himself to what is c osely connected with the subject of his memoirs. In this way, the
expectations of the intelligent reader will be met. He does
not take up a biography, that he may read a collection of
anecdotes, or that he may acquaint himself with the history
of a particular period. He expects to learn the history and
views of an individual, and to acquaint himself with the
history of the times, so far only as this individual is concerned.

The effect of neglecting the caution now given, and of
introducing notices of other individuals merely because they
lived at the same time, and narrations of other events, because they happened at the same period, is to render a
biography tedious and uninteresting.

2. A second direction is, to present a just statement of
facts and a fair view of character;— let neither partiality
nor aversion be discovered.

Memoirs are most frequently written by the particular
friends and associates of those, whose characters are described. The public are aware of this circumstance, and
make allowances for the partialities of friendship. But if
the eulogium is excessive, and the writer indulges himself
in praise and high commendation, an effect is often produced
different from that designed. It is much safer to state facts,
and leave the reader to make his own inference and reflections. We always suspect weakness, where there is an effort
to appear strong.

3. The style of Biographies should be characterized by
ease and perspicuity. The story should need no allurements
of style, to arrest and fix the attention of the reader.

Character-painting is often regarded as a difficult species
of writing, and he who attempts it, seems to gird himself
for some great effort. Hence productions of this kind are
often unnatural and labored. The sentences are short and

abrupt. There are striking contrasts and strong expressions. The picture is exhibited before us in bold relief and there is more effort that it may be striking, than that it be just. This kind of writing requires a skilful hand, and it rarely attempted with success. In some of the best modern biographies it is not found.

FICTITIOUS WRITINGS are extended fables, or tales, written with the professed design of combining instruction with amusement. Some are of a historical kind, and are designed to acquaint us with the manners and customs of a by gone age. Others lay claim to be considered of an ethical nature; they profess to detect and expose the springs of action; they shew the rewards of virtue and the evil consequences of vice; and thus they would be auxiliaries to those who seek to improve and reform men. There are others that are mirrors of the passing age: they catch and reflect back to us the fashions as they rise.

In estimating the merits of fictitious writings, our attention is directed to three particulars, — the plot, the characters, and the moral. Each of these will now be briefly considered.

By the plot of a fictitious work, is meant a connected series of incidents and actions, leading to some important and decided result. It is essential to success, that the course of events be not too obvious and direct. At least, there must be enough of intricacy in the story, and of uncertainty as to the final result, to awaken curiosity on the part of the reader, and lead him to form conjectures as to the event. Probability is another essential trait of a well formed plot. Men in fiction must feel and act as men in real life are wont to feel and act. It must be seen, that the force of circumstances is the same, and events must turn on universally recognized causes and principles of action Unity is a third requisite of a good plot. By unity, it is meant, that every occurrence and every event mentioned, should be a part of a connected series of events having some bearing on the object of the story. But while it is essential that unity be preserved, and probability be not violated, the story must be somewhat removed from the common current of human affairs. It must be full of incident, and give room for the free workings of the imagination. We must be hurried forward from one situation to another ;—unlooked for events and frequent changes must occur. This is justly regarded as a most difficult part of fictitious writing. It is no small task, to take beings, with the passions, opinions, and varieties of character, which may be found and imagined among men, and set them to work, subjecting them only to such influences, as the nature of the human mind and heart allows.

Next to the plot, the characters represented become objects of attention. And here it is requisite to success, that the characters be prominent, distinct and well supported. As the story goes forward, and different individuals are introduced to our notice, we must see in each one those distinct traits, which, as in real life, may cause him to be remembered and readily recognized, whenever afterwards met with. And further, there must be uniformity and consistency of action. After our acquaintance has been formed with the different characters introduced, we must be able to predict how they will act, under any given circumstances, in which they may be placed.

To conceive in this way, and exhibit a marked, decided character, acting with uniformity and consistency, when subjected to the various influences bearing upon it in the progress of a long continued story, requires no small ingenuity and skill. It requires also a thorough and intimate acquaintance with human nature. It is to this source, that the novel writer is to look for the modifying influences on his power. Under the limitations thus prescribed, he may compound the ingredients of human character at his will. He may form new and unknown characters, but not absurd and unnatural ones. It is an argument often brought in support of the utility of novels, that we thus obtain a knowledge of human nature. But unless the characters introduced are natural and well supported, no benefit of this kind will accrue; and it is to be feared, that the mass of fictitious works are in this respect more injurious than beneficial, since they often present false notions of men and things, and thus lead their readers astray.

That every fictitious work should be favorable to good morals, is universally allowed. At the end of a novel, as at the completion of the plans of a good moral government, it should be seen, that virtue has its reward, and that vice is punished. But it is not enough that such should be the conclusion of the tale. It should be borne in mind during its progress. In fact, the moral effect depends more on the impression made in the development of the story, than on a formal annunciation of some sound moral principle at its close. It is believed, that if the moral tendency of many novels were tested in this manner, they would be found to exert no favorable moral influence. There are and ever have been writers of fiction, and those too who profess themselves friends of morality and religion, who shew, in the course of their works, that they have not themselves strength of principle enough to resist temptations to amuse their readers, at the expense of what to every upright man is sacred.

The style of fictitious writings, since works of this class are addressed to the imagination, and are designed to please, may have both ornament and elegance. In an extended work, however, it must vary with the character of different parts. Some portions are simply narrative, requiring a plain, didactic manner. Others are descriptive, requiring more or

less e.evation of style. Occasionally also, as in ancient his
tories, letters, speeches, and discussions of various kinds,
are introduced, requiring correspondent changes in the style

Fictitious writings in some form have been known in
almost every age and nation. More than any other class of
literary productions, they exhibit to us the manners, and
feelings, and opinions, of the times when they were written.
Like an extended river, flowing through varieties of soil and
scenery, they show us the peculiarities of the region through
which they pass. English literature has its full share of
fictitious writing. It has been reserved to a writer of our
own age, to present it to us in a form, which, whether we
regard the skill and power with which it is executed, or its
value as combining instruction with amusement, has not
been surpassed.

An ARGUMENTATIVE DISCUSSION is the examination of
a subject with the design of establishing some position that
has been taken, or of maintaining some opinion that has
been advanced. It requires powers of research and investigation, joined with comprehensiveness and strength of intellect. When successfully executed, it is the effort of a well
disciplined mind, as it takes up a subject worthy the exertion of its powers, and placing facts and principles in due
order and connexion, presents before us a full and impressive view.

The most unportant directions to be observed in this
kind of writing are, 1. That the subject of discussion be
fully stated and explained. 2. That strict method be observed in the arrangement of the several parts of the discourse, and the object of the writer be kept constantly in
view. So much was said on these topics in the first chapter
of this work, that it is unnecessary here to enlarge upon them.

The style of the discussion should be dignified and manly;
forcible, rather than elegant. Expressions, which from the

figurative use of language are bold and striking, may be happily introduced; and the production should abound in illustrations and interesting facts.

An ORATION may be defined a popular address on some interesting and important subject. In listening to a performance of this kind, we expect the mind to be informed, the reasoning powers to be exercised, the imagination to be excited, and the taste improved.

In compositions of this class, much depends on the happy selection of a subject. Many err in supposing, that an oration should have declamation rather than argument, ornament rather than sense. In opposition to this, it should always be remembered, that it is a production addressed both to the understanding and the imagination. Instead then of selecting a subject, which may afford opportunity for contesting some disputed point, it should be one which requires a statement and elucidation of interesting facts and principles — a course of calm, dignified and persuasive reasoning. At the same time, it should allow of fine writing. There should be opportunity for description and pathos; for historical and classical allusions and illustrations, and for comprehensive and ennobling views. It should admit also unity of plan. The style of orations should be elevated and elegant; the forms of expression manly and dignified, and at the same time characterized by force and vivacity. The ornament should be of a high kind — such as ennobles and exalts the subject. Diffuseness, as has been remarked, is also desirable.

Selections from different authors, shewing the qualities of style mentioned in the different sections of this chapter, are found among the Exercises. (Ex. on Chap. 5.)

In concluding the attempt, that has now been made, to state the principles and rules of composition in English, I would enforce the following general directions for forming a good style.

1. Be familiar with the best models of style.

In observing this injunction, the attention should no doubt be principally directed to the best writers of the present day. There are peculiarities of style, which characterize the productions of different periods, no less than of different individuals; and to be esteemed a good writer some regard must be paid to the literary taste of the age The inquiries may here arise, what is the character of th prevalent style of our times, and where may the best models of writing be found? With the view of more fully answering these inquiries, I shall here introduce a short account of some prominent changes in the style of English writers.

If we go back to the time of Hooker, and Barrow, and Taylor, we find prevalent a rough, plain and energetic manner of writing. The literary men of that period were men of thought. Having but few books, and those difficult of access, they relied chiefly on the resources of their own minds. Hence their conceptions were distinct, and their expressions are marked by the freshness and strength of originality of thought. At the same time, from their famil iarity with Greek and Latin literature, and from their occa sionally composing in the latter of these languages, they acquired a harshness and stiffness of expression. Hence the style of the period may be characterized as forcible and often elevated, but at the same time harsh and labored.

Another period in the history of English style, worthy of our particular notice, is the reign of Queen Anne. The writers of that golden age were finished scholars — men of knowledge, wit and refinement, and we admire their skill in the use of words, their rich figurative language and the smoothness and harmony of their periods. We are pleased also with the thoughts which they convey to us, and with the allusions and happy illustrations, with which these thoughts are embellished. At the same time, we discern a marked difference between these writers and those before mentioned in their intellectual resources and energies. There is less of boldness of conception, less of comprehensiveness and exaltation of view, less of freedom of expression. The style of the latter period seems formed in one uniform mould, and the different writers exhibit not so much the characteristic marks of their own peculiar manner of thinking, as they do a conformity to some established standard.

That the influence of the polish and refinement of this period was most favorable, cannot be doubted. English style acquired an ease and elegance, which it had never possessed. Its forms of expression were idiomatic, its ornament had simplicity and beauty. The permanent influence of this progress has been felt in the improvement of our language itself.

But if we admit that the improvements in our language made at this period, and the ease and beauty of expression introduced, compensate for want of boldness and vigor of thought and expression, it must still be allowed, that the effect of the close imitation of these polished writers was injurious. For many years following the period of which we have last spoken, there was manifestly too great ambition among writers, to form their style on the model of Addisonian ease and simplicity. Hence freedom from faults, a negative sort of excellence, was the object at which they aimed; and in their painful efforts for polish and refinement of style they forgot to think for themselves, and nobly speak their thoughts. Such, with few exceptions, was the character of English writers for many years following the time of Addison

Within the last thirty years, another change in English style has been gradually making progress. The nerveless polish and refinement of the former period, have been giving

place to directness, and manliness, and strength of expression
In these traits of style, we seem to be going back to the
times of Hooker and Barrow. But the improvements of
intervening periods have not been lost. Our language has
become more definite in the use of words, more harmonious
in its sounds, and more copious in its terms.

The good writer of the present day seems ever to write
under a degree of excitement. He is full of his subject, and
his attention is directed to what he shall say, rather than to
the manner of conveying his thoughts. His expressions
have an air of originality about them. There is no toil-
some selection of words, no labored composition of sentences, no high wrought ornament; but the words, and sentences, and ornaments, are such as most naturally and obvious
ly present themselves to the excited mind. If a word is
more expressive of his meaning than any other, he uses it,
though it may never have been introduced to so good company before. If a form of sentence occurs to him, which is
more easy and idiomatic than another, he adopts it, and
stops not to inquire whether it end in a trisyllable, or a mon-
osyllable. If a figurative expression strikes him as pertinent and happy, he uses it, and leaves it for others to examine, whether it be found in the numbers of the Spectator,
and have the authority of classical writers for its support.
In short, instead of imitating the style of any other writer
as his guide, he has a style of his own, and observes the
maxim of Horace in the literal use of the term,

Nullius addictus jurare in verba magistri.

The most characteristic faults of the prevalent style of the
present day, are incorrectness and affectation of strength.
Though we could not condemn the writer, who, borne along
by the rapid and impetuous flow of his thoughts, disdains
the restraints of minor rhetorical rules, yet there are certain limits, beyond which no one can pass without censure.

19*

No one can be esteemed a good writer, whose manner of writing is not perspicuous. Hence no rule, the observance of which is essential to perspicuity, can be violated without the charge of incorrectness. If a writer uses words in a foreign or improper signification, no excellence can atone for these defects. If, in the composition of his sentences, he neglects to observe those rules, which require unity and a right arrangement of the several clauses and parts, to that degree which produces obscurity, he cannot receive the name of a good writer. It is too often the case, that modern writers, in the haste and ardor with which they compose, are guilty of violations of these rules.

The other fault which has been mentioned, is an affectation of strength of expression. This arises from the propensity, so natural to man, of going to extremes. Because strength is a characteristic of the style of the good writer of the present day, many are evidently laboring hard, through their whole composition, for its attainment. They are ever seeking after new and forcible forms of expression, ar searching for striking and dazzling illustrations. What is thus unnatural and forced must ever be disgusting.

In answer to the inquiry, where these models of writing are to be found, the study of which may aid in acquiring the style of the present day, I would first direct the attention to the literary Reviews of the time. This class of writings not only contains the best part of the literature of the age, but has done much towards the improvement of our style. Especially has the Edinburgh Review contributed much to this object. It was the first to lead the way in that fearlessness and boldness of thought and expression. which have succeeded to the tameness and excessive polish of a former period. The Orations and popular Addresses of the day, may be mentioned as another class of writings furnishing models of good writing. But I would recom end o him who would acquire a good style, that instead of confining the attention to models of good writing of the present day, he go back to an earlier period in English literature. Let him study the works of those great men of former days, who, conscious of an intellectual supremacy, stood forth with a noble spirit of independence and self-reliance, as the guides and instructors of their times; and who, feeling the responsibility attached to their high gifts and attainments, sought not the praises of their contemporaries only, but, to use the noble language of Milton, "that lasting fame and perpetuity of praise which God and good men have consented, shall be the reward of those whose published labors advance the good of mankind." He will indeed find in these writings inelegancies and inaccuracies of expression; — he will meet words and phrases which will appear to him strange and uncouth; but these deficiencies are amply compensated by a noble freedom and strength of thought, and a richness and directness of expression. Let him then study these models, that his mind may become assimilated to theirs, — that he may be actuated by the same spirit, and shew forth the same energy

2. Compose frequently and with care.

It should be remembered by all those who would attain a good style, that every good writer has made himself such. Instructors and works on Rhetoric may point out excellences, and give cautions, but they can never make good writers. A good style can be attained only by writing frequently and with care.

But it is not enough that efforts be made; they should be well-directed. The first object of attention should be to acquire a distinct and well-matured view of the subject. In this way a degree of interest in it will be excited, and the words and expressions, which offer themselves to the excited mind in conveying what it distinctly sees, will ordinarily be the best. There will, it is true, in the efforts of the

young writer, be inaccuracies and violations of rules, bu
these may be removed in revisal. There is danger, howev
er, lest, in this revisal, an attempt to refine and polish destroy the force and originality of the expressions. It is better merely to correct inaccuracies, and to leave a higher
degree of polish to be attained by an improvement of the
taste, resulting from the study of good models. Let not
then the young writer direct his efforts for improvement solely to the choice of his words, or the composition of his sentences, or waste them in a search after figurative expressions and the ornaments of style. Let him rather aim at the
attainment of distinct views of his subject, and the clear
and forcible exhibition of these views to others.

When a good style has been formed, it is still of impor
tance to compose occasionally with care and attention
The style of an individual in some respects resembles the
hand-writing. If he acquires the ability of writing a fair
and legible hand, and afterwards, in the hurry of business, is
led to write rapidly and carelessly, his hand-writing will de-
teriorate. If he continues to bestow on it a usual share of
attention, it will remain the same. If occasionally he
writes with attention, and labors to improve it, he will improve it. The same is true of style; and since, in the discharge of the common duties of a profession, it may be difficult to devote attention to the manner of composit on, it
may be well occasionally to discuss and exhibit some sub
ject with more than usual care.

A good style is an attainment, which amply repays all the
effort that is here enjoined. It is to the scholar, a consum-
mation of his intellectual discipline and acquirements. He,
who in this land of free institutions holds an able pen, has a
weapon of powerful efficacy both for defence and attack
and if this weapon be wielded with honest and patriotic motives, he who wields it, may become a public benefactor

EXERCISE 1.

First, therefore, every morning, make your private prayer unto almighty God, give him thanks for his protection of you the night past, and that he hath brought you to the morning, and desire him to bless and direct you by his grace and providence that day, and to preserve you from the evils and dangers of it, and to keep you in obedience to him.

Secondly, a little before you go to bed, make again your private prayers to God, returning him thanks for his protection, and for bringing you to the end of the day; desire him to forgive you the sins and failings of the day, and beg his protection over you the night following.

Always be attentive to your prayers, and keep your mind upon the business you are about, with all due seriousness and solemness, without playing or staring about, or thinking of other matters; for you must remember that in prayer you are speaking to the great God of heaven and earth, that doth not only see and observe your outward carriage, but also the very thoughts of your hearts and mind.

Let no occasion whatsoever hinder you from your private, constant devotion toward Almighty God, but be steady and fixed, and resolved in it; and not go about any business of importance (but only reading of a chapter, whereof in the next) till you have performed this duty; and although it be upon the Lord's Day, when you go to public prayers, morning and afternoon, and though there be morning and evening prayers in the schools or college where you live yet this must not make you omit your private devotions; for it must be a solemn and sacred employment, as a great and necessary means of your protection, and blessing, and safety, the ensuing day or night. I was ever distrustful of the success of that business which I undertook before I commended myself and affairs to Almighty God in my private morning prayers.

Let all your thoughts and words be full of reverence; think not of him lightly, nor speak of him, nor use his name vainly; consider, it is he by whose mercy and goodness you live and have all the blessings and comforts you enjoy, and that can call them away from you at his pleasure; it is he that knows all your thoughts, words and actions, and discerns whether they are such as are decent, becoming, and suitable to his will and presence; it is he that sees you though you see him not, and this is the reason of the third commandment, whereby you are forbidden to take his name in vain.

SIR MATTHEW HALE.

Analysis. 1. An injunction to pray every morning, with a brief statement of the objects of morning prayer.

2. An injunction to pray in the evening, and the objects of evening prayer.

3. Directions as to the conduct during time of prayer, with a reason assigned.

4. Injunction to be uniform and strict in the observance of the duty, enforced by a reference to the writer's experience.

5. Injunctions as to the general state of the thoughts and feelings towards God, with the reasons assigned.

In looking at this analysis, it is obvious, that though the different paragraphs are distinct from each other, they are connected together by their general bearing on the leading design of the writer; — they all tend to enforce the constant and right performance of the duty of prayer. We are also led to notice the directness and simplicity, which are found both in the thoughts and expressions. The amplification is for the most part explanatory; so far as reasons are assigned, they are briefly stated, and are such as commend themselves to the good sense and the moral feelings of the reader. The passage extracted is an example of didactic preceptive writing.

EXERCISE II.

Daily Prayer — Evening.

LET us now consider *another* part of the day which is favorable to the duty of prayer; we mean the *evening*. This season, like the morning, is calm and quiet. Our labors are ended. The bustle of life is gone by. The distracting glare of the day has vanished. The darkness which surrounds us favors seriousness, composure, and solemnity. At night the earth fades from our sight, and nothing of creation is left to us but the starry her.vens, so vast, so magnificent. so serene. as if to guide up our thoughts above all earthly things to God and immortality.

This period should in part be given to prayer, as it furnishes a variety of devotional topics and excitements. The evening is the close of an important division of time, and is therefore a fit and nat ural season for stopping and looking back on the day. And can we ever look back on a day, which bears no witness to God, and lays no claim to our gratitude? Who is it that strengthens us for daily labor, gives us daily bread, continues our friends and common pleasures, and grants us the privilege of retiring, after the cares of the day, to a quiet and beloved home?

The review of the day will often suggest not only these ordinar benefits, but peculiar proofs of God's goodness, unlooked for successes, singular concurrences of favorable events, singular blessings sent to our friends, or new and powerful aids to our own virtue, which call for peculiar thankfulness. And shall all these benefits pass away unnoticed? Shall we retire to repose as insensible as the wearied brute? How fit and natural is it to close with pious acknowledgment that day which has been filled with divine beneficence!

But the evening is the time to review, not only our blessings, but our actions. A reflecting mind will naturally remember at this nour that another day is gone, and gone to testify of us to our Judge. How natural and useful to inquire what report it has carried to aeaven! Perhaps we have the satisfaction of looking back on a day which in its general tenor has been innocent and pure, which, aaving begun with God's praise, has been spent as in his presence which has proved the reality of our principles in temptation; and shall such a day end without gratefully acknowledging Him in whose strength we have been strong, and to whom we owe the powers and opportunities of Christian improvement?

But no day will present to us recollections of purity unmixed with sin. Conscience, if suffered to inspect faithfully and speak plainly, will recount irregular desires and defective motives, talents wasted and time misspent; and shall we let the day pass from us without penitently confessing our offences to Him who has witnessed them, and who has promised pardon to true repentance? Shall we retire to rest with a burden of unlamented and unforgiven guilt upon our consciences? Shall we leave these stains to spread over and sink into the soul?

A religious recollection of our lives is one of the chief instruments of piety. If possible, no day should end without it. If we take no account of our sins on the day on which they are committed, can we hope that they will recur to us at a more distant period, that we shall watch against them to-morrow, or that we shall gain the strength to resist them, which we will not implore?

The evening is a fit time for prayer, not only as it ends the day, but as it immediately precedes the period of repose. The hour of activity having passed, we are soon to sink into insensibility and sleep. How fit that we resign ourselves to the care of that Being who never sleeps, to whom the darkness is as the light, and whose providence is our only safety! How fit to entreat him that he would keep us to another day; or, if our bed should prove our grave, that he would give us a part in the resurrection of the just, and awake us to a purer and immortal life! Let our prayers, like the ancient sacrifices, ascend morning and evening. Let our days begin and end with God.

CHANNING.

Remarks. This passage is an example of didactic persuasive writing, but it is not sufficiently extended to bring to view the plan and other peculiarities of this class of compositions. In the remarks made upon it, the attention will be principally directed to the amplification.

1. The evening is a part of the day in itself favorable to the duty of prayer. Under this head, the amplification is of the nature of proof, being an enumeration of those circumstances favorable to devotion, which are peculiar to the close of the day. These circum

stances are matters of common observation, and do not require to be
substantiated by authorities or arguments of any kind. The bare
suggestion of them is all that is necessary and all that is attempted
  2. The evening offers several topics and excitements favorable to
devotion.

Of these topics, the review of mercies common and special received
during the day, is first mentioned. The amplification here consists
of a brief enumeration of these mercies, with appeals to our gratitude
and to our sense of what is fit and natural to man in the relation
which he sustains to his Heavenly Benefactor.

Another topic which offers itself is a review of our actions. Here
a reference is made to our condition as accountable beings, and we
are led to consider what report respecting our conduct, the day has
borne to Heaven. Wherein we have been kept from wrong and enabled to do right, we are gratefully to acknowledge Him, in whose
strength we have been strong. Wherein we have done wrong, we
are penitently to confess our sins and to seek forgiveness. Here
also the amplification consists of an appeal to our emotions of grati
tude, to our conscience, and to our self-interest. In connection with
the last consideration, the writer is led to speak of a religious recollection of our lives as an instrument of piety.

Another distinct topic is now mentioned. The evening precedes
the period of repose. This lays the foundation of an appeal to what
is fit — to what our own safety and welfare require. We are to sink
into a state of insensibility and sleep. Shall we not commit our-
se.ves to the care of that Being, who never slumbers nor sleeps ?

EXERCISE III.

Defence of Literary Studies in Men of Business.

AMONG the cautions which prudence and worldly wisdom inculcate
on the young, or at least among those sober truths which experience
often pretends to have acquired, is that danger which is said to result
from the pursuit of letters and of science, in men destined for the labors of business for the active exertions of professional life. The
abstraction of learning, the speculations of science, and the visionary
excursions of fancy, are fatal, it is said, to the steady pursuit of com

mon objects, to the habits of plodding industry which ordinary busi
ness demands. The fineness of mind which is created or increased
by the study of letters, or the admiration of the arts, is supposed to
incapacitate a man for the drudgery by which professional eminence
is gained; as a nicely tempered edge applied to a coarse and rugged
material is unable to perform what a more common instrument
would have successfully achieved. A young man destined for law
or commerce is advised to look only into his folio of precedents, or
his method of book-keeping; and dulness is pointed to his homage,
as that benevolent goddess, under whose protection the honors of
station and the blessings of opulence are to be attained; while
learning and genius are proscribed as leading their votaries to bar
ren indigence and merited neglect.

In doubting the truth of these assertions, I think I shall not entertain any hurtful degree of skepticism, because the general current
of opinion seems of late years to have set too strongly in the contrary
direction; and one may endeavor to prop the falling cause of literature without being accused of blamable or dangerous partiality.

In the examples which memory and experience produce of idleness, of dissipation, and of poverty, brought on by indulgence of
literary or poetical enthusiasm, the evidence must necessarily be on
one side of the question only. Of the few whom learning or genius
has led astray, the ill success or the ruin is marked by the celebrity
of the sufferer. Of the many who have been as dull as they were
profligate, and as ignorant as they were poor, the fate is unknown
from the insignificance of those by whom it was endured. If we
may reason *a priori* on the matter, the chance, I think, should be on
the side of literature.

In young minds of any vivacity, there is a natural aversion to the
drudgery of business, which is seldom overcome, till the efferves-
cence of youth is allayed by the progress of time and habit, or till
that very warmth is enlisted on the side of their profession, by the
opening prospects of ambition or emolument. From this tyranny,
as youth conceives it, of attention and of labor, relief is commonly
sought from some favorite avocation or amusement, for which a
young man either finds or steals a portion of his time, either patiently
plods through his task, in expectation of its approach, or anticipates
its arrival by deserting his work before the legal period for amuse
ment is arrived . It may fairly be questioned, whether the most innocent of those amusements, is either so honorable or so safe as the

avocation of learning or of science. Of minds uninformed and gross, whom youthful spirits agitate, but fancy and feeling have no power to impel, the amusement will generally be either boisterous or effeminate, will either dissipate their attention or weaken their force. The employment of a young man's vacant hours is often too little attended to by those rigid masters, who exact the most scrupulous observance of the periods destined for business. The waste of time is undoubtedly a very calculable loss; but the waste or the depravation of mind is a loss of much higher denomination. The votary of study, or the enthusiast of fancy, may incur the first, but the latter will be suffered chiefly by him whom ignorance or want of imagination has left to the grossness of mere sensual enjoyments.

In this, as in other respects, the love of letters is friendly to sober manners and virtuous conduct, which in every profession is the road to success and to respect. Without adopting the common-place reflections against some particular departments, it must be allowed that in mere men of business there is a certain professional rule of right, which is not always honorable, and though meant to be selfish, very seldom profits. A superior education generally corrects this, by opening the mind to different motives of action, to the feelings of delicacy, the sense of honor, and a contempt of wealth, when earned by a desertion of those principles.

To the improvement of our faculties as well as of our principles, the love of letters appears to be favorable. Letters require a certain sort of application, though of a kind perhaps very different from that which business would recommend. Granting that they are unprofitable in themselves, as that word is used in the language of the world, yet, as developing the powers of thought and reflection, they may be an amusement of some use, as those sports of children in which numbers are used to familiarize them to the elements of arithmetic. They give room for the exercise of that discernment, that comparison of objects, that distinction of causes which is to increase the skill of the physician, to guide the speculations of the merchant, and to prompt the arguments of the lawyer; and though some professions employ but very few faculties of the mind, yet there is scarce any branch of business in which a man who can think will not excel him who can only labor. We shall accordingly find, n many departments where learned information seemed of all qualties the least necessary, that those who possessed it in a degree above their fellows, have found, from that very circumstance, the road to eminence and wealth.

But I must often repeat, that wealth does not necessarily create happiness, nor confer dignity; a truth which it may be thought declamation to insist on, which the present time seems particularly to require being told.

The love of letters is connected with an independence and delicacy of mind, which is a great preservative against that servile homage which abject men pay to fortune; and there is a certain classical pride, which from the society of Socrates and Plato, Cicero and Atticus, looks down with an honest disdain on the wealth-blown insects of modern times, neither enlightened by knowledge nor ennobled by virtue.

In the possession, indeed, of what he has attained, in that rest and retirement from his labors, with the hopes of which his fatigues were lightened and his cares were smoothed, the mere man of business frequently undergoes suffering, instead of finding enjoyment. To be busy as one ought is an easy art; but to know how to be idle is a very superior accomplishment. This difficulty is much increased with persons to whom the habit of employment has made some active exertion necessary; who cannot sleep contented in the torpor of indolence, or amuse themselves with those lighter trifles in which he, who inherited idleness as he did fortune from his ancestors, has been accustomed to find amusement. The miseries and misfortunes of the " retired pleasures " of men of business have been frequently matter of speculation to the moralist, and of ridicule to the wit. But he who has mixed general knowledge with professional skill, and literary amusements with professional labor, will have some stock wherewith to support him in idleness, some spring for his mind when unbent from business, some employment for those hours which retirement or solitude has left vacant and unoccupied. Independence in the use of one's time is not the least valuable species of freedom. This liberty the man of letters enjoys; while the ignorant and the illiterate often retire from the thraldom of business only to become the slaves of languor, intemperance or vice.

But the situation in which the advantages of that endowment of mind, which letters bestow, are chiefly conspicuous, is old age, when a man's society is necessarily circumscribed, and his powers of active enjoyment are unavoidably diminished. Unfit for the bustle of affairs, and the amusements of his youth, an old man, if he has no

source of mental exertion or employment, often settles into the
gloom of melancholy and peevishness, or petrifies his feelings by
habitual intoxication. From an old man whose gratifications were
solely derived from those sensual appetites which time has blunted,
or from those trivial amusements of which youth only can share,
age has cut off almost every source of enjoyment. But to him who
has stored his mind with the information, and can still employ it in
the amusement of letters, this blank of life is admirably filled up.
He acts, he thinks, and he feels with that literary world whose
society he can at all times enjoy. There is perhaps no state more
capable of comfort to ourselves, or more attractive of veneration from
others, than that which such an old age affords; it is then the twi-
light of the passions, when they are mitigated but not extinguished
and spread their gentle influence over the evening of our day, in
alliance with reason and in amity with virtue.　　　MACKENZIE.

Remarks and Analysis. In examining the preceding examples of
Argumentative writing, our principal object of attention will be the
plan or management of the subject.

The Introduction consists of an indirect statement of the question
to be agitated. We are told how those have thought and reasoned
whose opinions are opposed to the opinions of the writer. This
statement is distinctly, and fairly, and skilfully made. Our literary
taste is gratified by the illustrations and ornaments of language which
are found. Our curiosity is roused, and we are ready to enter with
interest on the proposed investigation. It should be noticed, that
there is no formal statement of the proposition which is to be supported, but that it is clearly and happily implied in the introductory
paragraphs.

After the introduction, follows the refutation of an objection.
That this is the proper place for considering the objection stated, is
evident, since, had it been unnoticed, or its refutation deferred to
the close of the Essay, the minds of readers might have been pre-
vented by its influence from giving due weight to the arguments adduced. There are two modes of refuting objections; one, by deny-
ing the premises from which a conclusion is drawn — the other, by
showing that the conclusion does not truly follow from the premises.

The objection here considered is — that facts establish the opposite of the opinion advanced by the writer — of course, the opinion
can have no good foundation. To refute the objection, the premise

is denied. Facts are otherwise, says the writer, and a satisfactory reason is assigned, why a different impression as to the bearing of facts on the case has prevailed. Having assigned this reason, the writer leaves the point at issue as to facts in the case, to be determined by the observation and the good sense of his readers.

Having thus introduced his subject to our attention, stating by implication the proposition to be examined, and having removed an objection, which presented itself at the threshold, the writer now enters on the direct examination of his subject.

The following proposition is supported. Men of business may advantageously devote a portion of their time to literary pursuits.

1st Argument. Young men of business should engage in literary studies, since in them is found a pleasant relaxation and security against nurtful indulgences.

2d Argument. Young men of business should engage in literary studies, because in this way they acquire a refinement and exaltation of mind which raises them above grovelling and selfish principles and conduct.

3d Argument. Young men of business should engage in literary studies, because the cultivation of letters is favorable to the improvement of the mind.

4th Argument. A man of business should engage in literary pursuits, because in this way he acquires an independence of feeling which prepares him to enjoy his wealth. Without cultivation of mind and a literary taste, the retirement of the man of wealth is wearisome and disgusting to him.

5th Argument. Men of business should cultivate letters that they may find in them grateful employment for old age.

This is the plan. Upon examination, we find that it conforms to the directions given in the text-book. The several heads are distinct from each other. They have a similar bearing on the leading proposition to be supported, and taken together, they give a unity to the subject.

The kind of argument here used, is the argument from cause to effect. Different reasons are stated, which account for and support the assertion that is made, and which forms the leading proposition.

Let us now take a nearer view of these different arguments, and see in what way they are supported. Under the first argument, the reasoning is as follows: 1. Young men in business will have relax ation and amusement: 2. Unless those of a salutary kind are provided, they will fall into such as are hurtful. Hence the importance of their being directed to literary pursuits, which may interest and benefit them. It may be asked, On what authority do these assertions of the writer rest? How do we know that young men thus will have relaxation and amusement? and that unless those of a salutary kind are provided, they will fall into such as are hurtful? I answer, that these assertions rest on the common observation and experience of men. Hence the writer takes it for granted that those whom he addresses will yield their assent to his premises, and consequently, if his conclusion is correctly drawn, will acknowledge the reality of his argument.

In analyzing the second argument, the inquiry arises, How is it known that literary studies give refinement and elevation to the mind, raising it above low and grovelling pursuits? Here the appeal is to consciousness. Men, who have thus cultivated their intellec tual powers are conscious, when they look in upon the operations of their own minds, that these salutary influences have been exerted upon them.

The third argument, which asserts that the love of letters is favorable to the cultivation of the intellectual powers, rests principally upon experience and observation. There is also found an illustration, which is of an analogical kind. It is where the writer refers to those sports of children, which familiarize them with the elements of arithmetic. This argument from analogy may be looked upon as an appeal to the common sense of the readers.

The remaining arguments rest in like manner on appeals to experience, observation, common sense and consciousness, and it is not necessary to analyze them. The student, in the analysis which has been made, has had an opportunity of seeing some of the grounds on which assertions and reasonings are founded.

EXERCISE IV.

Fortitude of the Indian Character

A PARTY of the Seneca Indians came to war against the Katawbas bitter enemies to each other. In the woods the former discovered a sprightly warrior belonging to the latter, hunting in their usual light dress: on his perceiving them, he sprang off for a hollow rock four or five miles distant, as they intercepted him from running homeward. He was so extremely swift and skilful with the gun, as to kill seven of them in the running fight before they were able to surround and take him. They carried him to their country in sad triumph; but though he had filled them with uncommon grief and shame for the loss of so many of their kindred, yet the love of martial virtue induced them to treat him, during their long journey, with a great deal more civility than if he had acted the part of a coward.

The women and children, when they met him at their severa' towns, beat him and whipped him in as severe a manner as the occasion required, according to their law of justice; and at last he was formally condemned to die by the fiery torture. It might reasonably be imagined, that what he had for some time gone through, by being fed with a scanty hand, a tedious march, lying at night on the bare ground, exposed to the changes of the weather, with his arms and legs extended in a pair of rough stocks, and suffering such punishment on his entering into their hostile towns, as a prelude to those sharper torments to which he was destined, would have so impaired his health, and affected his imagination, as to have sent him to his long sleep, out of the way of any more sufferings.

Probably this would have been the case with the major part of white people under similar circumstances; but I never knew this with any of the Indians; and this cool-headed, brave warrior, did not deviate from their rough lessons of martial virtue, but. acted his part so well as to surprise and sorely vex his numerous enemies:— for when they were taking him unpinioned, in their wild parade, to the place of torture, which lay near the river, he suddenly dashed down those who stood in his way, sprung off, and plunged into the water, swimming underneath like an otter, only rising to take breath, till he reached the opposite shore.

He ascended the steep bank, but though he had good reason to be in a hurry, as many of the enemy were in the water, and others running, like blood-hounds, in pursuit of him, and the bullets flying around him from the time he took to the river, yet his heart did not allow him to leave them abruptly. He chose to take leave in a formal manner, in return for the extraordinary favors they had done and intended to do him. So stopping a moment, he bid them defiance, in the genuine style of Indian gallantry, he put up the shrill warwhoop, as his last salute, till some more convenient opportunity offered, and darted off in the manner of a beast broke loose from its torturing enemies.

He continued his speed, so as to run, by about midnight of the same day, as far as his eager pursuers were two days in reaching. There he rested, till he happily discovered five of those Indians who had pursued him:—he lay hid a little way off their camp, till they were sound asleep. Every circumstance of his situation occurred to him and inspired him with heroism. He was naked, torn, and hungry, and his enraged enemies were come up with him; but there was now every thing to relieve his wants, and a fair opportunity to save his life, and get great honor and sweet revenge by cutting them off.—Resolution, a convenient spot, and sudden surprise, would effect the main object of all his wishes and hopes.

He accordingly crept, took one of their tomahawks, and killed them all on the spot—clothed himself, and took a choice gun, and as much ammunition and provision as he could well carry in a running march. He set off afresh with a light heart, and did not sleep for several successive nights, except when he reclined as usual, a little before day, with his back to a tree.

As it were by instinct, when he found he was free from the pursuing enemy, he made directly to the very place where he had been taken prisoner and doomed to the fiery torture, after having killed seven of his enemies. The bodies of these he dug up, burnt them to ashes, and went home in safety with singular triumph. Other pursuing enemies came, on the evening of the second day, to the camp of their dead people, when the sight gave them a greater shock than they ever had known before. In their chilled war council they concluded that as he had done such surprising things in his

defence before he was captivated, and even after that, in his naked
condition, he must surely be an enemy wizard; and that, as he was
now well armed, he would destroy them all should they continue the
pursuit : — they therefore very prudently returned home.

ADAIR.

Remarks. In analyzing this example of narrative writing, our attention is first to be directed to the leading purpose of the writer.
This evidently is to tell us of the successful escape of a young Indian
warrior from his enemies. Different facts are mentioned connected
with this leading fact, — such are the circumstances of his captivity,
of his being conducted in triumph through the towns and villages of
his enemies, of his revenge on those from whom he had suffered ills,
and of his triumphant return to his own tribe. These several facts
are stated in the order of their occurrence, and dwelt upon according
to their relative importance. Another purpose of the writer, which
is incidentally and skilfully effected, is the mention and illustration
of several traits of Indian character. Such are fortitude, manifested
in the patient endurance of extreme hardships and sufferings, — respect for martial virtue, rising at last to a superstitious reverence, -
the strong thirst for revenge, gratified at an imminent risk and
under the most perilous circumstances, and further, that cunning
and duplicity, by which the escape and flight were effected. Every
observing reader will also notice the deep interest, with which the
story is read, increasing with the progress of the narrative, and evidently to be ascribed to the natural connexion of the events narrated
We learn then from this example, that the plan, in narrative writing
is simply the statement of events in the order of their occurrence,
and further, that the amplification is the mention, with varying degrees of minuteness in their statement, of the different circumstances
connected with these events, accompanied by incidental remarks and
reflections

EXERCISE V

The first and last Dinner.

TWELVE friends, much about the same age, and fixed by their pursuits, their family connexions, and other local interests, as permanent inhabitants of the metropolis, agreed one day, when they were drinking wine at the Star and Garter at Richmond, to institute an annual dinner among themselves, under the following regulations:—That they should dine alternately at each other's houses on the *first* and *last* day of the year; and the *first* bottle of wine uncorked at the *first* dinner should be recorked and put away, to be drunk by him who should be the last of their number, that they should never admit a new member; that, when one died, eleven should meet, and when another died, ten should meet, and so on; and when only one remained, he should, on these two days, dine by himself, and sit the usual hours at his solitary table; but the first time he had so dined, lest it should be the only one, he should then uncork the *first* bottle, and in the *first* glass, drink to the memory of all who were gone.

Some thirty years had now glided away, and only ten remained, but the stealing hand of time had written sundry changes in most legible characters. Raven locks had become grizzled; two or three heads had not as many locks as may be reckoned in a walk of half a mile along the Regent's Canal—one was actually covered with a brown wig—the crow's feet were visible in the corner of the eye—good old port and warm Madeira carried it against hock, claret, red burgundy, and champagne—stews, hashes, and ragouts, grew into favor—crusts were rarely called for to relish the cheese after dinner—conversation was less boisterous, and it turned chiefly upon politics and the state of the funds, or the value of landed property—apologies were made for coming in thick shoes and warm stockings—the doors and windows were more carefully provided with list and sand-bags—the fire is in more request—and a quiet game of whist filled up the hours that were wont to be devoted to drinking, singing, and riotous merriment. Two rubbers, a cup of coffee, and at home by eleven o'clock, was the usual cry, when the fifth or sixth

glass had gone round after the removal of the cloth. At parting, too,
there was now a long ceremony in the hall, buttoning up grea:
coats, tying on woollen comforters, fixing silk handkerchiefs ovei
the mouth and up to the ears, and grasping sturdy walking-canes to
support unsteady feet.

Their fiftieth anniversary came, and death had indeed been busy
Four little old men, of withered appearance and decrepit walk, witr
cracked voices and dim, rayless eyes, sat down by the mercy of heav
en, (as they tremulously declared,) to celebrate, for the fiftieth time,
the first day of the year, to observe the frolic compact, which half
a century before, they had entered into at the Star and Garter at
Richmond. Eight were in their graves! The four that remained
stood upon its confines. Yet they chirped cheerily over their glass,
though they could scarcely carry it to their lips, if more than half
full; and cracked their jokes, though they articulated their words
with difficulty, and heard each other with still greater difficulty.
They mumbled, they chattered, they laughed, (if a sort of strangled
wheezing might be called a laugh,) and as the wine sent their icy
blood in warmer pulses through their veins, they talked of their
past as if it were but a yesterday that had slipped by them, and of
their future as if it were but a busy century that lay before them.

At length came the LAST dinner; and the survivor of the twelve
upon whose head four score and ten winters had showered their snow,
ate his solitary meal. It so chanced that it was in his house, and at
his table, they celebrated the first. In his cellar, too, had remained
for eight and forty years, the bottle they had then uncorked, recorked,
and which he was that day to uncork again. It stood beside him
With a feeble and reluctant grasp he took the " frail memorial "
of a youthful vow, and for a moment memory was faithful to her
office. She threw open the long vista of buried years; and his heart
travelled through them all: Their lusty and blithesome spring, —
their bright and fervid summer, — their ripe and temperate autumn
— their chill, but not too frozen winter. He saw, as in a mirror,
how one by one the laughing companions of that merry hour, at
Richmond, had dropped into eternity. He felt the loneliness of his
condition, (for he had eschewed marriage, and in the veins of no
living creature ran a drop of blood whose source was in his own;)
and as he drained the glass which he had filled, " to the memory of
those who were gor.   the tears slowly trickled down the deep fur
rows of his aged face.

He has thus fulfilled one part of his vow, and he prepared himself to discharge the other by sitting the usual number of hours at his desolate table. With a heavy heart he resigned himself to the gloom of his own thoughts—a lethargic sleep stole over him—his head fell upon his bosom—confused images crowded 'nto his mind—he babbled to himself—was silent—and when his servant entered the room alarmed by a noise which he heard, ne found his master stretched upon the carpet at the foot of an easy chair, out of which he had slipped in an apoplectic fit. He never spoke again, nor once opened his eyes, though the vital spark was not extinct till the fol. lowing day. And this was the LAST DINNER.

This example of descriptive writing is justly admired. The only point to which it is designed to direct the attention of the student, is the selection of circumstances. Let any one, after reading the extracts, especially the second and third paragraphs, notice with what distinctness and fulness the scene described is brought before his view—how, as it were, he is placed in the midst of the little group, and sees them, and hears them, and is made acquainted with their peculiarities. This, which in another part of this work is called truth to nature, is evidently effected by the skilful selection and arrangement of circumstances, and constitutes the amplification of descriptive writing. In some instances, especially where it is desirable that the description should be bold and striking, the enumeration of circumstances is less full and minute. But on this point, good sense and good taste must decide.

EXERCISES ON CHAPTER III.

In this exercise are found examples of the various ornaments of style which are brought to view in the chapter on Literary Taste. In examining them the student should institute the following inquiries :—

1 How is the example to be classed?

2 Viewing it in itself, and in its connection, is it to be approved or condemned?

In answering this second inquiry, the principles on which the attempt to excite the emotions of taste is founded, should be fully brought to view.

Example 1. President Kirkland, after mentioning the excitement which attended the public efforts of the late Fisher Ames as a speaker, says :—

"This excitement continued when the cause had ceased to operate. After debate his mind was agitated, like the ocean after a storm, and his nerves were like the shrouds of a ship torn by the tempest."

Example 2. The attentions of a respectful and affectionate son to his mother are thus described by an anonymous writer :—

"They are the native courtesies of a feeling mind, showing themselves amidst stern virtues and masculine energies, like gleams of light on points of rocks."

Example 3. Say, in his Political Economy, when describing the condition of the laborer in a manufacturing establishment, whose only occupation has been to fabricate a part of some article — the head of a pin perhaps — uses the following expression :—

"He is, when separated from his fellow-laborers, a mere adjective, without individual capacity or substantive importance."

Example 4. "Prayer must be animated. The arrow that would pierce the clouds, must part from the bent bow and the strained arm."

Example 5. The following passage is from W. Irving :—

"I recollect hearing a traveller, of poetical temperament, expressing the kind of horror which he felt in beholding, on the banks of the Missouri, an oak of prodigious size, which had been in a manner overpowered by an enormous wild grape-vine. The vine had clasped its huge folds round the trunk, and from thence had wound about every branch and twig, until the mighty tree had withered in its embrace. It seemed like Laocoon struggling ineffectually in the hideous coils of the monster Python. It was the lion of trees perishing in the embraces of a vegetable Boa."

Example 6 Webster, in his address to General La Fayette, has the following passage :—

" Sir, we have become reluctant to grant monuments and eulogies —our highest and last honors—further. We would gladly hold them yet back from the little remnant of that immortal band. *Serus in cælum redeas.*"

Example 7. " The mind is the great lever of all things."

Example 8. The following passage is addressed to time :—

" Go, bind thine ivy o'er the oak,
And spread thy rich embroidered cloak
  Around his trunk the while;
Or deck with moss the abbey wall,
And paint grotesque the Gothic hall,
And sculpture, with thy chisel small,
  The monumental pile.

Example 9 " Thus she (the vessel) kept on, away up the river, lessening and lessening in the evening sunshine, until she faded from sight, like a little white cloud melting away in the summer sky."

Example 10. Ferguson, the Scotch poet, was in poverty and distress. A friend sent relief, but it did not arrive till after his death. Of this generous act it is said,

" It fell a sunbeam on the blasted blossom."

Example 11. " The husbandman sees all his fields and gardens covered with the beauteous creations of his own industry ; and sees, like God, that all his works are good "

Example 12. "Literary immortality is a mere temporary rumor a local sound. Like the tone of a bell, it fills the ear for a moment—lingering transiently in echo—and then passing away, like a thing that was not!"

Example 13. Dr. Appleton thus closes an address to a Peace Society :—

"This society, and others formed for the same object, both in this country and in Europe, may now be compared to light clouds, far distant from each other, and no 'bigger than a man's hand.' It is for divine wisdom to determine, whether these clouds shall be speedily attenuated and dissolved; or whether they shall be thickened and enlarged, and uniting with others, yet to be formed in the intermediate spaces, shall cover all the heavens, and shall distil the dew of heaven; 'the dew that descended on the mountains of Zion.'"

Example 14. The following is from Canning's speech at Portsmouth, England :—

"Our present repose is no more proof of inability to act, than the state of inertness and inactivity, in which I have seen those mighty masses, that float in the waters above your town, is a proof that they are devoid of strength and incapable of being fitted for action. You well know how soon one of these stupendous masses, now reposing on their shadows with perfect stillness—how soon, upon any call of patriotism or of necessity, it would assume the likeness of an animated thing, instinct with life and motion; how soon it would ruffle, as it were, its swelling plumage; how quickly it would put forth all its beauty and bravery; collect its scattered elements of strength, and awaken its dormant thunders. Such is one of those magnificent machines, when springing from inaction into a display of its might—such is England herself; while apparently passive and motionless, she silently concentrates the power to be put forth on adequate occasion."

Example 15. The following is from the inaugural address of Professor Frisbie :—

" Miss Edgeworth has stretched forth a powerful hand to the impotent in virtue; and had she added, with the apostle, in the name of Jesus of Nazareth, we should almost have expected miracles from its touch."

Example 16. The same writer, describing the influence of the poems of Byron, says :—

" They are the scenes of a Summer evening, where all is tender, and beautiful, and grand ; but the damps of disease descend with the dews of Heaven, and the pestilent vapors of night are breathed in with the fragrance and balm, and the delicate and fair are the surest victims of the exposure."

Example 17.   " O, 'tis
A goodly night! the cloudy wind, which blew
From the Levant, hath crept into his cave,
And the broad moon hath brightened."

Example 18.   In a poem of Haley's, the following lines are adressed to Mr. Gibbon :—

" Humility herself, divinely mild,
Sublime Religion's meek and modest child,
Like the dumb son of Crœsus in the strife,
When force assailed his father's sacred life
Breaks silence, and with filial duty warm,
Bids thee revere her parent's hallowed form."

Example 19.   The following is from Kennilworth :—

" The mind of England's Elizabeth was like one of those ancien Druidical monuments, called Rocking-stones.   The finger of Cupid, boy as he is painted, could put her feelings in motion, but the power of Hercules could not have destroyed their equilibrium."

Example 20.   Another from the same author :- -

" The language of Scripture gave to Macbriar's exhortation a rich and solemn effect, like that which is produced by the beams of the
21*

sun, streaming through the storied representation of saints and martyrs on the Gothic window of some ancient cathedral."

Example 21. The following is from Percival :—

> "The quiet sea,
> That, like a giant resting from his toil,
> Sleeps in the morning sun."

Example 22. "Yon row of visionary pines,
> By twilight glimpse discovered : mark ! how they flee
> From the fierce sea blast, all their tresses wild
> Streaming before them !"

Example 23. The following is from Smollet's history :—

"The bill underwent a great variety of alterations and amendments which were not effected without violent contests. At length, however, it was floated through both houses on the tide of a great majority and steered into the safe harbor of royal approbation."

Example 24. "We are now advancing from the starlight of circumstance to the daylight of discovery; the sun of certainty is melting the darkness, and we are arrived at facts admitted by both parties.

EXERCISE ON CHAPTER IV.

The examples in this exercise are designed to illustrate the rules and cautions, which are found in the selections on Verbal Criticism, and on Sentences.

1. You stand to him in the relation of a son : of consequence you should obey him.
2. He came toward me, and immediately fell backward.
    His sermon was an extempore performance.
    It is exceeding dear, and scarce to be obtained.

5   He came afterward and apologized.

6.   He dare not do it at present, and he need not.

7.   Whether he will or no, I care not.

8.   He is vindictive in his disposition.

9.   These conditions were accepted of by the conquerers.

10.   I have followed the habit of rising early in the morning till it
/as become a custom with me.

11.   You have not money responsible to your views.

12.   They hold their own fortunes synonymous with those of their
country.

13.   Though some men reach the regions of wisdom by this path, it
is not the most patent route.

14.   He succeeded by dint of application, though he is not now a
whit better.

15.   He was engaged in the duties of his avocation.

16.   It was impossible not to suspect the veracity of his story.

17.   The conscience of approving one's self a benefactor to mankind
is the best recompense for being so.

18.   The servant must have an undeniable character.

19.   The calamities of children are due to the negligence ot parents.

20.   There soon appeared very apparent reasons for his partiality

21.   No man had ever less friends and more enemies.

22.   The reason will be accounted for hereafter.

23.   They wrecked their vengeance on all concerned.

24.   I expect he was the man you saw.

25.   The church was pewed after the old fashion.

26.   I will have mercy, and not sacrifice.

27.   We do those things frequently, that we repent of afterwards.

28.   It would appear, that for the cause of liberty, though paradoxical, neither hopes nor fears can be too sanguine.

29.   A clergyman is by the militia act exempted from both serving
and contributing.

30.   How few there are at the present day, who are willing to
make any sacrifice of their feelings or property for the public good
When by so doing they might ultimately benefit themselves and
society

31.   I have settled the meaning of those pleasures of imagination,
which are the subject of my present undertaking, by way of introduction, in this paper.

32   As it is necessary to have the head clear as well as the com-

plexion, to be perfect in this part of learning. I rarely mingle with the men, but frequently the tea-tables of the ladies.

33.　Many act so directly contrary to this method, that from a habit of saving time and paper, which they acquired at the university, they write in so diminutive a manner, that they can hardly read what they have written.

34.　Dr. Prideaux used to relate, that when he brought the copy of "Connexion of the Old and New Testaments" to the bookseller, he told him it was a dry subject, and the printing could not be safely ventured upon unless he could enliven the work with a little humor.

From the following example, the student may learn in what manner long and involved sentences may be broken up and made more plain, and also that the same ideas may be expressed in different forms, as the occasion may require.

"Since it is better to enter on the unaccustomed scenes of the world with that sorrow and dejection, which will make us heedful to our ways, rather than with an elation and giddiness which is careless of the present, and looks not to that which is to come, it is well that the breaking up of the attachments of our youth should for a time give us pain, and that thus we should be warned to prepare ourselves for the pursuits of life in such a manner, that we may obtain to ourselves other sources of happiness, which shall recompense us in a degree for those which are lost."

This sentence is long and involved. It may be improved by breaking it up into distinct sentences, and still further by changing the arrangement of its different clauses. I shall first divide it into several sentences.

"It is better for us to enter on the unaccustomed scenes of the world with that sorrow and dejection, which will make us heedful to our ways, rather than with an elation and giddiness, which is careless of the present, and looks not at that which is to come. Hence it is well, perhaps, that we are subjected to that pain, which attends the breaking up of the attachments of youth. We are thus warned to prepare ourselves for the pursuits of life. We are thus taught to obtain for ourselves other sources of happiness, which may recompense us for those which are lost."

The sentence may assume another form by changing the order of its members.

"It is well perhaps that the breaking up of the attachments of youth should for a time give us pain. We then enter on the unaccustomed scenes of the world with that sorrow and dejection, which will make us heedful to our ways, instead of an elation and giddiness, which is careless of the present, and looks not at that which is to come. We are warned to prepare ourselves for the pursuits of life in such a manner, as that we may obtain to ourselves other sources of happiness, which shall recompense us in a degree for those which are lost."

The sentence may assume another form, should the occasion and nature of the performance, in which it is found, require it.

"The breaking up of the attachments of youth gives us pain. This is well. We are warned to prepare ourselves for the pursuits of life. We are incited to obtain for ourselves other and different sources of happiness. Who would enter on the unaccustomed scenes of life with an elation and giddiness careless of the present and of the future? Better is it that we be familiar with sorrow and dejection, and thus take heed to our ways."

EXERCISE ON CHAPTER V.

The examples in this Exercise are particularly designed to lead the student to notice the characteristic traits of different styles; and have been selected with reference to what is said on this subject in the chapter on style. They are arranged miscellaneously, and without naming the authors, that the examination may call into exercise he knowledge and skill of the student

Example 1. "From him also was derived the wonderful workmanship of our fra nes—the eye, in whose orb of beauty is pencilled the whole orbs of heaven and of earth, for the mind to peruse and know, and possess and rejoice over, even as if the whole universe were her own—the ear, in whose vocal chamber are entertained harmonious numbers, the melody of rejoicing nature, the welcomes and the saluta-tions of friends, the whisperings of love, the voices of parents and of children, with all the sweetness and the power that dwell upon the tongue of man. His also is the gift of the beating heart, flooding all the hidden recesses of the human frame with the tide of life— his the cunning of the hand, whose workmanship turns rude and raw materials to such pleasant forms and wholesome uses—his the whole vital frame of man, which is a world of wonders within itself, a world of bounty, and, if rightly used, a world of the finest enjoyments.— His also are the mysteries of the soul within—the judgment, which weighs in a balance all contending thoughts, extracting order from confusion; the memory, recorder of the soul, in whose books are chronicled the accidents of the changing world, and the fluctuating moods cf the mind itself; fancy, the eye of the soul, which scales the heavens and circles round the verge and circuits of all possible existence ; hope, the purveyor of happiness, which peoples the hidden future with brighter forms and happier accidents than ever possessed the present, offering to the soul the foretaste of every joy, whose full bosom can cherish a thousand objects without being impoverished, but rather replenished, a storehouse inexhaustible towards the brotherhood and sisterhood of this earth, as the storehouse of God is inexhaustible to the universal world ; and conscience, the arbitrator of the soul, and the touchstone of the evil and the good, whose voice within our breast is the echo of the voice of God.

"These, all these, whose varied action and movement constitute the maze of thought, the mystery of life, the continuous chain of being— God hath given us to know that we hold of his hand, ana during his pleasure, and out of the fulness of his care."

Example 2. "One great cause of our inse sibility to the goodness of the Creator is the very *extensiveness* of is bounty. We prize but little what we share only in common with the rest, or with the gen erality of our species. When we hear of blessings, we think forthwith of successes, of prosperous fortunes, of honors, riches, preferments, i. e. of those advantages and superiorities over others, which we hap-pen either to possess, or to be in pursuit of, or to covet. The com-mon benefits of our nature entirely escape us. Yet these are the great things. These constitute, what most properly ought to be accounted blessings of Providence what alone, if we might so speak, are worthy of its care. Nightly rest and daily bread, the ordinary use of our limbs, and senses, and understandings, are gifts which admit of no comparison with any other. Yet, because almost every man we meet with, possesses these, we leave them out of our enumeration. They raise no sentiment, they move no gratitude: Now, herein is our judgment perverted by our selfishness. A blessing ought in truth to be the *more* satisfactory, the bounty at least of the donor is rendered more conspicuous, by its very diffusion, its commonness, by its falling to the lot, and forming the happiness of the great bulk and body of our species, as well as of ourselves. Nay, even when we do not possess it, ought to be matter of thankfulness, that others do. But we have a different way of thinking. We court distinction. That I don't quarrel with: but we can *see* nothing but what has distinction to recommend it. This necessarily contracts our view of the Creator's beneficence within a narrow compass; and most unjustly. It is in those things which are so common as to be no distinctions, that the amplitude of the divine benignity is perceived."

Example 3. " When public bodies are to be addressed on momentous occasions, when great interests are at stake, and strong passions excited, nothing is valuable in speech, further than it is connected with high intellectual and moral endowments. Clearness, force, and earnestness, are the qualities which produce conviction. True eloquence, indeed, does not consist in speech. It cannot be brought from far. Labor and learning may toil for it, but they will toil in vain. Words and phrases may be marshalled in every way, but they cannot compass it. It must exist in the man, in the subject, and in the occasion. Affected passion, intense expression, the pomp of declamation, all may aspire after it—they cannot reach it. It comes, if it comes at all, like the outbreaking of a fountain from the earth, or the bursting forth of volcanic fires, with spontaneous, original, native force. The graces taught in schools, the costly ornaments, and studied contrivances of speech, shock and disgust men, when their own lives, and the fate of their wives, their children, and their country, hang on the decision of an hour. Then, words have lost their power, rhetoric is vain, and all elaborate oratory contemptible Even genius itself then feels rebuked and subdued, as in the presence of higher qualities Then, patriotism is eloquent; then, self devotion is eloquent. The clear conception, outrunning the deduction of logic, the high purpose, the firm resolve, the dauntless spirit, speaking on the tongue, beaming from the eye, informing every feature, and urging the whole man onward, right onward to his object—this, this is eloquence; or rather it is something greater and higher than all eloquence,—it is action, noble, sublime, and godlike action."

Example 4. "Conceive a man to be standing on the margin of this green world; and that, when he looked towards it, he saw abundance smiling upon every field, and all the blessings which earth can afford scattered in profusion throughout every family, and the light of the sun sweetly resting upon all the pleasant habitations, and the joys of human companionship brightening many a happy circle of society,— conceive this to be the general character of the scene upon one side of the contemplation; and that on the other, beyond the verge of the goodly planet on which he was situated, he could descry nothing but a dark and fathomless unknown.
"Think you that he would bid a voluntary adieu to all the brightness and all the beauty that were laid before him upon earth, and commit himself to the frightful solitude away from it? Would he leave its peopled dwelling-places, and become a solitary wanderer through the fields of nonentity? If space offered him nothing but a wilderness, would he for it abandon the homebred scenes of life and cheerfulness that lay so near, and exerted such a power of urgency to detain him? Would he not cling to the regions of sense, and of life, and of society;—and shrinking away from the desolation that was beyond it, would he not be glad to keep his firm footing on the territory of this world, and to take shelter under the silver canopy that was stretched over it?
"But if, during the time of his contemplation, some happy island of the blessed floated by; and there had burst upon his senses the light of its surpassing glories, and its sounds of sweeter melody; and he clearly saw, that there, a purer beauty rested upon every field, and a more heartfelt joy spread itself upon all the families; and he could discern there a peace, and a piety, and a benevolence, which put a moral gladness into every bosom, and united the whole society in a rejoicing sympathy with each other, and with the beneficent Father of them all;—could he further see that pain and mortality were there unknown; above all, that signals of welcome were hung out, and an avenue of communication was made for him;—perceive you not that what was before the wilderness, would become the land of invitation; and that now the world would be the wilderness? What appeopled space could not do, can be done by space teeming with

...atific scenes, and beatific society. And let the existing tendencies of the heart be what they may to the scene that is near and visibly around us, still, if another stood revealed to the prospect of man, either through the channel of faith, or through the channel of his senses,— then, without violence done to the constitution of his moral nature may he die unto the present world, and live to the lovelier world that stands in the distance away from it."

Example 5. " Such was Napoleon Bonaparte. But, some will say he was still a great man. This we mean not to deny. But we would have it understood, that there are various kinds or orders of greatness, and that the highest did not belong to Bonaparte. There are different orders of greatness. Among these the first rank is unquestionably due to *moral* greatness, or magnanimity; to that sublime energy, by which the soul, smitten with the love of virtue, binds itself indissolubly, for life and for death, to truth and duty; espouses as its own the interests of human nature; scorns all meanness and defies all peril; hears in its own conscience a voice louder than threatenings and thunders; withstands all the powers of the universe, which would sever it from the cause of freedom, virtue, and religion; reposes an unfaltering trust in God in the darkest hour, and is ever ' ready to be offered up' on the altar of its country or of mankind. .Of this moral greatness, which throws all other forms of greatness into obscurity, we see not a trace or a spark in Napoleon Though clothed with the power of a God, the thought of consecra ting himself to the introduction of a new and higher era, to the exaltation of the character and condition of his race, seems never to have dawned on his mind. The spirit of disinterestedness and self-sacrifice seems not to have waged a moment's war with self-will and ambition. His ruling passions were singularly at variance with magnanimity. Moral greatness has too much simplicity, is too un ostentatious, too self-subsistent, and enters into others' interests with too much heartiness, to live a day for what Napoleon always lived,— to make itself the theme, and gaze, and wonder, of a dazzled world.— Next to moral comes *intellectual* greatness, or genius in the highest sense of that word; and by this we mean that sublime capacity of thought, through which the soul, smitten with the love of the true and the beautiful, essays to comprehend the universe. soars into the heavens, penetrates the earth, penetrates itself, questions the past, anticipates the future, traces out the general and all-comprehending laws of nature, binds together by innumerable affinities and relations

22

all the objec s of its knowledge; and, not satisfied witn what is finite frames to itself ideal excellence, loveliness, and grandeur. This is the greatness which belongs to philosophers, inspired poets, and to the master-spirits in the fine arts.—Next comes the greatness of *action;* and by this we mean the sublime power of conceiving and executing bold and extensive plans; constructing and bringing to bear on a mighty object a complicated machinery of means, energies, and arrangements, and accomplishing great outward effects. To this head belongs the greatness of Bonaparte, and that he possessed it we need not prove, and none will be hardy enough to deny. A man who, raised himself from obscurity to a throne, who changed the face of the world, who made himself felt through powerful and civilized nations, who sent the terror of his name across seas and oceans, whose will was pronounced and feared as destiny, whose donatives were crowns, who e antechamber was thronged by sub missive princes, who broke down the awful barrier of the Alps and made them a highway, and whose fame was spread beyond the boundaries of civilization to the steppes of the Cossack and the deserts of the Arab; a man who has left this record of himself in history, has taken out of our hands the question whether he shall bo called great. All must concede to him a sublime power of action, an energy equal to great effects."

Example 6. "The taste of the English in the cultivation of the land, and in what is called landscape gardening, is unrivalled. They have studied Nature intently, and discovered an exquisite sense of her beautiful forms and harmonious combinations. These charms, which in other countries she lavishes in wild solitude, are here assembled round the haunts of domestic life. They seem to have caught her coy and furtive graces, and spread them, like witchery, about their rural abodes.

"Nothing can be more imposing than the magnificence of English park scenery. Vast lawns that extend like sheets of vivid green, with here and there clumps of gigantic trees, heaping up rich piles of foliage. The solemn pomp of groves and woodland glades, with the deer trooping in silent herds across them; the hare, bounding away to the covert; or the pheasant, suddenly bursting upon the wing. The brook taught to wind in natural meanderings, or ex panded into a glassy lake; the sequestered pool, reflecting the quiv ering trees, with the yellow leaf sleeping on its bosom, and the trout roaming fearlessly about its limpid waters; while some rustic templ or sylvan statue, grown green and dark with age, gives an air of classic sanctity to the seclusion.

"These are but a few of the features of park scenery; but what most delights me is the creative talent with which the English decorate the unostentatious abodes of middle life. The rudest habitation, the most unpromising and scanty portion of land, in the hands of an Englishman of taste, becomes a little paradise. With a nice, discriminating eye, he seizes at once upon its capabilities, and pictures in his mind the future landscape. The sterile spot grows into loveliness under his hand, and yet the operations of art which produce the effect are scarcely to be perceived. The cherishing and training of some trees; the cautious pruning of others; the nice distribution of flowers and plants of tender and graceful foliage; the introduction of a green slope of velvet turf; the partial opening to a peep of blue distance, or silver gleam of water,—all these are managed with a delicate tact, a pervading yet quiet assiduity, like the magic touchings with which a painter finishes up a favorite picture.

"To this mingling of cultivated and rustic society may also be attributed the rural feeling that runs through British literature; the frequent use of illustrations from rural life, those incomparable descriptions of nature, that abound in the British poets—that have continued down from the 'Flower and Leaf' of Chaucer, and have brought into our closets all the freshness and fragrance of the dewy landscape. The pastoral writers of other countries appear as if they had paid nature an occasional visit, and become acquainted with her general charms; but the British poets have lived and revelled with her—they have wooed her in her most secret haunts—they have watched her minute caprices. A spray could not tremble in the breeze—a leaf could not rustle to the ground—a diamond drop could not patter in the stream—a fragrance could not exhale from the humble violet, nor a daisy unfold its crimson tints to the morning, but it has been noticed by these impassioned and delicate observers, and wrought up into some beautiful morality."

Example 7. "Every thing looked smiling about us as we embarked. The morning was now in its freshness, and the path of the breeze might be traced over the lake, wakening up its waters from their sleep of the night. The gay golden-winged birds that haunt the shores, were in every direction shining along the lake, while, with a graver consciousness of beauty, the swan and pelican were seen dressing their white plumage in the mirror of its wave. To add to the animation of the scene, a sweet tinkling of musical instruments came, at intervals, on the breeze, from boats at a distance, employed thus early in pursuing the fish of the waters, that suffered themselves to be decoyed into the nets by music.

"The banks of the canal were then luxuriantly wooded. Under the tufts of the light and towering palm were seen the orange and the citron, interlacing their boughs; while, here and there, huge tamarisks thickened the shade, and, at the very edge of the bank, the willow of Babylon stood bending its graceful branches into the water. Occasionally, out of the depth of these groves, there shone a small temple or pleasure house;—while now and then an opening in their line of foliage allowed the eye to wander over extensive fields, all covered with beds of those pale, sweet roses, for which the district of Egypt is so celebrated. The activity of the morning hour was visible every where. Flights of doves and lapwings were fluttering among the leaves; and the white heron, which had roosted all night in some date-tree, now stood sunning its wings on the green bank, or floated, like living silver, over the flood. The flowers, too, both of land and of water, looked freshly awakened;—and most of all, the superb lotus, which had risen with the sun from the wave, and was now holding up her chalice for a full draught of his light.

"Such were the scenes which now passed before my eyes, and mingled with the reveries that floated through my mind, as our boat, with its capacious sail, swept over the flood. * * * * * *

"Meanwhile the sun had reached his meridian. The busy hum of the morning had died gradually away, and all around were sleeping in the hot stillness of the noon. The Nile goose, folding her splendid wings, was lying motionless on the shadow of the sycamores in the water. Even the nimble birds upon the banks seemed to move more languishing, as the light fell upon their gold and azure hues. Over come as I was with watching, and weary with thought, it was not long before I yielded to the becalming influence of the hour. I felt my eyes close, and in a few minutes fell into a profound sleep."

Example 8. "Nearer the houses, we perceive an ample spread of branches, not so stately as the oaks, but more amiable for their annual services. A little while ago I beheld them, and all was one beauteous, boundless waste of blossoms. The eye marvelled at the very sight, and the heart rejoiced in the prospect of autumnal plenty. But now the blooming maid is resigned for the useful matron. The flower is fallen, and the fruits swell out on every twig.—Breathe soft, ye winds! O spare the tender fruitage, ye surly blasts! Let the pear-tree suckle her juicy progeny, till they drop into our hands, and dissolve in our mouths. Let the plum hang unmolested upon her boughs, till she fatten her delicious flesh, and cloud her polished skin with blue. And as for apples, that staple commodity of our orchards, let no injurious shocks precipitate them immaturely to the ground; till revolving suns have tinged them with a ruddy complexion, and concocted them into an exquisite flavor. Then, what copious hoards of burnished rinds, and what delightful relishes will replenish the store-room! Some, to present us with an early entertainment, and refresh our palates amidst the sultry heats. Some, to borrow ripeness from the falling snows, and carry autumn into the depths of winter. Some, to adorn the salver, make a part of the dessert, and give an agreeable close to our feasts. Others, to fill our vats with a foaming flood, which, mellowed by age, may sparkle in the glass, with a liveliness and delicacy little inferior to the blood of the grape.

" If it be pleasing to behold their orderly situation and their modest beauties, how much more delightful, to consider the advantages they yield! What a fund of choice accommodation is here! What a source of wholesome dainties! and all for the enjoyment of man. Why does the parsley, with her frizzled locks, shag the border? or why the celery, with her whitening arms, perforate the mold, but to render his soups savory? The asparagus shoots its tapering stems, to offer him the first fruits of the season; and the artichoke spreads its turgid top, to give him a treat of vegetable marrow. The tendrils of the cucumber creep into the sun, and though basking in its hottest rays, they secrete for their master, and barrel up for his use, the most cooling juices of the soil. The beans stand firm, like files of embattled troops; the peas rest upon their props, like so many companies of invalids; while both replenish their pods with the fatness of the earth, on purpose to pour it on their owner's table. Not one species, among all this variety of herbs, is a cumberer of the ground."

Example 9. "And now what shall we say to these things? Are they the dreams of a fervid imagination, or are they the words of truth and soberness? Will our blessings be perpetuated, or shall ours be added to the ruined republics that have been? Are we assembled to-day to bestow funeral honors upon departed glory, or with united counsels and hearts to strengthen the things that remain? Weak

22 *

indeed must be the faith that wavers now, and sinks amid waves less
terrific, and prospects more cheering, than any which our fathers
ever saw. Were it dark even as midnight, and did the waves run
high, and dash loud and angry around us, still our faith would not
be dismayed; still with our fathers we would believe, ' *Qui transtu
lit sustinet,*' and still would we rejoice in the annunciation of Him
that sitteth upon the throne, ' Behold, I create all things new. Our
anchor will not fail—our bark will not founder, for the means of
preservation *will* be used, and the God of our fathers *will* make
them effectual. The memory of our fathers is becoming more precious. Their institutions are commanding a higher estimation. Deep
er convictions are felt of the importance of religion; and more extended
and vigorous exertions are made to balance the temptations of pros-
perity by moral power. Christians are ceasing from their jealousies,
and concentrating their energies. The nation is moved, and beginning
to enroll itself in various forms of association, for the extension of
religion at home and abroad. Philosophers and patriots, statesmen
and men of wealth, are beginning to feel that it is righteousness
only which exalteth a nation; and to give to the work of moral
renovation their arguments, the power of their example, the impulse of
their charity. And the people, weary of political collision, are disposed
at length to build again those institutions which, in times of contention, they had either neglected or trodden down. Such an array
of moral influence as is now comprehended in the great plan of
charitable operations, was never before brought to bear upon the
nation. It moves onward, attended by fervent supplications, and
followed by glorious and unceasing effusions of the Holy Spirit. The
god of this world feels the shock of the onset, and has commenced
his retreat; and Jesus Christ is pressing onward from conquering to
conquer; nor will he turn from his purpose, nor cease from his work,
until he hath made all things new."

Example 10. "I know not how it happened, but it really seems
that, whilst his Grace was meditating his well-considered censure
upon me, he fell into a sort of sleep. Homer nods; and the duke of
Bedford may dream; and as dreams (even his golden dreams) are
apt to be ill-pieced and incongruously put together, his Grace pre
served his idea of reproach to *me*, but took the subject-matter from
the crown-grants to *his own family*. This is 'the stuff of which
dreams are made.' In that way of putting things together, his Grace
is perfectly in the right. The grants to the house of Russel were so

enormous, as not only to outrage economy, but even to stagger credibility. The duke of Bedford is the leviathan among all the creatures of the crown. He tumbles about his unwieldy bulk · he plays and frolics in the ocean of royal bounty. Huge as he is, and whilst 'he lies floating many a rood,' he is still a creature. His ribs, his fins, his whalebone, his blubber, the very spiracles through which he spouts a torrent of brine against his origin, and covers me all over with the spray,—every thing of him and about him is trom the throne. Is it for *him* to question the dispensation of the royal favor? * * * *

" Had it pleased God to continue to me the hope of succession, I should have been, according to my mediocrity, and the mediocrity of the age I live in, a sort of founder of a family; I should have left a son, who, in all the points in which personal merit can be viewed, in science, in erudition, in genius, in taste, in honor, in generosity, in humanity, in every · liberal sentiment, and every liberal accomplishment, would not have shown himself inferior to the duke of Bedford, or to any of those whom he traces in his line. His Grace very soon would have wanted all plausibility in his attack upon that provision which belonged more to mine than to me. He would soon have supplied every deficiency, and symmetrized every disproportion. It would not have been for that successor to resort to any stagnant wasting reservoir of merit in me, or in my ancestry. He had in himself a salient, living spring, of generous and manly action. Every day he lived he would have repurchased the bounty of the crown, and ten times more, if ten times more he had received. He was made a public creature, and had no enjoyment whatever, but in the performance of some duty. At this exigent moment, the loss of a finished man is not easily supplied.

" But a Disposer whose power we are little able to resist, and whose wisdom it behoves us not at all to dispute, has ordained it in another manner, and (whatever my querulous weakness might suggest) a far better. The storm has gone over me; and I lie like one of those old oaks which the late hurricane has scattered about me I am stripped of all my honors; I am torn up by the roots, and lie prostrate on the earth. There, and prostrate, I must unfeignedly recognize the divine justice, and in some degree submit to it. But whilst . humble myself before God, I do not know that it is forbidden to repel the attacks of unjust and inconsiderate men. The patience of Job is proverbial. After some of the convulsive struggles of our irritable nature, he submitted himself, and repented in dust and ashes

But even so, I do not find him blamed for reprehending, and with
a considerable degree of verbal asperity, those ill-natured neighbors
of his, who visited his dunghill to read moral, political, and econom-
ical lectures on his misery. I am alone. I have none to meet my
enemies in the gate. Indeed, my lord, I greatly deceive myself, if
in this hard season I would give a peck of refuse wheat for all that is
called fame and honor in the world. This is the appetite but of a
few. It is a luxury; it is a privilege; it is an indulgence for those
who are at their ease. But we are all of us made to shun disgrace
as we are made to shrink from pain, and poverty, and disease. It is
an instinct; and under the direction of reason, instinct is always in
the right. I live in an inverted order. They who should have succeeded me have gone before me. They who should have been to me
as posterity are in the place of ancestors. I owe to the dearest relation (which ever must subsist in memory) the act of piety which he
would have performed to me; I owe it to him to show that he was
not descended, as the duke of Bedford would have it, from an unworthy parent."

Example 11. "They stood pretty high upon the side of the glen,
which had suddenly opened into a sort of amphitheatre to give room
for a pure and profound lake of a few acres' extent, and a space of
level ground around it. The banks then arose every where steeply
and in some places were varied by rocks—in others covered with the
copse which run up, feathering their sides lightly and irregularly,
and breaking the uniformity of the green pasture-ground. Beneath,
the lake discharged itself into the huddling and tumultuous brook,
which had been their companion since they entered the glen. At
the point at which it issued from its 'parent lake' stood the ruins
which they had come to visit. They were not of great extent; but
the singular beauty, as well as wild, sequestered character of the spot
on which they were situated gave them an interest and importance
superior to that which attaches itself to the architectural remains of
greater consequence, but placed near to ordinary houses, and possessing less romantic accompaniments. The eastern window of the
church remained entire, with all its ornaments and tracery work
and the sides upheld by light flying buttresses, whose airy support,
detached from the wall against which they were placed, and ornamented with pinnacles and carved work, gave a variety and light-
ness to the building. The roof and western end of the church were
completely ruinous. but the latter appeared to have made one side of

a square. of which the ruins of the conventual buildings formed
other two. and the gardens a fourth. The side of these buildings
which overhung the brook, was partly founded on a steep and precipitous rock ; for the place had been occasionally turned to military
purposes, and had been taken, with great slaughter, during Mon
trose's wars. The ground formerly occupied by the garden was still
marked by a few orchard-trees. At a greater distance from the buildings were detached oaks, and elms, and chestnuts, growing singly,
which had attained great size. The rest of the space between the
ruins and the hill was close-cropt sward, which the daily pasture of
the sheep kept in much finer order than if it had been subjected to
the scythe and broom. The whole scene had a repose, which was
still and affecting without being monotonous. The dark, deep basin
in which the clear blue lake reposed, reflecting the water-lilies which
grew on its surface, and the trees which here and there threw their
arms from the banks, was finely contrasted with the haste and tu-
mult of the brook which broke away from the outlet, as if escaping
from confinement, and hurried down the glen, wheeling down the
base of the rock on which the ruins were situated, and brawling in
foam and fury with every shelve and stone which obstructed its passage. A similar contrast was seen between the level green meadow
in which the ruins were situated, and the large timber-trees which
were scattered over it, compared with the precipitous banks which
arose at a short distance around, partly fringed with light and feath-
ery underwood, partly rising in steeps clothed with purple heath,
and partly more abruptly elevated into founts of gray rock, chequer
ed with lichen, and those hardy plants which find root in the most
arid crevices of the crags.

Examp'e 12. " It is nearly impossible for me to convey to my
readers an idea of the ' vernal delight,' felt at this period, by the
Lay Preacher, far declined in the vale of years. My spectral figure,
pinched by the rude gripe of January, becomes as thin as that ' dag.
ger of lath,' employed by the vaunting Falstaff; and my mind, affected by the universal desolation of winter, is nearly as vacant of
joy and bright ideas, as the forest is of leaves, and the grove is of
song.

" Fortunately for my happiness, this is only periodical spleen
though in the bitter months, surveying my extenuated body, I exclaim with the melancholy prophet, ' My leanness, my leanness ; woe
into me ! and though adverting to the state of my mind, I behold it

'all in a robe of darkest grain,' yet, when April and May reign in sweet vicissitude, I give, like Horace, care to the winds; and perceive the whole system excited, by the potent stimulus of sunshine.

"An ancient bard of the happiest descriptive powers, and who noted objects, not only with the eye of the poet, but with the accuracy of a philosopher, says in a short poem, devoted to the praises of mirth, that

> ' Young and old come forth to play,
>   On a sunshine holiday.'

" In merry spring-time, not only birds, but melancholy old fellows like myself, sing. The sun is the poet's, the invalid's, and the hypochondriac's friend. Under clement skies, and genial sunshine, not only the body is corroborated, but the mind is vivified, and the heart becomes ' open as day.' I may be considered fanciful in the assertion, but I am positive that many, who, in November December, January, February, and March, read nothing but Mandeville, Rochefoucault, and Hobbes, and cherish malignant thoughts, at the expense of poor human nature, abjure their evil books and sour theories, when a softer season succeeds. I have myself, in winter, felt hostile to those whom I could smile upon in May, and clasp to my bosom in June. Our moral qualities, as well as natural objects, are affected by physical laws; and I can easily conceive that benevolence, no less than the sun-flower, flourishes and expands under the luminary of the day.

" With unaffected earnestness, I hope that none of my readers will look upon the agreeable visitation of the sun, at this beauteous season, as the impertinent call of a crabbed monitor, or an importunate dun. I hope that none will churlishly tell him ' how they hate his beams.' I am credibly informed that several of my city friends, many fine ladies, and the worshipful society of loungers, considered the early call of the above red-faced personage, as downright intrusion. It must be confessed that he is fond of prying into chambers and closets, but not like a rude searcher, or libertine gallant, for injurious or licentious purposes. His designs are beneficent, and he is one of the warmest friends in the world.

" Notwithstanding his looks are sometimes a little suspicious, and he presents himself with the fiery eye and flushed cheek of a jolly toper, yet this is only a new proof of the fallacy of physiognomy, for he is the most regular being in the universe. He keeps admirable hours, and is steady, diligent, and punctual to a proverb. Conscious

*f his shining merit, and dazzled by his regal glory, I must rigidly
inhibit all from attempting to exclude his person. I caution slug
gards to abstain from the use of shutters, curtains, and all other vil
lanous modes of insulting my ardent friend. My little garden, my
only support, and myself, are equally the objects of his care, and
were it not for the constant loan of his great lamp, I could not
always see to write "

Example 13. " There is great equability, and sustained force, in
every part of his writings. He never exhausts himself in flashes
and epigram, or languishes into tameness and insipidity; at first
sight you would say, that plainness and good sense were the predom
inating qualities; but, by the by, this simplicity is enriched with the
delicate and vivid colors of a fine imagination—the free and forcible
touches of a powerful intellect—and the lights and shades of an unerring, harmonizing taste. In comparing it with the styles of his
most celebrated contemporaries, we should say that it was more
purely and peculiarly a *written* style—and therefore rejected those
ornaments that more properly belong to oratory.

" It has no impetuosity, hurry, or vehemence; no bursts, or sudden
turns, or abruptness, like that of Burke; and, though eminently
smooth and melodious, it is not modulated to a uniform system of
solemn declamation, like that of Johnson, nor spread out in the richer
and more voluminous elocution of Stewart; nor still less broken into
that patchwork of scholastic pedantry and conversational smartness
which has found its admirers in Gibbon. It is a style, in short, of
great freedom, force, and beauty; but the deliberate style of a man
of thought and of learning; and neither that of a wit, throwing out
his extempores with an affectation of careless grace—nor a rhetorician, thinking more of his manner than his matter, and determined
to be admired for his expression, whatever may be the facts of his
sentiments.

" But we need dwell no longer on qualities that may be gathered
hereafter from the works he has left behind him. They who lived
with him mourn the most for those which will be traced in no such
memorial; and prize, far above these talents which gained him his
high name in philosophy, that personal character which endeared
him to his friends, and shed a grace and a dignity over all the society in which he moved. The same admirable taste which is con
spicuous in his writings, or rather, the higher principles from which
that taste was but an emanation, spread a similar change over his

whole life and conversation, and gave to the. most learned philoso
pher of his day the manner and deportment of the most perfect
gentleman."

Example 14. " HE IS FALLEN!

" We may now pause before that splendid prodigy, which towered
amongst us like some ancient ruin, whose frown terrified the glance
its magnificence attracted.

" Grand, gloomy, and peculiar, he sat upon the throne, a sceptred
hermit, wrapped in the solitude of his own originality.

" A mind bold, independent, and decisive—a will despotic in his
dictates—an energy that distanced expedition, and a conscience plia-
ble to every touch of interest, marked the outline of this extraordi
nary character—the most extraordinary, perhaps, that, in the annals
of this world, ever rose, or reigned, or fell.

" Flung into life in the midst of a Revolution that quickened every
energy of a people who acknowledged no superior, he commenced
his course, a stranger by birth, and a scholar by charity!

" With no friend but his sword, no fortune but his talents, he rushed
into the lists where rank, and wealth, and genius had arrayed themselves, and competition fled from him as from the glance of destiny
He knew no motive but interest—he acknowledged no criterion but
success—he worshipped no God but ambition, and with an Eastern
devotion he knelt at the shrine of his idolatry.   Subsidiary to this.
there was no creed which he did not promulgate; in the hope of a
dynasty, he upheld the Crescent; for the sake of a divorce, he
bowed before the Cross; the orphan of St. Louis, he became the
adopted child of the Republic; and with a parricidal ingratitude,
on the ruins both of the throne and the tribune, he reared the throne
of his despotism.

" A professed Catholic, he imprisoned the pope; a pretended pa-
triot, he impoverished the country; and in the name of Brutus, he
grasped without remorse, and wore without shame, the diadem of
the Cæsars.

" Through this pantomime of his policy, Fortune played the clown
of his caprices   At his touch, crowns crumbled, beggars reigned,
systems vanished, the wildest theories took the color of his whim,
and all that was novel, changed places with the rapidity of a drama
Even apparent defeat assumed the appearance of victory—his flight
from Egypt confirmed his destiny—ruin itself only elevated him to
empire.

" But, if his fortune was great, his genius was transcendent; decision flashed upon his counsels; and it was the same to decide and to perform. To inferior intellects, his combinations appeared perfectly impossible, his plans perfectly impracticable; but, in his hand, simplicity marked their development, and success vindicated their adoption.

" His person partook the character of his mind; if the one never yielded in the cabinet, the other never bent in the field.

" Nature had no obstacles that he did not surmount, space no opposition that he did not spurn; and, whether amid Alpine rocks, Arabian sands, or polar snows, he seemed proof against peril, and empowered with ubiquity. The whole continent of Europe trembled at beholding the audacity of his designs, and the miracle of their execution. Skepticism bowed to the prodigies of his performance; romance assumed the air of history; nor was there aught too incredible for belief, or too fanciful for expectation, when the world saw a subaltern of Corsica waving his imperial flag over her most ancient capitals. All the visions of antiquity became common-places in his contemplation; kings were his people; nations were his outposts; and he disposed of courts, and crowns, and camps, and churches, and cabinets, as if they were the titular dignitaries of the chess board."

23

HISTORICAL DISSERTATION

ON

ENGLISH STYLE

————

In the selection and arrangement of the following examples, it is designed to present a brief and connected outline of the history of English style. To carry this design into full execution, would obviously require far more extended limits than those here prescribed.

Of English Style before the Revival of Letters

There are few remains of English prose writers prior to the revival of letters, about the middle of the fifteenth century. Of the few productions that belong to early periods in English history, most are written either in Saxon or in Latin. Indeed, the origin of the English language is dated about the commencement of the fourteenth century, Sir John Mandeville being the first prose writer in the language. It is not, then, to be expected, that selections made from writers before the middle of the fifteenth century, will be of much interest or importance, as specimens of style. In these compositions, as in the first efforts of young writers, there is no distinctly formed style,—at least, no traits so well defined, and so prevalent, as to give a character to the style of the age. Still it will be noticed, that many of the words and phrases are idiomatic, and in common use at the present day

To the student of the English language, however, these early writings are highly interesting. He sees, in them, as hey become more and more intelligible, and bear a nearer resemblance to writings of later periods, the gradual formation of the language. He finds, also, an illustration of the remark, that the English language is a combination of different languages, or, in other words, that it is the Anglo-Saxon, with copious additions from the Norman, French, Latin, Greek, Italian, and German languages. He is further led to notice, that, during the time in which these additions and infusions were made, the language is in a transition-state, passing from the Anglo-Saxon to the English. Several causes conspired, during the fourteenth century, to bring about this change. A few distinguished poets appeared at this time, whose writings contributed much to the improvement of the language. Chaucer and Gower are especially worthy to be mentioned, the former having been styled the "father of the English language." Many translations were also made from the French and other languages; and in this way, new words and forms of expression were introduced. Trevisa's Translation of the Poly-chronicon, and other translations, made and printed by William Caxton, the first English printer, are examples. Several romances were also, at this time, either written originally in English, or translated from other languages; and this species of writing, as it called the attention of a new class of readers to the literature of the times, led to the advancement of the language. Thus poetry, history, and romance, in their rude forms, aided by the influence of a greater familiarity with foreign languages and nations, led to the gradual formation and improvement of native English.

I have made but three extracts from writers of this period

one from the Travels and Voyages of Sir John Mandeville written about 1370; the second, from the Poly-chronicon of Trevisa; and the third, from a romance entitled Morte Arthur, translated and published by Caxton, about 1475.

The following extract from Mandeville, gives us some knowledge of the philosophy of his times:—

"Ye have heard me say that Jerusalem is in the midst of the world, and that many men prove and shew there, by a sphere, that *pighte** in to the earth, upon the hour of mid-day, when it is so equinoctial, that sheweth no shadow on no side. And that it should be in the midst of the world, David witnesseth in the Psalter, where he saith, *Deus operatus est salute in medio terræ.* Then they that part from the parts of the West to go towards Jerusalem, as many journies as they go upward for to go thither, in as many journies may they go from Jerusalem, unto other confines of the superficiality of the earth beyond. And when men go beyond *tho†* journeys, towards Ind, and to the foreign isles, all is *euryronynge‡* the roundness of the earth and the sea, under our country on this half. And therefore hath it befallen many times of a thing, that I have heard counted when I was young; how a worthy man departed sometime from our countries, for to go search the world. And so he passed Ind, and the isles beyond Ind, where *ben mo* than 500 isles; and so long he went by sea and land, and so environed the world by many seasons, that he found an isle, where he heard speak his own language, calling on oxen in the plough such words, as men speak to beasts in nis own country; whereof he had great marvel; for he knew not how it might be. But I say, that he had gone so long by land and by sea, tnat he had environed all the earth, that he has come again environing, that it is to say, going about unto his own *marches,* if he would have passed forth, till he had found his country and his own knowledge. But he turned again from thence from whence he was come *fro;* and so he lost much painful labor, as himself said, a great while after, that he was come home. But how it seemeth to simple men unlearned, that men *ne* may go under the earth, and also that men should fall toward the heaven from under. But that may not be, unless that we may fall toward heaven from the earth, where we be. For

---

* fixed.   † these   ‡ passing round

from what part of the earth, where men dwell, either above or beneath, it seemeth alway to them that dwell, that they go more right than any other folk. And right as it seemeth to us, that they are under us, right so it seemeth to them that we be under them. For if a man might fall from the earth into the firmament, by greater reason the earth and the sea, that *ben* so heavy, should fall to the firmament; but that may not be; and therefore saith our Lord God, *Non timeus mei qui suspendi terram ex nihilo.*

The following passage from Trevisa reiates to the different languages of the inhabitants of Britain :—

"As it is knowen how many manner people *ben* in this island there *ben* also many languages *Netheless*, Welshmen, and Scots that *ben* not *medled* * with other nations, keep nigh yet their first language and speech ; but yet *tho* Scots that were sometime confederate, and dwelt with Picts, draw somewhat after their speech. But the Flemmings that dwell in the west side of Wales, have left their strange speech, and speaken like the Saxons. Also, Englishmen, tho they had from the beginning three manner speeches, southern, northern, and middle speech, in the middle of the land, as they come of three manner people of Germania, netheless by *commixyon* ǂ and *medling* ǂ first with Danes, and afterwards with Normans, in many things the country language is *appayred*.§ This appayring of the language cometh of two things; one is by cause that children that go to school, learn to speak first the English, and then ben compelled to construe their lessons in French; and that hath *ben* used *syn* the Normans came into England. Also gentlemen's children *ben* learned from their youth to speak French; and uplandish men will counterfeit and liken themselves unto gentlemen, and are *besy* ‖ to speak French, for to be more set by. Wherefore, it is said by a common proverb, "Jack would be a gentleman if he could speak French."

The following passage from Morte Arthur has been often quoted, as the perfect character of a knight-errant :—

* mixed.　　　† commixture　　　ǂ mingl ng.　　　§ inspired.　　　‖ busy

23 *

"And now I dare say, that Sir Lancelot, there thou liest that were never matched of none earthly knights hands. And thou were the curtiest knight that ever bare shield. And thou were the truest friend to thy lover that ever bestrode horse; and thou were the truest lover of a sinful man, that ever loved woman. And thou were the kindest man that ever stroke with sword. And thou were the goodliest person that ever came among prece* of knights. And thou were the meekest man, and the gentlest, that ever ate in hall among ladies. And thou were the sternest knight to thy mortal foe that ever put spear in rest."

From the Revival of Letters to the Reign of Elizabeth.

Several causes conspired, during this period, to the progress of society, and the advancement of English literature. The zeal with which the study of the Latin and Greek classics was pursued, led to a familiarity with these models of good taste, which could not fail to enrich and ameliorate the language, and improve the style. It was also the era of the Reformation—a time of great intellectual activity and power, and when writers, deeply interested in the subjects which they discussed, wrote with directness and simplicity. There appeared, also, in connexion with these great events, several individuals of learning and of superior minds, who thought with clearness and power. Such men were Sir Thomas More, Bishop Latimer, Sir John Cheke, and Bishop Fisher. It should be further mentioned, that the translation of the Bible, made, during this period, by Tyndale and Coverdale, especially the latter, which bears a near resemblance to that now in use, contributed much to the permanency of the language, and the simplicity of style.

From these, and, perhaps, other causes, there are found, partially developed, some of the more valuable traits of style. There is a degree of simplicity, strength, and directness

---

* press

which not only makes the writings of this period intelligible, but renders them grateful to the taste of even the present age. Still these excellencies are found united with many striking defects; and, looking at them as connected with the history of English style, they are rather to be regarded as favorable indications, than as established traits of style.

Sir Thomas More, who was a strenuous Papist, thus discourses on the writings of Luther :—

"But the very cause why his books be not suffered to be read is, because his heresies be so many and so abominable, and the proofs wherewith he pretended to make them probable, be so far from reason and truth, and so far against the right understanding of holy Scripture, whereof, under color of great zeal and affection, he laboreth to destroy the credence and good use, and finally so far stretcheth all things against good manner and virtue, provoking the world to wrong opinions of God, and boldness in sin and wretchedness, that there can be no good, but much harm, grow by the reading For if there were the substance good, and of error and oversight some cockle among the corn, which might be sifted out, and the remnant stand instead, men would have been content therewith, as they be with such other. But now is his not besprent with a few spots, but with more than half venom poisoned the whole wine, and that right rotten of itself. And this done of purpose and malice, not without an evil spirit in such wise walking with his words, that the contagion thereof were likely to infect a feeble soul, as the savor of a sickness sore infecteth a whole body. Nor the truth is not to be learned of every man's mouth; for as Christ was not content that the devil should call him God's son, though it were true, so is he not content a devil's limb, as Luther is, or Tyndale, should teach his flock the truth, for infecting them with their false devilish heresies besides."

From the sermons of Bishop Latimer much might be extracted to interest and amuse. The following passage is an example of his peculiar manner of writing :—

"We be many preachers here in England, and we preach many long sermons, yet the people will not repent nor convert. This was the fruit, the effect, and the good; that Jonas's sermon did, that all the whole city at his preaching converted, and amended their evi. loose living, and did penance in sackcloth. And yet here in this sermon of Jonas is no great curiousness, no great clerkliness, no great affectation of words, nor painted eloquence; it was none other but *adhuc quadraginta dies et Nineve subvertetur;* Yet forty days, *Nineve subvertetur,* and Ninevy shall be destroyed; it was no more. This was no great curious sermon, but it was a nipping sermon, a pinching sermon, a biting sermon; it had a full bite, it was a nipping sermon, a rough sermon, and a sharp biting sermon. Do you not here marvel that those Ninevites cast not Jonas in prison, that they did not revile him nor rebuke him? They did not revile him nor rebuke him. But God gave them grace to hear him, and to convert and amend at his preaching. A strange matter so noble a city to give place to one man's sermon. Now, England cannot abide this *gear,** they cannot be content to hear God's minister, and his threatening for their sins, though the sermon be never so good, tho it be never so true. It is a naughty fellow, a seditious fellow, he maketh trouble and rebellion in the realm, he lacketh discretion."

Little remains to us of the writings of Sir John Cheke He 's principally known from his zeal in the cause of ancient classical learning; and the influence of his familiarity with these writers is evidently seen in his style. The following passage is from an address to certain seditious persons, who disturbed the peace of England in 1549 :—

"Ye rise for religion. What religion taught you that? If ye were offered persecution for religion, ye ought to flee. So Christ teacheth you, and yet you intend to fight. If you would stand in the truth, ye ought to suffer like martyrs, and ye would slay like tyrants. Thus for religion, ye keep no religion, and neither will follow the council of Christ, nor the constancy of martyrs. Why rise ye for religion? Have ye any thing contrary to God's book? Yea, have ye not all things agreeable to God's word? But the new (religion) is different from the old; and therefore ye will have the old. If ye measure the old by truth, ye have the oldest. If ye measure the old by fancy, then it is hard, because men's fancies change, to give that is old

---

* matter.

Ye will have the old style. Will ye have any older than that as Christ left, and his apostles taught, and the first church did use? Ye will have that the *canons* do establish. Why, that is a great deal younger than that ye have of latter time, and newlier invented; yet that is it that ye desire. And do ye prefer the bishops of Rome afore Christ? Men's inventions afore God's law? The newer sort of worship before the older? Ye seek no religion; ye be deceived; ye seek traditions. They that teach you, blind you, that so instruct you, deceive you. If ye seek what the old doctors say, yet look what Christ, the oldest of all, saith. For he saith, ' Before Abram was made I am.' If ye seek the truest way, he is the very truth. If ye seek the readiest way, he is the very way. If ye seek everlasting life, he is the very life. What religion would ye have other now than his religion? You would have the Bibles in again. It is no nervail, your blind guides should lead you blind still.

" But why should ye not like that (religion) which God's word establisheth, the primitive church hath authorized, the greatest learned men of this realm have drawn, the whole consent of the parliament hath confirmed, the king's majesty hath set forth? Is it not truly set out? Can ye devise any truer than Christ's apostles used? Ye think it is not learnedly done. Dare ye, commons, take upon you more learning than the chosen bishops and clerks of this realm have?

" Learn, learn to know this one point of religion, that God will be worshipped as he hath prescribed, and not as we have devised. And that his will is wholly in the Scriptures, which be full of God's Spirit, and profitable to teach the truth."

Reign of Elizabeth

In directing our attention to English literature, during the reign of Elizabeth, we see more fully displayed the effects of those causes, which, as connected with the Revival of Letters and the Reformation, were in operation during the reigns of her immediate predecessors. Writers now appear, whose style is more distinctly marked, and whose works are more valuable. Still it must be acknowledged, that the literature of this period is not characterized by any well-defined and pervading traits of style. There is no standard to which the literary taste of the age is conformed. Each individual author, of intellectual power, writes in accordance with his own taste; and his influence is felt, in a greater or less degree, by the literature of the times. In noticing, therefore, the style of this reign, the attention will be directed to individual writers.

The first and second extracts are from the "Rhetoric" of Thomas Wilson, and the "Schoolmaster" of Roger Ascham. I have been induced to insert them, rather from the information they give us of prevailing notions respecting language and criticism, than from any marked peculiarity in the style. Still it may be noticed, that there is a good degree of perspicuity and vivacity of expression. Wilson came into notice in the preceding reign: his work, from which the following extract is made, is the first regular treatise on Rhetoric in the English language, and was deservedly, for many years, in high repute. Roger Ascham is well known as the tutor of Elizabeth. Both these individuals contributed much by their precepts, and their zeal for good learning, to the advancement of English language and literature.

Wilson, treating on plainness of style, has the following just remarks:—

"Among other lessons, this should be first learned, that we never affect any strange inkhorn terms, but to speak as is commonly received; neither seeking to be over-fine, nor yet living over-careless using our speech as most men do, and ordering our wits as the fewest have done. Some seek so far for outlandish English, that they forget altogether their mother's language. And I dare affirm this, if some of their mothers were alive, they were not able to tell what they say: and yet these fine English Clerks will say that they speak in their mother tongue, if a man should charge them with counterfeiting the King's English. Some far journied gentlemen, at their return home, like as they love to go in foreign apparel, so they will powder their ta k with over-sea language. He that cometh lately out of France, will talk French-English, and never blush at the matter. Another chops in with English Italianated, and applieth the Italian phrase to our English speaking; the which is, as if an orator that professeth to utter his mind in plain Latin would needs speak poetry, and far-fetched colors of strange antiquity. The lawyer will store his stomach with the prating of pedlers. The fine courtier will talk nothing but Chaucer. The mystical wise men and poetical clerks will speak nothing but quaint proverbs and blind allegories; delighting much in their own darkness, especially when none can tell what they do say. The unlearned or foolish fantastical, that smells but of learning, (such fellows as have seen learned men in their day,) will so Latin their tongues, that the simple can not but wonder at their talk, and think surely that they speak by some revelation. I know them that think rhetoric to stand wholly upon dark words; and that he who can catch an inkhorn term by the tail, him they count to be a fine Englishman and a good rhetorician."

Ascham, in his "Schoolmaster," thus remarks on the influence of Italian manners and books:—

"If some do not understand what is an Englishman Italianated, I will plainly tell him. He that by living and travelling in Italy, bringeth home into England, out of Italy, the religion, the learning, the policy, the experience, the manners of Italy. That is to say, for religion, papistry, or worse; for learning, less commonly than they carried out with them; for policy, a factious heart, a discoursing head, a mind to meddle in all men's matters; for experience, plenty of new mischief never known in England before; for manners, variety of vanities, and change of filthy lying.

"These be the enchantments of Circe, brought out of Italy to mar men's manners in England; much by example of ill life, but more by precepts of fond books, of late translated out of Italian into English, sold in every shop in London; commended by honest titles the sooner to corrupt honest manners; dedicated over boldly to virtuous and honorable personages, the easilier to beguile simple and innocent wits. It is pity that those who have authority and charge to allow and disallow books to be printed, be no more circumspect herein than they are. Ten sermons at Paul's cross do not so much good for moving men to true doctrine, as one of those books do harm, with enticing men to ill-living. Yea, I say further, those books do not so much to corrupt honest living, as they do to subvert true religion. More papists be made by your merry books of Italy, than by your earnest books of Lourain."

The Arcadia of Sir Philip Sidney was written about 1580. Regarding the time in which it was produced, it must be pronounced a work of uncommon merit—the product of a mind in advance of its age in elegant attainments and intellectual polish. To the reader of the present day, its faults are obvious. There is a looseness in the sentences, and a puerility in the thoughts, which belong to the childhood of literature. Yet with these faults is united much to interest and to please: a play of fancy, a sportiveness and sprightliness of thought, which offer a grateful relaxation to the mind. Something of his manner may be learned from the following specimen :—

"The third day after, in the time that the morning did strew roses and violets in the heavenly floor against the coming of the sun, the nightingales (striving one with the other, which could in most dainty variety recount their wrong caused sorrow) made them put off their sleep, and rising from under a tree (which that night had been their pavilion) they went on their journey, which by and by welcomed Musadora's eyes (wearied with the wasted soil of Laconia with delightful prospects. There were hills which garnished their proud heights with stately trees; humble vallies whose low estate seemed comforted with the refreshing of silver rivers, meadows enamelled with all sorts of eye-pleasing flowers; thickets, which being lined with most pleasant shades were witnessed so too, by the cheerful disposition of many well-tuned birds; each pasture stored with sheep feeding with sober security, while the pretty lambs with bleating oratory craved the dam's comfort. Here a shepherd's boy piping as though he should never be old; there a young shepherdess knitting, and withal singing, and it seemed that her voice comforted her hands to work, and her hands kept time to her voice-music. As for the houses of the country (for many houses came under their eye) they were all scattered, no two being one by the other and yet not so far off, as that it barred mutual succor; a show, as it were, of an accompaniable solitariness; and of a civil wilderness."

Sir Walter Raleigh, following the order of time, next offers himself to our notice. In this distinguished individual are found united the activity and enterprise of the adventurer and military leader, the practical common sense of the statesman and man of business, and the learning of the scholar. His style has those traits which his pursuits and the cast of his mind would lead us to anticipate. It is manly and forcible, and to a good degree natural and perspicuous; more like the style of later writers of good repute, than that of any of his contemporaries. Indeed, wherein it falls short of what in later times is esteemed a good English style, the defects are manifestly the faults of the age, above which he has partially and not entirely risen. His principal work is a History of the World; but his miscellaneous writings are numerous, showing him to have been a man of extensive knowledge and uncommon intellectual powers.

The following extract is from a work entitled the "Cabinet Council." It shows us the free use of classical authorities which at this period began to prevail.

"All virtues be required in a prince; but justice and clemency are most necessary; for justice is a habit of doing things as justly as well to himself as to others, and giving to every one so much as to him appertaineth. This is that virtue which preserveth concord among men, and whereof they be called good. *Jus et æquitas vincula civitatum.* CIC.

"It is the quality of this virtue also to proceed equally and temperately. It informeth the prince not to surcharge the subject with infinite laws, for therefore proceedeth the impoverishment of the subjects and the enriching of lawyers, a kind of men, which in ages more ancient, did seem of no necessity. *Sine causidicis satis felicis, olim fuere futuræque sunt urbes.* SAL.

"The next virtue required in princes is clemency, being an inclination of the mind to lenity and compassion, yet tempered with severity and judgment. This quality is fit for all great personages but chiefly princes, because their occasion to use it is most. By it also the love of men is gained. *Qui vult regnare, languida regnet manu.* SEN.

" After clemency, fidelity is expected in all good princes, which is a certain performance and observation of word and promise. This virtue seemeth to accompany justice, or is, as it were, the same; and therefore most fit for princes. *Sanctissimum generis humani bonum.* LIV.

" As fidelity followeth justice, so doth modesty accompany clemency. Modesty is a temperature of reason, whereby the mind of man is so governed, as neither in action or opinion, he overdeemeth of himself, or of any thing that is his—a quality not common in fortunate folk, and most rare in princes. *Superbia commune nobilitatis malum.* SAL.

" This virtue doth also moderate all external demonstrations of insolence, pride, and arrogance, and therefore necessary to be known of princes, and other, whom fortune or favor hath advanced. *Impone felicitate tuæ frænos, facilius illam reges.*" CURT.

John Lilly, a poet and romance writer, was esteemed in his day an unparalleled wit and scholar, " the darling of the Muses." His manner of writing, which is in a high degree affected, full of antithesis and quaint sayings, recommended him to the fashionables of his age. He was a favorite at court, " was heard, graced, and rewarded by Elizabeth ' Such indeed was his celebrity, that a manner of writing and speaking in imitation of his style, was called *Euphuism,* from the name of his most popular romance. I have thought him worthy of mention, since his celebrity, though short-lived, must have given his writings some influence on English style.

The following extract is from the romance before mentioned. Euphues had inveighed against woman to his friend

Philautus; afterwards he became enamored of English beauties, and is thus reproached by Philautus:—

"Stay, Euphues, I can level at the thoughts of thy heart by the words of thy mouth; for that commonly the tongue uttereth the mind, and outward speech betrayeth the inward spirit. For as a good root is known by a fair blossom, so is the substance of the heart noted by the shew of the countenance. I can see day at a little hole; thou must halt cunningly if thou beguile a cripple; but I cannot choose but laugh when I see thee play with the bait, that I fear thou hast swallowed, thinking with a mist to make my sight blind, because I should not perceive thy eyes bleared.

"A burnt child dreadeth the fire; he that stumbleth twice at one stone is worthy to break his shins; thou mayest happily forswear thyself, but thou shalt never delude me; I know thee now as readily by thy vizard as by thy visage; it is a blind goose that knoweth not a fox from a fern bush, and a foolish fellow that cannot discern craft from conscience, being once cozened. But why should I lament thy follies with grief, when thou seemest to color them with deceit? Ah, Euphues, I love thee well, but thou hatest thyself, and seekest to heap more harms on thy head by a little wit, than thou halt ever claw off by thy great wisdom. All fire is not quenched by water; thou hast not love in a string; affection is not thy slave thou canst not leave when thou listest. With what face, Euphues, canst thou return to thy vomit, seeming with the greedy hound to lap up that which thou didst cast up? I am ashamed to rehearse the terms that once thou didst utter of malice against women, and art thou not ashamed, now again, to recant them? They must needs think thee either envious upon small occasion, or amorous upon a light cause; and then will they be all as ready to hate thee for thy spite, as to laugh at thee for thy looseness.

"No, Euphues, so deep a wound cannot be healed with so light a plaster; thou mayest by art recover the skin, but thou canst never cover the scar; thou mayest flatter with fools because thou art wise, but the wise will ever mark thee for a fool."

During the reign of Elizabeth appeared several distinguished antiquarians and historians. Those writings of this class which acquired the greatest celebrity, and which still remain to us, are Holinshed's Chronicles, Stow's Survey of

London, and Camden's Britannia. These works discover great industry and research, and are the sources from which modern historians have largely drawn.

The only extract I shall make, is from Holinshed's Chronicles, a digression on the use of Venetian glasses.

"It is a world to see in these our days, wherein gold and silver most aboundeth, that our gentility, as lothing those metals, (because of the plenty,) do now generally choose rather the Venice glasses both for our wine and beer, than any of those metals or stone wherein before time we have been accustomed to drink; but such is the nature of man generally, that it most coveteth things difficult to be attained; and such is the estimation of this stuff, that many become rich only with their new trade unto Murana, (a town near to Venice situate on the Adriatic sea,) from whence the very best are daily to be had, and such as for beauty do well near match the crystal or the ancient *Murrhina vasa,* whereof now no man hath knowledge. And as this is seen in the gentility, so in the wealthy commonalty the like desire of glass is not neglected, whereby the gain gotten by their purchase is much more increased to the benefit of the merchant. The poorest also will have glass if they may, but sith the Venetian is somewhat too dear for them, they content themselves with such as are made at home of fern and burnt stone; but in fine, all go one way, that is, to shards at the last; so that our great expenses in glasses, (besides that they breed much strife towards those who have the charge of them,) are worse of all bestowed, in mine opinion, because their pieces do turn unto no profit. If the philosopher's stone were once found, and one part hereof mixed with forty of molten glass, it would induce such a metallic toughness thereunto, that a fall should nothing hurt it in such a manner, yet it might peradventure bunch or batter it; nevertheless that inconvenience were quickly to be redressed by the hammer. But whither am I slipped?"

There yet remains to be mentioned, among the distinguished men of his reign, the venerable Hooker. And it is pleasing evidence of the advance of the English nation in intelligence and learning, that a work written with the ability, the sound thought and extensive knowledge, found in

the Ecclesiastical Polity was rightly appreciated at the time
of its publication; while its continued reputation is evidence
how justly this celebrity was deserved. Perhaps the most
fit encomium ever passed upon this work, is that of King
James. "In it," says he, "there is no affectation of language: It is a clear, grave, and comprehensive manifestation
of reason. As a piece of composition, it is injured by the
inversion of clauses, and the imitation of foreign idioms,
which cause it to appear rough and unpolished, and at times
intricate and obscure. But in the midst of these faults are
found a dignity, and force, and elevation of style, which are
redeeming excellencies. There are also occasional passages of striking beauty and sublimity."

These peculiarities of the style of Hooker may be seen in
the following passage, in which he speaks of those who
would disparage the light of reason :—

"But so it is, the name of the light of reason is made hateful with
men; the star of reason and learning, and all other such like helps,
beginneth no otherwise to be thought of, than if it were an unlucky
comet; or as if God had so accursed it, that it should never
shine, or give light in things concerning our duty in any way towards him, but be esteemed as that star in the Revelation, called
Wormwood; which being fallen from Heaven, maketh rivers and
waters in which it falleth, so bitter, that men tasting them die
thereof. A number there are, who think that they cannot admire
as they ought, the power and authority of the word of God, if in
things divine, they should attribute any force to man's reason. For
which cause they never use reason so willingly as to disgrace
reason. Their usual and common discourses are to this effect. The
natural man perceiveth not the things of the Spirit of God; for they
are foolishness unto him, neither can he know them, because they
are spiritually discerned. By these and the like disputes, an opinion hath spread itself very far into the world; as if the way to be ripe
in faith, were to be raw in wit and judgment; as if reason were an
enemy unto religion, childish simplicity the mother of ghostly and
divine wisdom."

24 *

The following passage on death has more of simplicity and smoothness :—

" Is there any man o worth and virtue, though not instructed in the school of Christ, or ever taught what the soundness of religion meaneth, that had not rather end the days of this transitory life, as Cyrus in Xenophon, and in Plato Socrates, are described, than to sink down with them, of whom Elihu hath said, *momento moriuntur*, there is scarce an instant between their flourishing and not being? But let us, who know what it is to die as Absalom or Ananias and Sapphira died; let us beg of God, that when the hour of our rest is come, that patterns of our dissolution may be Jacob, Moses, Joshua, David, who, leisurely ending their lives in peace, prayed for the mercies of God to come upon their posterity; replenished the hearts of those nearest unto them with words of memorable consolation; strengthened men in the fear of God, gave them wholesome instructions of life, and confirmed them in true religion; in sum, taught the world no less virtuously how to die, than they had done before how to live."

If now we look back on the Examples of style during the reign of Elizabeth, we see that there is occasion to repeat the remark, that English style had not as yet assumed any distinct and well-defined character. It is not formed on any one model. And when we notice the prevalent faults of the best writers of this period, who are characterized either by a rambling, forceless manner of expression, or by intricacy, harshness, and obscurity, we must be convinced, that it is well this is the case. While, then, different writers have each contributed something to the advancement of English style, there is no one, who could with advantage have been looked upon as a standard.

Reign of James I.

Most of the writers who flourished during this reign, bear a resemblance to each other, not in any common excellen

cies of style, but ... certain pervading defects. Unnatural
conceits, antitheses, and false ornaments, are characteristic
traits. Especially do we find prevalent the absurd custom
of introducing, on all occasions, Latin quotations, thus often
expressing common thoughts in an imposing, affected manner. I propose therefore to make several extracts illustrative of these peculiarities of style, with slight notices of the
authors quoted.

The first extract is from a work, which may well be called
a literary curiosity, showing the most rare variety and extent
of literary attainments, and an uncommon, though eccentric
genius; I may add too, a work, the style of which, though
strongly marked by some of the faults just mentioned, possesses valuable traits. I refer to Burton's Anatomy of Melancholy, from which the following extract is made :—

'Thus much I say of myself, and that I hope without all suspicion
of pride or self-conceit; I have lived a silent, solitary, private life,
mihi et muses, in the University, as long almost as Xenocrates in
Athens, *ad senectam fere*, to learn wisdom as he did, penned up most
part in my study. Thirty years I have continued (having the use of
as good libraries as ever he had) a scholar, and would be therefore
loth, either by living as a drone, to be an unprofitable or unworthy
member of such a society, or to write that which would be any ways
dishonorable to such a royal and ample foundation. Something I
have done, though by my profession a divine, yet *turbine raptus in-
genii*, as he said, out of a running wit, and inconsistent, unsettled
mind, I had a great desire (not able to attain to a superficial skill in
any) to have some smattering in all, to be *aliquis in omnibus, nullus
in singulis*; which Plato commends, out of him Lipsius approves,
and further "as fit to be imprinted in all curious wits, not to be a
slave of one science, or dwell together in one subject, as most do, but
to rove abroad, *centum puer artium*, to have an oar in every man's
boat, to taste of every dish, and to sup of every cup;' which, saith
Montaigne, was well performed by Aristotle, and his learned coun-
tryman, Adrian Turnebus. This roving humor (though not with
like success) I have ever had and. like a ranging spaniel, that barks

at every bird he sees, leaving his game ' here followed all, saving that which I should, and may justly complain and truly *qui ubique est*, which Gestner *did in modesty*, that I have read many books, but to little purpose, for want of good method; I have confusedly turned over divers authors in our libraries, with small profit, for want of art, order, memory, judgment. And thus amidst the gallantry and misery of the world, jollity, pride, perplexities and cares, simplicity and villany, subtlety, knavery, candor and integrity, mutually mixed and offering themselves, I rub on *privus privatis;* as I have still lived, so I now continue, *statu quo prius*, left to a solitary life and my own discontents; saving that sometimes, *ne quid mentiar*, as Diogenes went into the city, and Democritus to the haven to see fashions, I did for my recreation now and then walk abroad, look into the world, and could not choose but make some little observations *non tam sagax observator, ac simplex recitator*, not as they did, to scoff or laugh at all, but with a mixt passion :

Bilem sæpe jocum vestri movere tumultus."

Strange as it may seem, this quaint, conceited, witty man ner of writing, found its way into the pulpit, and, united with the theological quibbling and the metaphysical subtilties of the age, became the prevalent style of preaching. Such a preacher was Bishop Andrews, a man of some learning, and of high repute with his contemporaries—being styled *stella predicantium*. Of the light emitted by this luminary, we may judge from the following extract, the subject of which is a comparison between men and angels :—

"What are angels? Surely they are spirits; glorious spirits, heavenly spirits; immortal spirits. For their nature or substance, spirits; for their quality or property, glorious; for their place or abode, heavenly; for their durance or continuance, immortal.

And what is the seed of Abraham but as Abraham himself? And what is Abraham? Let him answer himself: I am dust and ashes. What is the seed of Abraham? Let one answer in the persons of all the rest · *dicens putredini*, etc., saying to rottenness thou art my mother, and to the worms, ye are my brethren. They are spirits, now what are we, what is the seed of Abraham? Flesh. And what is the very harvest of this seed of flesh? what but corruption and rottenness, and worms? There is the substance of our bodies

They, heavenly spirits, angels of heaven; that is, their place of abode is in heaven above, ours is here below in the dust, *inter pulices et culices, tineas araneas et vermes;* our place is here among fleas and flies, moths and spiders, and crawling worms. There is our place of dwelling.

"They, immortal spirits; this is their durance. Our time is proclaimed in the prophet; flesh, all flesh is grass, and the glory of it as the flower of the field, (from April to June.) The scythe cometh, nay, the wind but bloweth, and we are gone, withering sooner than the grass, which is short; nay, fading sooner than the flower of the grass, which is much shorter; nay, (saith Job,) rubbed in pieces more easily than any moth.

"This we are to them if you lay us together; and if you weigh us upon a balance, we are *altogether lighter than vanity itself;* this is our weight. And if you value us, *man is but a thing of nought;* this is our worth. *Hoc* is *omnis homo;* that is Abraham, and this is Abraham's seed; and who would stand to compare these with angels? Verily, there is no comparison; they are incomparably far better than the best of us."

Dr. Donne is another preacher, who belongs to the same class, but he was a poet as well as a divine, and there is evidently more refinement of taste, than in the style of Bishop Andrews.

The following is the introduction to a sermon from the text, "For where your treasure is, there will your heart be also."

"I have seen minute glasses; glasses so short lived. If I were to preach upon this text (*where your treasure is, there will your heart be also*) to such a glass, it were enough for half the sermon; enough to show the worldly man his treasures, and the object of his heart, to call his eye to that minute glass, and to tell him, there flows, there flies your treasure, and your heart with it. But if I had a secular glass, a glass that would run an age; if the two hemispheres of the world calcined and burnt to ashes, and all the ashes, and sands, and atoms, of the world put into that glass, it would not be enough to tell the godly man what his treasure and the object of his heart is A parrot or a stare, docile birds, and of pregnant imitation, will sooner be brought to relate to us the wisdom of a council table than any Ambrose, or any Chrysostom, men that have gold and honey in their names, shall tell us what the sweetness, what the treasure of heaven is, and what that man's peace, that hath set his heart upon that treasure.'

Another short extract is perhaps a better example of his usual mode of writing:—

"Theudas rose up, *dicens se esse aliquem;* he said he was somebody, and he proved nobody; Simon Magus rose up, *dicens se esse aliquem magnum,* saying he was some great body; and he proved as little. Christ Jesus rose up, and said himself not to be somebody, nor some great body; but that there was nobody else, no other name given under heaven, whereby we should be saved, and he was believed. And, therefore, if any man think to destroy this general by making himself a woful instance to the contrary—Christ is not believed in all the world, for I never believed in Christ; so poor an objection requires no more answer, but that that will still be true in the general; man is a reasonable creature, though he be an unreasonable man."

Of the few writers of this age, who acquired any celebrity, the dramatist, Ben Jonson, may be mentioned. He has left but one piece of prose composition, and this, while it has in some degree the peculiarities of his time, has more good sense than is found in most of his contemporaries. I have selected the following passage because of the subject on which it treats:—

"Language most shews a man; speak, that I may see thee. It springs out of the most retired and inmost parts of us, and is the image of the parent of it, the mind. No glass renders a man's form or likeness so true, as his speech. Nay, it is likened to a man; and as we consider feature and composition in a man, so words in language; in the greatness, aptness, sound, structure, and harmony of it. Some men are tall and big; so some language is high and great. Then the words are chosen, the sound ample, the composition full, the absolution plenteous, and poured out, all grace, sinewy and strong. Some are little and dwarfs; so of speech, it is humble and low; the words poor and flat; the members and periods thin and weak, without knitting or number. The middle are of a just stature. There the language is plain and pleasing: even without stopping, round without swelling; all well turned, composed, elegant, and accurate. The vicious language is vast and gaping; swelling and irregular; when it contends, high, full of rock, mountain, and pointedness; as it affects to be low, it is abject and creeps, full of bogs and holes. And according to their subject, these styles vary, and lose their names; for that which is high and lofty, declaring excellent matter, becomes vast and tumorous, speaking of petty and inferior things; so that which was even and apt, in a mean and plain subject, will appear most poor and humble in a high argument.

"The next thing to the stature, is the figure and feature of language; that is, whether it be round and straight, which consists of short and succinct periods, numerous and polished, or square and firm, which is to have equal and strong parts, every thing answerable, and weighed.

"The third is the skin and coat, which rests in the well joining cementing, and coagmentation of words; when as it is smooth, gentle, and sweet; like a table upon which you may run your finger without rubs, and your nails cannot find a joint, nor horrid, rough, wrinkled, gaping, and chapt; after these, the flesh, blood, and bones come in question. We say it is a fleshy style, when there is much periphrasis, and circuit of words; and when with more than enough it grows fat and corpulent. It hath blood and juice, when the words are proper and apt, their sound sweet, and the phrases neat and picked There be some styles again that are bony and sinewy.

From these writers of vitiated taste, we turn o the illustrious Bacon, who is not only to be regarded as an ornament of this reign, but of English literature. This is not the place to enumerate his various works, or to speak of their influence on the advancement of science and good learning. We look only at his style. In this, as seen in his philosophical works, and in his miscellaneous productions, especially in his Essays, there is a striking difference In he former, there is evidently an improvement on preceding

writers. While the style has dignity, elevation, and force
and is free from the bad taste of his time, it has less of
harshness and of that involution of clauses, and consequent
intricacy, than are found in his immediate predecessors.
Still, to modern readers, it often appears rigid and unharmonious. It wants, also, that compactness and strength of
expression, to which good writers of the present day attain
But these defects disappear in many of those passages, in
which the intellectual greatness of the writer, his power of
thought, and grandeur of conception, are displayed. The
style of his Essays differs widely. The sentences are short
and antithetic, and devoid of ease and elegance. They are
a collection of striking thoughts and wise sayings, set forth
in sparkling expressions and illustrations.

The following passage from his Advancement of Learning,
is an example of Bacon's better style: —

"But the greatest error of all the rest, is the mistaking or mis
placing of the last or farthest end of knowledge, for men have
entered into a desire of learning and knowledge, sometimes upon a
natural curiosity, and an inquisitive appetite; sometimes to entertain their minds with variety and delight; sometimes for ornament
and reputation; and sometimes to enable them to victory of wit and
contradiction; and most times for lucre and profession; and seldom
sincerely to give a true account of their gift of reason, to the benefit
and use of men; as if there were sought in knowledge a couch
where to rest a searching and restless spirit; or a terras, for a wan
dering and variable mind to walk up and down with a fair prospect,
or a tower of state, for a proud mind to raise itself upon; or a fort
or commanding ground for strife or contention; or a shop for profit
and sale; and not a rich storehouse for the glory of the Creator,
and the relief of man's estate. But this is that which will indeed
dignify and exalt knowledge, if contemplation and action may be
more nearly conjoined and united together than they have been· a
conjunction like unto that of the two highest planets, Saturn, the
planet of rest and contemplation, and Jupiter, the planet of civil so
ciety and action; howbeit, I do not mean when I speak of use and

action, that end before mentioned of the applying of knowledge to
lucre and profession; for I am not ignorant how much that diverteth
and interrupteth the prosecution and advancement of knowledge, like
unto the golden ball thrown before Atalanta, which, while she goeth
aside and stoopeth to take up, the race is hindered,

' Declinant cursus, aurumque volubile tollit.'

Neither is my meaning, as was spoken of Socrates, to call philosophy
down from heaven to converse upon earth; that is, to leave natural
philosophy aside, and to apply knowledge only to manners and policy. But as both heaven and earth do conspire and contribute to
the use and benefit of man, so the end ought to be, from both phi-
losophies to separate and reject vain speculations, and whatsoever is
empty and void, and to preserve and augment whatever is solid and
fruitful.''

Charles I. and the Commonwealth.

This is the age of polemical and political controversy,
the very foundations of society seemed to be shaken. Or
rather, it was a period, when men of intellectual energy
and daring spirits came forth to the work of laying anew,
and with skill and solidity, these foundations. The first
principles of morals, of politics, and of ecclesiastical rule,
were subjected to examination, and the whole era, in church
and state, is one of revolution.

As might be expected, these commotions called forth the
intellectual energies of the most apt minds, and whatever
was written had a direct bearing on the interests of society.
Literature became more manly and practical in its character.
English style also felt most sensibly the change. Not that
the writers of this period are entirely free from those faults
which were stated to be characteristic of the last age. There
are remains of that affectation of manner and quaintness of
expression, which are indications of a taste wanting chasteness and refinement. Few also have laid aside the Latin

idioms and forms of construction, and none attain to tha unity, and compactness, and easy flow of the sentence, whic are found in later writers.

Of the ecclesiastical writers of this period, two are par ticularly conspicuous—Bishops Hall and Taylor.

Bishop Hall attained some celebrity as a controversia writer. He was the antagonist of Milton, and a strenuou supporter of episcopacy. Besides controversial writings, he .eft a work entitled "Occasional Meditations," which, from some resemblance in the turns of thought and expression to the Morals of Seneca, gave him the name of the Christian Seneca.—The following Meditation is upon the sight of a great Library.

"What a world of wit is here packed up together! I know not whether this sight doth more dismay or comfort me; it dismays me to think that here is so much that I cannot know; it comforts me to think that this variety yields so good helps to know what I should There is no truer word than that of Solomon:—there is no end of making many books; this sight verifies it; there is no end; indeed it were a pity there should; God hath given to man a busy soul the agitation whereof cannot, but through time and experience, work out many hidden truths; to suppress these would be no other than injurious to mankind, whose minds, like unto so many candles, should be kindled by each other; the thoughts of our de- liberation are most accurate; these we vent into our papers; what a happiness is it, that, without all offence of necromancy, I may here call up any of the ancient worthies of learning, whether hu- man or divine, and confer with them of all my doubts! that I can at pleasure summon whole synods of reverend fathers, and acute doctors from all the coasts of the earth, to give their well-studied judgments in all points of question which I propose! Neither can I cast my eye casually upon any of these silent masters but I must learn somewhat; it is a wantonness to complain of choice.

"No law binds me to read all; but the more we can take in and digest, the better liking must the mind's need be; blessed be God tha' he hath set up so many clear lamps in his church

" Now, none but the wilfully blind can plead darkness; and blessed
be the memory of those his faithful servants, that have left their blood,
their spirits, their lives in these precious papers; and have willingly
wasted themselves into these during monuments, to give light unto
others

The intellectual character of Bishop Taylor adapted him
to different times from those in which h s lot was cast; and,
indeed, it was not till the restoration of Charles II. that he
can be said to have acquired his celebrity. His distinguish-
ing trait is the richness of his fancy; and his intellectual
attainments are such as are connected with this faculty of
the mind, and adapted to its display. He was a fine classical
scholar, familiar with the learning of his times, thus possessing great resources for illustration, and an uncommon flow
of language. His sentences, though long and crowded, luxuriantly abounding in ornament, are often well modulated;
and hence the merit of contributing to the smoothness and
elegance of English style is ascribed to his writings.
I have selected, as a specimen of his style, the well-known
passage in which he speaks of anger as a hinderance to
prayer.

" Prayer is the peace of our spirit, the stillness of our thoughts,
the evenness of recollection, the seat of meditation. the rest of our
cares, and the calm of our tempest; prayer is the issue of a quiet
mind, of untroubled thoughts; it is the daughter of charity and the
sister of meekness; and he that prays to God with an angry, that
s, with a discomposed spirit, is like him that retires into a battle to
meditate, and sets up his quarters in the outposts of an army, and
chooses a frontier garrison to be wise in. Anger is a perfect alien-
ation of the mind from prayer, and therefore is contrary to that atten
tion which presents our prayers in a right line to God. For so have
I seen a lark rising from his bed of grass. and soaring upwards,
singing as he rises, and hopes to get to heaven, and climb above the
clouds; but the poor bird was beaten back with the loud sighings
of an eastern wind, and his motion made irregular and inconstant,

descending more at every breath of the tempest, than it could recover by the libration and frequent weighing of his wings; till the
little creature was forced to sit down and pant, and stay till the
storm was over, and then it made a prosperous flight, and did rise
and sing as if it had learned music and motion from an angel, as ne
passed sometimes through the air about his ministries here below,
so is the prayer of a good man; when his affairs have required
business, and his business was matter of discipline, and his discipline
was to pass upon a sinning person, or had a design of charity, his
duty met with the infirmities of a man, and anger was its instrument, and the instrument became stronger than the prime agent,
and raised a tempest and overruled the man; and then his prayer
was broken, and his thoughts were troubled, and his words went
up towards a cloud, and his thoughts pulled them back again, and
made them without intention; and the good man sighs for his in-
firmity, but must be content to lose the prayer, and he must recover
it, when his anger is removed, and his spirit is becalmed, made even
as the brow of Jesus, and smooth like the heart of God; and then it
ascends to heaven upon the wings of the holy dove, and dwells with
God, till it returns like the useful bee, loaden with a blessing and the
dew of heaven."

The philosophical writings of this period constitute an
important part of the literature of the times, and without
doubt contributed much to the advancement of style. In
this class Herbert, Hobbs, and Harrington, are most prominent, especially the philosopher of Malmesbury, who in
clearness of thought has rarely been surpassed. I have
room but for a single extract from his Leviathan. Having
given a description of a commonwealth, he thus discourses
on the manner of its formation : —

"The only way to erect such a common power as may be able to
defend men from the invasion of foreigners, and the injuries of one
another, and thereby to secure them in such sort, as that by their
own industry, and by the fruits of the earth, they may nourish themselves and live contentedly, is to confer all their power and strength
on one man, or upon one assembly of men, that may reduce all their

wills, by plurality of voices, under one will; which is as much as to say, to appoint one man, or assembly of men, to bear their person; and every one to own and acknowledge himself to be author of whatsoever he that so beareth their person shall act, or cause to be acted, in those things which concern the common peace and safety; and therein to submit their will every one to his will, and their judgments to his judgment. This is more than consent or concord; it is a real unity of them all in one and the same person, made by covenant of every man with every man, in such manner, as if every man should say to every man, ' I authorize and give up my right of governing myself to this man, or to this assembly of men, on this condition, that thou give up all thy right to him, and authorize all his actions in like manner.' This done, the multitude so united in one person is called a commonwealth, in Latin *civitas.* This is the generation of the great Leviathan, or rather (to speak more reverently) of that mortal God, to which we owe, under the immortal God, our peace and defence. For by this authority, given him by every particular man in the commonwealth, he hath the use of so much power and strength conferred on him, that by terror thereof, he is enabled to perform the wills of them all, to peace at home, and mutual aid against their enemies abroad. And in him consisteth the essence of the commonwealth; which (to define it) is one person of whose acts a great multitude, by mutual covenants one with another, have made themselves every one the author, to the end he may use the strength and means of them all, as he shall think expedient, for their peace and common defence."

It will readily be inferred even from this short extract that the effect of writers of this class, must have been to give to style increased clearness and strength, both of thought and expression.

But without doubt, the most favorable specimen of prose composition, during this reign, is found in the writings of Milton. These productions, from the nature of the subjects on which they treat, and of the occasions which called them forth, are now but little read yet they contain passages, which, for loftiness and strength, and even melody of style, are unrivalled in the literature of any age or any language

The inspiring mind rises above the faults of the age and of the individual, and even the stiff and involved idioms of the Latin language, which abound in his writings, are so much in accordance with the dignity and greatness of his thoughts, that they do not seem so unnatural and cumbersome, as in the writings of other men of less gifted minds.

Instead of selecting a passage from the writings of Milton, which might exhibit his style in his moments of poetic inspiration, I present the following, which owes its origin to the troubled times in which he lived :—

" Putting off the courtier, he (the king) now puts on the philosopher, and sententiously disputes to this effect: that reason ought to be used to men, force and terror to beasts; that he deserves to be a slave who captivates the rational sovereignty of his sou. and liberty of his will to compulsion; that he would not forfeit that freedom, which cannot be denied him as a king, because it belongs to him as a man and a Christian, though to preserve his kingdom; but rather die enjoying the empire of his soul, tnan live in such a vassalage, as not to use his reason and conscience to like or dislike as a king—which words of themselves, as far as they are sense, good and philosophical, yet in the mouth of him who, to engross this common liberty to himself, would tread down all other men into the condition of slaves and beasts, they quite lose their commendation. He confesses a rational sovereignty of soul, and freedom of will, in every man, and yet with an implicit repugnancy would have his reason the sovereign of that sovereignty, and would captivate and make useless that natural freedom of will in all other men but himself. But them that yield him this obedience he so well rewards, as to pronounce them worthy to be slaves. They who have lost all to be his subjects, may stoop and take up the reward. What that freedom is, which cannot be denied him as a king, because it belongs to him as a man and a Christian, I understand not. If it be his negative voice, it concludes all men who have not such a negative as his against a whole parliament, to be neither men nor Christians; and what was he himself then all this while, that we denied it him as a king? Will he say that he enjoyed within himself the less freedom for hat? Might not he, both as a man and a Christian,

have reigned within himself in full sovereignty of soul, no man re-
pining, but that his outward and imperious will must invade the
civil liberties of a nation? Did we therefore not permit him to use
his reason and his conscience, not permitting him to bereave us the
use of ours? And might not he have enjoyed both as a king,
governing us as freemen by, what laws we ourselves would be
governed?

"It was not the inward use of his reason and his conscience that
would content him, but to use them both as a law over all his subjects, in whatever he declared as a king to like or dislike, which use
of reason, most reasonless and unconscionable, is the utmost that any
tyrant ever pretended over his vassals."

Of a kindred spirit in his devotedness to republican
principles, was the patriotic and highminded Algernon
Sidney. His mind was not indeed cast in the same mould
with that of Milton, but his "Discourses on Government,"
which is the principal work he has left, discover an extent
of knowledge, and a power of thought, which entitle him
to a high rank as a philosopher and a scholar. His style
also, though less glowing than that of Milton, is marked by
purity, propriety, and strength.

The following passage, considering the period of the
world in which it was written, evidently comes forth from
a mind that thinks for itself, and dares to avow its thoughts.

"Such as have reason, understanding, and common sense, will
and ought to make use of it in those things that concern themselves
and their posterity, and suspect the words of such as are interested
in deceiving, or persuading them not to see with their own eyes,
that they may be more easily deceived. This rule obliges us so far
to search into matters of state, as to examine the original principles
of government in general, and of our own in particular. We cannot distinguish truth from falsehood, right from wrong, or know
what obedience we owe unto the magistrate, or what we may justly
expect from him, unless we know what he is, and why he is, and
by whom he is made to be what he is. These may be perhaps called
Mysteries of State,' and some would persuade us they are to

be esteemed 'Arcana;' but whosoever confesses himself to be ig.
norant of them, must acknowledge that he is incapable of giving
any judgment upon things relating to the superstructure; and in sc
doing evidently shows to others, that they ought not at all to hearket
to what they say."

In the preceding reign, I spoke of the style of Burton as
a literary curiosity; that of Thomas Brown, the author of
"Religio Medici," may be ranked in the same class. Brown
possessed an eccentric genius, and we find in his writings
many original and striking thoughts. What, however, particularly arrests our attention, is the extravagance of his
style. Many of his words are strange and unheard-of com-
pounds, or exotics, newly introduced from foreign languages
There is also so much of circumlocution and of unnatural-
ness in his forms of expression, that it is often difficult tc
divine what he would say. Two or three short extracts wil.
exhibit his peculiar manner better than any description.

"We hope it will not be unconsidered, that we find no open tract
or constant manuduction in this labyrinth, but are ofttimes feigned
to wander in the America and untravelled parts of truth. We are
often constrained to stand alone against the strength of opinion, and
to meet the Goliah and giant of authority, with contemptible peb
bles and feeble arguments, drawn from the script and slender stock
of ourselves."

—— "of lower consideration is the foretelling of strangers, from
the fungus parcels about the wicks of candles; which only signifieth
a moist and plurious air about them, hindering the avolation of the
light and parillous particles; whereupon they are forced to settle
upon the snast."

"Persons lightly dipped, not grained in generous honesty, are
but pale in goodness, and faint-hued in sincerity; but be thou wha
thou virtuously art, and let not the ocean wash away thy tincture
stand magnetically upon that axis where prudent simplicity hate
fixed thee, and let no temptation invert the poles of thy honesty

Hang early plummets upon the heels of pride, and let ambition have
but an epicycle or narrow circuit in thee."

I shall close the account of the writers of this age, with
the mention of one, who, from the time of his birth, is to be
ranked in this period, though, as was remarked of Bishop
Taylor, he might with some propriety be enumerated among
he writers of the next reign.   I refer to the poet Cowley.

In the few comments, that have been made on the style of
most of the writers who have been mentioned, there has been
occasion to speak of their harshness and stiffness of manner.
The poet Cowley, in the brief specimen of prose writing
which he has left us, exhibits to us a style of the opposite
character.   The following passage from his Essay on Agri-
culture, is written in his usual manner.—

" 'The first wish of Virgil was to be a good philosopher; the second,
a good husbandman; and God (whom he seemed to understand
better than most of the most learned heathens) dealt with him just
as he did with Solomon; because he prayed for wisdom in the first
place, he added all things else which were subordinately to be desired. He made him one of the best philosophers and best husband
men; and, to adorn both those faculties, the best poet; he made him
besides all this a rich man, and a man who desired to be no richer.
O fortunatus nimium, et bona qui sua novit. To be a husbandman is
but a retreat from the city; to be a philosopher, from the world; or
rather, a retreat from the world as it is man's, into the world as it
is God's. But since nature denies to most men the capacity or appetite, and fortune allows but to very few the opportunities or
possibility of applying themselves wholly to philosophy, the best
mixture of human affairs that we can make are the employments of
a country life.

" We are here among the vast and noble scenes of nature; we are
there (alluding to courts and cities) among the pitiful shifts of policy
we walk here in the light and open ways of the divine bounty; we
grope there in the dark and confused labyrinths of human malice
our senses are here feasted with the clear and genuine taste of their
objects, which are all sophisticated there, and for the most part over

whelme l with their contrarieties. Here pleasure looks (methinks) like
a beautiful, constant, and modest wife; it is there an unprudent,
fickle, and painted harlot. Here is harmless and cheap plenty, there
guilty and expensive luxury.

"I shall only instance in one delight more, the most natural and
best natured of all others, a perpetual companion of the husbandman,
and that is, the satisfaction of looking round about him, and seeing
nothing but the effects and improvements of his own art and diligence:
to be always gathering of some fruits of it, and at the same time to
behold others ripening, and others budding; to see all his fields and
gardens covered with the beauteous creations of his own industry
and to see, like God, that all his works are good."

In this passage, we find an easy flow and an unaffected
simplicity of expression. The words are happily chosen,
the sentences perspicuous and well modulated,—not crowded
and clogged by unnecessary clauses, as in most other writings
of the time, but having unity and naturalness.

Reign of Charles II.

Our attention is now to be directed to writers, who
appeared during a different state of public affairs, and
whose style, when compared with that of the preceding age,
corresponds to the change which had taken place in the
condition of the community. The Restoration gave to literature that court influence, which in almost every period of
English history has been powerful. In this instance, too, it
was of a kind so much in contrast to the preceding state of
the nation, that its effects are prominent. To the austerity
and affected plainness and coarseness of the commonwealth
succeeded the voluptuousness and elegance of the court of
Charles II., and the effects of this change are at once seen
in the style. The harshness and stiffness of former periods
give place to a smoother and more polished manner of

writing. The influence of an increased intercourse with the French nation had a similar tendency.

During this reign, the church offers to our notice several distinguished writers. Of Taylor I have already spoken; South, Barrow, and Tillotson, also require to be mentioned.

Dr. South is a favorable specimen of a class of writers who may be called witty preachers. Hardly any one is led to read his sermons for the religious instruction which they give, and for the cultivation of practical piety. They are read rather as a book of amusement, and many are the satirical and witty turns of expression, which excite a smile. It must be acknowledged, however, that there is often wisdom united with his wit; and some passages are found of great power and beauty. One of this class I have selected. It is a description of the passions before the fall of man

"And first for the grand leading affection of all, which is *love* This is the great instrument and engine of nature, the bond and cement of society, the spring and spirit of the universe. Love is 'such an affection, as cannot so properly be said to be in the soul as the soul to be in that. It is the whole man wrapt up into one desire; all the powers, vigor and faculties of the soul abridged into one inclination. And it is of that active, restless nature, that it must of necessity exert itself, and like the *fire*, to which it is so often compared, it is not a free agent, to choose whether it will heat or no, but it streams forth by natural results and unavoidable emanations; so that it will fasten upon an inferior, unsuitable object, rather than none at all. The soul may sooner leave off to subsist, than to love; and like the vine, it withers and dies, if it has nothing to embrace. Now, this affection in a state of innocence was happily pitched upon its right object; it flamed up in direct fervors of devotion to God, and in collateral emissions of charity to its neighbor.

"Next for the lightsome passion of *Joy*. It was not that, which now often usurps this name; that trivial, vanishing, superficial thing, that only gilds the apprehension, and plays upon the surface of the soul. It was not the mere crackling of thorns, a sudden blaze of the spirits, the exultation of a tickled fancy or a pleased appetite. Joy

was then a masculine and a severe thing; the recreation of the judg
ment, the jubilee of reason. It was the result of a real good, suitably
applied. It commenced on the solidities of truth, and the substance
of fruition. It did not run out in voice, or indecent eruptions, but
filled the soul, as God does the universe, silently and without noise
it was refreshing, but composed; like the pleasantness of youth tempered with the gravity of age; or the mirth of a festival managed with
the silence of contemplation."

The name of Barrow is known to us as being associated
with that of the illustrious Newton, in his contributions to
the advancement of science. His sermons also give him a
claim to be ranked among the most eminent preachers and
divines of the English church. He is said to have devoted
more than usual attention to the perfecting of his style, and
his freedom from some prevailing faults give evidence that
his efforts of this kind were not in vain. Not only are there
passages of great power and beauty, which indicate an elevated mind and refined taste, but in his writings generally,
there are a purity of diction, a correctness of construction
and a richness and copiousness of language, which are
rarely surpassed. And of the theological writings of this
period, it may be safely said, there are none read with more
interest and profit at the present day, than the sermons of
Barrow. The following extract is from a discourse on
Devotion :—

"Frequency is indeed necessary for the breeding, the nourishment,
the growth and improvement of all piety. Devotion is that holy and
heavenly fire, which darteth into our minds the light of spiritual
knowledge, which kindleth in our hearts the warmth of holy desires,
if, therefore, we do continue long absent from it, a night of darkness
will overspread our minds, a deadening coldness will seize upon our
affections. It is the best food of our souls, which preserveth their
life and health, which repaireth their strength and vigor, which ren
dereth them lusty and active; if we therefore long abstain from it,
we shall starve or pine away; we shall be faint and feeble in all re

.gious performances · we shall have none at all, or a very languid and meagre piety.

"To maintain in us a constant and steady disposition to obedience, to correct our perverse inclinations, to curb our unruly passions, to strengthen us against temptations, to comfort us in anxieties and distresses, we do need continual supplies of grace from God; the which ordinarily are communicated in devotion, as the channel which conveyeth, or the instrument which helpeth to procure it, or the condition upon which it is granted. Faith, hope, love, spiritual comfort and joy, all divine graces, are chiefly elicited, expressed, exercised therein and thereby; it is therefore needful that it should frequently be used; seeing otherwise we shall be in danger to fail in discharging our chief duties, and to want the best graces.

"It is frequency of devotion, also, which maintaineth that friendship with God, which is the soul of piety. As familiar conversation (wherein men do express their minds and affections) mutually breedeth acquaintance, and cherisheth good-will of men to one another,—but long forbearance thereof dissolveth, or slackeneth the bonds of amity, breaking their intimacy, and cooling their kindness,—so is it in respect to God; it is frequent converse with him which begetteth a particular acquaintance with him, a mindful regard of him, a hearty liking to him, a delightful taste of his goodness, and, consequently, a sincere and solid good-will toward him; but intermission thereof produceth estrangement or enmity towards him. If we seldom come at God, we shall little know him, not much care for him, scarce remember him, rest insensible of his love, and regardless of his favor; a coldness, a shyness, a distaste, an antipathy toward him, will, by degrees, creep upon us. Abstinence from his company and presence will cast us into conversations destructive or prejudicial to our friendship with him; wherein soon we shall contract familiarity and friendship with his enemies, (the world and the flesh,) which are inconsistent with love to him, which will dispose us to forget him or to dislike and loathe him."

Of an entirely opposite style to this forcible and impressive manner of writing, are the sermons of Bishop Tillotson. Drake has thus happily contrasted these two contemporary writers: "Whilst richness vehemence, and strength, characterize the productions of Barrow, simplicity, languor, and

26

enervation, form the chief features in the diction of Tillotson To the former belong a fervid fancy and a poetic ear, glow ing figures and harmonious cadences; to the latter, perspicuity and smoothness, verbal purity, and unaffected ease. If Barrow be occasionally involved, harsh, or redundant, Tillotson is too generally loose and feeble; and he seldom displays much either of beauty or melody in the arrangement or construction of his periods."

The following passage is a favorable specimen of the style of Tillotson : —

"Give me leave to recommend to you this new commandment that ye love one another; which is almost a new commandment still, and hardly the worse for wearing; so seldom is it put on, and so little hath it been practised among Christians for several ages.

" Consider seriously with yourselves, ought not the great matters wherein we are agreed,—our union in the doctrines of the Christian religion, and in all the necessary articles of that faith *which was once delivered to the saints,*—in the same sacraments, and in all the substantial parts of God's worship, and in the great duties and virtues of the Christian life,—to be of greater force to unite us, than difference in doubtful opinions, and in little rites and circumstances of worship. to divide and break us?

" Are not the things about which we differ, in their nature indifferent? that is, things about which there ought to be no difference among wise men? Are they not at a great distance from the life and essence of religion, and rather good or bad, as they tend to the peace and unity of the church, or are made use of to schism or faction. than either necessary or evil in themselves? And shall little scruples weigh so far with us, as, by breaking the peace of the church about them, to endanger the whole of religion? Shall we take one another by the throat for a hundred pence, when our common adversary stands ready to clap upon us an action of ten thousand talents?

This passage has more vivacity than is usually found in the writings of Tillotson. The extract found in the school books on the Advantage of Truth and Sincerity, is, perhaps, a fairer specimen of his style.

If now we turn from these dignitaries of the English church to the non-conformists of this reign, we find a class of writers of different, but not inferior, claims to our consideration. I refer to such men as Howe, Bates, Baxter, and Bunyan; men who, for intellectual vigor, for richness and originality, and, I may add, for poetical beauty of thought and language, are not surpassed in any period of English literature. It is true their tastes had not been fully subjected to the refining influences of classical learning, (some of them were uneducated men,) neither had they the same rich iterary stores for illustration and ornament, as were possessed by others; but these defects were well supplied by native genius, an intimate knowledge of men, and of things around them, and, above all, of the workings of their own hearts. They stand forth to our view, not as refined scholars, but as witnesses of the enlarging and exalting influence of the Christian religion on the minds of men. The writings of Baxter and Bunyan are familiar to all; I shall therefore confine the specimens given of this class of writers to two short extracts from Howe and Bates. The following is from Howe's "Blessedness of the Righteous":—

"To live destitute of a divine presence; to discern no beam of the heavenly glory; to go up and down, day by day, and perceive nothing of God, no glimmering, no appearance;—this is disconsolate as well as sinful darkness. What can be made of creatures, what of the daily events of providence, if we see not in them the glory of a Deity? if we do not contemplate the divine wisdom, power, and goodness, diffused every where? Our practical atheism, and inobservance of God, makes the world become to us the region and snadow of death, states us as among ghosts and spectres, makes all things look with a ghastly face, imprints death upon every thing we see, encircles us with gloomy, dreadful shades, and with uncomfortable apparitions. * * * * * Surely there is little heaven in all this

But, if we now open our eyes upon that all-comprehending glory
apply them to a steady intuition of God, how heavenly a life shal
we then live in the world! To have God always in view, as the
director and end of all our actions; to make our eye crave leave of
God to consult him before we venture upon any thing, and implore
his guidance and blessing; upon all occasions to direct our prayers
to him, and to look up, to make our eye wait his commanding look,
ready to receive all intimations of his will;—that is an angelic life.
* * * * This is to walk in the light, amidst a serene, placid, mild
light, that infuses no unquiet thoughts, admits no guilty fears,
nothing that can disturb or annoy us. To eye God in all our comforts, and observe the smiling aspects of his face, when he dispenses
them to us,—to eye him in all our afflictions, and consider the fra-
ternal wisdom that instructs us in them,—how would this increase
our mercies, and mitigate our trouble! To eye him in all his creatures, and observe the various prints of the Creator's glory stamped
upon them, — with how lively a lustre would it clothe the world, and
make every thing look with a pleasant face! What a heaven were
it, to look upon God as filling all in all! and how sweetly would it,
erewhile, raise our souls into some such sweet, seraphic strains,—
Holy, holy, the whole earth is full f his glory !' "

Bates, in a sermon on " Heaven," thus speaks of the pleasures that spring from knowledge in the regions of the blessed:

" When the soul opens its eyes to the clear discoveries of the first
truth, in which is no shadow of error, and its breast to the dear and
intimate embraces of the supreme good, in which is no mixture of
evil, and beyond which nothing remains to be known, nothing to be
enjoyed, what a deluge of the purest and sweetest pleasure will over-
flow it! We cannot ascend in our thoughts so high, as to conceive
the excess of joy that attends those operations of the glorified soul
upon its proper object. But something we may conjecture.
" Those who are possessed with a noble passion for knowledge,
how do they despise all lower pleasures in comparison of it! How
do they forget themselves, neglect the body, and retire into the mind,
the highest part of man, and nearest to God! The bare apprehen
sion of such things, that, by their internal nature, have no attractive
influence upon the affections, is pleasant to the understanding. A
the appearance of light, though not attended with any visible beau

ties, refreshes the eye after long darkness, so the clear discovery of truths, how abstract soever, that were before unknown, is grateful to the intellective faculty. * * * * * *

" But here are many imperfections that lessen this intellectual pleasure, which shall cease in heaven. Here, the acquisition of knowledge is often with the expense of health; the flower of the spirits, necessary for natural operations, is wasted by intense thought. How often are the learned sickly! As the flint, when it is struck, gives not a spark without consuming itself, so knowledge is obtained by studies. that waste our faint, sensitive faculties. But there our knowledge shall be a free emanation from the spring of truth, without our labor or pains. Here we learn by circuit, and discern by comparing things; ignorant darkness is dispelled by a gradual succession of light; but there perfect knowledge shall be infused in a moment. Here, after all our labor and toil, how little knowledge do we gain' Every question is a labyrinth, out of which the nimblest and most searching minds cannot extricate themselves. How many specious errors impose upon our understandings! We look on things by false lights, through deceiving spectacles; but then our knowledge shall be certain and complete. There is no forbidden tree in the celestial paradise, as no inordinate affection. We shall see God in all his excellencies, the supreme object and end, the only felicity of the soul. How will the sight of his glorious perfections, in the first moment, quench our extreme thirst, and fill us with joy and admiration! It is not as the naked conception of treasures, that only makes rich in idea; but that divine sight gives a real interest in him. The angels are so ravished with the beauties and wonders of his face, they never divert a moment from the contemplation of it."

While the theological writers of this period were thus contributing, in different ways, to the advancement of English style, there are found, in other departments of literature, writings of the same tendency. Sir William Temple, who flourished during this reign, may be ranked among the elegant writers that adorn the literature of England. He is said to have made the improvement of his style an object of special effort and study; and his uncommon purity of language, his ease and simplicity of expression, the rich ornaments which embellish his style, and the beauty and melody of his periods are evidence of his success. The following description of heroic virtue is a fair specimen of his style:—

"Though it is easier to describe heroic virtue by the effects and examples, than by causes or definitions, yet it may be said to arise from some great and native excellency of temper or genius, transcending the common race of mankind, in wisdom, goodness, and fortitude. These ingredients, advantaged by birth, improved by education, and assisted by fortune, seem to make that noble composition, which gives such a lustre to those who have possessed it, as made them appear to common eyes something more than mortals, and to have been of some mixture between divine and human race,—to have been honored and obeyed in their lives, and, after their deaths, bewailed and adored.

."The greatness of their wisdom appeared in the excellency of their inventions; and these, by the goodness of their nature, were turned and exercised upon such subjects as were of general good to mankind, in the common uses of life, or to their own countries, in the institutions of such laws, orders, and governments, as were of most ease, safety, and advantage, to civil society. Their valor was employed in defending their own countries from the violence of ill men at home, or enemies abroad, in reducing their barbarous neighbors to the same forms and orders of civil lives and institutions, or in relieving others from the cruelties and oppressions of tyranny and violence. * * * * * *

"I have said that this excellency of genius must be native, because it can never grow to any great height, if it be only acquired or affected; but it must be ennobled by birth, to give it more lustre, esteem, and authority; it must be cultivated by education and instruction, to improve its growth, and direct its end and application; and it must be assisted by fortune, to preserve it to maturity; because the noblest spirit or genius in the world, if it falls, though never so bravely, in its first enterprises, cannot deserve enough of mankind to pretend to so great a reward as the esteem of heroic virtue. And yet, perhaps, many a person has died in the first battle or adventure he achieved, and lies buried in silence and oblivion, who, had he out lived as many dangers as Alexander did, might have shined as bright in honor and fame. Now, since so many stars go to the making up of this constellation, 'tis no wonder it has so seldom appeared in the world; nor that, when it does, it is received and followed with so much gazing and veneration."

I close the specimens of prose writers of this reign, with two short extracts from "Dryden's Essay on Dramatic Poetry." The prose of this celebrated poet is characterized by originality and freshness of thought and language. We perceive at once in his style his intellectual superiority. He did much for the improvement of the language, and justly ranks high among the prose writers of English literature.

"To begin with Shakspeare. He is the man, who, of all modern, and perhaps ancient poets, had the largest and most comprehensive soul. All the images of nature were still present to him, and he drew them not laboriously, but luckily; when he describes any thing, you more than see it—you feel it. Those who accuse him to have wanted learning, give him the greater commendation; he was naturally learned; he needed not the spectacles of books to read Nature; he looked inwards, and found her there. I cannot say he is every where alike; were he so, I should do him injury to compare him with the greatest of mankind. He is many times flat, insipid; his comic wit degenerating into clenches, his serious swelling into bombast. But he is always great, when some great occasion is presented to him; no man can say he ever had a fit subject for wit, and did not raise himself as high above the rest of poets.

Quantum lenta solent inter viburna cupressi.

"The consideration of this made Mr. Hales of Eton say, that there was no subject of which any poet ever writ, but he would produce it much better done in Shakspeare; and however others are now generally preferred before him, yet the age wherein he lived, which had contemporaries with him, Fletcher and Jonson, never equalled them to him in their esteem.

"Of Chaucer, he says, as he is the father of English poetry, so I hold him in the same degree of veneration as the Grecians held Homer, or the Romans Virgil. He is a perpetual fountain of good sense; learned in all sciences; and therefore speaks properly on all subjects As he knew what to say, so he knows also where to leave off; a continence which is practised by few writers, and scarcely by any of the ancients, excepting Homer and Virgil.

"Chaucer followed nature every where; but was never so bold to go beyond her; and there is a great difference of being *poeta*, and *nimis poeta*, if we may believe Catullus, as much as betwixt a modest behavior and affectation. The verse of Chaucer, I confess, is not harmonious to us; but it is like the eloquence of one whom Tacitus commends—it was *auribus istius temporis accommodata*. They who lived with him, and some time after, thought it musical, and it continues so even in our judgment, if compared with the numbers of Lydgate and Gower, his contemporaries; there is a rude sweetness of the Scotch tune in it, which is natural and pleasing, though not perfect. * * * * We can only say, that he lived in the infancy of our poetry, and that nothing is brought to perfection at the first. We must be children before we can grow men. There was an Ennius, and in process of time a Lucilius and a Lucretius before Virgil and Horace."

My limits will not allow of continuing down, through later periods, this outline of the history of English style. Neither is it necessary, since the productions of more modern writers of eminence are well known, and the peculiar traits of their styles have often been pointed out. In looking back upon the specimens that have been given, we are able to trace the progress of English style from its early and rude state, towards the refinement and perfection it has since attained. At successive periods, writers have appeared, whose influence has been felt, and who have, individually, contributed something to the improvement of their native language and style. Perhaps their excellences have been united with many faults; but while the beneficial tendencies of the former have been felt, and become incorporated with the language and literature of the country, the latter have disappeared before the improvements of succeeding ages. There have also been periods, when, from the influence of some unpropitious causes, taste has become corrupt, and the progress of style has been stayed; but even in these periods, individuals have appeared, who have risen above the prevailing faults of their times, and exerted an influence, which, if not felt by their own age, has been powerful on the age which has followed.

To present a more connected and condensed view of the influence of different writers upon the progress of English style, I shall attempt a classification of them founded upon the different qualities by which they are characterized, and which they may have contributed to impart to the style of their age.

1 The first class consists of those to whom English style is indebted for its copiousness and dignity; copiousness, as they introduce many new words and forms of expressions: and dignity, as the words and phrases, thus introduced by them, were more elevated than those in common conversational use. In this class are to be enumerated those who flourished about the time of the Revival of Letters. Such are Wilson, Ascham, Cheke, More, and others of this date. In some of the succeeding reigns also, especially in that of James I., there were writers who were devoted to classical pursuits, and whose influence was of the same nature. In some of these writers, however, are found gross defects of style—harshness, obscurity, and what at the present day would be accounted downright pedantry.

2. The next class of writers is composed of those whose style is in some degree easy and idiomatic. These are either classical scholars of more than usual purity of taste, or uneducated, self-made men, of strong common sense and practical views. These are the writers who have given perspicuity, ease, and naturalness to English style, and their productions continue to this day to have a charm, both with the learned and with common readers. It is pure English undefiled, flowing in its own native channel, ard reflecting home objects and scenes. In this rank may be placed Raleigh, Cowley, and in latter days Swift and Paley, and also

the writers of the Bunyan school, who alike contributed to preserve the vestal flame of piety in the church, and the purity of their native language and style.

3. Nearly allied to this class is a third, consisting of those who have helped to give simplicity and purity to style. Such are the writers of Chronicles and of Essays and Treatises on practical common-place subjects—matter of fact men, who by the simple narrative, or the plain, practical exhibition of common truths, have sought to inform and improve those around them. Holinshed, Stow, and Bishop Hall are of this class.

4. I would next refer to those who have given precision and definiteness to style. They are writers of accurate, discriminating minds—the philosophers of their day—close thinkers and able reasoners—those whose favorite occupation it was, to search after truth, and either to invent or investigate the different theories, from time to time advanced The direct tendency of this class of writers to promote the attainment of the valuable traits of style just mentioned, is readily seen. Such writers are Herbert, Hobbes, Boyle, and especially Locke, to whom, perhaps, more than to any other author, English style is indebted for precision and accuracy.

5. Another class of writers embraces those who were men of poetical minds—those who possessed an active, playful fancy, and who were in no ordinary degree susceptible of emotions of taste. Their writings abounded in rich profusion of illustration and imagery, and their well-modulated periods show that they were not insensible to the harmony of numbers. It is from this source that style derives its richness, its melody and beauty; and when, as has sometimes been the case, such writers have appeared at periods in which these traits were peculiarly needed, their influence has been highly advantageous. The writings of Sir Philip Sydney, of Bishop Taylor, of Cowley, and of Temple, have thus enriched and adorned English style

6. Liveliness of fancy, where it has existed without the guidance of a chaste and correct taste, has sometimes taken a different direction. It has manifested itself in quaintness, in wit, and amusing conceits. Writers of this kind, though they abound in faults, have, without doubt, contributed something to the advancement of style. Their sentences are usually short, and their forms of expression striking and sententious. Thus they helped to break up the long, involved, intricate periods, which formerly prevailed, and to give to style vivacity and sprightliness. Lilly, Bacon in his Essays, Donne, Ben Jonson, Burton, and other writers of the reign of James I., may be ranked in this class.

7. There have appeared at different periods those, whose productions are examples of strength, force, and manliness of style. Such are most controversial writings that have been called forth in times of political or religious revolution. And whenever the nature of the subject, or the circumstances of the individual, have been such as deeply to interest the feelings, to stir up the soul, and to put into powerful action the faculties of the mind, we have writings, in which the qualities mentioned above are prominent. The extracts from Milton, Barrow, and Sidney, are examples of this manner of writing.

8. The only remaining class of writers, to whom I shall refer, includes those who have given elevation, richness, and every noble quality of style. They are those who, by their contemporaries, and by succeeding ages, have been esteemed intellectually great, and who, from their originality, their rich flow of thought and expression, and the strength, comprehensiveness, and clearness of their views, were well fitted to instruct and improve their race. A few such names are found in English literature; and as they have appeared at successive periods, it is easy to discern their powerful influence on the advancement of their native style. Such men were Bacon, and Milton, and Dryden.

CONTENTS.

www.ingramcontent.com/pod-product-compliance
Lightning Source LLC
Chambersburg PA
CBHW031030120726
47905CB00007B/2117